CW00385660

BRIGHT ROOMS

When Celia Masters learns that her thirteen-year-old niece has been found hanging from a tree, she is shocked. The police decide Tamsin's death is not murder but suicide and their investigation winds up. Celia, however, decides to learn what she can about the niece she never really knew and, haunted by the memory of Tamsin, determines to understand why she would have taken her own life. The more she searches, the stranger the official version of events seems to be. There are dark secrets that Tamsin was hiding, and Celia is determined to uncover them...

BRIGHT ROOMS

BRIGHT ROOMS

by

Jenny Maxwell

Magna Large Print Books
Long Preston, North Yorkshire,
BD23 4ND, England.

British Library Catalog

Maxwell, Jenny
 Bright rooms.

 A catalogue reco
 available from the British Library

 ISBN   0-7505-1892-8

First published in Great Britain in 2001 by Little Brown

Cover illustration © Black Sheep by arrangement with
Little Brown & Company Ltd.

The moral right of the author has been asserted

Published in Large Print 2002 by arrangement with
Little, Brown & Company

Magna Large Print is an imprint of Library Magna Books Ltd.

Printed and bound in Great Britain by
T.J. (International) Ltd., Cornwall, PL28 8RW

For Kobi Leins, with love.

Preface

I forgot to turn the telephone off that night. It had become a routine, because we were sick of wrong number disturbances. We'd lived in the house on the outskirts of Bonn for nearly six months, but still we received calls for a family called van Butler, and for somebody with the name Christine. Occasionally Heinrich. All these people seemed to have had nocturnal habits. Three o'clock in the morning was not unusual.

And so the bedtime routine included turning the little wheel on the side of the handset until the telephone bell was inaudible. It was a nuisance, because I so often forgot to turn it back in the morning, but that was better than being woken in the early hours, and being unable to go back to sleep afterwards.

That night there had been students in the house, talking to Anthony in his study, and when they left there was the usual German farewell, standing in the hall, then on the doorstep, then around the car, nearly fifteen minutes before they finally drove away. I was irritated, as always, by this pointless routine, and followed it with one of my own, a series of mantras all of which meant the same thing: why can't the Germans be like us?

Nearly eleven o'clock, and I'd been tired since nine, I snapped at my long-suffering husband, who'd been tired since February. His bloody students. It was doubly unfair since, only the night before, the house had been full of my bloody refugees, who'd stayed until long past midnight.

At four the telephone rang and woke us both, and I flung myself out of bed in a fury and screamed down into the mouthpiece.

'Es gibt hier keine scheisse van Butler. Auch keine Christine und kein Heinrich. Verstehst du?'

'Celia?'

I recognised the voice of my sister-in-law, Helen. My rage subsided, but irritation remained. I don't like her, and my reaction to her voice was, oh God, what the Hell does she want?

'Hello, Helen.'

She was crying, gasping sobs that sounded like panting.

'Helen, what's the matter?'

'Tamsin.'

Her daughter, my niece. It was not an answer to my question. I heard the words in my own voice inside my head. Tamsin, the name Tamsin, you stupid woman, is not an

12

answer to my question. Tamsin what? What's she done? What's happened?

'What about Tamsin? Why are you crying?'

'She's dead.'

And then, as I sank down onto the chair, there was a man's voice on the telephone. A stranger was speaking to me.

'I think you'd better come to England, Mrs Masters. It looks as though Tamsin may have been murdered.'

'Murdered?'

Incomprehension. This is a word that cannot apply, not to us. Murdered? No. This happens outside. You can't use that word, not to us. Murdered?

'Who are you?'

Murdered? Tamsin?

No.

'My name's Cooper, Mrs Masters. Detective Sergeant Cooper. I'm sorry to have such bad news for you. Mrs Simpson insisted on speaking to you herself first.'

I could hear Helen behind him, the sobs that sounded as if she'd been running, and a wailing noise, somebody else crying? And there were other voices in the background.

'Murdered?'

'So it would seem. If you can come, Mrs Masters, I think Mrs Simpson does need your help. I understand there are no other relatives available.'

'She's got a brother,' I protested. 'Giles.

13

Giles Baker, that's his name.'

'He's abroad.'

'So am I.'

Anthony had come into the room behind me. He walked quietly over to the window and waited, one glance at me, and then he looked out into the darkness.

'He can't be traced. He's travelling.'

I don't want to go. I can't go. Not now, and what could I do? I don't know anything about this sort of thing. There's Patrice's asylum hearing coming up in a week, and I have to take Anna to the lawyer tomorrow. I can't just drop them.

Helen was still crying, and those wailing noises were coming from her, too. It was as though she was singing a duet.

Her daughter had been murdered, and she'd asked for me.

'Yes, I'll come,' I said. 'I expect I can be there about noon tomorrow. Today, I mean.'

I told Anthony what had happened, and saw in his face my own reaction; shock, and the beginnings of sadness, but most of all astonishment.

It didn't take me long to pack, and Anthony called a taxi, and found my passport, and money, enough for the taxi, and a credit card.

'Will you be all right? Telephone me when you get there.'

'Can you find somebody to take Anna to

14

the lawyer?'

'Yes, I expect Gabi could do that. Listen, there's the taxi, give my love to Helen. Tell her I'm so sorry. Whatever sounds right, tell her.'

It wasn't a long drive to the airport, and I was in time to catch the early flight. It all seemed to be a scramble of papers, money and tickets and boarding cards, and then a magazine, and I was on the aeroplane, feeling the lurch and the swing as it climbed. I drank a cup of coffee, and I opened my magazine; something to distract me. There was nothing I could do.

Tamsin was dead. A dark girl, as I remembered her, rather quiet, nothing out of the ordinary. I'd never taken much notice of her. It was too late now; she was dead, she'd been murdered.

I was sad. I was truly sad, that she was dead, the dark girl who'd been quiet and not very noticeable. But still, over the sadness and the shock, the feeling that remained was one of amazement.

She'd been murdered.

1

There was nothing much to indicate the tragedy, not on the street. There was a police car parked a few yards away, but there were no blue lights, no tapes across the pavement. There wasn't even a policeman at the door, although one answered it when I rang the bell.

'I'm Celia Masters,' I said. 'I'm expected.'

Helen was still in a dressing gown, and she looked sloppy with anguish, as though something was melting, blurring her outlines. She reached out her arms to me, and I stepped into them and hugged her, trying very hard not to think of tears, and possibly snot, on my clothes. She was damp, rather disgusting. I'd always thought of her as flabby.

'Helen. My dear, I'm so sorry. My poor Helen.'

'Oh, Celia.'

She started to wail again, the noise I'd heard on the telephone, and I patted her on the back. She's not coughing, I told myself, but there didn't seem to be anything else to do.

'Anthony sends his love. He's terribly

16

shocked. And very sorry.'

'I don't know what to do,' she moaned.

'Have another cup of tea,' somebody suggested, and I felt her sniff.

'I've had tea. I've had tea all night. I don't want any more tea, thank you.'

'Have you seen a doctor?' I asked. 'He'll give you something for the shock.'

'Doctor Coburn's been. And it's she.'

Helen was a feminist, I remembered. In theory, at least.

'Did she give you anything?'

So trivial, I thought. Your daughter's been murdered, have you got a pill? Would you like a cup of tea because your daughter's been murdered?

Now that my astonishment was beginning to fade the enormity of the fact started to hurt. It was huge; overwhelming. There was no way to resist it, to combat it, and all we could do in response to it was fiddle around the edges, with our pills and our cups of tea and our polite acknowledgement of these strangers to whom it was something that had happened again; to whom it was not so vast and so appalling.

For ourselves, we couldn't yet bear to look at it.

Never going to see her again.

Have another cup of tea, dear. Sit down.

Somebody took that life and ... and *stopped* it. Those limbs will never move. Those eyes

17

will never see. There will never again be an
idea, a word, a laugh. Not from Tamsin.
Never again.

Never.

I began to gasp. I wasn't grieving. I hadn't
known the girl. But suddenly, as these ideas
came, it was hard to breathe. It was so big,
and yet...

Why couldn't we step back? Not far, just a
day. Only a day, and she was still alive. Just
that little time ago, we should be able to step
back just such a little time. Such a little step.

Have a pill. Cup of tea. When did you last?
Did she mention?

There were noises from upstairs.

'They're searching her room.'

Oh, yes, they do that, don't they? Crim-
inals and victims, no privacy any more. But
they have to find out. They mean us well, I
suppose. Or at least, no harm. They have to
find out.

My hand was on Helen's shoulder. I saw
one of the fingers move, and the sinews slid
under the skin, smoothly, so smoothly I
didn't feel it until I thought about it. Until I
turned my mind onto it, and then I moved
my finger again.

A miracle of engineering, that one finger
moving, such a little movement, so precise
and exact and perfect.

Tamsin could never move a finger again.
That marvellous piece of machinery, her

body, had been stopped.

'Mrs Masters, are you all right?'

Dead.

It means, finished. Never again. Stopped. The end.

But she's only thirteen. Not even grown. She's incomplete, there were the finishing touches still to be made. A few extra inches on her height, the muscles to harden, the breasts to swell, those long bones in her arms and legs, they were still growing.

'Mrs Masters?'

'I think she's going to faint. Sit her down.'

I can do that for myself. How do you sit somebody down? It's not a transitive verb, or whatever the term is.

I sat on the sofa, feeling my knees suddenly weak, and I seemed to drag Helen down beside me. I'd still been holding her, almost holding on to her. Rather ungraceful, suddenly plumping down onto the cushions, the pair of us, as though we were entangled. And my shoulder was damp, where she'd been crying.

'I feel sick,' I said, but I didn't really. Nausea wasn't what I was feeling. I was feeling outrage, and there was this cold gasping, as though I'd been punched in the stomach. The enormity of this had, quite literally, left me breathless.

'Are you going to *be* sick?'

The question came from a young police-

19

woman with spots on her chin. She didn't ask in a tone of concern. It was like an interrogation. If you *are* going to be sick, are you going to be sick into a bowl, or onto the floor? And when, exactly, will this event take place?

I didn't bother to answer.

What can I do? I thought. What can I do about this?

Never again. Not a single movement from that body. Not an idea from that mind. Not a response, not an emotion. Nothing. It's all been stopped.

It's been destroyed.

I'm not even close to this, but the force of that destruction has hit me. Like an explosion, a piece of the shrapnel has hit me. Hurt me. Left me gasping for breath, and too weak to stand.

It's too quiet for this. There should be shouting and screaming, rage. Defiance and fury, we cannot accept this. No, we cannot accept this.

I was crying, too. I could feel the tears hot on my cheeks.

Do not go gentle into that goodnight.

Dylan Thomas had been right. His anger, his furious rejection of death, he'd been right.

Rage, rage against the dying of the light.

Yes. You knew. When you wrote that, you knew, didn't you? Dylan Marlais Thomas,

20

saying what I feel, saying it loud and true.

Helen was wailing and gasping again, and I thought, stop. Stop this. Pull yourself together.

But I was thinking it at myself as well as at her, and I forced the ideas of Tamsin aside, pushing at them. Go away, let me think.

Huge, this thing. Huge and black and looming into my mind. Too dark, too big, can't think round this. Go away.

This is why we turn to trivia. We don't have to think, when we say have a cup of tea, have you seen the doctor. We can't think, with this, this thing here, it overpowers us.

Dear Helen. Poor Helen. I'm so sorry. Sorry to be so trite and banal, just here, with my hand still on your shoulder, still thinking of your tears wetting my clothes, and please I do wish you would blow your nose, and the spots on the policewoman's chin. I wish I could say something to you, something that would at least let you know I really am sorry. Sorry for you. Sorry that there's no more Tamsin.

Something, there must be something to say.

'Who could have killed her?'

I was choking on the words.

'I don't know,' Helen wailed, and then she fell forward against me, and my arms were round her, holding her close, palms of my hands against her back, against the soft fat

21

under the slippery fabric of her dressing gown.

'Helen. Helen, dear Helen. You'll feel better if you have a shower, and get dressed. Why don't you do that?'

'We haven't finished upstairs yet, Mrs Masters.'

It was a man who had spoken, and I looked up, vaguely surprised to hear another voice.

'They won't *let* me,' moaned Helen.

'But that's ridiculous. It's your house, isn't it? You can go where you like.'

'We won't be much longer.'

It was a very calm voice. His face was calm, too. He'd been there all the time, listening to us, watching us, as if we were something to be studied, and it was his right to watch us, and listen to our private conversation.

'Who are you?'

'Welland. Chief Inspector Welland, Mrs Masters.'

'Are you in charge here?'

'For the moment.'

He was middle-aged, brown hair turning grey, and he looked tired. Or perhaps it wasn't tiredness. The droop to the corners of his eyes, his slow movements, perhaps it was sadness. Perhaps, even though for him this was something that had happened *again*, he was truly sad about it.

22

'Then perhaps you'd be kind enough to let Mrs Simpson use her own bathroom.'

I hadn't meant to sound arrogant and sarcastic. I really hadn't. I'd wanted to help Helen, and a shower or a bath, and some clean clothes, they would have helped. She would have felt better, washed, and in clean clothes.

Welland looked at me, no particular expression on his face.

'If you think that fighting with me and being obstructive to the police will make life easier for Mrs Simpson, then please go ahead.'

'Oh, don't, Celia. Please don't. Please don't.'

She was clinging to me again, so I turned away from Welland, glad of an excuse not to answer him. I was shocked by his words. I felt as if I'd been hit, hit again, firstly by this monstrous thing that had happened, then by him. It was a slap in the face, and couldn't he understand that I, too, was a victim? How dared he speak to me like that?

And I'd been right. It was Helen's house, and she could go where she liked in it. She could have a shower if she wanted one, they couldn't stop her.

How dared he?

He'd left the room. I could hear footsteps on the stairs, slow and heavy, and then his voice, but I couldn't make out the words.

There were other voices, and then quick steps above our heads.

What a flimsy house this is. You can hear everything, every sound. What was going on up there?

Was her body here? Was it here that she'd been killed?

I knew nothing about it. Was her body still here? Lying here?

Almost frantically, I looked up at the policewoman.

'Is Tamsin here?' I whispered, and it seemed as if she didn't understand my question.

'Her body? Is it here?'

'Oh, no. We wouldn't bring her here.'

She'd died somewhere else, then. Been killed. Been finished.

Where? What had happened to her? How had she been killed?

I wanted to know, but with Helen still there, still crying onto my shoulder, I couldn't ask.

'What are they doing up there?' I asked, and she shrugged.

'Routine,' she said.

It would be better not to ask. Better to leave it alone. Talking, or arguing, it would only invite more rejections, more rudeness.

Why had he spoken to me like that?

The doorbell rang, and somebody came down the stairs. I could hear voices again, one of them repeating the word 'no'. Then the door closed.

It might have been somebody Helen would have liked to invite into the house. It might have been a friend, or somebody who could have helped.

It could have been somebody else for her to hold, another shoulder for her to soak with her tears.

She was moaning again, repetitions of a quiet gasp and then a long, blurred moan. When I looked at her I saw her eyes were open, but not focussed. They were red and swollen, they looked drowned. And her mouth was moving in a way that seemed uncoordinated.

'Do you think the doctor might have given her something a bit too strong?' I asked, and the policewoman looked at Helen, consideringly.

'Shouldn't think so. Probably just shock. I'll turn on the fire.'

Helen seemed to watch as the girl crossed the room and bent to the controls. Then her head rolled on my shoulder, and she gave a huge, hiccoughing sigh.

'She's exhausted,' I said.

'I don't suppose they'll be much longer. She can go to bed soon.'

I didn't know what to do. There was nothing, nothing to be done, nothing to say. I could only hold Helen, feeling her body move at the little gasp, and then go slack as the long, burbling moan droned through her lips.

Poor Helen.

What must it be like, to lose a child? It was the worst of all bereavements, or so I understood. So people said. I had no children, and so I couldn't imagine.

Dreadful. It must be dreadful.

And what could I do? She'd asked for me, and I was here, so there must be something I could do.

The funeral, I could arrange the funeral. I was good at organising things, I could take that business on for Helen. That would be a help.

It would help me, too.

'Helen, have you got a Yellow Pages? The telephone directory thing, have you got one?'

Funeral Directors, that's what they call undertakers now, isn't it? The nearest one would probably be best. Or I should call and see, try to find one that's not too shabby. If necessary Anthony and I could help with the expenses.

And there'll be letters to write, I don't suppose she's even got a typewriter, let alone a computer. I could probably hire one.

'Helen, a Yellow Pages directory, darling. Have you got one?'

And the newspapers, we'll have to fend them off, but a statement might make it easier. I can draft something.

The policewoman was handing me the directory, looking inquisitive. Nosy. But it doesn't hurt to be polite to people, so I smiled at her and thanked her.

Funeral Directors, here they are. When Helen's safely asleep I'll go out and find one. I ought to have a map. I can buy one at the corner shop, I expect. It'll do me good, to walk around this town.

'You can't do anything about a funeral until we've finished.'

She was looking over my shoulder, looking at what I was reading.

The cheek of it.

'Don't be silly,' I said. 'And would you mind? You're standing in my light.'

She wasn't, and she knew it, but she backed away.

'The coroner will give directions about the funeral at the inquest.'

There was just a hint of triumph in her voice. Got you that time, you snotty bitch, she was thinking.

Was it true, though? Could we really not arrange the funeral? Did they have that much power over us, these people?

I stood up and went to the door. A young policeman was standing on the stairs, and he looked down at me.

'Inspector Welland?' I asked. 'Is he there?'
'*Chief* Inspector Welland.'

Oh, God. Another pip on his shoulder, and I forgot about it. Probably worked for it for twenty years.

'May I speak to him?'

It seemed he'd heard me, because he came to the top of the stairs and looked down.

'This policewoman says we can't arrange the funeral.'

'She's quite right.'

It must be the law. He wouldn't dare just forbid it, unless it was the law. Would he?

'Is that the law?'

'It is.'

This is dreadful. And it's cruel, too. How long can all this take? It could be months. What happens if they never solve a murder? Can they just keep a body in some sort of freezer, for ever?

I was staring at him, and he was waiting, looking down the stairs at me, quite courteous, waiting in case I had another question.

It's like being in limbo, between the death and the funeral. It's dreadful. And it could go on and on.

I can't go back to Germany until the funeral's over. I can't just desert Helen. She asked for me.

'How long is all this going to take?' I asked, knowing even before I spoke that he could not possibly give me an answer.

But he was kinder than I deserved.

'We may not need to keep the body for very long. It depends on what the pathologist finds at the post mortem examination.'

It was a very precise manner of speech, I noticed. 'Post mortem examination,' he'd said, where most wouldn't have bothered with 'examination', or would at least have abbreviated it.

I walked up the stairs towards him, and the policeman flattened himself against the wall to let me pass.

'Where and how did she die?' I asked.

I spoke softly. I didn't know how much Helen could hear, in this badly built house with its thin walls.

'On a piece of waste ground behind the railway tracks. She was hanged.'

His answer seemed to mean nothing. I looked away from him, looked into the little whirling pattern on the wallpaper of the landing, and I thought, hanged. She was hanged. That could have been horrible. A horrible thing.

'It's not a cruel death.'

He was kind. He would shut off the nightmares, if he could.

'Pressure on the carotid arteries would have caused unconsciousness quite quickly. I don't believe she choked.'

There were tears in my eyes, a silly

response to his sympathy.

'Thank you,' I whispered, and I went back down the stairs before he could see.

Does Helen know? I wondered. If not, I'd have to find some way of telling her.

Behind these thoughts was beginning to grow the worry of the time I would have to be away from Germany. I told myself that nothing serious could go wrong because of my absence, but I wasn't at all sure.

Gabi would have taken Anna to the lawyer, but next week there was the date for Patrice's asylum hearing, and I would have to be back in time for that. I was a witness for him. I was needed.

But I couldn't leave a woman whose child had been murdered.

Helen was still slumped on the sofa when I went in, and I didn't think she'd noticed that I'd gone. Her hands were lying in her lap, the palms upwards, the fingers curled.

'What are they looking for?' she asked as I closed the door, and suddenly she sat up straight and stared at me, her eyes wide.

'I don't know.'

'What, then?' she demanded of the police-woman. 'You know, don't you? What are they looking for, then?'

'It's just routine.'

'They're not going to find anything, are they? Not up there.'

She was beginning to sound desperate. I

didn't want to sit beside her again, so I walked behind the sofa and dropped a hand onto her shoulder, patting her. There, there, then. Don't worry.

She looked up at me, and her eyes were even wider than before. They were almost bulging.

'They won't find anything, will they?'

'They might,' I said, hoping to encourage her.

Her jaw dropped and she looked towards the door. She began to moan again.

'There's nothing up there. Nothing. There's nothing.' I watched her for a moment, and then I turned to the policewoman.

'I think we ought to get that doctor back. This is more than shock; she's ill. She's had a bad reaction to that pill.'

'It was only Valium.'

'Perhaps she's had a bad reaction to the Valium, then.'

'I shouldn't think so.'

I was beginning to feel angry again, and with the anger came the thought of Tamsin, who would never move or think again.

No. Not now, Tamsin. Wait a minute.

And the anger, I couldn't afford anger. This girl in uniform, perhaps she spent so much of her time talking to the stupid and the uneducated that she couldn't help behaving as though she was the only one with an opinion worth having.

'Helen, I'm going to call the doctor again,' I said. 'Coburn, was it? Was that the name?'

She wasn't listening to me.

'I wish they'd go away,' she said. 'They won't find anything, there's nothing there.'

She was frightened. Sedatives can have that sort of result, I'd heard. It's dangerous to sedate animals. Doctor Coburn had given Helen Valium to calm her, but Helen wasn't calm, not any more.

The number was in an address book that lay open on the little table by the telephone. Doctor Coburn was out on her rounds, I was told. Was it an emergency?

I didn't know.

I tried to explain to the receptionist, but she said she thought it was unlikely that Mrs Simpson would have had a reaction to Valium.

Were receptionists, too, only accustomed to speaking to the stupid and uneducated?

Irritated, I hung up, and Welland came into the room as I did so.

'We've finished in the bathroom,' he said, and he looked at the policewoman.

'Mrs Masters was telephoning the doctor,' she said. 'Mrs Masters thinks Mrs Simpson isn't suited by the Valium.'

'Mrs Masters speaks English, too,' I snapped. 'And is quite capable of answering questions, if she thinks they're relevant.'

But Welland was looking at Helen, his

32

head on one side and his eyes narrowed.

'There's *nothing* up there,' she said. 'Nothing.'

'Where, then?' he asked, and his voice was very gentle.

She pressed herself back against the sofa, her hands gripping the edges of the cushion. She was trying to get away from him. She really was frightened.

'You see?' I said. 'I think it's a backlash, if that's the right term. You sometimes get it from sedatives. It has the opposite effect.'

He looked at me, but only briefly, as if I was a distraction, and then he was concentrating on Helen again.

'Where should we look?'

For a moment I thought she would answer him, but instead she resorted to tears. Her hands went up to her face, her head dropped, and her voice was muffled.

'Oh. Oh, Tamsin. My little girl.'

Was she crying? I wondered, and I knew he was asking himself the same question. But there was clearly nothing to be done.

'She can have a shower if she'd like one,' he said to me. 'By the time she's finished we'll be out of her bedroom. She might sleep.'

I might sleep, too. I was very weary; I was almost light-headed with tiredness, or so I told myself. How else could I account for the dream-like atmosphere in this room?

Here was a woman whose child had been killed and who was pretending to cry, and a man backing away from the situation but never taking his eyes off it. Even the smell of burning dust from the elements of the electric fire contributed to the air of unreality.

Over it all, dark and sad, hung the fact of Tamsin's death, and soon we would no longer be able to take refuge in the hackneyed conventions that we used to hide disaster; soon, we would all have to turn, and face it.

2

The house was almost empty, and it felt stale, as though there had been a party and nobody had cleared up after it. Too many people had been there. It was hot in the living room, and cold and stuffy everywhere else, except, perhaps, in Helen's bedroom.

I had done my best there. It had been searched, but not vindictively; nothing had been broken, and it had been left tidy, but everything had been moved. It had looked out of balance when I went in while Helen washed herself in the bathroom.

I'd turned on the fire and straightened the bedclothes, plumped the pillows, found a clean nightdress, and then I'd tried to put the ornaments where I thought they should be, to give some appearance of symmetry. There were framed photographs on the dressing table, and I picked up the one of my brother and looked down into his face, smiling out from the silver frame.

I could have been looking into a mirror, if I'd gone back ten years.

It wasn't a thought I liked. John and I had never been very close, and in the days that had followed the crash that killed him and my father immediately, and my mother three weeks later, I'd hardly thought of John at all.

Daddy was dead. Ten years had passed, and still, of the three of them, Daddy was the one who came into my mind first, and stayed as the other two drifted away.

I put the photograph down, took a paper handkerchief out of a little box and used it to wipe up some talcum powder that had been spilled on the glass tray.

Had they been looking for drugs? I wondered. Why not? People aren't murdered for nothing. Once they knew why, they might know who.

Perhaps Tamsin had been using drugs. Or selling them. Even at thirteen, it wasn't unknown.

The sounds of the shower in the bathroom stopped, and I shook my head, and put a silver-backed hairbrush and a matching comb in line with each other, diagonally across the centre of the dressing table, and a clothes brush and hand mirror behind them. They were probably not in the places Helen had chosen, but they were at least laid out, not set to one side in a stack.

My mother had said the word 'mirror' was vulgar, and incorrect. It was a looking glass, not a mirror. But mother had said 'lahndry' instead of 'laundry', and pronounced the word golf without the L.

I still thought in terms of 'Daddy' and 'my mother'. And I hardly thought of John at all.

Helen came out of the bathroom, seeming to be stumbling, although she showed no signs of falling. She hardly looked at me. She did fall across the bed, scrambling into it and pulling the duvet up over her shoulders before rolling away so that her back was towards me.

'G'night,' she said. She sounded drunk.

I picked up the nightdress she'd ignored, and laid it on the stool in front of the dressing table.

'Will you be all right?' I asked.

'You're not going away?'

Suddenly she was alarmed, twisting her head round to look at me, her face anxious.

'Oh, no. No, of course not. I'll stay while you need me. Perhaps I'll go for a walk, though.'

I could buy a map. I could make a note of the addresses of those undertakers, and look in their windows, perhaps pick out a couple that might be suitable. We could both visit them later.

'Will you be long?' asked Helen.

'Two or three hours? While you're sleeping? I'll cook us something to eat when I get back, shall I?'

I tried to sound reassuring, but she might as well not have heard me. She was still staring at me, her mouth open as though

37

she was about to speak, but could think of nothing to say.

'Don't go,' she said at last.

'All right,' I answered. 'I'll stay in the house, if you'd rather I did.'

She nodded, and then turned away, rubbing her face against the pillow, and sighing.

She didn't speak again.

I left her door slightly open when I went out, so that I would hear her if she called me.

There were still people downstairs, the spotty policewoman and a man in a white overall who'd been up here when I first came. Somebody had told me they were diverting all the incoming telephone calls to make sure Helen wasn't bothered by cranks, or by reporters, and the policewoman was waiting to hear that it had been done. Helen had said she only wanted to hear from her brother, Giles.

'Oh, and my husband,' I'd remembered to tell them. 'Anthony Masters. He'll probably call.'

I stood at the top of the stairs, wondering whether to go down and make myself a coffee, but I decided to wait until I could have the place to myself. In the meantime I'd look around up here, perhaps do some housework.

There were only two bedrooms. For such a small house it had taken them a long time to search. But perhaps there hadn't been as many of them as there'd seemed. I could only remember the feeling of a crowd, not individuals.

I cleaned the bathroom. Helen hadn't wiped out the bath after her shower, and the towel had been dropped onto the floor, damp and a little grubby. She did tend to give the impression that she wasn't a very clean person.

It was rather nice, the bathroom, a little out of place in this house, I thought. It had concealed lighting, and the shower controls looked like something out of a science fiction film.

There was nothing else to do, so I decided to make myself my coffee, or find a book. If I really couldn't stand Spotty I'd have to sit on the stairs and read it.

In the living room she looked up as I came in.

'Can I get you anything?' she asked, as if it was her house and I was a not very welcome guest.

'I thought I'd find a book.'

'I don't think Mrs Simpson's much of a reader.'

She was right. I looked in the cupboards under the display cabinet, and found nothing but magazines. None of them were of any interest to me.

I did wish I could go out.

It seemed almost blasphemous, to be bored in such a situation, but now that Helen was asleep and the shock that had hit me so hard earlier in the afternoon had worn off, that was what I felt. Tired, and bored.

There was nothing to do, and nothing to read.

I turned on the television, and flicked through the channels, then turned it off again. I looked at a small collection of compact discs, and found nothing that I wanted to hear.

Nothing. It's a nothing house, with a nothing woman in it, and I ought to be in Germany, where I'm needed, not slouching around in this room being stared at by a teenager in uniform.

'How long will you be here?' I asked, and she jerked her head towards the kitchen.

'Waiting for him,' she said. 'And the telephone.'

'I can answer the telephone. I'm not going to be upset by a crank.'

I looked in through the kitchen door, and the man in the white coat looked back at me. He didn't seem to be doing anything at all, other than standing in the middle of the room, but I supposed he was some sort of technician, and possibly knew his job.

'Will you be long?' I asked.

'No.'

It was a fitted kitchen, something I usually dislike. I glanced around, and then looked at an open cupboard door, looked more closely.

The wood was solid. Oak, I thought. Solid oak kitchen units? Helen? And in this silly, flimsy house?

Perhaps you can make a silk purse out of a sow's ear after all, I thought as I closed the door again, postponing my coffee. That kitchen looked rather nice. It looked as though people who knew what they were doing had spent some time and thought on it.

But the living room was hopeless, quite hopeless. The furniture had probably been chosen out of a catalogue, and it would take a great deal more than matching wallpaper and curtains to disguise its awkward shape. And the wall unit, with its flashy bits of glass with gold edges, it was frankly trashy. Somewhere on there, among those bits of china, there'd be something claiming to be A Present from Blackpool, Made in Taiwan.

Anthony had sometimes accused me of intolerance and bigotry, but I didn't see why I should pretend to like anything that I felt was second-rate. I wouldn't criticise the room, not to Helen. I wouldn't want to hurt her feelings. Nevertheless, I was perfectly entitled to my own opinions, and to express them, if I so wished.

However, Anthony was right. At least, he was partly right. Word of my opinions had, on occasion, got back to my victims, and had caused trouble. One or two of his colleagues now only invited him to their homes when it was known I wouldn't be able to come.

I'd been dreadfully upset when I had realised, but Anthony had pointed out that I'd always hated those social occasions anyway. I'd never had a good word to say about them afterwards. The food had been nasty, the people boring, why would I want to come?

I hadn't wanted to come, but I hadn't wanted to be excluded, either.

'Perhaps you'd better start keeping your opinions to yourself, then,' he'd said.

But what was there to talk about? To those people who smiled at me politely, being nice to the professor's wife, and they'd damned well better, hadn't they?

'Did you enjoy Doctor Neubacher's party?'

'Oh, yes. It was very nice.'

The conversation would come to an end, and we would be left smiling politely at each other, wondering what to say next.

'*Was* that really lamb we had? I did rather wonder whether somebody in the kitchen had difficulty distinguishing between a sheep and a donkey.'

There would be laughter, and a joke in response, and we would relax, and that lamb, yes, truly, it was, that was nothing. You should have tried the venison at New Year.

I never had meant to hurt anybody. I'd only wanted to make people laugh, and relax, and enjoy the conversation.

I thought about describing this house to Anthony when I got home. There wouldn't be anything much to say about Helen's living room, but I wished the man in the white coat would come out of the kitchen. That might be worth seeing again.

Only a minute or so later he did come out, and the policewoman stood up.

'Will you be all right, then?' she asked. I said I expected so, and she told me to ask for her if we had any problems, and she gave me her name, which I promptly forgot. They'd keep the telephone calls diverted for a few days, don't be upset if there are nasty letters, there are some right freaks about. Better open Mrs Simpson's mail for her unless I was sure I knew what was in it. And make sure it was me who answered the telephone until I got the call to say the diverter was on.

She'd be in touch, she said as they left.

If I had any problems it would be Welland I'd contact, not her. There's never any point in expecting the rank and file to solve prob-

43

lems; one has to go to the top.

Helen's kitchen astonished me. The units were, as I'd thought, solid oak. The drawers slid, silently and politely, on brass runners. The doors were hung precisely, opening and closing at a touch, close fitting, and the tiny gaps where they met the frames seemed to be absolutely parallel, exactly the same width at the top as they were at the bottom.

Daddy had once told me that that was the signature of a master craftsman.

My own kitchen was nothing like as good as this.

The use of space was clever, without being slick or smart. In the corners the shelves had been shaped and curved, and there were soft lights behind hanging plants, and a clear lamp over a slanted rack by the bookshelf, so you could prop a recipe book open and read it easily from the broad work surface where you would be preparing the food. There were marble slabs in the larder, with some sort of air conditioning over them, perfect for storing cheese and butter. The floor was covered with some substance that felt warm underfoot, and yet was smooth. There were creamy-coloured tiles behind the oak, beautifully fitted. The hob seemed to have been made of golden bronze, with a satiny finish, and gas thumped softly into blue flame at my first tentative touch.

How had Helen managed to afford this?

I found I was feeling slightly resentful. I'd understood she was finding it a little hard to manage, since John had died. And she'd never worked. Had she?

Well, if she could afford a kitchen like this, I certainly wouldn't have to worry about helping with funeral expenses.

I was being spiteful and childish, and I acknowledged it, and looked around the kitchen once more, longingly. I'd have to ask her who'd designed it. Perhaps one day I could get them to do one for me.

But I would have to save up for it. Save up for a long time. Thousands of pounds had been spent on this, thousands.

Helen seemed to be asleep when I looked in on her. The drawn curtains made it seem shady and cool in her room, but there was a smell of scent that I disliked. It was a deodorant, or something like that, an acrid smell overlaid with perfume.

This time, I closed the door behind me.

I stood on the landing, looking around, wondering. There was nothing out of the ordinary here, nothing I wouldn't have expected in Helen's house.

The third door was in front of me, and I stood there for what might have been several minutes before I opened it.

Tamsin's room.

It was lovely.

The colours were pale and warm, and they blended into each other, milky white into cream, into apricot, into a deep, glowing orange. This was difficult work, something I'd never seen outside exhibitions or in photographs in good magazines. I almost gasped as I looked at the evenness of the paintwork. Airbrushing can seem simple, but I knew it wasn't. Nowhere could I find a fault in it. It was seamless, as if it had grown that way. The sheen of silk in the white that surrounded the window, where did it become cream? As my eyes searched I was already looking at the delicate apricot, and still no sign of where, or how, the effect had been achieved.

And the wood, I didn't know what it was, a soft gold with a coppery grain, was smooth and beautifully worked.

For all its luxury, it was a room for a young girl. There was a teddy bear on the bed, and I caught my breath as I recognised it. That had been John's. It was shabby, and not very clean, but she'd tied a blue ribbon around its neck. She'd loved it.

Plum, John had called that bear.

'Hello, Plum.'

I would cry if I looked at him any longer. There was nothing else in the room that was familiar to me, and there was nothing else that was worn, and old.

There were school books on a shelf over a

desk, and I went across and sat on the chair in front of it. It was like an office chair, but a good one, and the fabric I had thought was woven turned out to be suede.

Anthony had bought himself a good chair, because he spent so much of his time working at his desk, but even that would have seemed cheap alongside this one.

How had they managed this? And why?

I ran my fingers over the arms and turned, swivelling on the smooth castors, to look at this extraordinary room.

It was a bad shape. It was long and narrow, but it had been so skilfully planned that I hadn't noticed until I analysed it. The colours made it seem broader and lighter. The awkward angles vanished behind curved woodwork, or were used in a way that made them seem part of the overall design. It all looked smooth and simple, as if it could not be any other way, as if it had grown naturally. There was nothing that seemed contrived, nothing artificial.

Helen has this in her house? *Helen?*

That silly, flabby, affected woman has *this?* For *Tamsin?*

But this house was nothing. It was nothing at all, a semi-detached lump in a little suburb, it might as well have been a council house, and in it, in *this* house, is a room fit for a palace.

And that kitchen.

47

And, come to think of it, the bathroom.

I stood up quickly and went out onto the landing, listening as I did so in case Helen might be awake.

The bathroom, I hadn't really noticed it when I'd gone in to clean up after Helen. But, yes. This was the same. This, too, showed the hand of a master craftsman, perhaps even an artist. It had the same simplicity, the same colours that seemed normal, even neutral, but then, if you did look, if you did turn your mind to it, were perfect. It all blended, and it was all of the highest possible quality. It was small, this room, with the door in a corner, and a difficult, high window, but there was no feeling that anything was cramped.

The shower screen over the bath slid smoothly into place, and then back, folding perfectly into a deep recess in the tiles, with none of the awkward aluminium or artificial rubber to which I had become accustomed, and I had thought our bathroom was a good one, modern and efficient.

But this? And it was all porcelain, it was good. It was more than good, it was the best.

What had happened to this family since my brother had died?

Helen had said she was poor, she'd said she couldn't manage. John's pension hadn't been enough, and she'd complained bitterly about our parents' will. She did have cause, although nobody could have anticipated the accident that had killed all three of them, not outright, but leaving my mother to survive for three weeks.

Daddy had done his best with the wills. He and my mother had agreed that they would only inherit from each other if the survivor outlived the one who died by two weeks. Otherwise everything would go in taxes, Daddy had said, and John and Celia wouldn't get much. Suppose we're both run over by the same bus?

It had all been a horrible muddle, the solicitor had said afterwards, and he was very sorry.

They had both been run over by the same bus, or rather, the same bus had fallen off a crumbling viaduct in Portugal onto their car. John had been driving, Daddy beside him, my mother in the back.

It had been the worst road accident in that area for twenty years, and nobody, absolutely nobody, was to blame. A mud slide after heavy rain had loosened the old brickwork at one end of the viaduct, and an engineer was already on his way to inspect it when it gave way. Fourteen people had died in the bus, including the driver, and Daddy and John, and a lorry behind them had swerved to try and avoid it and gone out of control and hit a little car, knocked it down into a ravine, and both the people in that had died, too.

They'd only stopped to try and help.

I wiped a tear away from the corner of my eye. I really should be over this by now, I told myself, and I was. I had got over their deaths, Daddy and John and my mother, but sometimes when I thought of those two young men who'd stopped their little Fiat and were about to get out to see if they could help, and the lorry coming round that bend and sliding on the mud, it did upset me. It still upsets me.

Helen had been shocked by John's death, but I'd never thought she'd really grieved. She'd insisted on going to the airport to meet the aeroplane when it brought the bodies home, and her brother had gone with her. It had all been pointless. They'd had to wait for three hours, and the Customs people had forgotten they were there. Anthony had arranged for an undertaker to collect the two coffins and take them back, but nobody had thought to tell the driver about Helen and Giles, sitting and waiting.

Helen had decided to believe that Anthony had done it on purpose. She did not intend to allow the funeral to take place without some sort of quarrel. She'd telephoned the undertaker and told him she wanted to make the arrangements for John's funeral herself.

'There's been a family dispute,' she'd said grandly.

I'd been in Portugal at the hospital, waiting for my mother to die.

The nuns had said they were praying for a miracle, and that I should do the same. I just prayed for a quick end, and didn't even get that. Sometimes she was almost conscious, but with that came pain, and so more drugs, and even if she'd known I was there, would she have cared?

They kept her alive for three weeks, and it was so pointless, so utterly pointless, all they did with their machines and their consultations, and perhaps their prayers, was thwart Daddy's careful plan. With the taxes, and the cost of bringing the bodies home, and the lawyers' fees, there was very little left.

'Don't let them bury Daddy,' I'd begged Anthony, and he'd guessed that I couldn't believe my mother would live. Bury them together. At least Daddy had loved her.

But John had been cremated that week, and later I heard Helen had told people that I hadn't even bothered to come to my brother's funeral.

How could I have gone? I couldn't be sure my mother wouldn't live, might even recover, despite that terrible wound in her head. She might have opened her eyes and looked at me, instead of giving that frantic

51

glare, and the little flicking movements which was my signal to press the bell for the nun to come in with the hypodermic syringe.

I couldn't have gone, I thought. Why did she say that? Did she expect me to leave my mother? How could I have gone?

'She didn't mean it,' said Anthony, and then I thought, she did. It was a deliberate piece of malice. Damn her, she's telling people I couldn't be bothered to attend my brother's funeral, out of sheer bloody malice.

'Is she telling them where I am?' I demanded, and Anthony had no answer.

I wrote to her. I shouldn't have done it, and, had I been less exhausted, had I been able to think at all, I wouldn't have. I would have turned it aside, without so much as an acknowledgement. But I was exhausted, and I was angry, and I wrote some very hard words to Helen. I don't think she ever forgave me.

There was nothing for Helen in my mother's will. My mother's property was to be divided equally between any surviving children, and that meant me.

'I want half,' Helen had said when we'd met at the church, on the way in for the service. She couldn't even wait until they'd been buried.

She'd been dressed in deep black, and the

toddler by her side had worn a black ribbon in her hair.

'That was what they meant, with that will. Not just you. I want half.'

'Then want,' I'd said coldly, 'must be your master.'

A few days later Anthony had suggested I should give Helen a share of the money, if only for Tamsin.

'She told everybody I couldn't be bothered to go to John's funeral.'

'She didn't say it like that. It's not the child's fault.'

I'd sent Helen two thousand pounds. It wasn't half, but it was something at least. She never thanked me, never even acknowledged it, but the cheque was cleared the following day. She paid the few pounds extra to have it done quickly, probably because she thought I might change my mind.

We'd exchanged letters and Christmas cards, and her letters were mostly complaints, the government, prices, schools, nothing was right, everything was a struggle. She wasn't going to work, because no employer would give her what she was worth. Equal Pay for Equal Work was a joke, so they could pay through their taxes to keep her and Tamsin, serve them right.

No doubt everything was much better in Germany.

We'd met again at a wedding, and Helen had put on weight. She'd been pretty, but now she simply wasn't bothering. Tamsin was a bridesmaid, and when Helen had introduced us she'd referred to me as 'Your Auntie Celia', which had set my teeth on edge, but I'd smiled at the girl, and tried to talk to her. I'd asked her about school, and her favourite subject.

She hadn't got one.

'You look like your father,' I'd said. 'You've got his eyes. They were his best feature.'

I must look again at those photographs, I told myself. It had been true when I'd spoken, so far as I could remember John's eyes. I could compare photographs of John and Tamsin.

When Helen woke up I would do that.

And would I ask her about these rooms? Probably not outright, that would be rude, but I could compliment her. I could ask for the name of the designer. She couldn't object to that, if I said it was an absolutely splendid kitchen, who designed it, Helen? Well, my dear, you may think that every-thing's better in Germany, but I've never seen a kitchen up to that standard over there.

It must have cost a fortune.

Or perhaps I wouldn't say that. I'd leave that for a little while. I wouldn't want her to think I was prying.

But I did want to know what these rooms had cost, and how she'd managed to pay for them.

I was feeling tired, but very alert. I knew I wouldn't sleep that night, and then I thought, sleep where? Helen had said nothing, and I hadn't thought to ask. I shouldn't leave her alone, but I certainly wasn't going to sleep on that horrible sofa.

Tamsin's room, then?

It hardly seemed right. Helen would be sure to object, although Tamsin couldn't mind any more. Helen might take a 'What would people say?' attitude.

But if she wanted me to stay in the house, she would have to let me use Tamsin's bed. Otherwise, I would go to a hotel. And I wouldn't stay long, either. The air fare had cost me enough, for a woman I didn't even like. Hotel bills on top was going too far.

I was building myself up into a state of irritation again, which was silly, when Helen might easily say that of course I could sleep in Tamsin's room. She might even offer to reimburse me for my ticket, although I'd probably refuse that. Probably. Although, with rooms like these, couldn't she afford it?

But no, that wasn't the point.

I went back into Tamsin's room, and this time I managed to smile at Plum. I'd thrown him in the canal once, when I was about four and John two, and Daddy had waded out to rescue him. I'd had to spend the rest of the day in my room, with no toys. Think about what you did, you nasty little girl, my mother had said. That night I'd apologised to Plum, and Daddy had laughed, but my mother had been annoyed.

Poor old bear, all soggy and out of shape, hanging on the washing line pegged up by his ears.

A couple of years later, when John was being a cowboy, Plum had been dragged around at the end of a lariat. He was being a longhorn steer. Now he had a nice blue ribbon round his neck instead of an old piece of sash cord.

I sat in the suede chair again, and moved a sliding panel on the desk top to one side. A keyboard rose out of the recess.

Oh, come now. This is ridiculous. This, for a thirteen-year-old, this is *right* over the top. What on earth could Helen have been thinking of, to give a child this sort of thing?

Another panel hid the monitor, and wasn't that one of the new ones? The ones that cost thousands and doubled up as televisions? There were speakers over my head, the fabric tinted to blend in with the wood, and they were Bang and Olufsen. Weren't they?

What had she been doing, with this computer?

I switched it on, and watched as it ran through the routine.

There were a few games, but most of the files seemed to be schoolwork. Perhaps she'd finally found a favourite subject. And perhaps this was why so much time had been taken, searching up here. Somebody would have looked through all these files.

I chose the one labelled History, and there was an essay on the Treaty of Versailles, the last piece of work she'd done under that file.

I do not think the Treaty of Versailles was fair. It is not fair when people are blamed for things they did not do and the people in Germany got blamed for the first world war when they had not been born. Even in the first world war, I would not like it if I had to do what people said when they did not even speak my language and I could not vote for them. I do not like being bossed about and I do not think the Germans liked being bossed about so they got angry and made a war about it. If you get angry and you want to fight somebody anything can let you do it. When the duke was killed I do not think anybody really minded but it meant they could have a war.

When you are fighting you do not think about right or wrong you think about winning and not getting hurt.

If the treaty of Versailles had been fair maybe there wouldn't have been another world war because the people of Germany would not have been angry and fed up of being bossed about and they would not have thought Hitler was so clever and brave and a good leader.

I looked in Tamsin's history file on the shelf over the desk, and found the printed version of her essay. At the bottom, in red ink, was her mark, a C+, and the comments:

Once again, you have not been listening. You have taken no account of the economic factors, nor the situation in North Africa, nor was Germany being governed by people who did not speak German. However, your ideas about democracy are basically sound and intelligent.

Do not let your own feelings run away with you. Facts must take precedence over theory, and you cannot hold well informed opinions without information.

In the margin, against Tamsin's comment 'when the duke was killed I do not think anybody really minded,' appeared the question 'Except, perhaps, the Duke?'

It wasn't a very good essay, but I found I could sympathise with Tamsin's indignation on behalf of Germany. After all, I thought, what are a few facts in the face of injustice?

There was something in the Geography file about the rubber trade in South-East Asia, in which Tamsin was more concerned about the burning of the natural forests than international trade, as her teacher remarked. Another low mark, but at least she had some opinions of her own, even if they weren't very well founded.

I think I would have liked you, Tamsin.

I thought I heard Helen, so I went to the door and listened for a few moments. There was no sound from her room.

She must be exhausted, I thought. Shock and grief must have that effect.

And yet, after the accident in Portugal, it had been three days before I'd slept. I hadn't been able to sleep at all, not even short naps. I'd wanted to talk. Some of the nuns had spoken English, and had listened to me, and the doctor, when he'd had time. After the three days he'd said firmly that I must sleep, and he would give me something to help me. No more talking now, take this. One of the sisters would stay with my mother.

But Helen was sleeping, and this time yesterday Tamsin had been alive.

Or perhaps not, I wasn't sure when she'd been killed. How, and where, but not when, and not, not yet, by whom.

The telephone rang, and I went down the stairs as quickly as I could to answer it, but I heard Helen's feet on the floor above my head as I picked up the receiver.

'Yes?' I asked cautiously, not sure what words I should use here, and in this situation.

'Is that Mrs Masters?'

'Yes.'

'Just ringing to tell you the call diverter's in place now.'

'Thank you. Could I speak to Chief Inspector Welland?'

He was out. Could somebody else help? Could they give a message?

Helen was standing in the doorway, staring at me.

'I wanted to ask somebody to keep us informed. About the case. Well, of course, about the case. Can you ask him?'

'Who is it?' asked Helen.

'The police,' I said as I put down the telephone. 'They were only ringing to tell us about the call diverter. I'm sorry it woke you.'

'Have they found Giles?'

'They didn't say so.'

'Well, didn't you *ask?*'

I supposed it was natural, that she would want her brother at such a time.

'If they'd found him I'm sure they would have told me,' I said.

'They've *got* to find him,' she said. 'They've *got* to.'

There were tears in her eyes again, and she started to shiver.

'Helen, come and sit down. Poor Helen. Shall I cook us something to eat? You're probably getting hungry by now. Would you like something?'

She sniffed, and then nodded at me, and tried to smile.

'You're very kind, Celia. I'm sorry. I am

60

grateful, really. Really, I am.'

She began to cry again, and all I could do was take her into my arms and hug her. It would have been heartless not to.

'Poor Helen,' I said again.

What can you say to somebody whose child has died like this?

'Poor Helen.'

Once she was calmer I led her over to the sofa and left her there while I went into the kitchen. Soup, I thought. Hot, and nourishing, and easy.

There was nothing with which I could make a proper soup, but there were packets in one of the cupboards. I'd have to go shopping. If I was to cope here I would have to buy the ingredients I was used to.

Oh, this lovely kitchen.

I heated bread in the microwave and found the remains of a roast chicken in the fridge, chopped it and added it to the packet mixture. And cream.

When I carried the tray into the living room Helen was watching the television. I took the remote control from her slack hand, and turned it off.

'I don't think you should watch tonight,' I said. 'It might upset you, if there's...'

'Why are you always so *bossy?*'

'I don't mean to be bossy, but I do think...'

'I'll do what I like in my own house, thank you very much.'

61

I gave her back the remote control.

Stupid woman, I thought. Well, if there's something about Tamsin, she'll be the one who'll suffer.

'I'm sorry,' she said a few minutes later.

'That's all right. Drink your soup, it might make you feel better.'

I wanted to ask, how long will you need me to stay here? If I was going to be snapped at every time I tried to help, it would be impossible. For myself, I would have liked to have watched the news. I'd only been thinking of Helen.

'I don't think I've ever met Giles,' I said.

'He was at John's funeral.'

Oh, for God's sake. I would have been at John's funeral too, if you hadn't contrived that stupid quarrel. Yes, well, all right. If that stupid quarrel had not arisen. Anyway, I will not answer your childish jibes.

Now, if I say something nice about your kitchen, you'll probably come back with something unpleasant about Daddy's will.

'Does he travel a lot? Giles?'

'He's in business.'

Is he indeed? So's the cashier at the supermarket, and that filthy old creature who used to sell clothes pegs on the corner of Deakin Street.

'What line of business?'

I tried to sound interested, but Helen shrugged. She wasn't sure. He had investments in lots of things. He had his own office.

I was trying to think of some way of continuing the conversation when the telephone rang again. Helen jumped, and I gave her an enquiring look before going over to it.

'Hello?'

'Is that Mrs Masters?'

It was Chief Inspector Welland. He had news of a sort, and wasn't sure whether we would regard it as good or bad. He'd like to come over, if that was convenient. He could be with us in about five minutes.

3

He came alone, but I saw a driver in the car, a man in uniform. I caught a brief glimpse of a chequered cap band in the headlamps of a passing van.

Helen had been upset when I'd told her he was coming with some news, and kept demanding of me what it could be. I'd answered every time that I had no idea, but that we'd learn soon enough. I cleared away the plates and bowls as I spoke to her. This wasn't my house, but in a way I was in charge, or at least responsible, and I dislike it when visitors find me in a room that is anything short of immaculate.

Helen was frightened.

'Please don't upset yourself,' I kept repeating. 'He's only being kind, he's coming round to keep us up to date.'

I was glad he did only take five minutes. By the time he arrived Helen was in tears again, begging me not to go, wishing Giles was here, and when I showed Welland into the room she shrank back into the corner of the sofa and raised her hands to her mouth. Her eyes were wide.

Why was she so frightened? I wondered if

it could still be a reaction to the drug, and if so, for how long it would last.

'May I sit down?' Welland asked, but she didn't respond, except with a gasp, and her hands raised even higher.

'Please, do,' I said.

It didn't take him long to give us his news.

'Tamsin wasn't murdered. She took her own life.'

Helen moaned, and I reached out and put a hand on her knee. I could think of nothing to say. She was dead, and we'd thought somebody had killed her. Now, we had to think again, but still, Tamsin was dead.

'Mrs Simpson?' Welland asked. 'Did you understand what I said?'

She moaned again, and there were tears welling up into her eyes. Still she said nothing. She was staring at him. She seemed even more scared than before.

Why?

How far could I go here? I wondered. She'd already accused me of being bossy, and I didn't want to interfere, but we could hardly sit here for ever, with her staring at him and saying nothing, and him waiting for her to answer.

'Are you absolutely sure?' I asked him, and he looked at me.

'That it was suicide, I mean?' I added.

'Quite sure.'

I wanted to know, why did you think it was

murder, then? I wanted to ask, what have you found out? You can't leave us like this; Tamsin's been murdered; Tamsin took her own life: you have to tell us.

But perhaps not just now, not with Helen seemingly hypnotised, sitting there staring and white with the tears rolling down her cheeks.

Why would she have killed herself? She was thirteen years old, she was indignant about the Treaty of Versailles and the burning of the forests, why would she have ended her life?

Murder had been dreadful, but was suicide any better?

At least it had been her own choice.

What do we do now?

'Does this mean we can start arranging the funeral?' I asked.

'There'll have to be an inquest,' he answered, 'but I don't think there'll be a long delay. The coroner's officer will be able to advise you.'

He glanced at Helen, and then dropped his voice as he spoke to me again.

'The post mortem examination has been scheduled for tomorrow afternoon.'

I hardly heard him. Other questions, and not addressed to him, had come into my mind.

Why, Tamsin? Why not live, and campaign for the rainforests, and write angry letters about unfair treaties and injustice? Why end it? Why not go on? You *cared*, didn't you?

There were tears in my own eyes now, and Welland stood up, nodded to Helen, and smiled at me.

'I'll go now. You'll want to know more at some time. You can ask the coroner's officer for the details.'

I saw him out, and when I went back into the living room I didn't want to sit beside Helen and comfort her. I wanted to cry for Tamsin myself.

'I won't be a minute,' I said, and I walked through into the kitchen, and seized a handful of paper towels and wiped at my eyes with them.

Oh, Tamsin. All the things you could have done. All the marches and the demonstrations and getting arrested, all that stuff that's such a bloody nuisance for everybody else and sometimes does get results anyway, wasn't that worth it? Weren't white clouds in the sky, and sunshine on silver birch bark and some boy in the school playground looking at you long and hard and turning a bit red when you looked back, weren't they worth it?

All the things you left behind, wasn't there one worth living for? The things you must have been looking forward to. Growing up, being an adult, the ideas that all turn out to be wrong, but at that age it doesn't matter.

You can do what you like when you're grown up, there's nobody bossing you about when you're grown up. Weren't you looking forward to that? You'd hardly even started being a teenager, weren't you looking forward to pop concerts? To missing the last train home, and to those telephone calls; I'm staying with a friend don't worry. And then up all night with just exactly the sort of people your mother hoped you'd never meet. Saying 'no', I hope, but it had been exciting to be asked. There was all that to look forward to. Wasn't it enough?

'Celia?'

'I'm coming, Helen.'

I stifled the feeling of irritation at the sound of her voice. I'd come over to help her, after all. What an incredibly silly woman, sitting there like a scared rabbit, when that nice man had come to give us the news himself. He could easily have delegated that, but he did care, at least a bit. At least enough to come himself, to tell us the news. He hadn't known whether we'd see it as good or bad.

Good, I suppose, I thought. Or, what could have made her so wretched? No, it was bad news. Murder is horrible, but to want to die, at thirteen, to want to die so much that you did actually kill yourself, wasn't that worse? Just how miserable did you have to be to do that?

It was nearly dark outside, so I drew the curtains as I went into the living room. This time yesterday I'd been making coffee for Anthony and his bloody students, laying out a tray with a plate of biscuits and wondering if that girl with the frizzy hair who couldn't sit still and kept rocking on her chair was sitting on my nice little Edwardian nurser again. I'd reupholstered it myself, and I knew just how fragile those legs were. She'd break it if she wasn't careful, and think it was *so funny*, this little chair just collapsed under me, but it's all right, I'm not hurt, Frau Masters.

Would you like another cup of coffee, Fräulein Thing? Sugar, or ground glass?

I shouldn't be thinking like that. Not now, with Tamsin, maybe not even one day dead. I didn't know when she'd done it, when she'd hanged herself. Not a cruel death, Mr Welland had said. He didn't think she'd choked. While I was making coffee and wishing Anthony would tell that girl to sit still or move onto the sofa she, maybe, was tying a rope around her own neck.

I went back into the living room and sat down beside Helen, laying a hand on her knee. It was just a gesture of sympathy, to say, I'm here; I'm here for you.

I don't think I am, though, I thought. Not now. I think I'm here for Tamsin, now.

Was there *any* way this could have been an

accident? I wondered, hardly noticing Helen beside me, sniffing into a paper handkerchief. After all, at first they'd said it was murder. Then suicide, they'd said, so maybe they could be wrong again. Maybe she'd been swinging on a rope, the way children do, and it had got caught around her neck, wasn't that possible? Wasn't it possible that it had been nothing more than an accident?

Then she wouldn't have been miserable before she died. She'd have been happy, playing. She'd have been swinging on a rope, liking the movement, liking the wind in her face and her hair. I could remember doing that. One foot in a loop of rope, and leaning back away from it, getting the momentum up, and higher, and higher, swooping through the air, with the rope creaking on the branch of the tree, might break, might break, go on, higher and higher, nothing can happen to me, I'm invincible, I'm immortal, I'm *young*. Up at the highest point, when the rope goes slack just before you turn and bend your knees and the rope could, couldn't it? Suppose you really twisted around instead of that simple turn, it could, it could possibly get caught around your neck.

So there'd be nothing more than a moment of surprise, and fright. This can't be happening to me. And then, all over.

Not a cruel death. Unconsciousness, very

70

quick, something like that, he'd said, that nice man with the sad brown eyes.

Beside me Helen made the same moaning sound, and I turned to her, trying to smile.

'Tomorrow, we'll find...' What did they call them? 'We'll find a funeral director, shall we?' I asked Helen. 'We'll arrange something lovely for her. Shall we do that?'

She nodded at me, and began to cry again.

This time I'll go on talking, I thought. I do not want to hug her. I don't like the feel of her body, all soft and saggy. I don't like it.

'Lots of flowers,' I said. 'I expect she liked flowers, didn't she? And the right sort of hymns for a young teenager.'

Were they Church of England? Or even Christian? I didn't know. But we could have something with a bit of a swing to it, something she would have liked. What was there? It was years since I'd been in...

Don't be bossy, I told myself. Don't try to organise this, just help and support her, this woman whose daughter killed herself.

Oh, yes. Killed herself. Murder, they'd said, or at least something like that, they'd never actually said definitely. 'It looks as if...' those had been the words. 'It seems.' But never outright, she was murdered. Then, took her own life. New words, new meanings, and very clear.

They wouldn't have said that if there had been any chance that it could have been an accident. They wouldn't have said that to her mother.

Who *surely* should have *known* she was in trouble.

Don't judge, I told myself. You don't know. You don't know anything about it. If you did know you would understand. And if you understood you would forgive, or, even better, realise that there is nothing to forgive.

Apart from anything else, it is none of your business.

But at that thought another part of my mind rebelled. Oh, yes, it is. I might not have got on well with my brother, but Tamsin was his child too, and I'm the only one left, apart from this flabby woman.

He'd married her when she was three months up the duff as he'd put it, trying to make a joke of it, but with an edge to his voice, even through the smile, that did suggest he'd felt trapped.

And your ghastly mother at the reception, I remembered, trying to patronise everybody, referring to her dead husband as 'The Colonel', and mentioning how premature *Helen* had been, something she got from The Colonel's side of the family.

Your ghastly mother, covering your tracks six months in advance, because people can count up to nine, and certainly would. Did she really think, then, that when your child was born only six months after the wedding, those people would remember, and believe? Premature births run in the family, you know. Her mother said so at the wedding.

Mrs Henry Baker, *nee* Brotherton-Radcliffe. A two-generation-old double-barrelled name conferred a distinction, we were to understand. Certainly upon a Simpson.

I'd introduced Anthony as 'The Professor', which had annoyed Anthony considerably but had made Daddy snort with laughter, and bury his face in his handkerchief.

'So sorry,' he'd said, and contrived a cough. 'Smoky in here.'

None of that had been Helen's fault.

This may be the wrong time to ask, and she may feel it's nothing to do with me, but I don't really care.

'Why do you think she would have done it?'

She sighed, and the sigh turned into a yawn. I knew it was nothing more than nervousness and exhaustion, but a part of me of which I was immediately ashamed thought, I'll keep that. One day I may say, when I asked you why your daughter killed herself, you yawned.

Mrs Henry Baker, *nee* Brotherton-Radcliffe, was now in a home where the medical staff referred to her, tactfully, as 'confused'.

Mad as a bloody hatter, Anthony had said when he'd read her Christmas letter two years ago, babbling about a Ming vase that her aunt had been given by the Empress of China with whom she'd been on such intimate terms.

She was certainly in no position to offer any help or support to her daughter, and probably wouldn't even understand what had happened. Indeed, it would be cruel to try to explain it to her.

There was only me, until Helen's brother could be found, and I could think of nothing except spiteful little anecdotes against her and her family. Ever since Welland had said it was suicide, at the back of my mind and forcing its way forward all the time was the thought, why didn't you know? Why didn't you stop her?

The verdict at the inquest would be suicide while the balance of her mind was disturbed, wasn't that how they phrased it? So that she could be buried in consecrated ground. It meant, she killed herself, but she didn't mean to. It wasn't her fault. It wasn't a mortal sin.

'Tell me about Tamsin,' I said to Helen.

Go on, talk, I thought. It's supposed to be cathartic.

When I'd met that lovely woman from

Somalia, two of whose children had been bayoneted in front of her, Gabi had told me to let her talk about them. Never mind if she cries, Gabi had said. It will help her.

But the only time I'd ever seen Feduna cry was when she'd thought she couldn't buy winter shoes for her family, because the shoe shops wouldn't take the tokens the social services gave refugees instead of money. God knows how she'd managed to save tokens, when the others swore they couldn't manage at all, let alone save.

I'd sorted that out for Feduna, taken her to the Sozialamt, where for once they'd been sympathetic and anxious to help. They'd given her enough money to buy the shoes, even a few marks extra, and had said she should bring the receipts and any change when she was next in the town.

I'd been astonished.

'We know her,' Frau Scharf had said to me.

Feduna didn't talk about the two children very often, and I think it was because she saw that it upset me, not because she wanted to forget them. I'd let Feduna down, by not being able to listen without showing my rage, and my sorrow.

Why, when I had heard so many horror stories from the refugees I tried to help, could I not be better prepared for the horror of my own niece's death?

'Tell me about Tamsin.'

'What do you want to know?'

'I want to know what she was like.'

Helen sniffed.

'She had nearly black hair. Sort of, half long, down to her shoulders.'

I wanted to shout at her.

Oh, you *stupid* woman. Not what she *looked* like, I can see photographs. How could John have married you? Somebody so stupid, how could he? He wasn't a fool, surely he could have found *some* way of ducking out of that ridiculous wedding, and spending nearly three years in your company. Three *hours* has been enough for me.

Tamsin. It's quite a pretty name, although I wouldn't have chosen it, not for a child. A nice name for a dog, a spaniel perhaps. John hadn't seemed very interested in his daughter's name. Helen's godmother had been called Tamsin, he'd explained. Perhaps Helen had thought there might be something in the will for the girl, if she used a little bit of flattery.

'Everybody said she was pretty,' Helen went on. 'She was, too. Not that it matters, not to me, but it's still a man's world, isn't it? More's the pity.'

'What did she like doing?' I asked.

Helen shrugged, and sniffed again.

'Going out with friends. Never at home if she could help it. Art, at school, she liked that. Always painting trees, got some of them up on the wall in the art studio. She was quite good at that.'

'Was that her favourite subject?'

'I suppose so.'

Then she turned towards me and she was crying again.

'Why are they doing that post mortem? They know she killed herself, don't they? What do they want to cut her up for?'

This time I could sympathise.

'Oh, poor Helen, that must be horrible for you. Yes, poor Helen, I do understand that.'

I put my arms around her and let her drop her face onto my shoulder. Poor, poor Helen, thinking about that.

'Why can't they just leave her alone?'

'It's the law.'

'It's all wrong, that. Cutting her up. It's wicked. Can't you stop them? I bet Giles could stop them. He's got influence, Giles, I bet he could stop them.'

'I'm sure they'll find him soon,' I said, trying to sound positive. 'Or he'll come home. Is he often away for long? Or is it just short trips?'

She wasn't sure. Sometimes a few days. No, she didn't know where he went, he'd tell her he was going to be away, and then he'd go. Europe, she thought. He had lots of investments. He had important things to see to, he always said he didn't want to be disturbed when he was abroad.

'Somebody must know where he is,' I commented, but Helen didn't know who.

Giles didn't have a secretary. Giles said you couldn't get good staff these days, and a laptop computer could do everything a secretary could.

Giles was on the Internet. He had something called a website, she thought.

'If he's got an E-mail address he could be contacted through that,' I said. 'He's bound to check his mail, no matter where he is. Isn't he?'

She didn't know.

'Did you tell the police his E-mail address?'

She hadn't.

'Helen, have you got his E-mail address?'

No, she hadn't. She didn't know anything about all that technology.

I thought, I bet Tamsin's got it on her computer. But if I say so, Helen will know I've been looking in that room, and I don't want her to know that. It'll seem as if I've been snooping.

Let there be a long pause, then, I thought. And another sympathetic pat on that soft knee.

'Was Tamsin interested in technology, Helen?'

'Sort of. Did all her homework on a computer. Giles bought it for her. He's got contacts, he said he'd get the best. He was very good to Tamsin. It's going to break his heart, this.'

Another pause. Give it a moment or two. Then the idea.

'Did Tamsin use the Internet?'

'No. I wouldn't let her. There was a note from the school about pornography. I wouldn't have that.'

'I think you can block it now. There are parental control systems. I'm sure I heard that somewhere.'

But I'd no idea how it worked. I remembered thinking, when I saw an advertisement mentioning it, that a lot of children were a great deal more computer literate than their parents. It wouldn't take an intelligent young enthusiast long to find a way round *that*.

It was too late to worry about it for Tamsin.

'Would you like me to telephone the police and tell them Giles might be contacted by E-mail?'

Welland had gone home. I was put through to CID, and a man there said he knew about the case, but the police weren't taking any further action. It had all been handed over to the coroner's officer. A message had been left on an answering machine for Mr Baker. He didn't think he could commit himself to tracing Mr Baker through the Internet.

He wasn't rude. He sounded quite sympathetic. But he did repeat, twice, that so far as the police were concerned the case was closed, and they were taking no further action, and what he meant was, stop bothering us.

'They can't help,' I said as I hung up, but Helen seemed to have lost interest. She was yawning again, and she looked very strained.

Poor woman, she must be exhausted. I did feel sympathetic, even though my irritation persisted.

'Did you sleep at all this afternoon?' I asked, and she shook her head, and then nodded.

'A bit.'

Then she put her hands up to her face again.

'I do wish they wouldn't do that post mortem. I do wish they wouldn't.'

'Try not to think about it, Helen. Did the doctor give you something to help you sleep?'

'I don't *want* to sleep.'

But I did. I was feeling drained now. I'd had less than four hours' sleep on the previous night, there'd been the flight over here, and then that bout of shock, in which I'd suddenly realised what death meant, and what I'd thought was murder meant. Dylan Thomas's poem still echoed in my mind, but it had a different meaning now. I hoped she had gone gentle into that goodnight, young Tamsin, but I could rage against the dying of the light. For her.

There were tears on my cheeks again, and Helen looked up and saw them, and seemed surprised.

'You didn't know her,' she said.

'I'm sorry,' I answered. 'I'm just feeling rather tired. I didn't mean to get all emotional.'

To my surprise, she was concerned. She touched my hand, and tried to smile at me.

'You must be,' she said. 'Tired, I mean. I woke you up in the middle of the night, didn't I? Do you want to have a lie down on my bed?'

I shook my head, and smiled back at her.

'No, I'm all right. But I am going to have to think about where to sleep tonight.'

She looked around the room, as if expecting to see a bed materialise in front of her.

'I could check into a hotel,' I suggested.

'Oh, no.'

'No, I don't think you should be alone yet.'

Come on, I thought. Offer me Tamsin's room. Be sensible, not sentimental. I'm not going to desecrate her memory by sleeping in her bed.

She tried to find an alternative, but I told

her I suffered from back trouble, I really couldn't sleep on the sofa. And Helen, luckily, did not offer to do so herself, so that I could have her bed. I hadn't believed she would. She could only sleep in her own bed, she never got a wink in a strange bed, she brought out all the usual excuses.

'Well,' she said at last, a little doubtfully, 'I don't suppose it would matter. If it wouldn't upset you? I mean, Tamsin's bed? We could put clean sheets...'

'I can do that,' I said. 'No, it wouldn't upset me. Thank you for suggesting it.'

She shivered.

'I'm ever so hungry. Is that heartless? Is that cruel of me, to be hungry when she's just dead?'

'No,' I said. 'Of course it's not cruel, Helen. You're exhausted. When the body's exhausted, it needs fuel, that's why you're hungry. I'll cook something, shall I?'

The soup earlier in the evening had been enough for me, but Helen was obviously used to something more substantial, so I made us a meal, and Helen said there was a film on the television, it might take our minds off things. I forget what it was, but I found I quite enjoyed it. It was a good film. Helen kept dozing off and jerking into wakefulness, and at last I said I really did think she should go to bed, and take that pill. Making herself ill with tiredness was no good, not for anybody, least of all Tamsin. I was sure it was the last thing Tamsin would have wanted.

'She wouldn't have cared,' said Helen, and began to cry again.

I ran her a bath, and put some scented oil in it. I laid out the new nightdress again, and I made up her bed with clean sheets, as well as Tamsin's. Helen's bed looked as inviting as I could make it, with smooth pillows and the duvet turned down, the bedside light with the shade tilted away so it wouldn't be in her eyes.

I stayed in her room until she fell asleep, quite soon after she took the single pill which the doctor had left in a little plastic box, and then I went out, leaving her door open, and the light in the hall on in case she woke.

I fell asleep almost immediately, although I'd thought I was so tired I'd probably have one of those nights when sleep would not come, and that I'd be useless to Helen the next day.

Yes, to Helen. I tried to remind myself that it was for Helen I was there. She had lost her child, and needed somebody to support her. There was only me.

Then why could I only think of Tamsin? I could hardly remember the dark girl I'd met for the first time at that wedding, apart from the glimpse I'd had of her as a toddler. I could remember only that she'd been quiet, with very little to say for herself, but polite.

Tamsin had cared about fairness, and about forests. She'd liked painting trees, and she was good at that.

Tamsin was locked up somewhere, and I had a key, but I couldn't remember. It was lost, the key was lost, I must find it.

I woke up suddenly, sitting up in the bed, remembering immediately where I was, and why I was there, but still thinking of the key I must find. I don't even know where to look, I thought. And then, stupid. Only a dream.

It was a dream that came back.

She was trying to escape, from that place where she was locked up, and I could help, if I could find the key. There was only me now. All the others who might have freed her had gone. There was only me, and I didn't know where to look.

'Let me out. Let me *out* of here!'

She was battering against something, there was a banging noise, a crash as china broke, what was she doing? What was happening?

'Tamsin?'

'Let. Me. Out.'

She was frightened, but she was hiding it very well. There was nothing but determination and anger in her voice. She smashed something else, and I caught a flash of triumph through the fear.

Hope it was valuable, she spat through my mind. Hope it mattered.

What else could she break? And where's the key? There has to be a key somewhere, if there's a lock.

'Please let me out. Please help me.'

'I'm trying,' I said. 'Where's the key?'

She'd moved away from the door now, it must have been a door. What else could it have been? I didn't know. It was all confusion and noise. She was sitting, hunched and furious, on a bed. Is that a bed?

'Tamsin? Tam?'

'Don't call me Tam.'

'Sorry. Where's the key?'

Her voice had been harsh. She was trying not to cry. She was determined not to cry, so give her time to answer. Don't push.

'Tamsin, can you remember where the key is?' It wasn't a matter of remembering. It was up to me, this. That was why I was here. I had to find the key.

'Let me *out*, let me *out*, let me *out*.'

Stamp, and again, and something crunched. She'd broken it, whatever it was, that crash, that china, and it was not going to be mended, either.

Right, glue that together if you can, you bastards. Hope it cost a fucking fortune.

'*Tamsin!*'

'Sorry.'

85

Thirteen years old, language like that, and she wasn't in the least sorry. She was angry, and scared.

Find the key, but I don't even know where we are. It's dark; at least, I think it's dark. I can't really see.

But I'm here, and she's trapped, so I have to do something, don't I?

'Let me out.'

'I'm trying.'

I wasn't. I wasn't doing anything. I was just being there. Not seeing, because of the dark, or maybe I'm blind. I can't see. I don't understand this. There's a key, and I have to find it.

'You're stupid.'

She hadn't meant me to hear that. It was a sullen mutter, but I can hear very, very well. Much better than she knows.

She was thinking, you've got the key. If not you, then there's nobody.

'Oh, please. Let me out.'

I woke then because I couldn't bear to hear her defeat. She had tried so hard not to cry, young Tamsin, but it had been too much. She was only thirteen, after all.

I sat up in her bed, and I picked up Plum and hugged him.

Dreams, I thought, and I wondered how often Tamsin had hugged this shabby old bear, who had heard so many whispered secrets, and stood between children and their nightmares.

Dear old Plum.

There was light from the streetlamps shining on the ceiling. I should have drawn the curtains, but I wanted fresh air. I didn't want barriers.

Tamsin was locked in.

Killed herself, at thirteen. How much misery does it take, to do that?

I lay on my back, looking up at the ceiling, my chin resting on Plum's head, my hands holding his arms.

Some nightmares are just too big, aren't they, Plum? Too much for one shabby old bear. Whatever it was, you couldn't fight that one. You couldn't win.

Maybe I shouldn't be in this lovely room after all. Silly, to let it affect me like this. Silly dreams, and I'm so tired.

Go back to sleep. Never mind the streetlamps, reflected light on the painted ceiling. Tired, go back to sleep.

She's angry, she's desperate, there's a whirling in this room, flailing and thrashing, Tamsin, be still!

No. No. I will not.

But what do you want? You're dead, Tamsin. Whatever it was, you've escaped now.

You'll have to do it. There's only you.

What? What will I have to do?

No, this is too much, this rage. I can't cope

with this, it's intolerable.

Had I been asleep again? The duvet was twisted, half under my sprawled legs. I must have fallen asleep and somehow, turning, got it crumpled like that. I must have been restless, moving in my sleep.

There's a boiling in this room, in the still, quiet air, in the silence of the night, a thunder of anger and despair tearing at the serenity.

'Tamsin?'

I whispered her name into the silence, and felt the rage swirl around me.

Dreams, but I'm awake.

'Tamsin?'

Be quiet. Don't disturb Helen, oblivious in the next room, drugged and heavy. Don't disturb the sleeping mother.

What do you want me to do?

She's snarling, really snarling, I've never known people do that, like dogs, like lions, and her dark hair's flying around her face, so much anger, a turbulence of fear and ferocity. How can she be so strong?

I could see very clearly, shapes and angles, light and shadow, and it was all very still, which was wrong. With this wildness of fury there should be movement here, there should be a tornado. Those books, they should be flying through the air, pages ripping in the storm, the windows should be rattling. There is a whirlwind in this room, why is it so still? Why do the heavy curtains hang in graceful folds? Why is the clear light so serene?

My heart was beating fast. I could feel a pulse in the side of my head, and I turned my face into the pillow, suddenly frightened, not by Tamsin, but by myself.

Be quiet. Be calm. Don't be so silly. The girl's dead. You're a sensible woman, stop being so hysterical. It's ridiculous, letting your imagination run away with you like that. Stop it.

'Tamsin, be quiet now.'

She's dead, you fool. Why are you trying to speak to her? Hanged herself, and it's so sad. Yes, it's shocking, so you're suffering from shock, obviously.

All right, that's quite normal.

Now, breathe slowly and deeply. Slowly. And again.

'Tamsin, go away.'

Slowly, breathe slowly. Is the air forcing itself into my lungs? Slowly, but it's like facing a hurricane, this. I can't...

I was gasping, the pulse in my temple thudding harder and harder, and my hands were in front of my face, trying to shield it from the storm.

'Tamsin, please, please, don't.'

I could hardly speak, but I heard my own voice, a frantic whisper of fear, and did I hear another voice?

'I *am* here. I *am*.'

'All right, I know. All right.'

I sat up in the bed, shuddering, and pressed myself into the corner, feeling the angle of the wall and the headboard hard against my shoulders. There were tears on my cheeks, and I wiped them away and tried to suppress the urge to cry.

'All right. All right.'

Shock. I was really suffering from shock, much worse than I'd thought, I really am, Tamsin. Really. Just give me a few moments, please. I'm sorry, but I've got to have a little time, please.

At least I could breathe again, at least I could do that. Now, breathe slowly, and I could do it. Count, slowly, one, two, three, breathing in, and hold for a moment, and one, two, three, breathing out, and again. Is my heart still racing? Is that pulse in my temple still so fast? Or slower now?

'Don't forget I'm here.'

'No, Tam. Tamsin. I won't forget.'

'I'm sorry I frightened you.'

It sounded more like a warning than an apology. I had to frighten you, and I'll do it again, if I have to. If you make me.

I was awake. I knew I was awake. I knew exactly where I was, and what had happened. I looked towards the window, where the curtains hung so incongruously still, where the light shone through the clear,

90

dark glass.

That, too, was special; that wasn't normal window glass.

There'd been a telephone call to say Tamsin was dead. Murdered, they'd said, and I'd come to help Helen, because there was nobody else. Then they'd said it was suicide, and now I was in Tamsin's room, and I'd had a dream.

But I was awake.

'Yes.'

'Tamsin, I'm trying to think.'

I'd been asleep, and I'd had a dream, and I was still suffering from shock, so I'd woken up and had some sort of panic attack, whatever that meant. Difficulty in breathing, and a vague hallucination, not all that surprising. But perhaps, if that doctor came back the next day I should ask about it.

My pulse had slowed, almost back to normal, and I could breathe again. I was still trying to do it slowly, not to gasp and pant as I had done during the panic attack, but the feeling of a hurricane forcing air into my lungs had gone.

It had been horrible. I really had been quite frightened.

I was wide awake now, and my watch gave the time as three o'clock. Early hours of the morning, I might not be able to go back to sleep, and I was desperately tired. That was part of the problem, of course. I was not

91

only emotionally drained, I was physically exhausted.

I got out of bed and put on my dressing gown. I would make myself a hot drink, and perhaps read until I fell asleep again, or until morning.

But there is nothing to read in this stupid house. That stupid woman, she only buys stupid magazines.

Helen was sleeping heavily when I looked into her room. The drug seemed to have taken effect. It was unfair of me, to feel even mildly resentful and contemptuous.

I heated some milk and put a spoonful of honey in it, something that usually helps me to sleep. As the milk warmed I looked enviously around the kitchen, wondering how Helen had paid for it, and why she had done it. To me, she seemed like the sort of woman who would go to a kitchen centre in the High Street, or choose something from a catalogue. But this kitchen, this was a long way from anything a local shop would provide.

So, why had she done it?

I was feeling light and very alert, but I knew this was only because I was close to exhaustion. Ideas that now would seem sensible and intelligent would later reveal themselves as foolish.

I had better think only of the unimportant. Puzzle over this enigma.

I sipped the hot milk, and wondered how Helen had met the designer, and how she had found enough money to pay him.

But nothing came to mind.

Back in bed I took down two of Tamsin's school books, a grossly over-simplified and abbreviated account of the First World War, and a French novel about schoolchildren on holiday. I drifted off to sleep trying to remember what the word '*ane*' meant.

'Donkey,' said Tamsin.

Oh, yes. So it does. There would probably have been a picture, if I'd turned the page, and that would have reminded me. Perhaps I had turned the page just before I fell asleep, and so this dream had come.

'I'm not a dream.'

I must sleep. I'm so tired.

'No. I'm here. Wake up!'

'Tamsin, you're a dream. If I wake up, you'll go. Let me sleep.'

Had there been a noise? Yes, there'd been a terrible noise, crashing in the room, something that shook the walls, something that...

It's still. It's quiet, there's no sound at all, only a distant murmur, traffic on the road behind the houses. It's quiet.

What was that noise? What had shaken the room and thrown me into wakefulness?

'Tamsin?'

'I'm *not* a dream. You wake up, you. You've

got to do it. There isn't anybody else.'

'You're a hallucination. Go away.'

'No. I'm here. This is *my*...'

'I'm not listening. I want to sleep, I'm tired. Tamsin, you go away, you're dead and...'

'I won't let you sleep. Listen to...'

'I won't listen. *Our Father, who art in Heaven, hallowed be thy name, thy...*'

'It won't work. I'm not an evil spirit, I'm just me.'

'*...kingdom come, thy will be done, on Earth, as...*'

'Please. Please help me. There really is only you.'

'*...it is in Heaven. Give us this day...*'

'Oh, please. Please.'

'*...our...* Tamsin? What do you want me to do?'

She was crying again, and I shivered, suddenly very cold, sitting in the corner pressed against the wall. I wrapped the duvet around my shoulders, drawing up my knees and hunching into the warmth of the soft feathers. Stop crying, I thought, and I was speaking to myself as well as to her. There were tears on my own cheeks, too.

'Tamsin? Tell me, then. Stop crying, sweetheart. Tell me what you want me to do.'

There was only quiet sobbing as an answer, and she thought I couldn't hear her.

She was ashamed, there was something she was too ashamed to tell me. Something horrible? What can I do? Tamsin, sweetheart, what can I do?

'There's only you.'

Such a tiny whisper, so faint.

'What about your mother?'

Little laugh, stifled, back of the hand against the eyes, I can't see her, how do I know that? Rubbing away the tears, quickly, hoping nobody had noticed.

'She won't. She's too frightened.'

Helen had been frightened of that policeman. She'd looked at him with her hands against her mouth, her eyes bulging. It was the drug, wasn't it? She'd been drugged, there'd been a reaction. Drugs can do that sort of thing. Every person reacts differently. Only Valium, that's what the spotty policewoman had said, and Helen had been frightened.

I jerked awake again. There was light in the sky now, it was dawn, and here I was, sitting on the bed, a warm feather duvet around me, and I was still tired, because I hadn't slept well. There'd be a lot to do, and I was tired, and I should have slept better. Now it was daylight, and I would have to get up and face the day, and I didn't want to.

Say it again, and then again, if you have to. Say it, because then you won't have to say those other words, not yet. But soon, because you can't escape them.

I am so tired. I do wish I'd slept better. I don't want to get up yet.

Tamsin is dead. She's killed herself. I need to know why, because there's something horrible, and I have to find out.

4

Helen slept late the next morning, and I let her do so, looking in now and then to see that she was all right. It must have been quite a powerful drug that Dr Coburn had left for her.

I telephoned Anthony and told him what had happened. I should be able to come home in a few days, I said. I couldn't leave Helen alone, and her blasted brother was abroad, nobody could find him. He might turn up at any time, and then I'd be on the next plane home. Or perhaps I'd stay on for the funeral. Perhaps I should do that, provided it wasn't delayed for too long.

'How is Helen?' he asked.

'Upset,' I said. 'She's asleep at the moment.'

She was more than upset, though, I thought, after I'd hung up. She was truly frightened. Why was she frightened? I could understand the grief and the shock, I could understand the distress at the idea of the post mortem examination, but the fear was something I could not comprehend. Of what was she so afraid? What did she think would happen?

Surely the worst had already occurred; there could be nothing more. Certainly nothing worse.

I found dusters and furniture polish, and cleaned the living room. There was a Hoover in the cupboard under the stairs, but I didn't want to wake Helen, so I went back into Tamsin's room and sat in front of the computer, and did a search through the files.

Giles. Uncle. Baker.

'Uncle' and 'baker' turned up in her French file in vocabulary lists, but the name 'Giles' was nowhere.

I browsed through a few of her school files.

There was an essay on friendship that struck me as strange. She said that friends are people you want to help.

I like being with friends. I like going to different places with them when I have time. Being with friends is nice because they don't hassle you or make you do things, like people who aren't your friends.

If I have a friend whose in trouble I want to help if I can.

Some people say they have lots of friends but I don't think they do. I think they mean they know lots of people. I know lots of people but I only have about six friends.

Some people say I am their friend when I am not. I do not like it when people pretend to be friends.

A bit wary, for a thirteen-year-old, I thought.

A real friend is somebody you want to help.

She'd got a B+ for that essay, as I found when I checked in her folder. The remark at the bottom of the page read 'Quite good, Tamsin', and I felt that the teacher, too, had been puzzled by what she had written.

I went back further into the file, and opened one with the name 'Trees'.

Trees are the most beautiful things there are. They make dirty air clean again and there are millions of different sorts of trees. Some are very big and some are only little but they are all beautiful.

Some trees have roots so big they are as big as all the branches, but you can't see the roots because they are under the ground. If you could see the roots it would be like looking in a mirror with the branches not in the mirror and the roots being the reflection.

Not all trees have green leaves. Some trees like copper beech and maple have brown or red leaves and they are beautiful too but I like green leaves best. I like silver birch trees best of all because they can move and in the wind they look as if they are sort of dancing and liking the wind in their leaves. Silver birch trees have green leaves but the bark is not brown except in little places, it is all silvery.

Some trees are green all the year round and they are called evergreen. They are like fir trees

99

and pine trees and some more. Most trees drop all their leaves before the winter and new ones come in spring. They are called deciduous. The biggest tree of all is the Redwood and some of them are thousands of years old.

I think it should be a crime to hurt a tree just like it is to hurt a person.

I leaned back in the chair and stared at the screen. I tried to remember being thirteen, and feeling passionate and angry as Tamsin had done.

Tamsin, you could have been in the trees, making rope walkways and living on the platforms you built high among the leaves, in Newbury or wherever trees are threatened. You could have done that, Tamsin. You could have been clinging to the branches and shouting defiance at the people who would eventually win, this time, but maybe not next time, or the time after. You would have cried when those trees were felled, if you could have borne to have watched, but you could have gone on to the next place, and fought again, until in the end it might be a crime to hurt a tree.

Or at least so bloody expensive that nobody could afford to do it.

I brushed angry tears out of my eyes, and this time I didn't even wonder why.

I'd have paid your fines, Tamsin. I would. If I'd known you before you killed yourself. I'd have bought you ropes, too, and a good knife, whatever you need to live in a tree and fight for its life.

The folder of English essays lay on the desk by the side of the keyboard, but I didn't bother to look. I didn't care what anybody else thought of Tamsin's essay.

'What are you doing?'

Helen was standing in the doorway, and I swivelled around in the chair, and smiled at her. I felt slightly guilty, having been caught using the computer.

'I think I'm getting to know Tamsin.'

But I didn't want her to see what I'd been reading, so I turned back, quickly, and closed the file.

'I'll get you something to eat,' I said, standing up. 'The next few days may be a bit of an ordeal. You'll have to keep yourself as strong as possible.'

If I change the conversation back to you, maybe you won't ask me what I've found out about your daughter.

'I don't know how I'm going to manage,' she said.

Good. It worked.

I made toast, and boiled a couple of eggs, put the coffee on, and sat her down at the table. I talked to her as I worked. We ought to find a funeral director today, I said. Somebody good, who could advise us. Did she think a private family funeral would be best? Or would she like to invite Tamsin's friends? What about flowers, or was there a charity?

Helen became quite animated, talking about the funeral. She wanted flowers, she wanted Tamsin's coffin covered with flowers. And a really good coffin, not one of those veneered chipboard things. And a proper funeral in a church, and Tamsin was to be buried in a proper churchyard, not a town cemetery.

'Did Tamsin go to church?' I asked, but Helen said no.

'I don't believe in all that,' she said.

You'll have a job getting her buried in a churchyard then, I thought, but I said nothing. Helen would have to find that out for herself.

Any burial was likely to be expensive. Had she thought of that?

'Have you got any insurance to cover this?' I asked.

'Giles will pay,' she answered. 'Giles has always been very good to us. I don't know how we'd have managed, without Giles.'

I had no idea how much a funeral would cost today. Hundreds at least, I'd heard, and if all Helen's plans were allowed to take place, possibly thousands.

'Try to eat that second egg,' I said. 'You really ought to, Helen.'

There was a small show of reluctance, but she did. She liked her coffee made with hot milk in the microwave, and sugar. She supposed she ought to have a bath and find something nice to wear if we were going out, she must look a fright.

'You look exhausted,' I said, and got a wan smile by way of thanks.

We'd have to go shopping, she said. She'd have to buy some black clothes. Black made her look a frump, but it was the least she could do, for Tamsin.

I cleared away the breakfast things and ran the Hoover over the living room carpet while Helen had her bath. I supposed being a sort of housekeeper was one of the best ways in which I could support her, and at least it was something to do. While she was buying black clothes, I could find a decent book to read.

We took a taxi into town, and I'd thought we could split up and meet later, but Helen begged me not to leave her alone. Resignedly, I went with her, and we spent what seemed like hours while she tried on black dresses, and then black coats, and then a black hat which she said would just have to do, but which I thought looked like a upturned flowerpot with rope wound around it. Helen was the sort of person who could not choose without trying on every-thing at least twice, and asking the opinions of the shop assistant each time, as well as mine.

I tried to be tactful.

'I think that one makes you look a little old. I know you don't want to be frivolous, but you can still be well-groomed, can't you? Somehow, that dress makes your legs look a bit stumpy.'

The dress had made her look old, but it had done so by being too short. Helen's knees were of the type best left covered.

I couldn't be in her company for more than fifteen minutes at a time without my thoughts becoming spiteful.

Why did she have to insist that she was a size sixteen, so time was wasted on clothes that were too small? Why should she care that the shop assistant and I knew she took an eighteen?

We still had to find an undertaker.

Say nothing, I told myself. About now they might be carrying out the post mortem on Tamsin's body. Don't remind her.

I found it hard enough myself, thinking of that. Perhaps Welland shouldn't have told us when it was to take place.

'I preferred the coat with the velvet collar. The fur makes your neck look a bit short, it stands up too high.'

Honestly, you'd need to be about twenty years old and as thin as a stick to look like anything other than a box on stilts in that. Surely she must see.

What sort of flowers would you like,

Tamsin? I can't see you having a high opinion of hothouse lilies. Do you want a wreath? Or what they call a spray, or a bouquet, or something in a particular shape?

'Helen, you might be standing out of doors for quite a long time, and there's nothing worse than cold feet.'

'But these are the only ones that don't look like ... *boots*.'

'Walking shoes?'

She insisted on a high heel. I suppressed a shrug. Buying the clothes seemed to lift her spirits. She suggested we have tea in the store, there was a nice cafeteria on the fifth floor. She could do with a cup of tea. Couldn't I?

I smiled, and nodded, and thought, undertaker and florist. You bloody woman, what about arranging the damned *funeral*?

'I do have to eat, don't I? I've got to keep my strength up.'

What sort of flowers would be best for a young eco-warrior? I'd buy a spray of silver birch branches, but that would hurt the tree, wouldn't it? I can't do that.

'Would you like one of these cakes, Celia?'

'No, not for me, thanks.'

'I don't really feel like eating, but I've got to, haven't I?'

'Yes, Helen, you've got to.'

Light green leaves and white flowers. I can

at least give you the colour scheme of your lovely silver birches, Tamsin. Maybe something blue, for the blue sky behind them, what about that?

'You're very *quiet*. Haven't you got anything to say?'

'I'm sorry, Helen.' I pulled myself together, and smiled at her. 'I was just thinking about the flowers.'

Her lips trembled, and she reached into her handbag for a handkerchief.

'I don't want to arrange the funeral today. I don't think I could *bear* it.'

'We'll do it tomorrow, then.'

We won't be able to have the funeral before the inquest anyway, I thought. We need the coroner's permission, don't we? How long is all this going to take?

Helen wanted to go home in a taxi, and I found I was longing for a chance to stretch my legs. Do you never take any exercise at all? I wondered. I'm feeling stiff, and stuffy.

And I am going to buy something to read. 'Have they got a book department in this store?' She wasn't sure. She thought there might be something in the basement. Did I want a magazine? She had plenty of magazines at home, I only had to ask.

'No,' I said. 'I want a book.'

Tamsin, I'll plant a tree for you. You'd like that, wouldn't you? It won't really matter where I put it, so long as it's not somewhere with outline planning permission for a bloody motorway. Which would you prefer, a redwood or a silver birch?

Are they *really* thousands of years old?

'Are you coming, then? We have to pay on the way out. Celia?'

'Oh, I'll do that. No, let me, Helen. Please. My treat.'

I wondered when she'd remember about the post mortem, and she did, in the taxi on the way home. She drew in her breath, sharply, and looked at her watch. Her lips began to tremble, and there were tears in her wide eyes.

I handed her a packet of paper handkerchiefs.

'Oh, Celia,' she whispered.

'I know,' I said. 'But it'll be over by now. I don't think she'd have minded, would she?'

What are they going to find out by cutting her open? And why is Helen so frightened?

'Will they tell us?' she asked when we were in the house again. 'Will they come and tell us?'

'Do you think she was ill?' I asked, and I wondered, could that be a reason for suicide? For a thirteen-year-old?

'I don't know. How should I know? She never said anything.'

I didn't answer, but I couldn't control my angry thoughts.

You were her mother. You don't know if

she was ill? You've no idea why she killed herself?

'They'll have to find out why she did it,' I said, and Helen burst into tears.

'I wish they'd just leave us alone. It's too late anyway, isn't it? She's dead, so it's too late.'

She backed away from me when I went towards her, and she began to shout, and to beat at her knees with her hands. I stopped, and watched her, horrified, but somehow fascinated. She was bending forward, her fists clenched, raised in front of her face and then banging down onto her knees, onto her thighs, and then raised again as her voice rose higher and higher, a scream, almost a shriek, it was hard to distinguish the words.

'It's too late, isn't it? They ought to leave her alone. Cutting her up, and snooping and all that, it's not right. I want them to leave us alone. I don't want them prying, with their questions.'

I couldn't think what to do. She was out of control, completely hysterical.

'Helen, pull yourself together. I mean it, Helen. Stop that!'

She gasped, and gulped, and looked at me, shocked, but the hysterics seemed to have subsided almost as quickly as they had risen.

'I'm *allowed* to be upset. I'm *supposed* to be upset.'

Now there was indignation in her voice. Don't you try to stop me, she was saying.

Tears smeared her cheeks and her nose was running. I tried to suppress my distaste.

'I know. Naturally, you're upset. You'd be a monster if you weren't. But you'll make yourself ill if you lose control like that.'

'I don't want them snooping.'

I tried to reason with her. A girl of thirteen who kills herself, surely it's important to find out why? Helen, something terrible might have been happening. I didn't necessarily mean Tamsin, but in any case like this, there could be awful things going on. Bullying, or abuse, or maybe illness. They have to find out, Helen. It might stop the same thing happening to another young girl.

But she wouldn't listen. She cried, and she began to scream again, and then she started the same sequence, hands beating at her legs, voice rising, screaming again that she wanted to be left alone, she didn't want anybody snooping and prying. Leave us alone, leave us alone.

I telephoned the doctor, and the receptionist put me straight through. I told her Helen was hysterical and I didn't know what to do, and she said she was coming over. She'd be there in about ten minutes.

She sounded sensible, and sympathetic, and when she arrived she handled Helen well. She made her sit down, and be quiet, and take long, deep breaths, and she spoke with the sort of authority that made Helen do as she was told.

She asked me to bring a glass of water, and she gave Helen another pill.

After a while, when Helen seemed to be calm again, she said she'd like to have a word with me, if I wouldn't mind.

We went into the kitchen, leaving Helen sitting on the sofa, staring at nothing.

'Tamsin was nearly three months pregnant,' she said.

Pregnant. Oh. Tamsin, you poor kid. Did that seem like the end of the world? Was there nobody to help you?

'Mrs Masters?'

'Poor Tamsin.'

She nodded, waited for a moment, and then went on.

'It's a little hard to say, but the pathologist doesn't think it was her first pregnancy.'

Oh, no. No. That must be a mistake. That *must* be wrong.

'Hard to say?' I asked, and my voice sounded sharp in my own ears.

'It's not always possible to be sure. But he is certain that Tamsin was very experienced, sexually.'

I heard her words, but I could feel nothing, couldn't even think. This had to be wrong. It made no sense. This could not be true.

'He must have got the results mixed up. I mean, two post mortems? This can't be...'

I put my hands up to my face. Ridiculous. No, mistakes might be made, but nothing like that.

'You never knew her?' asked Dr Coburn.

No. I never knew her. Never knew her, never knew anything about her, except dark hair down to her shoulders and brown eyes. That was it, you were right, Helen. Tell me what she looks like, that's enough. There won't be much more than that, will there? A shallow little tart.

'Was that why she killed herself, then?'

My voice was light now. This is small talk, this conversation, just polite chat, nothing that really matters. What lovely weather we're having, did you see that film last night, is that why she killed herself? So sorry, I must go now, I've got an appointment at the hairdresser's.

Tacky little tart. Sleeping around and getting yourself knocked up. Got rid of one, why didn't you get rid of this one, too? What's the problem, Tamsin? In the club again, oh, tough luck. Costs a bloody packet, doesn't it? Never mind, a couple of evenings under the railway arches should scrape up enough, if you'll excuse the use of the term 'scrape'. You little bitch.

'I think you'd better sit down, Mrs Masters. You've gone quite white.'

'I'm so sorry. How stupid of me.'

Yes, how stupid. Thinking I was getting to know a girl who was dead. Thinking how much I would have liked her. What sort of flowers would you like, Tamsin? Something a bit blowsy and overblown, I think. Cabbage roses, a bloody great wreath with a sentimental message on a gold card. Nothing white, darling, that's for sure.

'I'd no idea it would be such a shock for you.'

She was apologetic, and a bit puzzled. She must think I'm some sort of prude, I thought, an extreme sort, well on the borderline of obsession. Mention pregnancy and I nearly faint, and I didn't even know the girl.

'I've been reading her schoolwork,' I explained. 'I liked what I read.'

'Was she clever?'

'No. No, not particularly. About average, I suppose.'

I thought for a moment, and then tried to smile.

'She seemed to care about things that I feel are important, too.'

I pushed the hair back off my face, and then shook my head.

'Well,' I said. 'I suppose everybody's a mixture of good and bad. Maybe she would have grown up to be the tart with the heart of gold.'

She smiled briefly, and said:

'Maybe she would have grown up, anyway. Are you all right now?'

'Oh, yes. I'm sorry I was so stupid.'

'They're going to do some more tests. They are very busy, so I'm not sure when they'll get the results. Tamsin could be HIV-positive. They'll need to find that out, and maybe try to trace her partners. There could be some boys at her school who've been infected.'

Oh, yes, I thought bitterly. Yes, indeed, Tamsin. Leave a few souvenirs, won't you? A few boys who'll never forget you, not for the rest of their lives.

'Well,' I said at last, 'I suppose she could have seen that as a good enough reason to kill herself. Couldn't she?'

Helen called out from the living room.

'Celia? Are you there?'

'Could you break the news to her?' asked Dr Coburn.

'Yes. Yes, I'll do that.'

She left me some more pills in case Helen became distressed again, and two of the strong ones for sleeping. She asked if I needed anything, but I didn't.

Not unless she had an antidote for foolishness. After Dr Coburn had gone I sat in the living room with Helen, and asked if there was anything she wanted to watch on television. She seemed dazed by the drug, or perhaps it was more than that. In any event, I would have to wait until she was more aware before I could tell her about Tamsin.

It was quite late that night before I felt she would understand, and when I told her she pressed her hands against her eyes, and began to cry again.

For myself, I was less angry and upset by then. Perhaps I'd been unfair to Tamsin, and I'd certainly been stupid, dreaming up this vision of a child who didn't exist, and then blaming her for not fitting the image.

'Do you know who the father of her child is?'

'No. No.'

'She never brought her boyfriend home?'

'She was hardly ever at home at all. Always out. You've no idea what teenagers are like these days. No matter what I said. What I did. She never listened to me. And now look what's happened. It's not my fault. I couldn't help it. What could I do?'

'Nobody's blaming you, Helen.'

'They will. You'll see, they will. They always blame the parents, don't they? Whenever anything goes wrong, it's always the parents. They should try some time, bringing up a child these days. They're all the same. And it's worse, when you're on your own. It's impossible.'

She choked, reached for another handful of tissues, and buried her face in them. She said something else, but it was muffled, and I couldn't hear.

'Helen, I'll make you a cup of tea. On top of everything else, it must be a shock.'

She raised her face from her hands, and it was bleary with misery.

'It's illegal, too. She was breaking the law. What else will they find? Oh, God, I wish I'd never had her. I wish I'd never had her.'

I had no answer for that, and I could hardly blame her for saying it. Perhaps even for feeling it. I'd been as guilty as anybody else of blaming parents for the short-comings of their children. Whenever I heard of teenage hooliganism, or juvenile crime, I'd thought, parents. What were the parents doing? It must be their fault.

But even children are individuals, and have free will. Adolescents have always rebelled, often against their parents' beliefs, so why not against the law? If the parents were decent people, and a child wanted to rebel, how better than with a gesture that said, this is what I think of the law. Laws are just for breaking. Much I care for your stupid laws.

There'd be telephone calls in the early hours of the morning, from the casualty department, or a police station, can you come down straight away?

Why? What's happened?

Overdose, vandalism, somebody else's car,

pocketful of drugs, answers that would have been unthinkable only a few years ago.

And there was so much shoplifting, with children taking things for which they could have no possible use, gangs, led on by the others, the slightly older ones. Perhaps it was only a handful of sweets, but in nearly every town now newsagents wouldn't let school-children through the door in groups of more than two or three at a time, and some of them put barriers up in front of the counters just before the children came out of school.

Stay that side. That's right, sunshine. That way you can't reach the display.

Parents sometimes complained; my child's not a thief. Yours may not be, madam, but I've lost hundreds of pounds over the last few months. Can't make any exceptions.

Right, you miserable old sod, you think I'm a thief, I'll be one. Got longer arms than you think.

And we'll smash in your window tonight, me and the boys. And girls. Teach you to treat me like a criminal.

Didn't, did you? Old Parker's window, was that you? You're *wicked*, you are.

Think that's wicked, you keep watching the papers, darling. You watch for next Saturday.

I don't care anyway. Parker's a nasty old bugger. Should see the way he looks at us.

I know. Like you're dirt.

You *don't* know, then. I never said he was a poofter.

He's a bloody pervert, we all know that.

The kettle lid rattled, and I poured the boiling water into the teapot.

Was it all new, this crime wave among children? Had they always been like this, so angry, so demanding, so defiant?

Blame the parents. Blame the other children. Blame the *other* parents.

Blame the schools, blame the television, blame society.

One day, they might try blaming the children.

'It wasn't my fault,' Helen said again when I took the tray into the living room.

'Nobody's going to say it was your fault. Every day you hear the same sort of thing on the radio, don't you? Teenage pregnancies, teenage crime. Any parent whose child doesn't get into some sort of trouble is just downright lucky, so far as I can see. Of course it's not your fault, Helen. What could you do? You can't make them prisoners, can you? You can't watch them every minute of the day.'

She smiled at me, and took her cup in hands that were almost steady again.

'Well, I don't know,' I said. 'I haven't got children. I think I'm rather glad of that. What sort of a world are they growing up in?'

No sort of world that I could imagine, it seemed. Nothing that I'd managed to dream of, in these last two days.

Tamsin. Sexually experienced, at the age of thirteen. I hadn't even had a moment to come up with the idea that my imaginary eco-warrior had been raped. Not her first pregnancy, let alone her first sexual encounter. Two young teenagers imagining themselves in love, undying passion, never be anybody else but you, I swear it, I promise; that, I could have understood and accepted.

HIV-positive, perhaps. Not very likely, the teenage romance.

Teenage tart. Adult men have more money, don't they?

Forget it, but that reminds me.

'Your kitchen, Helen. It's absolutely spectacular. Who designed it?'

She told me it had been a friend of Giles's, who lived in Belgium. His name was Neville. He'd come over, he was so nice. Giles had given it to her and Tamsin for Christmas last year. He'd said, spare no expense, nothing but the best for Helen and Tamsin. And Neville had talked for ages about what she wanted in a kitchen and then said leave it all to him, and Giles had taken Tamsin off for a holiday, and Helen had stayed in a hotel, waited on hand and foot, all part of the Christmas present.

'I don't know how I'd have managed without Giles,' she said. 'Oh, Celia. I don't know what he's going to say about this. He'll be heartbroken. He adored Tamsin. Nothing was too good for her.'

We sat in silence for a little while. I felt sad again, but I knew I was really only grieving for the Tamsin I'd imagined. These facts, this hard information about the real girl, my brother's daughter, this made everything different. I could only be sad for her in the abstract. What a shame; so young; what a waste. They were words that rose from my mind like bubbles, thin and empty.

Silly girl.

'I suppose, in a way, knowing why she did it helps. It's better than wondering, isn't it?' I asked, but Helen looked at me blankly, as if I'd put forward some complicated theory that she couldn't understand.

Now that I'd lost my Tamsin, my sympathy for Helen was stronger, even though I did think she should at least have known. What sort of a mother? was the question that throbbed in my mind. What sort of mother wouldn't have known? A few encounters with a boyfriend, that might easily have been kept a secret, but the sort of promiscuity Dr Coburn's words had implied, surely there must have been signs. Something a mother should have seen.

'I'm tired,' said Helen, and I looked at my

watch. It was past midnight.

We should have slept well, Helen with her pill, and me, weary and perhaps illogically disillusioned, but when I couldn't sleep, and crept out onto the landing I could hear Helen, restless and moving in her bed, moaning.

'Helen?'

There was no answer. There was a quick, indrawn breath, the head jerking on the pillow, and then a sigh.

'Helen?'

Bad dreams. Perhaps I had broken a nightmare. Perhaps now she would be quieter, less distressed.

I did feel sorry for her. I did try, I tried not to judge her, not to accuse.

As I lay in her bed I tried to think of Tamsin, tried to find some compromise between the girl I had imagined, and the girl she must have been. It was very difficult to reconcile the two, the one who had felt so passionate about trees, and the other in the third month of her second pregnancy, a teenage tart.

So tired now. I must sleep. It's been three days since I slept well. There'd been those panic attacks last night, and the hallucinations, because I'd been suffering from shock. I must sleep properly tonight. I'll be no good for anything, if I go on like this. I must sleep properly now.

It was with a waking dream of a dark girl climbing in old trees that I finally fell asleep, and then I dreamed again.

'Get me out of here. Please. Please. Look for the key.'

'I can't find the key, Tamsin.'

'You're not even looking.'

Once again I was suddenly awake, sitting up in bed, staring around me.

The light from the hall glowed softly on the beautiful colours of Tamsin's room, and it should have been soothing, it should have calmed me.

'Tamsin?'

Nothing. My imagination again, I must be even more tired than I'd thought. Weird dreams, these. Perhaps I shouldn't be here. Perhaps I should sleep on that sofa, or move out. Hotel, or something. Until Giles gets back.

She did have John's eyes. She didn't look much like Helen, although maybe Helen as a young girl had had that lift of the head and that way of tilting it as she considered a new idea.

Silly ideas, fantasies. You never knew her, never saw her move. Hardly noticed her when you met her that time. How can you know how she moves her head? Or that she isn't a teenage tart, and she died angry and desperate?

'Tamsin?'

There's only you now. Please, believe me. Believe in me. Find the key. Oh, please, don't leave me. Please. There is only you now.

5

I walked down to the police station the next morning. I told Helen I simply had to have some exercise. I gave her one of the pills Dr Coburn had left, put on my raincoat, and walked out of the house.

I asked at the desk for Chief Inspector Welland, and somewhat to my surprise he came down about five minutes later, showed me into a room where we sat on opposite sides of a table, and asked what he could do for me.

'Tamsin was pregnant,' I said, and he nodded. He'd been sent a copy of the report, and he'd read it.

'That's a crime, isn't it? For a thirteen-year-old?'

'Yes.'

'Are you going to investigate it?'

He didn't answer at first. He was tapping one of his fingers on the polished wood of the table, not impatiently, but as if it helped him to think of an answer. When he looked at me again he smiled.

'Would you like a cup of coffee?'

I was struck once again by the precision of his speech. Not, would you like a coffee, but, a cup of coffee.

'Yes, I would, please.'

While he was away I looked around the room, intrigued rather than genuinely interested. I supposed it was used for interviewing people, suspects or witnesses. It was small, with a low ceiling, and there was a tape recorder in the corner, set on a black stand with a cupboard underneath it. All the chairs had metal frames and blue cushions, a rough synthetic fabric, but the table was out of place. It should have been like the chairs, metal-framed, and it should have had a veneered top, but it was old; it was solid wood. I thought it might be cherry. It had a dark red lustre, and there was depth to the shine.

It was a strange place to find an antique table.

Welland wasn't gone long, and when he returned he bore a tray. There were, genuinely, cups on it. Cups and saucers and teaspoons, and a jug of coffee, a bowl of sugar, and milk.

He caught my look of surprise; and shrugged, almost as if embarrassed.

'There are coffee machines around here,' he said. 'I find everything tastes of a mixture of vegetable soup and sweet tea.'

'Does CID have special privileges?' I asked.

'No. CID has a coffee percolator,' he

answered, and we both laughed.

As he poured the coffee I asked him about the table, and he smiled, and ran his hand over the wood, almost as if he was caressing it.

He told me it belonged to one of the sergeants. It had been left to him by his grandmother. The man had a foster son who'd had a difficult early childhood. Now, the boy was destructive, and at times quite dangerous. He liked breaking things. Sergeant Roberts didn't want his table spoilt, and had nowhere to store it. This was as safe a place as any. Vandals and hooligans in this room were at least under some sort of supervision.

I was sure there must be other places where Sergeant Roberts could have left his table, but I was much more interested in the foster son. I asked if it was common for policemen to have foster children, and Welland smiled at me.

'We're people,' he said. 'We do what other people do. Bill Roberts is good with children. He'll probably be able to take this home again in a month or so.'

I mulled over the idea of a police sergeant with a destructive foster son as I drank my coffee. I'd never thought about the home lives of policemen. My surprise that one would be a foster father seemed, upon reflection, to be a little offensive.

'I hope he sorts him out,' I said. 'I hope he does. At least he won't have to worry about pregnancy.'

'Not for a while, anyway,' Welland agreed. 'Danny's only eight. Pregnancy still takes two, but they're usually older than that.'

It brought us back to Tamsin, and he put his cup down in its saucer, carefully, and leaned back in his chair.

'I wish I could follow it up,' he said. 'Unfortunately, for one thing there are just too many pregnant children. We haven't the time, or the resources. Anyway, most of the fathers are the same age as the mothers. What should we do about it? I mean, we as police. What is the point in prosecuting a fourteen-year-old boy for getting a twelve-year-old girl pregnant?'

I had no answer. There could be no point. He was right.

'Where Tamsin was concerned, I would have liked to have found out a bit more,' he went on. 'I don't think this was the usual story, not if the pathologist was right. But I've got other things to do. There's a series of burglaries in two housing estates, and the residents are getting sick of it, small blame to them. There was a ram raid on a tool hire shop last night, that was probably drugs-related, like a few more unpleasant incidents we still haven't sorted out. Seven cars disappeared from the same car park in one afternoon a couple of days ago, which is a puzzle. Where could I find the time to ask about Tamsin? On the paperwork, if you'll excuse my saying so, she was just one more promiscuous young girl.'

'No great loss?' I asked, a little bitterly, and he shook his head at me.

'That's not fair. I do regard her as a victim, Mrs Masters. But, as I said, if I were to investigate every teenage pregnancy in this town, I doubt if I'd have time to do anything else at all.'

It wasn't unreasonable, and I hadn't expected him to respond in any other way. But I had hoped.

'May I ask you what led you to think Tamsin had been murdered?'

It took him quite a long time to answer that, and when he did he told me that he personally had not believed in the murder, once he had been to the place where she had died, and had seen her body. She'd been found by a woman walking her dog.

'It's always somebody with a dog,' he said.

She was a very sensible woman, which was unusual. She'd lifted Tamsin down, laid her on the ground, and tried to resuscitate her with mouth-to-mouth artificial respiration. She'd tried for about half an hour, and then she'd gone to the road, flagged down a taxi, and asked the driver to call the police through his radio.

Tamsin's hands had been tied behind her back. There were scratches on her face. Some bushes nearby had been trampled and broken, which could have been caused by a struggle.

I felt my jaw drop.

'And you tell me this *wasn't* murder?'

Her wrists had been tied with a cord, using a simple slip knot. There was no bruising on her arms or hands, as you would expect if it had been done forcibly. There was no sign that she'd been unconscious either, no bruise on her head, nothing like that. Footprints around the bushes had all been made by Tamsin, those of them that could be identified, and there were plenty that could. And the blood and skin under Tamsin's fingernails had been her own.

'She was very determined, and not unintelligent,' said Welland. 'But she wasn't very well-informed.'

Why? I asked myself. Why did she do this?

Welland was looking at his watch, and I thought, he's going to tell me he has to go now. But instead he offered to buy me lunch.

At first I was mildly startled. And then I thought, why not? Why shouldn't I go out to lunch with him? Aren't policemen allowed a social life? I'd already made one mistake there, with my surprise about a foster child.

We went to a small restaurant where he

was known, and while we were waiting for a table I said:

'Tamsin wanted something investigated.'

'Yes,' he agreed.

'Of course, you'd have realised that. I was thinking aloud. But what? And why? I mean, why not leave a note?'

'Perhaps because a murder investigation is so much more dramatic?' he suggested, and I thought, I suppose that could be it. I suppose.

Was it just a way of making yourself important, Tamsin? A demand for attention? A very effective one, if it had worked.

'But to want somebody accused of murder,' I protested.

He didn't answer then, but later, when we'd talked about other things for a while, he suggested, diffidently, that she might have wanted to get her boyfriend into trouble, if he'd dropped her.

It was the most likely explanation. A spiteful retaliation for hurt pride. How banal, and how obvious.

Oh, Tamsin.

'If you *had* believed it was murder,' I began, and then couldn't think how to go on.

'If we had believed it was murder,' he said, 'quite a lot of us would have been working on it, quite hard. We really do take murder seriously. Particularly when it's a child who's died.'

There didn't seem to be anything else to say about Tamsin.

I found myself liking Frank Welland. I couldn't seem to reconcile this pleasant, friendly man with the one who had delivered such a verbal slap in the face when I'd first met him only two days earlier. I'd thought he not only disliked me, but despised me as well. It seemed I'd been wrong.

He told me about a burglar who'd tried to escape from the house in which he'd been trapped by breaking a hole in the roof and climbing out between the slates. Frank hadn't been in the force long at the time, and was not at all prepared for such a situation. He'd been told to stay in the garden and keep his eyes open, and now here was the suspect scrambling around on the roof, and slates were falling all around him, and there was nobody to tell him what to do next. So he just dodged the slates, and shouted up at the man to give himself up, he was surrounded, all the things he'd seen on television, and the burglar was sitting on the roof and shouting back things they weren't allowed to say on television, and all the neighbours came out to watch, and wouldn't go away. Then his sergeant had come out and sworn at him because the street was full of people, and nearly got hit by a falling slate. They'd had to borrow a ladder from a window cleaner, and when the burglar had finally come down, apparently realising the situation was hopeless, and therefore resigned to his fate, he'd made a sudden dive for the garden gate and got clean away, running down the street like an Olympic athlete. A sergeant and three constables, one of them admittedly a bit on the green side, and it hadn't been enough for one small burglar.

It wasn't a hilarious story, but it was amusing, and I enjoyed hearing it told in his slightly rueful and self-deprecating tones.

For my part, I told him a little about Germany, and how, when I had tried to report a break-in at a block of flats where we had lived when first we moved to Bonn, I'd been told to call back later, because everybody was at lunch.

It was a surprisingly relaxing interlude, and I enjoyed it, but at last I looked at my watch, and said I had to get back to Helen. Frank asked me how she was, but it was politeness. I knew he didn't much care about Helen, although he might have felt sorry for her.

He, too, thought she should have known.

For myself, as I walked back to the house, I wondered if there was anything I could say to Helen that would comfort her. Nothing I had learned that morning, certainly. To sexual promiscuity I could now add vindictiveness.

Perhaps it would have been difficult for a thirteen-year-old to envisage the appalling damage a charge of murder would do. Teenagers have not had time to develop a sense of proportion.

Were Helen to learn about Tamsin's attempt to have somebody blamed for her death, this would be an argument I could put forward, something to comfort her.

But Helen was not interested in hearing what I had been doing. Anthony had telephoned, and she hadn't known where I was, and she'd been upset, and shouldn't have been left alone for so long.

'I'm sorry,' I said. 'I had to get some fresh air. I don't sleep well if I don't get enough exercise.'

I cooked her something to eat, an omelette, and asked her if she felt ready to arrange the funeral. Or at least to visit a florist. She had said she wanted Tamsin's coffin to be covered in flowers, and I thought it was a lovely idea. We'd have to choose a coffin, too. Weren't they usually white, for children?

Helen said she thought we might do that. The flowers, anyway. But she wanted Giles to arrange the funeral, not me.

I was hurt, and a little angry. I hadn't intended to arrange the funeral, I said. I'd asked if she felt ready to do it. In any event,

I doubted if anybody could do much until after the inquest. Didn't the coroner have to give permission?

Somebody would have to identify the body, too, wouldn't they? I thought, but I didn't say that. Shouldn't that have been done before the post mortem?

Perhaps they, too, were waiting for Giles.

If he didn't turn up soon, I would have to go back to Germany. There was nothing much more I could do for Helen, and after her remark about the funeral arrangements, I was less inclined than ever to try.

But Giles arrived the next morning, and Helen collapsed into grateful acquiescence with everything he had to say.

To me, he was polite, but cool. He thanked me for coming to help Helen, but his acknowledgement of what I had done carried with it the suggestion that there was now no further need of me. I could leave, as soon as I wished.

'I would like to stay for the funeral,' I said, and although he raised an eyebrow he could not, without being extremely rude, deny me.

I will buy you a spray of blue and white flowers on light green leaves, Tamsin. And I will plant your tree.

I can't say I disliked Giles. I'd hardly been able to remember him before he came back, but I'd felt he had probably encouraged

Helen in her demands about the wills. I reminded myself of that now and then, when Helen irritated me, or when I was tired, but it was a little like trying to attribute a character to a piece of furniture. I didn't dislike Giles, but it was because there seemed to be nothing to arouse any sort of emotion.

He was affectionate to Helen, constantly hugging her, calling her pet names and telling her not to worry, he'd do everything. He referred to himself as 'Big Brother'. Don't you worry, sweetheart, Big Brother's here now. Leave that to Big Brother.

And Helen reverted to childishness. Want this. Don't want to. Shan't, then.

Don't you bother yourself, my love. Big Brother can do that.

I made a point of handing everything over to Giles, Helen's pills and the doctor's instructions concerning them, what I had understood to be the procedure about the inquest and the permission of the coroner for the funeral, and Helen's desire to cover Tamsin's coffin with flowers, and to have her buried in a churchyard.

He frowned at that, and I felt a small surge of satisfaction.

I didn't tell him about my visit to the police station, or what Welland had said.

If Giles grieved for Tamsin, he did so in private. When I was there, he confined

134

himself to saying what a lovely girl she had been, and how heartbreaking it all was for Helen.

Letters began to arrive, and I offered to draft replies on the computer, so that Helen would only have to copy them out. I put it as tactfully as I could.

'When you're distressed it's so difficult to find the right words,' I said. 'Please let me do something to help, I feel so useless.'

Giles had already been using Tamsin's computer, and I wished I could protest. When he was in that room I had a sense of claustrophobia, as if he took up too much space, and was trespassing.

Tamsin, I thought, was wary of Giles.

I pushed the idea away. I had already made too many mistakes about Tamsin, and it was all becoming rather silly.

That night I dreamed I heard her crying. She was still trapped, and I wasn't even bothering to look for the key.

Giles identified Tamsin's body, and came back looking rather white. He told me he hadn't really taken it in until then.

'I wanted to tell her to wake up,' he said. 'As if it was a joke, gone too far.'

It was rather the way I had felt, when I had thought Tamsin had been alive such a short time before, and we should be able to step back into that time, and change it, because it was only such a short time. As you did when you caught words before you spoke them, an instant when you so nearly said the wrong thing, but just in time you stopped yourself.

Just in time, we could have stopped her. No. Don't do that, Tamsin. Stop.

On the brink, and almost falling, and catching your balance at the last moment, so near. Such a narrow escape.

Nearly a narrow escape. But that little time was too long.

How long had she been hanging, before the woman with the dog found her, and tried to save her?

'I can't believe she's not going to walk through that door,' said Giles.

I could sympathise with him, but I couldn't like him. I kept thinking of him as sly, but there was nothing in his manner or his behaviour to give me reason for my opinion. He'd been polite to me, and he'd thanked me for looking after Helen while he was away. In fact, he was quite charming, and he was dealing with the arrangements for the funeral, and the coroner's office, efficiently and quietly.

Why did I think he was sly?

Why was Tamsin so quiet?

I made myself a coffee, and told myself it really was time I got out of this environment. I was obviously under too much pressure, and my imagination was getting out of hand.

Usually, when I'm too tired, or stressed, I start seeing dead animals where there are none. A small heap of gravel by the road, is that a dog? A tussock in a field, not a dead rabbit after all. A black tarpaulin stretched over something by a farmyard, a second look, and of course it's not a dead horse.

But it is time to stop working quite so hard, perhaps to try to delegate.

There was nothing to delegate. It had all been taken over now. I wasn't doing anything much any more, just waiting, for the inquest in two days' time, and for the funeral the day after, assuming, as everybody did, that the coroner would give his permission.

I spent a lot of time walking around the town. It was cold and grey and misty, but nevertheless it wasn't a gloomy place. There were a few small industrial estates where new businesses were starting up, and the bright paintwork on the boards over the doors seemed hopeful. There was an air of optimism. It should have been spring, not late autumn.

I went to the place behind the railway lines where Tamsin had killed herself. I told myself it would be morbid to do so, but in the end my curiosity got the better of my good sense.

Some bushes had been sawn down. I

stood looking at the cut stems, and thought, this is where she staged the scene of a fight. This is where she trampled the leaves and the grass, and didn't know enough to do it convincingly. That broken stem, lower than the cut ones around it, that had felt the imprint of her foot. The bare earth around it, which in places showed signs of a rake where it had been sheltered from the recent rain, there she had stamped, and scraped, and tried to make clues.

I was attacked, she was thinking. Come on, believe me. Start it up, that huge machine you call a murder investigation. I was murdered. Find out.

She'd scratched her own face.

Even now, I winced when I thought of that. It hurts, a scratch on the face. For a child, that showed a lot of determination.

She hadn't thought about cleaning her fingernails after she'd done that. She hadn't known much about forensic science.

It was a bit easy, sweetheart. Poor baby, setting yourself up against the experts, and losing so quickly. Poor little Tamsin. You didn't stand much of a chance there, did you?

I wiped the tears off my face, and looked around again.

That tree, that must have been it. That branch.

Don't look at that. At least there was a tree

for you, Tamsin.

I didn't look at the branch, but I leaned back against the trunk and let my fingers rub against the bark. It seemed to be warm, as though life pulsed through the trunk, just underneath that tough, thick skin.

At least there was a tree for you.

Teenage tart, promiscuous little slut, all that had gone. It may have been true, but it didn't seem to matter any more. If I've got you wrong, Tamsin, who am I hurting? If that's what you were, there's nothing I can do about it.

I shall pretend to remember you as a girl who loved trees, and thought people should be treated fairly, and not bossed about.

I bet you'd have been an anarchist by the time you were fifteen. Wish I could have joined you. Gone back to that time, that age, that innocence.

Easy to put the world right, if we just get rid of the old lot. Ban the arms trade, make organic farming compulsory, be a vegetarian and hang all the politicians.

We could have gone on demonstrations together, carrying our hand-painted banners and yelling our defiance and sitting side by side in the back of a Black Maria and trying to think of a way out this time, feeling just a bit scared behind our nonchalant airs.

You and your aunt, I thought, trying to

bring myself back to reality.

I could have been in the background, though, couldn't I? That telephone call you're allowed, call me.

'Celia? I'm in the nick again.'

'Are you, sweetheart? How much is it this time?'

I would have liked to have helped. Help you get a criminal record, help you live it down. It was important, what you thought and felt. It's still important.

Why are you so quiet now? Why don't I wake up in the night in your room, knowing you're angry and lost? Have you gone away, Tamsin? Aren't you there any more?

I pushed myself away from the trunk of the tree, and walked across the waste ground to the road. I didn't look back.

6

The inquest was a curiously informal affair. I'd expected lawyers, but it was the coroner who asked questions, and it hardly took any time at all. The pathologist said Tamsin had hanged herself, and had been about three months pregnant, and the woman who'd found her, who was a staff nurse at the local hospital, told how she'd gone on trying mouth-to-mouth resuscitation, until she'd been quite sure Tamsin was dead.

'How did you make sure?' asked the coroner, and she said she'd been wearing a brooch. She'd used the pin, stuck it into Tamsin's arm, and the little wound hadn't bled. Then she'd gone to the road and waited until a taxi came. She'd flagged it down, and asked the driver to call his control room. They'd telephoned the police.

The coroner asked somebody if the taxi driver was to give evidence, but the man he spoke to said, no. We could probably get him if you want him, but it'll mean an adjournment.

The coroner smiled, and said he didn't think it was necessary.

The verdict was suicide while the balance

of her mind was disturbed, and the funeral could be carried out as planned.

He spoke rather briskly about the emotional instability of young teenagers, and offered his condolences to the family.

Was that all? Was there to be nothing about this not being her first pregnancy, about the beginnings of a murder investigation?

Was there to be nothing about who she'd been, and what we had lost? Nothing?

They're drawing a line under the total of your life, Tamsin. Finished.

'Is that all?' asked Helen as we left, and I looked at her with a flash of sympathy. It was exactly what I'd been thinking, and she'd said it.

Giles, who had his arm around her shoulders, smiled at her.

'That's all,' he said. 'It's like I told you, pet. Just a formality.'

But there had to be more. There was to be the funeral tomorrow, and then, I was to fly home to Germany. And...

And, what?

I was feeling almost bewildered. There was no logic in it. I hadn't expected revelations, I hadn't thought we would learn anything new, but the inquest had been standing ahead of us for these last few days, with its attendant phrases: can't bury her until after the inquest; the coroner will give permission for the funeral at The Inquest; and now The Inquest was over, and it had been nothing.

There had just been that surprisingly young man with a small handful of questions, and something written down, and that's the end of Tamsin Simpson.

But it can't be the end. It can't just finish like this.

Can it?

'I suppose you're going for another walk, then, are you?' asked Helen, and I nodded. I didn't want to go back to the house. I was no longer welcome. Neither Helen nor Giles had said anything, but the silences when I came into a room, the artificiality of the smiles, they made it clear.

I tried to be unobtrusive, and to be helpful when I could. I'd responded to Helen's cry for help, and could not, as a result, be asked to leave, at least not before the funeral. But I was given little to do, and most of the offers I made were turned down.

So, I thought, I will go for a walk, and I will find your flowers, Tamsin.

I'm sorry I was so spiteful and angry, when I first heard you were pregnant.

There was a young boy standing at the side of the steps, watching us. I wondered if I'd seen him, sitting at the back. I hadn't taken much notice of anybody, except Helen. She was wearing her new black clothes, and she was still taking the pills, which made her seem vague, as if she was always thinking about something else, until the effect wore off, when she'd become angry, or start to cry, and go on and on, wailing about Tamsin.

I'd telephoned Dr Coburn and asked, are these pills addictive? No, she'd said, but they can become a habit.

That incident brought Giles very close to telling me to mind my own business.

'I'll look after her,' he'd said. 'I'll telephone the doctor, if I think she needs one.'

Stay away from him, I thought. Keep as far away from him as you can.

Oh, that's silly. It's only for another day. I'm going home tomorrow. After the funeral, I'll catch the next flight back to Bonn, and a taxi home. In thirty-six hours I'll be away from all this.

The boy who'd been standing by the steps was following me, and I turned to look at him. I wasn't frightened, although he was quite tall, a lot bigger than me. He didn't look threatening. He was young, sixteen or so, and he was tidy and clean.

He stopped when I did as if he was uncertain of what to do, but then he walked forward again, holding his hands out in front of him, palms towards me, as if to show me he wasn't carrying a weapon. It looked a little odd.

'Were you there?' he asked, and then,

before I could answer, he went on, 'I know you were. I saw you. Did you know Tamsin, then?'

'I'm her aunt,' I said.

'I didn't know she had one.'

Why should you? I thought. I doubt if Tamsin ever spoke about me, unless there was some sort of question-and-answer session in a lesson at school. French, perhaps.

'J'ai une tante. Elle s'appelle Celia Masters.'

'What they said back there about her being pregnant,' the boy said, and he was looking down into my face, quite close to me, his eyes very wide.

'Yes?'

'It's not true. They got that wrong.'

Oh dear, I thought. Oh, Tamsin. What do I say to him?

'Who are you?' I asked.

'Andrew Harper.'

He held out his hand, as if suddenly reminded to do so.

'How do you do? I'm very pleased to meet you.'

Half man, half child. A horrible age.

'I'm Celia Masters. I'm pleased to meet you, too, Andrew.'

'They got her mixed up with somebody else. She couldn't have been pregnant.'

This was very curious.

'Why not, Andrew?'

He was embarrassed.

'Because she wouldn't have been. She wouldn't. She never did. I mean, she couldn't get pregnant, without *doing* it, could she? And she wouldn't ... you know.'

'I know what you *mean*,' I said gently, and he blushed, and tried to laugh.

That was a mistake, because he was still half a child, and the laughter turned to a choke, and he was brushing tears out of his eyes.

I turned away, as if there was something very interesting to be seen further down the road, and then I said I was thirsty.

'Do you come from around here?' I asked. 'Do you know where we could get a cup of tea?'

'I haven't got any money,' he said, and then added, quickly, 'not on me, I mean. I forgot my wallet.'

He should have been in school.

'I've got some money,' I said.

He took me to a Wimpy Bar on the corner of the main shopping street, only a five-minute walk into a different world, where people carried shopping bags and looked in bright windows, and didn't have to think about sudden endings. It seemed a little shocking, this lack of awareness, as if the people going about their own lives were being disrespectful and uncaring.

That woman shouting at her children, she should be quiet in the face of death. And the two girls laughing. They shouldn't laugh.

Suicide while the balance of her mind was disturbed. The funeral may take place. May I offer my sympathy to the family. Teenage, emotional, unpredictable, a tragic event. Thank you, ladies and gentlemen.

These were the words floating through my mind, disjointed, and almost meaningless now.

Andrew was waiting for me at the door of the Wimpy Bar, looking back at me, wondering why I was standing in the street staring around at the people. I smiled at him, and walked past him into the brightly lit room.

It really was time I got back to normality. This illogical way of thinking was becoming quite disturbing. It was one thing to daydream about a girl called Tamsin, and pretend I knew her; those daydreams intruding into my thoughts and actions at any unexpected moment was intolerable.

I bought two cups of tea and carried them back to the table, where Andrew waited, looking a little uncomfortable.

'Sorry,' he said as we sat down. 'I should have brought my wallet.'

'You can pay next time,' I answered.

He wasn't sixteen, I realised. He was very tall for his age, which was where I had gone wrong. I didn't think he was much more than fourteen. He was very young, very uncertain. Did I mean he was going to have to buy me a cup of tea at some unspecified future date?

He didn't know what to say to me.

'It's Tamsin's funeral tomorrow,' I said. 'Will you be there?'

He nodded.

'Some of us from school, we've got permission. We're being, sort of representatives. And Mrs Clarkson, she's Tamsin's form teacher. Was. She's coming. We're going in her car.'

There was to be a service in the local church, but Giles hadn't managed to buy a grave in a churchyard. Nowadays even regular churchgoers were lucky to get that. You had to have been a warden, or a verger, some sort of serving official, and to have been one for a long time as well.

Giles had offered money, but had been refused. Helen had had hysterics when he told her, this time a genuine fit of hysterics, and I'd left the room so that he could cope with it as best he could.

'I don't want her buried in that big cemetery with everybody else. I want her buried somewhere special. They can't do that. Find another churchyard. There's got to be somewhere nice for Tamsin.'

Giles suggested cremation, so we could scatter her ashes somewhere she would have liked.

Helen cried again. She wanted to put flowers on Tamsin's grave. She wanted to visit Tamsin's grave. How could Giles suggest cremation, and no grave for Tamsin?

Giles had fed Helen another pill. Come on, sweetie, Big Brother's got a nice pill for you. Leave it all to Big Brother.

He hadn't found a churchyard willing to take Tamsin.

'Mrs Masters?'

'I'm sorry, Andrew. I was miles away.'

'I just asked if you knew Tamsin well.'

So I told him, because I thought it might be easier for him if I talked first, that I'd met her at my parents' funeral, when she was just a toddler in a dark blue coat with a black ribbon in her hair, and then at a wedding a couple of years ago. We'd only exchanged a few words. I'd sent her Christmas cards and birthday cards, and a little money each time, with a short message, to tell her to buy herself something she wanted. She hadn't written to thank me. I'd never had a letter from her.

Then there'd been the telephone call in the middle of the night, and I'd stayed in her room, and read some of her essays. I felt I knew a little bit about her, from them.

I'd been shocked, when I'd learned she was pregnant.

I stopped talking then. I didn't look at him.

Andrew, were you the father of her baby? I wondered. Because if so, I may have very bad news for you. For you, and for your parents, for people who love you. If she really was HIV-positive, Andrew, there is a dreadful time ahead for you.

'I don't believe that,' he said. 'They made a mistake.' I let the silence hang between us for a while before I spoke again.

'They don't make that sort of mistake, Andrew.'

He was fighting back the tears again.

'You know what they used to call her? In the playground? Iron drawers.'

He stopped, and sniffed, felt in his pockets, found a packet of paper handkerchiefs. He muttered something about a rotten cold, and I nodded. A rotten cold, of course.

'Iron drawers? That's a peculiar sort of name. Isn't it?'

If I didn't ask direct questions, about him and Tamsin, I might learn something.

'Do all the girls have weird nicknames? I mean, I assume it's the boys who make them up?'

He shook his head, and then shrugged.

'Sixth formers, mostly. They sort of, boast. You know. Bragging about the girls.'

'Did they brag about Tamsin?'

'Nobody believed them.'

He looked up at me, and his eyes were

150

swimming with tears.

'Not about Tamsin, nobody believed them. Brag, they can brag all they like, we all knew. She wouldn't. She never would. Wouldn't even kiss you, not properly, not the way the others do. You know.'

'I know,' I agreed.

He drank his tea, and stared down into the empty cup.

'She'd let you hug her.'

He didn't seem to want to say anything else. I waited for a while, trying to choose my words, but at least I could reach out and touch his hand.

'Andrew, she *was* pregnant.'

Stubbornly, he shook his head, refusing to meet my eyes.

'No. She *couldn't* have been.'

'I don't say they never make mistakes, Andrew, but I don't think they did this time.'

He looked up and there was bewildered misery on his face.

'I don't understand.'

'You weren't the father, then?'

'No. *No.*'

Giles, I thought. Giles, you bastard. No wonder I thought you were sly. No wonder Tamsin was so wary.

I caught myself up, quickly.

Stop that. This time you use logic, not your daydreams. This has gone far too far

151

for your silly imagination.

Giles took Tamsin away on holiday while his friend did that kitchen. Helen went to a hotel, but Giles took Tamsin on holiday.

That was nearly a year ago. Helen had said it was a Christmas present, the kitchen, a Christmas present for her and for Tamsin.

Not the first pregnancy, was it?

He'll be heartbroken, she'd said.

'Andrew, have you any idea who might have been the father?'

'Nobody.'

He would hold, obstinately, to his belief in a mistake. Tamsin never would, he'd said. So she couldn't have been pregnant.

But something else he had said had brought the tears to my eyes.

She wouldn't even kiss you properly.

She did know, then, that she had been infected by the virus, and she wouldn't put her friends at risk. Tamsin's friends were people she wanted to help. She would have been careful not to harm them. She knew she was HIV-positive, but she didn't know enough about it, because there was nobody she could ask. How had this happened? There must have been a test, and she'd been told the result. Told that, and nothing else. Frightened, and alone, and with nobody to tell her what it meant. Only rumours and playground gossip, spiteful remarks, God, I wouldn't kiss *that*, you might *catch* something. Bloody scrubber's probably got AIDS, they ought to give her a separate lavatory.

Had there really been nobody she trusted?

'Andrew, if Tamsin was in trouble, who would she talk to?'

'Me.'

I couldn't be sure of that. Andrew was grieving now, and I could remember how much loss hurt at that age. The pain was made worse by the lack of understanding shown by adults. You'll get over her. You're still young, there'll be plenty of other girls. Nobody would dream of saying that to somebody only ten years older.

We seem to think children should only be deeply hurt by the death of a parent, or a brother or sister. Only close members of the family should be loved enough at that age. Love, fenced in by our conventions. Beyond the safe borders of the family, love is only permitted to be transitory, and shallow. You'll get over her *because* you're young. You cannot possibly, at fourteen, know what love really is, and therefore this pain isn't so bad.

When I was sixteen my boyfriend dropped me for somebody prettier and more sophisticated. I'd wanted to die. Hurt pride, my mother had commented on her way out to a whist drive. Daddy had said it seemed like a good opportunity to get drunk for the first time in my life, but it had better be white wine. We'd leave the hard stuff for the next emotional crisis.

My mother's best friend wrote to her about a week later, saying she was divorcing her husband for adultery, and my mother packed a suitcase and went off to stay with her. It was an utter disaster, she said. Poor Louise, what a dreadful, dreadful thing to have happened, we must all rally round.

Louise was nearly forty, and I was sixteen. Louise's husband had left, and Sam was only a boyfriend, and not a very suitable one at that.

I could not only remember the pain. I could remember the resentment.

Now, Andrew would be thinking of Tamsin as the only girl he could ever love, and even if I, thirty years older, knew it wasn't true, my knowledge couldn't help him now. Nor could my experience, but I would try.

I told him about the crash in Portugal, leading around to it by saying the funeral had been the first time I'd ever set eyes on Tamsin. I told him how pretty she'd been, and how solemn she'd looked in her dark clothes with the black ribbon in her hair. Daddy had been such a special person to me. He'd always seemed to understand me, although that had been a mixed blessing: just as he would know when my intentions had been good, even if my actions hadn't proved it, he also spotted instantly any attempts I made to wriggle out of the blame for my childhood crimes and sins.

'I gave up lying to Daddy when I was about eight, I think,' I told Andrew. 'I went on lying to my mother until I was well into my twenties. Until I didn't much care whether she approved of me or not.'

I'd been married for about four years when they'd died, and I'd still been very much in love with my husband, but even that hadn't helped. I thought nothing would ever heal that ragged black hole in the side of my life. It felt as if I was going to fall through it, because everything was out of balance now Daddy was dead. I didn't see how I could ever even *manage* again, let alone enjoy my life. What was I going to do, without Daddy?

But only about a month later I'd woken up in the morning, and the sun was shining, and my first thought wasn't 'Daddy's dead'. It was, sunshine. Then, 'Daddy's dead.'

I knew then that I was just beginning to heal. I knew that one day I would be all right again. And that not going on being crippled wasn't being disloyal to Daddy. It was being a bit like him, because he'd been brave, and cheerful, and kind, and trying to be a bit like him was as loyal as I could be.

Andrew was listening to me, politely, not quite believing what I said. It was still too new, and too raw. He could not yet envisage

155

a time when he could think of sunshine again.

'How old are you?' I asked, and I'd been right; he was fourteen.

I'd been dreaming about pop singers at the age of fourteen, and wondering what was wrong with me, because I hadn't got a boyfriend. How had they crashed through that barrier so young, these children? Tamsin had been pregnant at thirteen, and Andrew hadn't thought she couldn't have been pregnant because she was too young; he'd said, she couldn't have been pregnant because *she* wouldn't. She, as opposed to the other thirteen-year-old girls, who would.

'I want to go for a walk,' I said. 'And I want to buy Tamsin some flowers. Have you got time? Would you come with me?'

I asked him what they had done when they went out together. Nothing special, he said. Just, going out.

But as we walked along the roads he began to talk about her. They'd gone fishing once, but she didn't like it. She got angry with him. She didn't believe it didn't hurt the fish, having a hook in its mouth and being pulled out of the water. If it didn't hurt, why was the fish struggling? So they hadn't gone fishing again.

There'd been the day they'd gone for a walk in the country, and there was a farm where they were dipping the sheep, and they'd stopped and helped. It had been great. Once again, Tamsin hadn't liked it at first, because it had seemed hard on the sheep, but the farmer had told her about ticks, and the parasites in the fleeces, and when she'd understood she'd been all right. She hadn't worked very fast, because she kept telling the sheep it was for their own good, and she wouldn't push them hard enough, in case she hurt them. But the men on the farm had been really nice to them. They'd laughed at Tamsin a bit, but she didn't mind. One of the men had kicked a sheep, and Tamsin had protested. She'd said he was cruel. The farmer had agreed with her. 'Vic, don't do that again,' he'd said.

They'd worked until quite late in the afternoon. They'd been filthy dirty, and a bit smelly, by the time they'd stopped. They'd walked home, really tired, taken a short cut across some fields, but there was a stream, quite wide.

He'd carried her across the stream.

When he'd told me that, Andrew fell silent for a while, and I didn't want to interrupt his memory of a day in heaven.

Hold on to that for as long as you need it, I thought. Carrying the girl you loved across that stream.

'Were you in the same class as Tamsin at school?' I asked.

No, he was one year ahead of her. The only lessons they did together were art and music. He'd have given them up at the end of the summer term if it hadn't been for Tamsin. He wanted to concentrate on physics and chemistry, but it had been nice, doing painting with Tamsin in the art studio. But he'd already said he was chucking in the music. He couldn't sing a note anyway, and didn't see the point.

'She wasn't allowed to sit next to you, then?' I asked, and he smiled.

No, she had to be on the other side of the hall. She was a soprano, and he wasn't.

I laughed, and he began to relax.

She hadn't been that keen on singing, either. Art, that was what she wanted to do, but she hadn't thought she was good enough, not to do it for a job. What she'd hoped to do was work for a landscape gardener, painting pictures of gardens as they'd be when they were finished, to show to the customers.

'Computers can do that now,' said Andrew. 'When they told us about those programs in the IT lesson, I thought, that's the end of Tamsin's idea, then. But I didn't tell her. Maybe there are places where they'd rather have them painted. I don't know.'

'IT? That's information technology, isn't it?'

'That's right. Computers.'

We walked on in silence for a little while. It was beginning to get dark, and lights from the shop windows reflected on his young, hurt face.

Every time we stopped talking he was thinking, and the thoughts were almost too painful to bear. She was pregnant, and it wasn't me. But she couldn't have been, because she wouldn't do it. Something's wrong, it's all a mistake.

And in the end, the unbearable. She's dead.

'Her mother told me she's got some of her paintings on the wall at school,' I said. 'She must have been quite good.'

We'd come to a florist as I spoke, and we stopped and looked in the window. The display was mainly of potted plants, but in the background I could see big buckets of cut flowers, and two girls working at a table.

'You wouldn't happen to know what her favourite flowers were, would you?' I asked, and I wasn't surprised that he didn't. Roses, he supposed, but I knew that was guessing, and that he'd guessed wrong.

We went into the shop, and I said I wanted some of them, and them, and, yes, them. And light green leaves. No, not those, they look too heavy. Yes, those.

I didn't know the names of any of them. Tamsin would have been disgusted with my ignorance. I should learn at least a little bit about flowers. You should know at least a little bit about everything.

I do know what a silver birch looks like, I thought, smothering a feeling of resentment.

Andrew was looking between the buckets of flowers and my choices, which lay in a heap on the table. Roses, he'd said, and I hadn't chosen any. So I picked out three white roses, and some dark ferns, and I gave them to him.

'You helped me,' I said, 'so call this a sort of thank-you present. It's only right that her favourite flowers should come from you.'

I paid for them, and wrote a card. 'With love, Celia', and I left Andrew pondering painfully over the wording of his. There was something else I wanted to do that afternoon before I went back to the house, to Helen and Giles.

Frank Welland was still in his office when I asked for him, and he came down almost immediately, his coat over his arm, smiling when he saw me waiting for him.

'Is this too official for a pub?' he asked, and when I said I thought it might be there was a fleeting look of disappointment on his face, and an instant reversion to formality that I found a little daunting. Had I offended him?

'Please, come in.'

160

We went into the same room, and I looked around, almost as if I was checking that every-thing was still there. I wanted a few moments in which to phrase my question, and so I paid attention to the blue upholstered chairs, to the recording equipment in the corner, to the polish on Sergeant Roberts' antique table.

I sat down opposite Frank, and looked into his enquiring face, and asked:

'Is there any possibility that there could have been a mistake at the mortuary? *Could* they have sent the results of a different post mortem?'

He became a little wary.

'May I ask why you think that could have happened?'

I'd wondered what to say when he asked, as I knew he would.

Her boyfriend doesn't think she could have been pregnant. Pregnancy doesn't fit in with how I imagine her to have been. I dream about her, and she isn't like that.

'I've been reading her schoolwork. I can't tell for sure, Frank, but it doesn't seem to tie in. She seems like the sort of girl who tries. And she takes things seriously.'

He was looking doubtful, but at least interested, and he'd relaxed at my use of his first name, so I went on.

'Dr Coburn told me she might have been HIV-positive. They were going to test for it.

They didn't say anything at the inquest, I don't know why. The other thing Dr Coburn said was that it might not have been her first pregnancy. What sort of girl, at the age of thirteen, does that suggest to you? I mean, usually. I'm sure there are exceptions.'

He nodded. He'd understood immediately.

'What do you want me to do?' he asked.

'Find out if there could have been a mistake? Could you?'

He was gone for quite a long time. I was beginning to think he'd been called away on something urgent and had forgotten about me by the time he came back.

'There were only three post mortem examinations of teenagers that week,' he said, 'and the other two were boys.'

I had only wanted to make sure. Mistakes did happen, sometimes.

'I'm thirsty now,' I said. 'You mentioned a pub?'

And he smiled again.

7

I had hoped to sleep well that night. I was certainly tired, but there were so many questions still unanswered that it felt as if I was looking into the entrance to a maze. Every question had too many possible answers, and every answer raised questions of its own.

Giles, you bastard, I'd thought when he'd answered the door to me that evening, but I was doubtful. I could find no conviction in my dislike. There was more to it than this, and the biggest question of all remained unanswered.

Why had Tamsin said nothing?

I wanted to go home. I wanted to be back in Germany, dealing with facts; with statements and witnesses for the refugees I was trying to help. I wanted to be back in a situation in which I felt no guilt and no responsibility, no matter what the outcome, where I could only do my best, and then leave it to the courts.

Why did I feel responsible here, then? Tamsin had been my brother's daughter, but my help had never been sought. I'd had no reason to think there was anything

163

wrong, no reason to interfere, which is what I would have been doing.

Tomorrow I will go home, I told myself as I lay in Tamsin's bed and stared up at the ceiling. I will be dealing with facts. I just can't cope with all this, with Helen and Giles and Tamsin. I can't. I'm not that sort of person, coping with the fantastic, and I don't like Helen and Giles.

I'll have a meeting with the translators when I get back. I can think about that, I can plan that. Maybe I should draw up an agenda and circulate it.

Apologies for absence, Tamsin. You won't be there. I can't manage, because I don't understand. I cannot translate whatever it is you keep trying to tell me, I cannot.

So please let me sleep well tonight. Please, no noises, stop waking me up in the early hours. I am sorry, but you are dead. Your case is closed, and I have to help people who are still in trouble. They will not send you back, because you are dead. They said so at the inquest, they drew the lines underneath and they closed the file, and now it will be on a shelf somewhere, and soon there will be dust.

Don't go. There's only you.

Yes, I remember you saying that. Or dreaming you'd said that. I suppose I could believe in ghosts, if I were a different person. Somebody asked me if I'd like to go to a medium so I could talk to Daddy. I was amazed. Do I look like that sort of idiot? I'd asked. Not very polite. Perhaps he'd meant well, that man with the big teeth and the bottle-glass spectacles.

What will I do when you've gone?

Be dead. Aren't you beyond harm now? I'd always thought that was the good thing about being dead.

It depends.

I am very tired, Tamsin. It's been a week since I slept properly. Well, you know that, it's you who keeps waking me. But I don't seem to mind any more, lying here, talking to you. I wonder why Helen never hears? I'm sure I'm speaking out loud. If I'm not I'd have to assume you're inside my head, and I don't believe that. I don't believe in all that sort of stuff. That's as silly as ghosts.

I'm a ghost.

Are you? All my life I've heard that word said in such scornful tones. You don't believe in *ghosts*, do you? Like being frightened of something silly, like spiders. Well, I am. Afraid of spiders, I hate the things. But that's a phobia, that's allowed. I know spiders won't hurt me, but they frighten me, and revolt me, I know I'd scream if one touched me. I wouldn't scream if you touched me, Tamsin. I'm not afraid of you. I like you. I think you're a bit like me. I don't mean when I was thirteen, either.

Will you miss me, then?

Oh, yes. Yes, I'll miss you. I'll never forget you.

But this is...

I seem to be living in two worlds. It's like driving through a bank of fog, on familiar roads in which I'm sure of my direction, and then I slow for the swirling clouds, and there's a brief interlude in which I'm uncertain, and then I'm on the other side, and everything's changed.

That's like dying.

Oh, Tamsin. Tamsin.

I was sitting by the window. The duvet lay on the floor, twisted. I must have thrown it off. My head hurt, not like a normal headache, but stabbing pains. What is this? Am I ill?

I'm shaking. I'm sweating. My mind's wandering, or something. Go away, Tamsin. I can't help you. Lie still and be quiet. Whatever happened, it's over. It can't hurt you any more, it's over.

Isn't it?

Nobody can do anything more to you. Not now. You stepped over that line, and you escaped. But I have to go back to Germany to help people who haven't escaped, not yet, not completely. You must understand. Nobody can make you go back, but there are others, they need me. They have their stories, but sometimes they aren't believed.

You, you're different now. Your story is entirely convincing, Tamsin. They believed you. They won't make you go back, it was all proved, for you. The noose around your neck, your tied hands, the nurse who stuck the pin of her brooch into your arm and waited to see if the little wound would bleed, it was all proved.

But they don't really care. Suicide, nothing more to investigate, another closed case, move on to something else, no time, not enough money, not enough people to look into it. Officially closed, and thank God for that. How are we getting on with those burglaries? Any word on the ram raid?

Don't be angry, Tamsin. It's not their fault.

That boy, Andrew Harper. Are there no answers for him? All his life, not knowing? Wondering who, because it was never him?

He's nice. He never bragged. He never said anything much. But there was love there, wasn't there? It really was, love?

'Don't you start that. I spent an hour in his company, do you think that means I owe him something? Oh, and those white roses, they're from him. That I do owe him, all right? For his time.'

'Who are you talking to?'

Helen was standing in the doorway, staring at me, and I jumped, so startled I felt sick for a moment, felt my heart thudding

167

fast in my chest.

'Oh. Oh, God, Helen. You did make me jump.'

'I heard you talking.'

'Was I?'

Helen was still looking at me, staring almost.

'Oh. I'm so sorry, Helen. Did I wake you up? I've got a case coming up. Well, that sounds a bit grand, doesn't it? I've got a case. One of the asylum seekers, he's a bit special to me. He was tortured, you see. I was sort of thinking around it. I'm one of his witnesses.'

'To torture?'

Oh, don't be so stupid, I thought, and this time I had to try quite hard not to show my anger.

You really are. Stupid.

'No. No, not that,' I said. 'I took him to a psychiatrist, I've helped him a bit. With lawyers. I know him. His lawyer wants me as a witness. I suppose I was thinking about the questions they might ask, how I could answer them.'

I must indeed start thinking about that. I really must plan a little bit.

Helen came into the room and sat on Tamsin's bed.

'Would you like me to make you a hot drink?' I asked, but she shook her head, leaned across the pillows and switched on the lamp.

'I wish there could be somewhere nice for Tamsin,' she said, and I thought, Oh, God. Not that again.

Try to be kind I told myself. It's only for another few hours, after all.

'I walked through there a couple of days ago. It seems very peaceful. And from the top of the slope, you know where I mean? Up by the chapels? There's a view, right across the town.'

I didn't think she was listening to me.

'Would you like one of your pills, Helen?'

'Giles says I should try to sleep without them. There's a couple for the funeral. Then I've got to do without them.'

'Don't be too hard on yourself,' I said. 'Give yourself time. Ask Dr Coburn.'

But she shook her head again.

'Giles says I don't need a doctor.'

And this is the woman who calls herself a feminist, I remembered, and then I told myself that that wasn't fair. At a time like this she was surely permitted to lean on somebody.

Even Giles.

Helen lay down on Tamsin's bed and tucked her feet up, kicking off her slippers. Both her hands were folded under her head, a child's mime of the word 'sleep'.

From tomorrow, she'd be on her own, unless Big Brother moved in. Into this room.

I shuddered.

'Are you cold?' she asked, and her eyes were wide.

'No. Goose walked over my grave.'

Oh, what a stupid thing to have said.

But Helen didn't seem to notice. She would have taken it as an excuse for tears if she had.

'It's really warm for the time of year,' she said, and closed her eyes.

She looked sleepy, and relaxed. I wondered if she had kept some of the pills, not given them all to Giles.

'Who do you think was the father of Tamsin's baby?' I asked, and I kept my voice very soft. Very unalarming.

Now, why should I think Helen would be alarmed by that question? She must know it would be asked.

'I don't know. She wouldn't tell me, would she? Never told me anything.'

'You didn't know she was pregnant? You never suspected?'

She'd already told me that. I didn't know, she'd wailed. How could I know? Tamsin never told me anything. She was that sly.

Did the sly ones kill themselves?

Helen moved her head on her hands, a small gesture of negation. A small shrug? Didn't know? Didn't want to know?

She was bound to find out soon, though, wasn't she? Not necessarily. This hadn't been Tamsin's first pregnancy. Had she known about the first one? And, if so, what had she done about it?

'Did Tamsin have an abortion?' I asked, and Helen's eyes were suddenly open again. Open, and wary.

'She never said anything to me. Not about anything. Ever.'

She was angry and defensive, and her hands were clenched into fists. I'd gone too far.

'I'm sorry,' I said. 'I just can't help but wonder. When Dr Coburn said it looked as if it hadn't been her first pregnancy. Mind you, she wasn't sure. I expect that was a mistake, don't you? I can't see Tamsin as that sort of tart.'

'Can't you?'

She was still sharp, still defensive. Did she want me to take her part *against* Tamsin? Was there some sort of antagonism behind all this?

I should probe, then; but carefully, and gently.

'It must be so difficult. On your own. Probably even worse with a girl.'

My voice was musing, and I wasn't looking at her, or so it would seem. I was looking out of the window, talking to myself, looking at the lights in the road.

Looking at Helen's reflection clear in the dark glass. Watching her eyes, fixed on me, on the back of my head.

'This is such a lovely room. Such a nice home.'

Too blatant, surely. Wouldn't she see through that? Wouldn't she be warned by the flattery?

But she was relaxing again. The clenched fists uncurled, and, palm to palm, her hands lay under her cheek, although she was still watching me.

'Sometimes I wish I'd had a child,' I lied. 'Then I hear things, and I wonder. It always seems to be the parents who get blamed, it isn't fair. Television, there's so much violence. Or sex. We can't expect them not to notice, can we? And if it doesn't have any effect, why do they use it for advertising?'

I was talking as if to myself, letting my ideas speak, not thinking. And Helen was nodding, slow small movements of her head.

'They arrested a boy in Bonn a few weeks ago for dealing in drugs. He was ten years old. Can you believe it? Only ten, and he was selling drugs. He said he was saving up for a car. He wanted a Mercedes. I remember, when I read that, I thought, is that company responsible for the child's crimes? If he hadn't wanted that car, he might not have been selling drugs, and if they hadn't advertised it, he might not have wanted it.'

'I don't know,' said Helen.

'You can't protect them from advertising, can you?' I continued. 'I suppose you could refuse to have a television. Not buy any newspapers or magazines, but what about billboards and posters? It's everywhere, isn't it? It's not just, wouldn't it be nice to have this. It's so insistent. It's more like, you *must* have this. *Now.* And if you haven't got it, you're inadequate. You're a failure. You're not like everybody else. And even if you protect your own children from advertising, what about their friends? What about the ones they meet at school? It's like an infection, isn't it?'

I turned my head to look at Helen. She was still watching me, but sleepily, her eyes half closed.

'Or maybe it's more like a war,' I said. 'Some sort of fight, anyway, and you're always outnumbered, aren't you? There's only you against the advertisers. Against your child's friends. What can you do? It must be so exhausting, always fighting so many. They've got everything. Marketing expertise, money, and what have you got? Your own efforts to teach them the difference between right and wrong. That's all you've got. The same boring arguments, pitted against colour television and avarice and fear and greed, and they're really powerful, aren't they? All children want to fit in, don't they? They all want to be popular. I suppose. And if that means having the latest fashions, that's what they want.'

Was she asleep?

'It's years since I've had much to do with young people,' I said. 'Are they still desperate to conform?'

'Hmm?'

'When I left school I pinned my prefect's badge to the hatband of my ghastly school uniform Panama, and I slung it off the end of Brighton pier. I can still see it, spinning away over the waves, and the bloody thing floated. Still, it didn't matter. The tide was going out. It must have got waterlogged in the end. Then I went to university, and we could wear what we liked. And we all wore jeans and cotton blouses and leather belts. Levi's, they had to be Levi's. You could get away with Lee Coopers, but only just. No sooner was I out of compulsory school uniform, I put myself back into a voluntary one.'

'John always wore suits.'

'He had to, he was a civil servant.'

Where was this conversation going? Would she pick up anything I said? If I stopped talking now, would she start?

I don't know this woman. I don't know how to handle her.

'Tamsin was very like John. She was such a snob.'

Oh, here we go again. Those ridiculous quarrels you used to have with John, and drag everybody you could into them. He thinks he's so much better than me, well, let me tell you. His bloody stuck-up family. Looking down their noses.

'Telling lies. Horrible. I don't know where she gets it from. I said, you stop watching those videos. Putting ideas like that in your head, disgusting. Go and wash your mouth out, you dirty-minded little thing.'

She had, she'd kept some of those pills back from Giles. There was that vague look, that, here I am but I'm somewhere else feeling about her.

Those words, they were angry, but she'd said them quite calmly, slowly and quietly.

Have another pill, I thought, and then, quickly, no. Don't say anything. Be quiet, don't be interested, just be calm. Listen.

I'm nothing, Helen, I'm only here to help a little bit, I'm not a threat to you. It's quite safe.

Tell me more.

'Dirty-minded little slut. I didn't want her in the house, not talking like that. I said, I don't want dirt like that in the house. Hold your tongue. It's disgusting.'

You tried, then, did you, Tamsin? You tried to tell her?

'Never there when I wanted her. Out till all hours. No consideration. Used the house

175

like a hotel. Come and go as she pleased. I used to say, come home before ten. If I feel like it, she'd say. Did what she liked, I couldn't stop her.'

Say nothing, I told myself again. Just wait, and listen.

It was a very long time before I turned my head to look at her again, and even though her eyes were open, very slightly open, I think she was asleep.

Who will listen, if your mother won't? And if she won't, what can you do? On your own, at thirteen, pregnant, and carrying that terrible virus, and she won't listen.

Did you ever kiss her good night, Tamsin? Did you ever take your revenge? Thinking, as it seems you did, that you could pass it on by kissing? And would this stupid, selfish and ignorant woman know any better?

I shall ask her. I shall plant that little seed of frenzy. HIV-positive, poor little Tamsin.

Oh, Helen. Did she ever kiss you?

Helen, are you sure?

8

It had been a long time since I'd been to a funeral. I was surprised at the number of people. The small church was crowded, with only two or three pews right at the back empty of all save a couple of old men in black, who wore the air of those who had the right, and the duty, to be there.

Helen seemed to be drugged almost into oblivion. When I'd spoken to her on the way to the church she'd looked at me, blank and slightly perplexed. Then there'd been a small frown, a sigh, and apparently she'd forgotten I'd said anything. Her eyes had turned once more to the car window, to the houses and the gardens we were passing, to the people on the pavement.

Now Giles sat beside her in the front pew, her arm tucked into his, his hand patting hers. As we'd entered the church he'd been just a few inches ahead of her, and her face had been turned towards his shoulder. If anybody had spoken to her, she'd made no response. It was Giles who'd looked into people's faces, and smiled, and nodded, and occasionally murmured a reply.

I wondered whether she really needed so

many of Dr Coburn's pills, but she'd placed herself entirely in her brother's hands, and I'd been warned off. I was not to interfere.

In fact, I was to leave.

My suitcase was in the boot of the limousine that had brought us to the church and was to take us to the cemetery afterwards. From there, Giles had said, I could easily get a taxi straight to the station, and a train to the airport, and he really was so grateful for all I'd done for Helen. He was sure I was anxious to get home now.

The funeral was taking place in a church on the outskirts of the town, and I was sitting two pews back from Tamsin's mother and her uncle. I had told Giles I would rather not sit in the front pew, since he seemed to be trying to keep me away from Helen as much as he could without making his efforts too obvious.

'I hardly knew Tamsin,' I'd said. 'The front pew seems a bit pushy.'

In my grey coat, with a black hat and bag, I made no impression as a close relative. I could have been anybody, and was probably nobody.

Andrew Harper was on the other side of the church, looking across at me. When I noticed him he nodded to me, and seemed somehow relieved that I had seen him. I smiled at him, and looked further back into the congregation, where people were still taking their places, whispering to each other and shuffling along the narrow spaces between the pews.

Frank Welland sat towards the back against the wall, reading from a piece of paper. Beside him there was a man I thought I recognised from the first day, when I'd come to the house. Was it the young policeman who'd been on the stairs? I couldn't be sure.

I watched them for a while, but neither of them looked up.

Why had they come? I wondered. This was a suicide. They were taking no further action. Was this an exercise in community relations? Or was there something more?

Somebody touched my sleeve, and I looked around to see an old woman in a black coat peering up at me through thick spectacles.

'Did you know her?' she whispered to me.

'Not very well, I'm afraid,' I answered.

'Such a nice young girl. Shocking, isn't it?'

'Shocking,' I agreed.

'My son keeps the shop across from the school. She used to come in sometimes. Such a nice girl. I do like a nice funeral, don't you? I do hope there's lots of flowers.'

I smiled at her, and tried to turn away, but she hadn't finished. She touched my sleeve again.

'My son would have come himself, but he

couldn't leave the shop. So I said I'd go, like a representative. To show our respects, for the business. It wouldn't do to be disrespectful, would it?'

'No.'

I wished she would be quiet, or talk to the man on her other side. I wanted silence. I wanted to think.

'We would have sent a nice wreath, but the instructions weren't very clear. We didn't know if it was family flowers only.'

I didn't know what to say to her about that. I made a non-committal noise.

'So we didn't,' she added unnecessarily.

I don't suppose you could tell Tamsin from the Queen of Sheba, I thought uncharitably, but I didn't have to say anything because the organ started, something solemn in a minor key that I didn't recognise.

Tamsin's coffin was indeed covered in flowers, and I was glad to see Andrew's three white roses among them on the lid.

The vicar was standing on the steps in front of the altar, watching as it was carried towards him. He looked truly sad, as though the tragedy had touched him personally.

Perhaps it had. I knew so little about her.

The service was brief, and so was the eulogy, if that is what it was. Her life had been short, so there was not much to be said. Only that we were sorry, and we missed her, and wished it could have been different.

Goodbye, then, Tamsin, I thought. Go with God, if that is what happens.

The vicar closed his prayer book and stood behind the coffin with his head bowed as Giles led Helen back down the aisle towards the door, and after a few moments I followed them, part of the crowd, nobody in particular, just a woman in a grey coat who may have looked a little sad, and perhaps puzzled.

Frank Welland was standing by the path as I came out, and he walked beside me towards the waiting cars.

'Are you coming to the cemetery?' I asked, but he said he couldn't. He was sorry.

'It was nice of you to come to the church,' I said, and he smiled.

'Will I see you again?' he asked.

I turned to face him, and found myself thinking, I hope so. I hope I see you again. I like you.

'I'm going back to Germany tonight,' I said.

'Oh.' His voice was flat, expressionless. He was disappointed.

'It's been nearly a week,' I explained. 'I work with refugees. I help with translators, that sort of thing. But I am needed. Well, I like to think I'm needed.'

'Translators always are,' he said, smiling at me, and I didn't tell him I wasn't one. My German is very bad, very limited. Please,

Frank Welland, think of me as efficient and useful. Don't see me as one of those pushy do-gooders who get in the way and see every nasty thug as the victim of an oppressive society and its uniformed minions.

I held out my hand, and he took it.

'I hope I see you again,' I said.

There was another journey in the black limousine, following that hearse, and this time I felt a little impatient. It had been a bad idea, the service in the church, and the burial three miles away, breaking everything up. It would have been better if the service had been in the chapel on the hill, but Helen had insisted. A proper church for Tamsin, and somewhere nice.

Some things cannot be done, no matter how much you scream.

Hardly anybody came to the cemetery. Even the little ghoul in her black coat had ducked her head to me and said she'd better be going, it had been ever so nice meeting me. It had been ever such a nice funeral too, and hadn't the flowers been lovely?

She had to go back to her son's shop, and I had to go back to Germany, because there, at least, I could be useful.

I had packed my suitcase with everything except the few items I needed for my last night in England, in Tamsin's lovely bedroom, and I had settled myself into her comfortable bed, under her duvet, with my brother's teddy bear on her pillow, and I had waited for the dreams.

Are you really leaving?

I don't think there's anything more I can do.

Suicide while the balance of your mind was disturbed. They can't make you go back, you see. Your case has been heard. You are safe. Patrice is not.

I thought you liked me. I thought you really liked me.

Oh, I do. There are so many things I wish for you. So much, if I'd known you. I think I could have helped.

But do you know what they did to Patrice, Tamsin? They beat him, again and again. His head. He's got broken teeth, and he can't hear properly, and those bloody electric shocks. Well, I'm not going into that.

He's younger than you now, Tamsin. Mentally. Physically I think he's about thirty.

When I say Patrice's a bit childish, people ask if he's been castrated. No, he hasn't. They came damned close to it, but he hasn't. And you, I don't care how often you've been pregnant, or what virus you carry, you are still only thirteen and I am not going to tell you what they did to Patrice. It's going to be bad enough listening to it all again in that court. Bad enough for me, and pure hell for that poor young man.

I've got to stop him crying, you see, Tamsin. And if, just after he's heard all that again, he sees a policeman, he may start screaming. Then they may say he's not well enough for the hearing, and it'll be adjourned, and that's the worst of all. There's a saying about hope deferred. How does it go? 'Hope deferred maketh the heart sick', that's it. Biblical, I think.

They'd mean well, but he gets so confused.

'What are you thinking?' asked Giles, and I pulled myself back to the present. To the over-luxurious interior of the long car, to Helen gazing out of the window with her eyebrows slightly raised behind the thin black veil that she hadn't lifted away from her face since we'd walked towards the church.

'I was thinking about somebody I have to visit on my way home. An African. His case is coming up in a couple of days.'

Satisfied, he looked away from me, and down at his sister.

'Nearly done now, sweetheart,' he said. 'Just a bit more, and then it'll all be over.'

Should that be a comfort? All over. It'll all be over. That's the end of it then, that's the end of Tamsin.

I tried to stop myself from shivering.

I'd thought the cars would stop in front of the chapels, but they drove straight on down

184

the narrow road to within a few yards of the new grave. Some people were already there, among them the group from the school. The heap of earth beside the deep and narrow trench had been covered with a sheet of artificial grass. It was a bright green, garish, almost glaring. The bare earth would have been better. That tufted stuff, it was a nasty euphemism. This is not earth. This is not the soil that will be thrown, and then dug, back onto the coffin. This is a bank of green grass, ever so nice and clean and neat and tidy and inoffensive, and look, we've even put some of the flowers on it.

We are burying her, and we all know it. Why do we have to pretend, with plastic grass? What are we trying to hide?

Solemn faces were staring as the coffin was slowly lowered into the earth, and the vicar's voice was a dim drone in the background. And then the undertaker's men, they had earth in their hands, and they were dropping it into the grave. It fell with soft noises onto the flowers that they had left on the coffin.

It fell onto the three white roses that glowed against their dark ferns. It fell onto carnations on a bed of moss, onto lilies.

There's nothing like silver birch, is there?

It doesn't matter. She isn't there.

I hope they didn't embalm her. I hope there isn't a lead lining to that coffin. She wouldn't have wanted that. She probably never thought about it, but Tamsin wouldn't have wanted all that, all sanitised and hygienic and nasty. Let her rot down decently, the way she was meant to. Let her body become nourishment for the flowers and the grass and the trees.

I, too, wish there could have been somewhere nice for Tamsin; somewhere in a sunny wood, near her lovely silver birch trees, where the young roots would have grown through her young bones, grown strong.

I wish there could have been somewhere nice for Tamsin.

That dark-haired woman standing beside Andrew Harper, that must be the teacher. Mrs Clarkson, he'd said. She did look sad. There was a handkerchief clenched in her black-gloved hand. It wasn't some official piece of lace with a dark border, but a real one, blue checked.

Did you teach her history? I wondered. I think you may be a good teacher. Tamsin didn't listen much to what you said about the Treaty of Versailles, and didn't take account of the economic situation, nor what was happening in North Africa, but she had sound ideas about justice, and you did see that, and you did say so.

You saw something worthwhile in young Tamsin Simpson, didn't you?

She turned away as I watched, and the girl beside her, and Andrew, they both turned with her, and I looked up to see everybody walking away.

The undertaker's men still stood by the mound, waiting for us to go.

It was all over. She'd been buried, or would be, when the men, workmen, probably, wearing overalls rather than the striped trousers and black jackets, shovelled that covered earth back into the trench, and turned it into a grave.

They'd all said their goodbyes, all except me.

Because she hadn't left it at that, last night as I lay in her bed, and then sat by the window, and told myself it was time I stopped all this stupid imagining and went back to where I could handle the problems that came my way.

Once again, I'd driven through that bank of fog in my mind, into the unfamiliar place where I didn't know where I was, where I was sure of nothing.

Tamsin, I have to go back. I have to. For Patrice.

But what about me?

What do you *want?* I don't understand, Tamsin. What do you want?

Why could I hear crying in the room? She wasn't the sort of girl who cried, was she? Snap back at you, defy you, argue with you, but Tamsin tended her own wounds, in secret.

Tamsin? I do like you. Really, I do. I am so sorry.

It wasn't enough. I could hear her. She didn't want me to hear her, she'd turned away from me. But I could hear, and she was heartbroken. I'd been the one who'd listened, and now I was going. I was leaving her.

Tamsin? Listen, Tamsin. Listen to me. I have to go back for Patrice, I have to. I can't leave him. But I'll come back to England for you. Not to this house, I can't come back here. And I don't know what you want. Honestly, I don't understand, but I'll try. I will come back.

Don't cry, Tamsin.

I promise, I will come back.

9

I kept the promise I'd made to a ghost, although it was two weeks before I came back to England, and by the time I did so I was tired, and I was sad.

'A promise is a promise,' I'd said to Anthony, and he'd watched me, and only now and then did his eyes stray back to the screen of his computer, where the words of the lecture beckoned.

'Perhaps you're overtired,' he'd suggested. 'It must have been very difficult for you.'

Of course that was the answer. I'd been overwrought, and I'd had some sort of breakdown. Only a minor one. I really should go to a doctor, not let one small part of it grow into an obsession. It was ridiculous, this idea of going back to England. After all, I don't believe in ghosts, do I?

Do I?

'Do you believe in ghosts?' I asked lightly, glancing across the room to catch him looking at the screen again.

He was polite as he evaded the question. Only a year or so ago there'd have been banter. Oh bloody hell, Celia, of course I do, spend half my life digging them up. I'd

189

have narrowed my eyes and thought about his reply. Archaeology, yes, digging up the past, and this man always was a bit too clever for me.

Now, though, it rather depended upon what I meant by the term.

As we drifted apart we became more and more courteous. The jokes we cracked at each other's expense had become quite rare.

I should do something about this. I should try to revive what we had had, try to bring it back to life. It had been good, wasn't it worth the effort?

But as I'd tried to frame the words, I'd found I was just too tired.

I'd tried to sleep on the aeroplane, and found myself wondering whether Tamsin would be waking me at night once I got back to her town. Half asleep, listening to the muted drone of the big engines, eyes almost closed against the dim lights, I let my thoughts drift back to the girl I believed I knew, and I let the belief take hold.

If I was coming back to keep my promise to her, I should believe in her.

Will you be there, Tamsin? Or am I returning to silence and emptiness? I'll miss you, if you're not there.

But I couldn't sleep, and the flight only took just over an hour, so I sat up, and turned on the reading lamp, and accepted the stewardess's offer of a cup of coffee.

We landed in the half light of a winter morning, a cold rain beating against the windows, and then there was the train into London, and a taxi because it was close to rush hour and I couldn't face the press of people in the Underground, and chose instead the frustration and delay of the traffic.

I should have planned the timing of my journey better than this, I thought. I used to be efficient.

'On holiday, love?' asked the driver, and I suppressed the rude reply that rose to my lips. Holiday, in November? In England? Grow up.

'No, family business,' I answered. 'Sorting out a will.'

Tamsin, if I can, I'll give something of yours to Andrew Harper. I'd like to give him that computer. It can only be about six months old.

Plum. If I can get back into that house, I'll steal Plum, and I'll give him...

I'll keep him. I'll keep Plum. I'll get him back somehow. Helen won't want him, John's teddy bear, and then yours. I'll get him back.

'That's twelve quid, love. Good luck with the will.'

I looked at him blankly, and he smiled back at me, reaching through to open the door for me.

I gave him fifteen, and yielded to the raised eyebrows and the questioning grin.

'Keep the change.'

'Ta, love. Have a safe journey.'

I'd left my car in the university car park. I'd taken the little one, the one we called the Tin Wimp, because Anthony preferred to drive the big, shabby one that we should have sold. We didn't need two cars, not really.

But then I'd met a family of refugees, and they'd asked me to help them in the supermarket, very polite, rather shy. They didn't understand the money. I'd gone round with them, telling them what, in my opinion, was good value, and I'd given them a lift home, because there'd been two young children and quite a lot of heavy shopping. Potatoes are cheap, and nourishing.

Diffidently, they'd shown me a letter. They didn't understand it. Please, what did it say, this official-looking document?

And I'd met others, other families, and the young men who were on their own in the strange country, and within a week I was trying to organise German lessons for them, and I'd found two friends who were willing to help with translations, and now, only months later, nearly all my time was taken up.

Yes, we do need two cars.

But now there was the train from Liverpool Street, and the memory of Anthony's cool kiss as I'd left, and the thought that I really should try, I should. It had been good, our marriage, it was worth an effort.

Perhaps I was drowning. My life had become aimless. I was clutching at anything to give myself some purpose, some sense of worth. Refugees, who could certainly manage without me, or maybe not, but it was none of my business, if they missed deadlines because they couldn't understand the letters. I'd let it become quite a burden, and so now I was running away again, on a wild-goose chase, back to England at the behest of a ghost.

Will you be there, Tamsin? Are you waiting for me?

I left my suitcase at the station, and I walked out of the town centre, looking for somewhere to stay. I don't like hotels. They bring out the worst in me. I look for faults, for reasons to complain.

In any case, I didn't want to be in the middle of the town. I didn't want to risk meeting Helen. Vaguely, I was apprehensive at the idea, and I'd told myself I wanted to be fairly close to Tamsin's school, and within reach of the town, but not on a busy street.

So as soon as I could I turned into the quieter roads, the older part of the town, leaving the bus station and the coffee bars behind me, and walking down a small hill and over a canal bridge, and I found myself in a wide road with trees and big houses on either side. It was a dark place, and the trees made it seem sombre in the early winter light.

One of the houses had a sign over the black front door, 'Brackenhills Hotel', and a hand-printed notice in the front window, 'Vacancies'.

The old Indian woman who answered the front door greeted me with a smile, and said yes, they did have a room free, which she hoped I would like.

She led the way up the wide stairs and then stood aside so I could go in and look at it.

'It is cheap,' she said. 'Only twenty-five pounds a night.'

It was small, and had not been decorated for some time, but it was very clean. There was a double bed that looked new, a wardrobe and a small chest of drawers that had been painted white in an effort to make them match, and a table with a printed cloth on it, two upright chairs set against it. The window behind it was not very big, looked out over an unkempt garden, and was framed in crimson plush curtains.

'May I have a lamp for the table?' I asked.

The room really was very dark. I didn't want to spend my evenings in such a gloomy atmosphere.

She would ask her husband when he came home that night. In the meantime, would I like a cup of coffee in the lounge? Coffee or tea could be served in the lounge in the mornings, but not, she was very sorry, in the afternoons. There was nobody in the kitchen in the afternoons, but because I had only just arrived, she would be pleased to make me some coffee. Nonono. Notrouble.

'But as you see, there is a kettle and tea and coffee bags in every room. And of course the television is colour, and a nice bathroom on the next floor up, only to share with two other guests, very clean people, and very quiet. No noise.'

I told her I would take the room, for about a week, probably not more.

Her name was Mrs Sambhi, and I liked her. She had the naturally graceful movements that are said to be part of the Asian inheritance, and certainly seem to be, where the older women are concerned. Mrs Sambhi, or Mrs Sam as she said most people called her, asked in some embarrassment if I would mind paying for the room in advance, each day. Twice in the last month people had left without paying, so now they had to ask for the money. She was sososorry and hoped I would understand. And, cash, if I would not mind. Of course she would write a receipt.

There was a pay telephone in the hall, and

while Mrs Sam made coffee I carried out the next part of the plan I had made in the aeroplane, and telephoned Tamsin's school. I told the secretary who answered that I would like a meeting with Mrs Clarkson. On a personal and confidential matter. No, I was not a parent, I was a close relative of a girl who had recently left. Yes, it was important. And, as I had said, personal and confidential.

Next week would be too late.

It developed into an argument, and I hung up.

Damn.

Mrs Clarkson had looked sad at the funeral, and had been holding a blue checked handkerchief with which to wipe away tears and blow her nose, not some frilly piece of lace with which to make a show. I hoped it meant she cared about Tamsin, and that it would make a difference, so I decided to confront her. I would wait for her outside the school. Surely she couldn't refuse to speak to me?

I laid my plans as I drank my coffee.

I thought of the words I would use, the invitation, and some sort of explanation, if it became necessary.

I was fairly sure I would know her again. She had been dark-haired and not very tall, quite smartly dressed, but then she would have been, for a funeral, wouldn't she?

Will I know her if she's wearing a shabby mackintosh and a headscarf? I wondered. Will I spot her if she's shielding herself with an umbrella?

I was thinking myself into a state of nervousness, and it lasted until I did see her in the doorway of the big building turning back to say something to somebody who was still inside, and then crossing the concrete towards the iron gate, where I waited.

'Mrs Clarkson?'

'Yes?'

'I'm Tamsin Simpson's aunt. My name's Celia Masters. I would very much like to talk to you.'

As I had known she would, she looked at her watch.

But I was ready for that.

'What subjects do you teach?'

'History and English.'

'I have a degree in English. I'll happily help you with some marking to make up the time I take.'

It wasn't really a serious offer, and I made it with a half-joking smile, but it did acknowledge the burden of her work, and she laughed in response.

'I wouldn't inflict that on you. Was it you who telephoned this afternoon? Ah, well, that's one mystery solved. Jeanette was quite excited about it.'

There didn't seem to be an appropriate

answer to that, so I waited.

'What do you want to know about Tamsin?'

'Everything.'

She gave another brief laugh, and once again looked at her watch.

'May I buy you dinner?' I asked, and then added: 'and your husband, naturally.'

'I'm divorced. Look, I have to catch my bus, can we walk together?'

'Of course.'

'I'm not sure what I can tell you,' she said as we set off down the pavement, but I didn't want this conversation to take place here, with schoolchildren running past us and half her words drowned by the noise of the traffic.

'I've come over from Germany just for the one purpose of finding out about Tamsin,' I said, and then, on impulse: 'Funnily enough, I really could help you with your marking. I do know enough. The degree's genuine.'

'It sounds like heaven, but it's not allowed,' she answered, and she muttered something I couldn't quite catch. 'Look, I simply haven't got time to go out tonight. I'm sorry. Time, tide, and marking history essays wait for no man. But if you want to talk about Tamsin, you could come to my flat later. And if you were serious about a meal, an Indian takeaway would be marvellous. So long as you understand, the bloody history essays do have to come first?'

She gave me her address, and I watched her striding away down the pavement, looking down at her feet rather self-consciously as though she knew I was still there, and still watching. She had made an impulsive response to my request, and I thought she might already be regretting it, so I turned away and went down a side road before she could change her mind, and come after me in order to tell me she had done so.

'Proper Indian food or British Raj Indian food?' Mrs Sam demanded when I knocked on her door and asked her for a recommendation, and I said British Raj. Later I heard her husband in the kitchen, scolding her. I didn't understand the language, but I caught the tone quite clearly, and the words 'British Raj'. She'd been rude, suggesting that British Raj Indian food was not proper Indian food.

Mrs Sam had plenty of replies to his strictures. She was not in the least over-awed by her husband.

To me, he seemed a rather forbidding man, tall for an Indian, and very upright, without his wife's ready smile, but he had bought a lamp for my table. It wasn't a stylish one, but it was new, and it did make the room a little brighter.

I thought I'd made a good choice, with the Brackenhills Hotel.

I was nothing like so certain about Mrs Clarkson.

'I hope you like samosas,' I said as she opened her door to me late that evening, and she said she loved them, and then she stood aside and gestured to me to come in.

Wearing jeans and a thick sweater, and with her hair loose around her face, she seemed much younger than the woman who'd hurried to catch her bus that afternoon. I could have been her mother. In fact, at her age I'd looked a little like her.

I could have been a teacher, had I liked children. My mother had thought it a good sort of career for a woman, which might have been why I'd chosen journalism instead.

'How very strange,' she'd remarked distantly, when I'd told her I'd been offered a job on a local paper in Swindon. 'You may have to mix with some most peculiar people.'

Daddy had said he hoped I'd made the right choice; and for the right reasons.

I doubt if I'd have been a very good teacher. I wasn't a particularly good journalist either, but at least I'd done no harm, writing my pieces for newspapers that few people read, and fewer remembered.

It was a tiny flat into which Mrs Clarkson

showed me, with a little kitchenette screened off from one corner of the room by a bead curtain, and a bookcase that reached from floor to ceiling acting as the wall between living room and bedroom. There was a smell of emulsion paint, and of new cotton fabric.

'I've only been here a couple of weeks,' she said. 'Let me have your coat.'

She seemed a little flustered, talking quickly and making excuses about the flat, not yet got a proper desk which was why the table was covered in exercise books, hoped the smell of paint didn't bother me, it had all been rather a rush since she'd moved, not sure whether the flat was right for her, it was so small.

I'd had practice with nervous students. I made soothing noises, saying things about potential, it really could be rather dramatic if she was a bit clever with lights, and after a few minutes she began to relax.

'Tamsin?' I suggested, and she sat down on the sofa beside me, put her hands on her knees, and shook her head at me.

'I couldn't believe it.'

I waited, and there was quite a long silence before she spoke again.

'When I got back here this afternoon I did regret asking you. I hope you don't mind me saying that? It wasn't anything to do with you personally, of course. I mean, I don't know you, do I? But it was such an odd thing to do, wasn't it? Never having met you, and that joke about helping me with the marking.'

'It was only half a joke,' I protested. 'I'll do it. I've even got a pen.'

She laughed, and shook her head again.

'No, but apart from it being odd, I thought, what can I *tell* her? I mean, I'd thought I knew Tamsin, but I didn't. I couldn't have done. And I feel so *dreadful* about...'

Suddenly there were tears in her eyes, and her voice broke, so she bent over quickly, her hands to her face.

'I'm so sorry. How silly.'

She went over to the kitchenette, hiding her face from me, and I said:

'I never knew her at all, and the same thing keeps happening to me, just when I don't expect it.'

And it had, that very afternoon.

While I'd been in Germany, telling myself how ridiculous it would be to come back to England on a crazy crusade, I'd been quite unemotional about Tamsin. But in my dark little room in Mr and Mrs Sam's hotel I'd thought of her again. I'd remembered my ideas about her, and there'd been that sudden, shocked breathlessness, and the stinging in the eyes.

'I do wish she'd talked to me.'

Mrs Clarkson came back to the sofa,

trying to smile, and still dabbing at the corners of her eyes with a paper kitchen towel. There was a smudge of mascara, which made her look even younger, like a teenager experimenting with make-up and not always getting it right.

'I do wish she'd felt able to do that, and I feel I've let her down, because she didn't. She didn't feel she could talk to me. That must be my fault.'

'She didn't talk to her mother, either.'

'No. Well, that's something else. Teenagers often can't.'

She sat down again, gave me a wavering smile, and apologised.

'I'm sorry. So silly.'

'I'm glad you cared enough about her to cry for her,' I said, and she sniffed into her paper towel, and smiled again.

'My name's Mandy,' she said.

'Thank you. I'm Celia.'

'I think it's still a bit of a shock,' she went on. 'I've never encountered suicide before, not so close. That was bad enough. And then, it was like a slap in the face. I've never been so *wrong* about anybody before. I'd thought I was quite a good teacher. Not marvellous, but, I mean, I thought I *knew* them. Well enough, anyway.'

'Was Tamsin special?'

She looked at me, a little undecided. Could she tell me Tamsin was nothing out of the ordinary? Would I be offended?

'Did you really never know her at all? That does seem a bit strange. But, no. Tamsin wasn't particularly special, not really. Just one of the class. Average, or a little bit better, but you wouldn't *despair* about Tamsin. I mean, some of those girls, you might as well give up now. You don't, because there's always hope, a little bit, but honestly, you might as well.'

'I read one or two of her essays,' I said.

'Yes. Done on a computer. When they come to calculating marks, I don't know if anybody's taken the spelling checker into account. It made quite a difference to Tamsin's, certainly.'

She sniffed again, and wiped her eyes vigorously.

'If you've read her essays you might understand, then. I mean, she certainly wasn't going on to university, not unless there was a dramatic change for the better. But she would have voted in the elections. She wouldn't have got married to get out of going to work. It could have been a life worth having. Tamsin wasn't a complete waste of space.'

'But she was pregnant,' I said, and Mandy fell silent, and looked down at her hands, clasped in her lap.

'Yes,' she said at last. 'So they told me.'

'You were surprised?'

'I was ... *astounded*. I still think they might have made a mistake. It seems the most likely explanation.'

I thought her choice of words was extreme. Astounded?

She must have realised I was doubtful, because she went on to explain.

'To kill herself for that. I mean, if Tamsin had come to me and said she was pregnant, I would have been a bit surprised. She was rather, arm's length if you see what I mean, when it came to boys. But, well.'

She looked away, and sighed.

'Nowadays it seems it can happen to anybody. One of my colleagues has just had her second abortion, which was careless if nothing worse. But if it had happened to Tamsin, I can't see why she would be so extreme. I mean, can you? Not a word to anybody, just go off and hang herself? *Why?*'

There were tears in her eyes again, but this time she didn't apologise, or try to hide them.

This was why I had come, wasn't it? But I'd had no answers from Mandy Clarkson, only a reaffirmation of the questions.

She put the British Raj meal in her oven to reheat, and we both sat at her table. There were protests about my offer to help.

'Honestly, it isn't allowed, but I do have to get through all this today. I'm sorry to be such a rotten hostess. Wouldn't you rather read a book?

'Well, look, in that case, could you take over 5C's blasted comprehension tests? Just mark in pencil in the margins anything really gross in the way of grammar? So I won't have to read all the bloody things, only pick them out quickly and make my comments in red ink? You're not to bother with split infinitives, or sentences ending with prepositions, or punctuation unless it's impossible. If the brat can be understood at all, astonishing progress has been made. Then I can get on with the history essays. If you're absolutely sure? And keep taking breaks, or you'll think you're losing your mind, let alone your grammar.'

This all came out in a disjointed series of comments as she pushed papers around on the table, dropped pens onto the floor, and sorted the books into tidy stacks.

There were thirty-five of them for me to mark.

Mandy was a mutterer, and I found myself smiling when I caught the odd phrase, usually of irritation, but sometimes of surprised pleasure. Good God, Brian Freeman, distinct evidence of a grey cell. Susan Platt, what a triumph, two whole paragraphs. Yes, Theresa, Mummy's written quite a good essay this week. Let's wait for the class test, you little bitch, we'll have you then.

Occasionally one of us would read out something, either because it was funny, or now and then because it was interesting, a new idea. Twice, we found ourselves in quite heated arguments about whether what somebody had written showed a total misunderstanding of the situation, or was just possibly a new interpretation that might be worth exploring.

As Mandy had suggested, after about ten examples of the comprehension exercises I began to wonder whether my own grasp of grammar was failing, and when that happened I took a short break, and looked at the titles of the books on the shelf between the living room and the bedroom.

Mine was by far the easier of the two tasks.

Gradually, we found ourselves slipping into an easy way of talking. We became a little less polite. We laughed at each other. We argued about the importance of apostrophes. We took books off the shelves, hunted for references, and probably wasted a great deal of time, but it became fun.

'Something's burning,' I said in the middle of one of our disputes, and Mandy jumped to her feet.

'Oh, God. I'm sorry, sorry, sorry. I'm not used to that oven, there's something wrong with the thermostat. Oh, your lovely meal. Celia, I'm sorry.'

'One *mea culpa* will do.'

It was nothing very serious. A couple of the tinfoil boxes needed their contents turning out and the edges removing, and then we sat on the sofa again with trays on our laps in order to eat, because the table was hidden under a chaotic heap of papers.

We ate in near silence, but it was a companionable silence, enjoying the taste of the food and realising how hungry we had become without noticing it while we'd been working.

For a moment, I wished I'd been a teacher; and even more briefly, I wished I'd had a daughter. There was a chance she might have been like Mandy.

'Do you often work this late?' I asked. It was past ten o'clock.

'No. But then I don't often find myself trying to defend Mussolini. Tonight's your fault.'

She put her tray on the sofa beside her, leaned back and sighed.

'Oh, that was good. That must have been about a thousand calories a mouthful, and I don't give a damn. No wonder we fought to keep India.'

I began to speak, and she threw up her hand.

'No, no, I give up,' she protested. 'Whatever side you're taking, you win. I'm not going through all that again, not after that meal.'

So I smiled, and pushed my own tray away, and for a little while we sat quietly, simply enjoying each other's company.

'I would have liked to have talked to Tamsin about the Treaty of Versailles,' I said at last.

'Hmm. Little things like being a few decades out of date would have done for Tamsin in an argument with you.'

'Mandy,' I said after another long silence, 'if I were to tell you that it wasn't Tamsin's first pregnancy, and that she was HIV-positive, what would you say?'

She turned her head and stared at me, and I looked into her face, and wished I'd known Tamsin as she had.

'I don't think I'd believe you,' she answered.

10

The Wimpy Bar seemed to be a favourite meeting place for schoolchildren. It wasn't too far from the school, and it was big, with plenty of places to sit and a wide pavement outside for anybody who could neither find a seat nor bear the crush of teenagers standing in groups sucking drinks through straws and chewing huge hamburgers, or picking chips out of cardboard containers.

I stood outside, looking into the brightly lit room and wondering which of the many groups might have known Tamsin.

I'm not very good at judging ages. I'd had some strange idea, which I now saw as ridiculous, that Tamsin would help me. She'd haunted me, I'd told myself, and I'd promised to come back. But last night, when I'd returned to the hotel and fallen asleep, there'd been no dreams. There was nothing left of Tamsin.

But I was here. I'd given myself a week to play detective, and although I could now, in the reality of a November afternoon, see that my ideas were merely fantasies, I would use that week to find out what I could. There were questions to be answered, even if not for Tamsin's sake.

There was noise, and talk, and there were protesting screams from girls determinedly unaware of the impression they were making on the boys. This was the background against which I had to ask my questions.

'Tamsin Simpson,' I yelled at three girls who looked about the right age, and they stared at me and shook their heads.

'Did you know her?'

'No.'

'She went to your school.'

One of them shrugged indifferently, and another whispered something behind her hand that made the third girl giggle.

'Thank you so much for your help,' I snapped, and the whispering girl gave me a big, artificial smile.

'You're welcome, I'm sure.'

Yes, Mandy, I, too, would despair, I thought.

There had to be somebody here. If I was to learn about Tamsin it would be from these noisy and uncaring brats. I would have to persist, despite the urge to walk out into the comparative peace of the street.

I thought, I am so glad I am not a mother. And I could *never* have been a teacher, I'd have turned into a screaming wreck. I'd have belted that little blonde tart for a start, and probably ended up in jail for it.

'Tamsin Simpson? Did anybody here know her?'

'What's it to you?'

'I'm a reporter,' I said, and then thought, Oh, God. What a stupid thing to have said. What on earth induced me to say that?

'Oh, yes? What paper, then?'

'I'm freelance.'

'My dad says that means you can't get a job.'

There were more giggles. I couldn't believe they could be so rude to a stranger.

'Do I look as if I'm unemployed?' I demanded, and then decided that I could be as rude as they were, and if they didn't like it they shouldn't have started it. I pushed my way onto the bench beside a fat girl, neither apologising for shoving at her nor asking if they minded. They shifted along to make room for me, apparently quite accustomed to this way of taking a seat.

'I earn a bloody good screw for what I do,' I said, and they began to giggle.

'In bed and out of it, if that's what I want,' I added, and the girl who'd started the giggling looked surprised.

'Did you think I didn't know what a screw is?' I asked her, speaking quite loudly so that the teenagers at the next table turned to look, wide-eyed with exaggerated astonishment. 'You probably think it's just another word for a fuck. Well, it's not. It's a particular position and the routine that goes with it. If you are very, very good I might explain it to you. Granny could tell you a bedtime story or two.'

A girl in a paper hat and a bright uniform pushed her way through to our table and began to wipe it.

'You lot buying, or just taking up space?'

Then she saw me, and apologised.

'Sorry, missus. Didn't notice you there.'

Before anybody could answer her I turned to the fat girl I'd pushed along the bench.

'Did you know Tamsin Simpson? No, just a minute. What can you drink in this place? Is the coffee any good?'

The uniformed girl smiled.

'I drink it,' she said, and went off to another table, where I heard her asking the same question in the same tone of voice.

'Are you buying, then?' asked a boy at the end of the bench, and I said, 'Yes, I suppose so. If you're carrying.'

I took my purse out of my bag, making sure that anybody who looked could see a thick wad of notes and several credit cards, and gave him ten pounds.

'Okay, who knew Tamsin Simpson? And I don't mean just by sight. I mean to talk to. I want to hear something interesting.'

I made myself sound as though I had every right to demand answers.

'Like what?' asked the girl who'd giggled.

'Like it had better be true. If I write fiction I want to know I'm doing it.'

This was a most peculiar act I was putting on, but it did seem to be effective. They tried to appear sophisticated, these young people, but they didn't yet have the experience to distinguish between a fast-talking act and the real thing.

Around us more children in uniform, older this time, pushed their way towards the bar, brightly coloured bags slung from shoulders, the girls tall in big blocky shoes, the boys pulling at tie knots and kicking at the floor as they moved, a ritual I hadn't seen before, that made them laugh.

'You got a press card, then?' asked a boy at our table, and I gave him a cynical smile.

'Would you know one if it jumped out and bit you? Did you know Tamsin Simpson?'

'No.'

'Make the most of your coffee, then.'

'Are you paying?' asked the girl.

'That depends upon what you're selling.'

They were beginning to enjoy themselves. They, too, began to act, to put on the air of people who were quite experienced at bargaining with the press. They lounged around on the benches. Heads lolled in an ultra-relaxed manner, and eyelids drooped. At any moment cigarettes might appear, so that they could hang from the corners of world-weary mouths.

This had gone far enough. I leaned forward and pointed at the girl.

'Did you know her? Were you in the same class as her? If so, I've got a few questions, just for a start, before we even think about your second cup of coffee, let alone cash. Don't get funny ideas about chequebook journalism. She wasn't a Spice Girl and neither are you.'

'I knew her.'

She spoke in exactly the tone I had expected, bored and uncaring.

The boy came back with a tray, holding it high and shouting at anyone who might bump into him, and everybody shifted around, pushing paper cups to each other, handing out packets of sugar and little plastic stirrers. He passed me some change, and I thanked him, mildly surprised that he hadn't put it in his pocket.

'Were you in the same class as Tamsin at school?' I asked the girl, and she hesitated, and then shrugged.

'No.'

'I was.'

It was the fat girl sitting beside me, and I looked at her enquiringly.

'Tell me about her, then.'

'What do you want to know?'

'First of all I want to be sure you knew her. So talk. I know enough to recognise a word picture, if you're telling the truth.'

I don't think she knew what I meant, but she did start to talk about Tamsin, and after a little while I believed she had known her. They hadn't been close friends, but there was something to go on. She spoke of Tamsin's paintings, of how she'd been a bit upset when one of them got torn at the end of the term when they were taken down. A painting of a swan on a river, that one had been. Tamsin didn't much like drawing people. She liked drawing countryside things. Trees, and all that.

The others were talking as well, reminding her and each other of things Tamsin had done. There was that time she got detention for writing on the playground wall and it hadn't been her. One of the girls repeated what Sarkie Clarkie had said about her spelling, and I didn't bother to suppress a grin at an unflattering description of Mandy Clarkson.

A dark-haired boy said she'd come back from Amsterdam with a shirt with that picture on it, that scientist, that old one. Einstein, yes. Something written on it about blowing your mind. She gave it away, didn't she?

'Who did she give it to?' I asked.

He couldn't remember. Maybe she gave it to a charity shop or something. Anyway, she didn't like it. She said it was stupid. She said Amsterdam was boring.

I thought, Amsterdam? A teenager had found Amsterdam boring? She must have been very hard to please. Or more likely he'd got that wrong.

'Did you go out with her in the evenings?'

The fat girl shrugged, and the other one sneered at her.

'Nobody goes out with Fatty Baldwin.'

'Did you, then?' I challenged her, and she laughed, trying to be scornful.

'Go out with Tamsin Simpson? Got better things to do, thank you very much.'

'And I do go out,' said the fat girl.

'Yeah, with your mum and dad. To the dentist. See your granny.'

She didn't like not being the centre of attention, the sneering girl.

'What did Tamsin do when she went out, if you think you had better things to do?' I asked her, and she gave me a look which was intended to indicate her amazement at my innocence and stupidity.

'Tamsin Simpson? You *are* talking about *Tamsin Simpson*, aren't you? Iron drawers Tamsin Simpson? Tell you this, Tamsin Simpson goes to the pictures, she can tell you what the film was about next day.'

The boys laughed at that, building a camaraderie out of the image they all wanted to share, and would lose no opportunity of enhancing.

Yes, I thought, they had known her. I was

on the right tracks now. But did that girl who sneered about her know she'd died pregnant? What had been said, in the school, about Tamsin's suicide?

'Why did she kill herself?' I asked, and the girl sighed, a deep and long-suffering sigh. I was beginning to find her act very tiresome.

'Because she was in the club and didn't know what to do about it, that's why. Everybody knows that.'

'She didn't join the club in the back seat of a cinema, though?'

They all looked at each other, and the fat girl smirked across the table.

'Got you there, didn't she? Or was it a virgin birth?'

'So why are you so sure Tamsin didn't finish her evenings out being shagged, like you?' I asked, and the girl protested.

'Hey, you, just a minute.'

I'd caught her now, and she was defensive. It was one thing to put on airs of experience and sophistication, quite another to be faced with what they meant.

'I'm not *that* easy,' she said, but now the tone was sullen.

'Not as easy as Tamsin Simpson?'

'Bloody hell,' said the fat girl.

'Language, Fatty.'

'What about you lot, then?' I asked the boys, who'd been listening without commenting, and they looked at each other, but wouldn't meet my eyes.

'*Was* she easy?'

They were embarrassed. They didn't want to answer. One of them laughed, and started stacking up the paper cups onto the tray, making a castle. It fell over, splashing coffee dregs across the plastic table, and that created a diversion. The girls protested, more angrily than was necessary, and made a play of mopping up with the paper napkins.

There were more screams of laughter from across the room, younger girls who happened to be looking in our direction, but, when the boys glanced towards them, scornful shoulders were turned. Drop dead, you lot.

I supposed I must have played these games myself. They hadn't seemed so obvious, then.

There were four boys at our table, and I smiled around at them, brightly.

'So, which of you lot shagged Tamsin Simpson?'

They wouldn't even look at each other now. They were grinning, but their faces were turned elsewhere, and two of them were blushing. It might be one thing to brag in the playground; it was something quite different to make the same claims to an adult who seemed to know quite a lot already.

'How much are you offering?' demanded the girl.

'For the name of the father of her baby, at least two hundred pounds. There'll be DNA tests. Anything but the truth gets the liar a very nasty write-up in a paper all her friends will read.'

They fell silent, most of them looking down at the table, some exchanging surreptitious glances, but nobody spoke to me.

The room wasn't so crowded now. Almost all the younger children had left, and there were only two tables packed with teenagers in school uniform. It was quieter, and somehow brighter.

The games with the spilled coffee had stopped.

'Names of boys who *could* have been the father would be worth a bit.'

There was still no reply, but the sneering girl pushed her yellow hair off her forehead and laughed.

'Don? What about it? You said.'

'Oh, belt up.'

He was a dark boy with greasy hair and school ink tattoos on the back of his hand.

'You said you had.'

'Karen, I'm warning you. Shut it.'

'A bit of an exaggeration, was it, Don?' I asked.

'And you don't warn *me* about *nothing*, you dago shit.'

'Cruising for a bruising, Karen.'

'Okay, Don, when did it happen?'

But he would neither answer nor look at me. He laughed, and muttered something to the boy sitting next to him.

'Any chance you could have been the father?'

He shrugged, and then shook his head.

'No bird catches me like that. No way.'

Karen was still smirking, but the girl she'd called Fatty spoke up loudly, and she was angry.

'None of them. Not this lot.'

'Which lot, then?'

She didn't know. She, too, shook her head, but she was looking at me. I don't know, she was saying, and she was telling the truth.

'Andrew Harper?' she suggested, but she sounded very doubtful.

'*Harper?*' Scornful incredulity from Don.

'Karen?' I asked. 'Is this all an act, or do you know something?'

'I know what they said.'

'Who?'

'That lot.' She tossed her head in the direction of the four boys. 'Listen to them, they've had every bird in the county. In their dreams.'

'Had you, anyway, that was no dream.' 'Bleeding nightmare, more like.' 'Me, I can't remember. *Have* I had you, Karen?'

'That's not the question,' I interrupted.

221

'Have you had Tamsin Simpson? That was the question.'

Again, there was silence, so I added:

'I'm not publishing a list of Tamsin's lovers, if that's what you're all afraid of. It goes no further, unless the DNA tests come up.'

'Me, then,' said Don, but he was lying, and I don't think anybody there believed him. Defiantly holding to the bragging position he'd adopted, nothing would make him admit it wasn't true.

'Simple Simon met a pieman going to the fair,' chanted Karen, and a stocky boy with the beginnings of sideboards narrowed his eyes at her.

'That aimed at me, is it?'

'Simon?' I asked. 'You too?'

He gave me a grin, a little shame-faced, and a shake of the head.

'Nah. Not me.'

'You said,' challenged Karen.

'I did not. I don't need to name names.'

'All right, darlings,' I said. 'Leave the sex bit aside for a moment. Who went out with her? Who took her to the cinema and came out knowing what the film was about?'

'I did,' said Simon. 'Couple of times.'

'To the cinema?'

'Once. And we went swimming.'

'Dead sexy,' commented Karen, and she laughed.

'You'd be surprised.' Simon was annoyed. 'She had a better figure than you, anyway.'

'Exclusive interview, Simon,' I said. 'In private. Twenty pounds.'

'Thirty?' he ventured.

'Not unless a cabinet minister turns up in the conversation.'

'Okay.'

'Anybody else?'

Don didn't bother. He knew I hadn't believed him. I waited for the other boys, but they only looked at each other, not at me.

'And what about you?' I asked the fat girl. 'What's your name, by the way?'

'Susan Baldwin.' She looked a bit undecided, and then shook her head.

'I don't know any more.'

'Honesty's the best policy,' I remarked, and I gave her a ten-pound note. 'All right, Simon. Let's go.'

He hadn't finished his coffee, but he stood up, hoisted his bag onto his shoulder, and pushed his way behind the seats to follow me out of the bar. Once outside he walked alongside me, and began to look anxious. He looked younger, too, now that he'd dropped the swaggering act, and far more intelligent.

'I don't think there's much I can tell you,' he said.

'Don't worry. Where can we go to talk?'

We went to the park, because he said

everywhere else would have kids from the school in it. I suppressed a shiver. He seemed to be impervious to the cold. As we walked I asked him, why had he taken Tamsin out?

It was difficult to get him to talk, but as it grew darker I think he forgot how much older than him I was, once he couldn't see me so clearly, and he began to relax.

Tamsin hadn't been bad-looking. Not top glamour, but okay. You wouldn't mind being seen with her. She was nice, too. You could talk to her. And he'd wanted to see that film, not spend the whole evening grappling, he'd really wanted to watch it. You can't go on your own, can you? So he'd asked Tamsin. Come and see *Braveheart* with me? And she'd wanted to see it, so they'd gone together, just like friends. It had been nice.

'Did you ever kiss her?' I asked.

'Course I did.'

'Think about it,' I said. 'I want to know about that. Maybe you can remember the details. Maybe you confused her with somebody else.'

He didn't answer, and we walked on down the path, kicking at fallen leaves, enjoying the feel and the sound of them around our feet.

'Tamsin didn't like kissing,' he said. 'She told me. So I said, okay, no tongues, but she wouldn't. Not anything.'

They'd sat together at the back of the cinema and watched the film. They'd each paid for their own tickets, but he'd bought the drinks. Afterwards, when they'd left, he'd had his arm round her, and she hadn't minded.

'Look, would you not write that in, please? That I never even kissed her?'

'No problem, Simon.'

He'd walked all the way home with her. She hadn't asked him in, nothing like that. But it had been nice, just walking, talking about the film. Once or twice he'd tried to kiss her, like you have to, but she'd pushed him away. She really meant it, she didn't like kissing. When they'd got back to her house she'd hugged him. But she still wouldn't kiss him.

It hadn't mattered. There were plenty of other girls for that.

'What happened when you went swimming?' I asked.

'There was that really hot spell in June, I'd come out of school just thinking about going swimming. I'd have done anything to get cool, and there was Tamsin, just happened to be there, so I asked her, come swimming? And she said okay. We met down at the pool. I paid, that time.'

It seemed important to him, who'd paid.

'So, we sort of splashed around. Had a bit of a laugh. But there were lots of other kids there, from the school. Afterwards we went to the canteen. They call it a restaurant, but it isn't really, just a grotty little place where you can buy drinks and crisps, things like that.'

'What happened?' I asked.

'Nothing. She went home.'

And then he spoke quickly, and quite loudly.

'I *told* you there wasn't much. I'm sorry. I just went out with her a couple of times, that's all. Like I said. But you asked.'

'That's all right, Simon.'

'Doesn't seem like much for twenty pounds.'

He was a little hopeful, but a little dejected too, as if he was not going to argue if I wouldn't pay him.

'Who fathered that baby? Would you like to try a guess?'

He didn't know.

'How did you find out she was pregnant?' I asked, and he said, it was in the papers, about the inquest. He'd thought, bloody liars. Say anything to sell their papers. But then, they wouldn't write that about an inquest, would they? Not if it wasn't true.

'Who was her best friend at the time she died?' I asked, and again he didn't know. He didn't think she'd been a best friend sort of person. But, Linda Gregson might have been. It might have been her.

'You could try her,' he said.

11

I telephoned Mandy Clarkson at school the next day. She said she'd ask, and she called me back a few minutes later with Linda Gregson's telephone number. Mandy had had to ask Mrs Gregson's permission first. Linda herself hadn't come to school; she had a cold.

'I think you're wasting your time with Linda,' said Mandy.

I called the number she'd given me, and Linda's mother answered.

I told her who I was. Tamsin Simpson's aunt.

She was dubious. Linda had been very upset at the time, she said, and she didn't want her upset again. It was bad for her schoolwork, and Linda was sensitive.

'Mind you, we were all upset. I don't want to be unhelpful, but I'm not sure, really, I'm not.'

I told her I only had a few questions, nothing difficult, and in the end she agreed I could come to the flat. But she'd want to be there all the time, just to be on the safe side. She didn't want Linda upset again.

I didn't learn anything much from Linda.

She was a disappointingly commonplace child, with no opinions, and her favourite phrase was 'I suppose so'. She supposed she'd been Tamsin's best friend. But Tamsin had only been interested in the country, that sort of thing. Countryside, yes, sort of cows and trees and things.

I asked her why she and Tamsin had been best friends. What did they do together? Had she ever visited Tamsin at home?

Who was her best friend now?

She didn't have one.

Did Tamsin have a boyfriend?

Andrew Harper, sort of. She supposed.

Had Tamsin talked about killing herself?

Linda decided to cry at that point, and her mother said she was getting upset.

We left Linda in the living room, and as she showed me out I repeated the question to Mrs Gregson. Had Tamsin ever talked about killing herself? Surely Linda would have told her mother, if she had.

But she didn't know. Linda had been too upset to talk about it.

Suppressing my irritation, I thanked her, and left.

I thought Simon had probably been right; Tamsin wasn't a 'best friend' sort of person. She and Linda had sat together in class, but they had to sit next to somebody. They had spent little or no time together outside school.

Tamsin had usually been alone.

'I think that's right,' said Mandy when I met her later. 'What's this I hear about a reporter?'

I had a very specific question for Mandy, and I think she'd been expecting it.

'Could she have been the victim of a paedophile?' I asked her, and she nodded.

'Do you think I should have spotted it?' she asked.

She looked so desperately unhappy I didn't know what to say to her.

'There are thirty-seven in that class,' she said. 'Since Tamsin died I've tried to look at every one of them. I've thought about them, all of them. Celia, there are ten of them who could be victims of abuse, if you just look at the symptoms. I don't know. I mean, what am I supposed to do? I don't think they are, not really. But they don't mix very well, they're uncommunicative, underachieving. What do I do?'

All day I'd been thinking that there had to be some sort of procedure for a teacher who thought a child was in trouble. Didn't there?

'What are you supposed to do if you suspect abuse?' I asked.

'I don't suspect it,' she said. 'I think that's just the way they are. They don't come in covered in bruises. We're told to look out for children who seem withdrawn, that sort of thing. I try, but how do I know? Quite a lot of them just don't like me. Sarkie Clarkie, that's what they call me. Not every child wants to spend break times running around in a gang. I mean, some people like being alone, and that means children, too.'

'Let me buy you a coffee,' I said, and this time she agreed, and we went into a little café.

She told me that one boy from the school had been taken into care only a couple of months earlier. Nobody had suspected what was happening to him, and none of the symptoms had applied. He wasn't in the least withdrawn, he was noisy to the point of being disruptive, and hardly ever alone. He was a member of a gang, too. So far as they could see, he was perfectly normal.

But his father had been beating him, and he'd been taken to hospital with a broken arm after a fall down the stairs, or so they'd said. At the hospital, they hadn't let him go home.

People from the Social Services had been to the school, and poor Tony Rivers had been accused of negligence. He'd been the boy's class teacher. He'd offered to resign, but they'd all said the same thing; there was nothing he should have seen, because there hadn't *been* any symptoms.

'Teenagers are so damned moody,' said Mandy. 'I mean, one day to the next, you just don't know. Should we keep charts?

Graphs, or something? Mark them on a scale of ten?

'And, I don't want to sound as if I'm making excuses, Celia, but *when* do you talk to them? I have twelve free lessons a week. If somebody's ill, you can forget your free lessons for that day, because you're standing in for them, and taking all their classes. It's tough bloody luck, you have to catch up with your own work after school, in your so-called spare time. Or parents come to see you, and that's usually a waste of time, too, but you've still lost your free lesson. Or there's a staff conference. So, when do you have time?'

Her voice wasn't quite steady, so she stopped speaking and stirred her coffee instead.

'Sometimes I do tell one of them to stay behind after school, but if they'll talk to you, there's nothing much wrong. And if they won't, you don't know. Which is it? Damned if I'll talk to Sarkie Clarkie, or, I can't talk about it, it's too bad and I don't know what to say.'

'Mandy, I'm not blaming you for what happened to Tamsin.'

'Why not?' she responded. 'Isn't it supposed to be my job?'

There were tears in her eyes, and I reached across the table and took her hand.

'I *should* have known,' she said. 'She

should have been able to tell me. I should have seen something wrong. I know they don't like me much, but they should be able to come to me for help. It *is* my job.'

I couldn't think of anything to say to comfort her, and she desperately needed comfort, poor Mandy. But as we sat in silence, with my hand still lying across the fist she'd clenched on the table, I thought, why should this be up to her? History and English was what she taught. This is what happened a hundred years ago, and this is the effect it has on you today. Or, put these words together like this, and it means something. Change the order, and put a comma here, and it means something else.

'I think Tamsin's uncle is a paedophile,' I said. 'I'm going to tell the police.'

She nodded, and met my eyes again. Hers were swimming in tears.

'I know you don't blame me, but I am very sorry.'

Then she brushed the tears away, and choked on a laugh.

'I call teenagers moody. I really thought I was getting over this.'

'And I'm bringing it all back.'

I couldn't apologise. Perhaps she should have known. A child desperate enough to kill herself must have shown some signs of her misery, and just because I liked Mandy didn't mean she was blameless. The fact that there were mitigating circumstances didn't mean there was nothing to excuse.

She had to go back to the school, and I asked if I could go with her. I wanted to see where Tamsin had worked; I wanted to sit at her desk, and perhaps to see the pictures on the wall of the art studio, although Mandy said there wouldn't be much time. She only needed a few minutes in the staff room with a colleague.

But she was longer than she'd thought she'd be, and when she came back to collect me, she found me in tears still sitting at the table where Tamsin had been only a few hours before she'd gone to the tree on the waste ground behind the railway tracks.

I'm here. It was all right, here.

Tamsin?

There was something like a miasma in my mind; a voice I told myself I'd never heard speaking to me, but it was a familiar voice, and I had a feeling she'd been half expecting me.

I wish you could be at peace, I thought.

Help me?

I came back. I said I would.

She seemed very tired now, young Tamsin. Where was she, then? Only in my mind, or with me, wherever I was? And why me?

I never knew you.

There's nobody else, now.

Here I am, sitting at your table. I'd

233

thought there'd be desks, but it's all plastic tables, all sitting around tables, how can you do schoolwork like this? What a very strange sort of place in which to learn. Most of the time you were just bored. Or was that me? I remember being bored, at school. I was always thinking about something else, my mind wandering off. Then you find you've missed something, don't you? You weren't listening. Well, if it's not interesting, you don't, do you? Then you get it all wrong.

Didn't matter. It's not what happened that matters, it's why.

Oh, yes? Whose philosophy's that?

She wasn't listening. She wasn't interested. Or perhaps she was too tired now. You don't listen if you're very tired.

I wanted to see your pictures. I wanted to sit here, and see where you'd worked. I suppose Linda sat here beside you, did she? She said she was your best friend, she supposed. Or ... no, it was Simon who said that. Nobody seemed very sure. Why didn't you have a best friend?

What for?

To do things with. To be with. To talk to.

That's why. I didn't want to talk. Best friends, talk. Tell you a secret. Then they tell everybody else. It's better not to talk.

You're right. Rosamund, she was my best friend at school, for a while. I told her secrets. Well, one. We had a row, and she

234

told everybody. I wanted to die.

Die? You wanted to die?

No. No, I didn't. I was just angry.

Now it was faint, and fading, like a mist in my mind. Was this all my own memories, tied up with the tragedy of another child? Was that my own voice I heard, from the past? Rosamund, who'd played a trick on me for a joke, and I'd thought it was stupid and said something hurtful to her, and she'd whispered all around the class. Celia hasn't got a boyfriend at all, she made it up. Those letters she hides, she wrote them herself.

I could always write. I could write love letters, romantic gush good enough to fool half a dozen schoolgirls. But I couldn't paint. I wasn't any good at that. You were. I wanted to see your paintings.

Something stirred in my mind, and I stood up and went over to the shelves that lined the far wall of the classroom. Here, and here, papers and books, boxes. Dusters for the blackboard, a thing like a scrubbing brush with a sponge instead of bristles, all worn out and a bit dirty. A box of coloured chalk.

Draw on the blackboard?

Don't be silly.

A tree. Draw me a tree.

Brown for the trunk, no. It's not, is it? It's not. Grey, sort of green, but that's leaves.

Not brown, come on.

Just, draw, it doesn't matter.

That's right. And the branches, for shelter, they spread. So the leaves can get the light, that's why they spread. Wide.

There was a rope here.

No. No, I won't.

Wipe it off, then.

It's quite good, that tree. When I was learning how to draw trees I was told, birds can fly through them, and birds can nest in them. You have to remember that, when you're drawing a tree.

I could never draw very well, but that tree's quite good.

Leave it, then. Nobody will mind. Even if they know who did it, nobody will mind, will they?

I'm glad you came back.

I love you, Tamsin.

Why am I here? To draw a tree on a blackboard, and not to draw the rope. To sit here, and look around, and listen to something that might be your voice, and might be mine. I find answers to questions when I ask them, and every answer raises more questions, and this is my imagination, isn't it?

If you're here, why don't you tell me? Who fathered that baby, Tamsin?

It's not what happened that matters. It's why.

Who did you want to punish, when you tried to make it look like murder?

236

She was still there, still in my mind, listening. I looked at her tree, and thought, it's good. You had talent. A bird could fly through that, a bird could nest in it. And I have seen that tree, when I went to the place behind the railway lines. There were still some leaves on it, then. I don't suppose there are now. It was quite windy, wasn't it? Yesterday, when Simon and I walked down the paths in the park, we were kicking the fallen leaves aside.

He liked you. You wouldn't kiss him. He tried, but you wouldn't. He wanted to see the film, not spend the evening groping around in the back row of the cinema, so he took you. You paid for your own ticket.

If a boy pays, he thinks he's bought you.

Oh, you cynic.

What about Andrew Harper? I had to buy the tea, he said he'd forgotten his wallet. Simon didn't know when I asked him, Andrew won't believe it. They made a mistake.

They didn't though. You wouldn't kiss them.

Don't like kissing.

I leaned back in Tamsin's chair and closed my eyes, and tried to remember. Teenage kisses, quite a long time ago. It had been summer, hadn't it?

Lips on lips, hesitating, what now? Lips again, and again, like a question that hasn't been answered, what now? Harder, pressure, open your mouth, and what now? What now?

Hands against my back, arms pressing mine close, hard to move, and lips, again, open your mouth. Tongue in my mouth, I don't like this. No, I don't like it. Stop. Let me go. Head twisting away, no.

Arms, and hands, can't move, can't get away. Please, stop. No, I don't like this. Please, don't.

But it hadn't been like that, had it?

Tamsin?

I was frightened, and there were tears on my cheeks, and I was staring at a drawing of a tree on a blackboard, and the door opened and Mandy came in.

'Celia, I'm sorry I was so long. What's the matter?' It hadn't been like that, when I was fifteen, the first time that boy from the farm had kissed me. It had been on a summer holiday, in Cornwall, and I'd never been kissed before, I'd only boasted about it at school, just like those boys in the Wimpy Bar. Then, what was his name? Alan? He was doing a summer job before college, on the farm near the hotel. He kissed me; on the cheek, on my eyelids, his hands had been gentle on my shoulders. He'd kissed me on the lips, just brushing. And my arms had been around his waist, then we'd been cheek to cheek, standing by the gate.

There'd been nothing more.

But I remembered something else. I didn't like it, not being able to get away, that tongue in my mouth. There'd been hot breath, a smell of beer, somebody had been panting.

'Celia?'

'Oh, Mandy. Mandy. I'm sorry, I was miles away.'

'Why are you crying?'

'Old memories. How silly of me. God, the smell of chalk does bring it back. There's nothing like a smell for inducing senti-mental nostalgia.'

I was talking too fast, I was embarrassed, and thoughts were racing through my mind. How very silly, sitting at this table and crying, making excuses. I think, when I get home, I will go and see a doctor. I can't stand much more of that. It really was rather frightening, that. My imagination, getting out of control, and frightening me. And the hands, and the hot breath, and the tongue in my mouth.

'Did you do that?'

I laughed, and followed Mandy's eyes to the tree in smudged coloured chalks on the blackboard.

'Do I get detention?'

'It's good. It's very good. That's almost spooky, Celia. She got her talent from her father, then.'

But she hadn't. I can't draw. I never could draw.
And neither could John.

12

I told Frank Welland everything I had found out, and he listened to me, quite attentively, and occasionally he asked me a question.

'I'm back,' I'd said on the telephone, and he'd replied:

'I'm glad.'

I'd gone to the police station, and he'd been expecting me, and he'd shown me into the same room with the blue upholstered chairs and the polished wooden table, and we'd sat opposite each other and he'd smiled at me.

I felt happy, sitting there with him. Happy, and a little excited. He'd been pleased to see me. He'd greeted me quite formally when he came down, but as he turned away from the uniformed constable at the desk his smile had become warmer, it had spread to his eyes, and when he opened the door for me his hand touched my back as I went through it.

'Why did you come back?' he asked. 'Is Mrs Simpson in trouble?'

'I hope so,' I answered, and one of his eyebrows rose.

So I told him about Mandy Clarkson, and

used her word, astounded. Simon, I said, had been disbelieving, had thought the papers might be lying. And I told him about Andrew Harper, who'd refused to believe it. I told him she wouldn't even kiss, and surely that was unusual? But I believed she'd known she had the virus. Otherwise, even if you didn't like it much, you would kiss, on a date, wouldn't you?

'If my memory serves me correctly,' I said, and Frank grinned at me.

'Wouldn't almost any teenager do that? But both Andrew and Simon had said she wouldn't, not properly.'

I explained, Tamsin hadn't been special. She hadn't been particularly gifted, except perhaps at drawing and painting, and even there she hadn't been outstanding. She'd been good, though. She'd been interested in the countryside, in trees; very interested in trees. She'd had a strong sense of justice.

'How do you know all this?' he asked.

'I've read some of her schoolwork. I've talked to her friends.'

'It's very vivid,' he commented. 'You make it sound as if you knew her.'

I ignored that, and I went on, telling him what I'd heard about Tamsin; what had been said, and what had been believed.

And then I fell silent, and waited for him to speak.

I waited for quite a long time.

'I was never happy about that case,' he said at last.

'Will you reopen it?'

But he wouldn't go that far. It wasn't his decision to make. Tamsin had killed herself, victim and perpetrator were one and the same, there was nothing for him to investigate. For a teenage pregnancy, he couldn't even start. You'd need the equivalent of traffic wardens, to enforce that one.

But a paedophile, oh yes, he could get his teeth into that. Yes, if he could persuade the superintendent that she'd been the victim of a paedophile, he would be able to ask some questions. Paedophiles merited serious attention.

'It's Giles,' I said. 'I know it. He took her away on holiday.'

'And you don't like him,' suggested Frank.

Which was true, and I had to acknowledge it.

He'd ask tomorrow, he said. The superintendent was at a meeting that afternoon, and wouldn't be back. Then, unless some member of the criminal fraternity did something dramatic, he'd have some questions for Giles Baker.

I didn't even pretend to consider it when he asked me to have a meal with him that night, although later, at the restaurant, I told him that a teenager had said that if a boy pays he thinks he's bought you.

243

'Which of them said that?' asked Frank, smiling, and I tried to remember, and then shook my head.

'What's the matter?'

'Nothing. Why?'

'You looked as if something had made you jump.'

It had been Tamsin who'd told me, that afternoon. The memory of her voice had come back, so clearly it was as real as Karen calling Don a dago shit. It was a memory, a recent one. There hadn't been time for it to become indistinct.

I wondered what Frank would think, or say, if I told him that Tamsin was haunting me. Anthony had been calm, and polite, and reasonable. Frank would probably be the same, but if I ever saw him again I doubted if it would be in a quiet little French restaurant a few miles from the town.

'I suppose I am a little nervous,' I answered. 'I've taken on too many responsibilities.'

'Why did you come back?' he asked.

Now I would have to lie to him, and he might know I was lying. I was having a meal with him in the late evening, and this was a social occasion, but he was, after all, a detective, and an experienced one. He might recognise a lie, even in a setting in which he wouldn't expect it.'

'Like you, I was never happy with the

explanations,' I answered, and it was only an evasion.

If his eyes became a little steadier, that was the only response. Simple good manners demanded that he shouldn't press me for the whole truth.

He leaned back in his chair and smiled.

'What responsibilities have you taken on that are so onerous?'

So I told him a little more about the refugees, explained about their difficulties with the German language. He asked if it was my job, dealing with immigrants and asylum seekers.

Hausfrau, that's my job, I told him, a little wryly. Keep the house clean. Cook meals, iron shirts. *Kirche, Kinder, Küche*, the German housewife. Church, children, cooking, although I was at best agnostic, and had no children. Most people seemed to think I was quite a good cook.

'So where did the asylum seekers come in?'

I supposed I was seeking something, too; something more important than a cheese soufflé rising properly. But no, I couldn't call it a job, although I did think it was important.

Frank said that sometimes he had to deal with illegal immigrants, and it always left a nasty taste in his mouth. His job was the law, but often, in those cases, he couldn't be

245

happy, because it seemed so unfair. They'd been born in a poor country, he in a rich one. His country had made a substantial proportion of its wealth from theirs. Lines drawn on a map could mean the difference between prosperity and starvation, between freedom and oppression.

It was wrong, but neither of us had any suggestions as to how to put it right.

'Ask your teenagers,' he said. 'They'll know.'

'How many of them would care?' I asked, and then corrected myself. 'No, that was unfair of me. They do care, don't they? But they don't know enough. It seems such a shame, when a lousy fact blows a good theory away.'

The lousy fact came back to me the next day, when Frank came to collect me from the hotel.

I'd been waiting all day, hoping he'd telephone to say he'd arrested Giles, but there'd been nothing until he arrived in the evening, punctually at seven, as he'd said he would, and when I demanded news he laid an admonishing finger on my lips and told me to wait until I'd had my first glass of sherry.

Giles could not have fathered Tamsin's child, because he had had a vasectomy three years earlier. Frank would check it with the surgeon as a matter of routine, but he would offer very long odds that Giles had been telling the truth.

I don't think I was very good company during that meal. I had been so sure it was Giles. I seemed to have given myself the idea that all I had to do was demonstrate that Tamsin was not the tart the medical evidence had suggested, and Giles would be arrested. The one would follow the other.

'Who, then?' I demanded miserably. 'Who could it have been?'

He leaned forward and took my hands, and looked into my face. He was concerned, but it was answers he wanted, and this time he would insist upon having them.

'Celia, why don't you believe it happened in the normal way?'

'Because she wasn't like that.'

That was all I had. Only one card to play, and it wasn't enough.

I told myself that what lay behind his doubts was so reasonable. Not every teenage girl who became pregnant was a tart, far from it. It was possible this was her first pregnancy. The pathologist had used the word 'probably'; he wasn't prepared to commit himself in court, so he wasn't sure. Tamsin could have fallen in love, and been unlucky. Her lover had not only impregnated her, but infected her as well.

But it wasn't like that, was it? I thought. Frank was so reasonable, and so wrong.

In my mind I went over every objection he

might make, every argument he could use to persuade me.

In the summer, when she'd been going out with her friends, and had refused to kiss them, she'd known she was infected, perhaps. If that was the interpretation I wanted to put on her reluctance. She could still have been in love with whoever it was who'd infected her. Perhaps she'd met him again, and this time she'd become pregnant.

No, I thought. She didn't love him. She hadn't liked it, even when he'd kissed her. She'd hated having her arms trapped at her sides, and the smell of beer, and that disgusting tongue in her mouth, and not being able to get away.

I shuddered, and Frank looked enquiring.

'Goose walked over my grave,' I said. 'Is that it, then, Frank?'

'What more do you want me to do?'

It was a genuine question, not another way of saying he'd finished, and would do nothing. If there was anything, he would at least listen as I suggested it.

'I don't know,' I said.

I wanted to say, I feel this is wrong. I *know* it. I'm sure she wasn't like this, she wasn't in love, there's something very wrong. I feel it.

But I thought, if I say this I will see the look of concern change into a patronising smirk. Woman's intuition, is it?

It was stupid and unfair to allow these

feelings of anger to arise, on the grounds of something that might happen, if.

'One night when I was in Tamsin's room, I couldn't sleep, and Helen came in. She'd taken some of those drugs. Sleeping pills. She was half asleep. She told me that Tamsin had...'

How had she put it? What had she said, that told me Tamsin had looked for help, and not found it?

'Tamsin had asked for her help. Frank, I can't remember the words. She said what Tamsin told her was disgusting, that's it. Disgusting. She'd refused to believe her. Told her to wash out her mouth.'

'Go on.'

'There wasn't any more. It was difficult enough to get that much. She wouldn't have said it, if she'd been awake.'

'What were you trying to find out?'

Why Tamsin was asking for my help, I thought. Why she'd come back to that bright room and woken me, and left me knowing her, and knowing there was more, and more, and every question answered raised more questions.

I couldn't answer him.

I told him instead about Patrice. I said he was one of the Africans, just another one, from Zaire, he looked a bit of a thug, actually, until he smiled, and then he was a child. It's amazing, how a smile like that can transform a face. This is the sort of smile that mothers see in the faces of their children, I suppose.

Nevertheless, delightful smile or not, Patrice was just another African, who needed a bit of help with his papers, and was in trouble with the police. It had all been a bit silly. He'd bought a bicycle. It was a child's bicycle, far too small for him, but everybody needed bicycles, so Patrice had to have one. Riding around on it, his knees were nearly bumping into his chin.

It turned out it had been stolen.

The man who'd sold it to him said he thought the bicycle had been put out with the rubbish, and it was quite a convincing story. Every two or three months each household could put out big items of rubbish, furniture, that sort of thing, and the council would collect them. It was a treasure hunter's paradise. People would come from miles away, in pick-up trucks, even in big lorries sometimes. You could furnish your house, with what Germans threw away. Sometimes there were quite valuable antiques.

Well, anyway. Patrice had bought this bicycle, and it was stolen, so he was summoned to the police headquarters in Bonn.

I didn't know his story, then. I don't mean about the bicycle, I mean what had happened to him. So I read the letter the police had sent him, and I told him what it said, and then I looked up to hand it back to him, and I saw that he was terrified. I've never seen such fear.

I calmed him down as best I could, and said I'd take him. No, he didn't want to go. Please, don't make him go.

He was crying.

It was shocking. He was a grown man, and he was crying, not even trying to hide it.

Frank was listening, his face very intent. This story had caught him.

I told Patrice nothing would happen. I said, we'll go to the police, see this Herr Ganzweber, explain what has happened, and then we will come home.

I might as well have said, we will jump off this cliff, and then we will come home.

In the end, four of us went; I, to translate from German into English; Dongo, to translate from English into French; Tchile, to translate from French into Lingala. And Patrice walked between me and Tchile, with no expression at all on his face that morning. I think, in his own mind, he was already dead.

He was not a very well-educated man, Patrice. He'd been a good mechanic, I suppose, although by then I wouldn't have let him anywhere near *my* car. Tchile was nervous, too. None of them were very happy anywhere near a uniform.

In the office, under the amazed eyes of about a dozen other policemen, we played our game of Chinese Whispers. Translation, translation, translation, reply. Translation, translation, translation.

Frank was grinning at me. He could picture this.

Had it been a serious case it probably wouldn't have been allowed, but by then they just wanted to close the file. The brat had got his bicycle back, after all. Next time, they'd warned him, don't leave it propped up against a fence alongside, or at least reasonably near, a heap of rubbish.

So it was all right. Herr Ganzweber had typed it out on some whirring electronic nightmare, and handed it to Patrice to sign. Laboriously, he had done so, one letter at a time, not very straight, and I don't think in the right place, but that was the end of it. Patrice had lost his bicycle, and the money he'd paid for it, but we walked out of the police station into the sunshine, and back to the car.

That was it. Just as I had said, we would go home.

The unbelievable had happened, and it must be because Momma Celia had power over the police.

A week later, he had come to my home, troubled and bewildered. Momma Celia, problem too much.

He had failed to keep an appointment with the social services, or something like that. He hadn't answered a letter. There was no money for him that week, and no food, and he didn't understand.

'Momma Celia, problem too much.'

I had looked at the letters he'd brought with him, crumpled and stained with coffee, some of them missing, and I couldn't understand them myself. Something had gone wrong, and Patrice was in serious trouble. This wasn't far from repatriation.

I took him to see the jurist I knew. That's the equivalent of a JP, I think. A nice man. I'd helped his two daughters with their English when they were falling behind at school. He looked at the letters, and said Patrice needed a lawyer in a hurry. Now, on what grounds was he asking for political asylum?

That was the first time I'd heard about the torture chambers in the prison in Kinshasa, although not the last. But as Herr Stephans questioned Patrice, as gently as he could in the face of the man's growing distress, I knew that what I was hearing was the truth. It was not a matter of the balance of probabilities, of evidence, let alone of proof, it was simply, clearly, and unmistakably, the truth.

Over the next few weeks I had taken Patrice to see doctors and psychiatrists and his irritating, excellent lawyer. I had pinned him down in a dentist's chair and shouted into his face, as if he had been a naughty child. You *will* sit there, and you *will* sit still and let the nice dentist do something about your broken tooth. I had behaved like an angry mother with a naughty child, because poor Patrice had become childish, and needed a mother.

Doctors had examined him, and had written prescriptions, and psychiatrists had talked, and listened, and run tests, and said yes, he is telling the truth. He has been tortured.

I already knew.

Of course I had heard plenty of stories. This man had escaped from a prison camp, where he'd been held hostage because of his father. That, a taxi driver, had taken somebody fleeing the country to the airport, hadn't known the man was wanted by the army. How should he? He was only a taxi driver. Now he was labelled as an accomplice.

Maybe, I'd thought. I suppose that's possible.

It hadn't been any of my business. It wasn't up to me to decide.

I wasn't indifferent; I liked them. But I did manage to keep my distance in some way, to offer practical help without committing myself completely to their causes.

Except for Patrice, for whom, if I had to, I would break the law.

I looked at Frank very directly as I said that, perhaps seeking some sign of shock or disapproval, and finding none.

He ignored it.

'Is this how you feel about Tamsin?' he asked. 'Nothing to do with proof or evidence, but you know you're right?'

'"Know" is a very strong word,' I said.

It wasn't an answer. It was, if anything, an evasion. No, Frank, I cannot 'know' about Tamsin as I know about Patrice. Most of the time I do not believe I know the girl at all. I find rational explanations, and make decisions about seeing a doctor when I get home. I'm suffering from stress, or something. My imagination's playing tricks on me.

Frank's hands were still clasped around mine, and he was looking into my face very intently. My opinions about Tamsin mattered to him, it seemed. We'd been sitting like that all the time I'd been telling him about Patrice, leaning towards each other across the table, quite close. But just as I became conscious of his grip on my hands he released them, and sat back in his chair.

'I know I can't be happy with the conventional explanation,' I said. 'But that doesn't mean you can't. I do understand that.'

Go back to Germany, then? I thought. See

a doctor and put all this behind me and get on with the things that mattered to the living?

Somehow the idea made me feel sad, almost forlorn.

'I never was happy with this case,' Frank said again, as he'd said the night before.

'Why?'

'At first, because Mrs Simpson was so frightened. I couldn't stop asking myself why. She was frightened of me, as a detective. Doesn't that mean frightened of something I might find out?'

It had been obvious to him, and I'd missed it, or forgotten. But I hadn't thought as he had. Distress, and a bad reaction to Valium, hadn't that been my explanation? He had seen beyond that. I had wondered, why is she so frightened? He, why is she so frightened of *me*?

What don't you want me to know? was the question he'd asked himself.

It hadn't been kindness, that had brought him back to the house that evening to tell us Tamsin hadn't been murdered. It had been that characteristic that isn't quite determination, but is akin to it, which had been aroused by the obstacle of Helen's refusal to answer. Stubbornness, perhaps. Something that would always respond to an unanswered question.

The reaction to it would be: find out. Dig

a bit deeper. Ask a different question, ask somebody else, come back to it again and again and again until you know the answer. Don't be happy until you know the answer, and Frank wasn't happy with this case and never had been.

'I don't like Giles Baker either,' he said.

'What did he say when you asked him?'

He laughed, and signalled to the waiter to bring the bill.

'It was the reaction I'd expected. Of course not, what an appalling idea, the usual bluster. It proved nothing either way.'

'It was a complete waste of time, then?'

The waiter was beside him, and he didn't reply until he'd signed the piece of paper and the man had left.

'Oh, no. No, I don't think I'd call it a waste of time.'

He wasn't trying to tantalise me, with these delays in his answers, these long pauses. He wanted to choose his words carefully.

'He told me Tamsin was wild, and disobedient, and almost out of control. He said that her mother had wanted to put her into care, because of her behaviour. Specifically, she was out until all hours of the night, and sometimes all night. Then she'd refuse to say where she'd been. He told me I could check the police records because his sister had reported Tamsin missing on three occasions.'

'A pack of lies, then,' I said, and he shook his head.

'No, it wasn't. I did check. There were three occasions when Mrs Simpson telephoned the police late at night because Tamsin hadn't come home. On two of those occasions she didn't come home until the next morning. Giles says he thinks she was with a man. What do you think, Celia?'

'No!'

'She wouldn't be the first,' he said. 'She might have been quite clever, making everybody think she was so different. Don't you think it possible?'

It had to be possible. I had no answer for him. I could only feel as I had done when I'd first been told she was pregnant, shocked, and disbelieving, and most of all angry, but with myself more than with her.

'Shall we go?' he suggested when I didn't reply, and I could only nod.

Once outside he took my arm, and we began to walk back to the car park. There was something comforting about Frank's presence beside me, something in the undemanding pressure of his hand that said, never mind. It's all right. It was only a mistake, never mind.

'Where had she been?' I asked at last, and he told me she'd refused to say.

There hadn't been a great deal of alarm, when she'd first been reported missing. A teenager, late home, later than she'd said, you'd make a note of it, but at that point there wouldn't be much the police could do. The note was made in case something else happened, a report of a road accident with a teenager involved, something like that. If there were no means of identification on them, the question, 'Has anybody been reported missing?' would be asked. It was for cross-reference more than anything else.

The next day, when Mrs Simpson had telephoned to say Tamsin had returned, a WPC and a sergeant had called at the house. They'd questioned Tamsin. She'd been quiet, rather sullen. She would not answer their questions.

That was the first time. On the second occasion, she'd come home in the early hours of the morning, and nobody had been to see them. The third time, again she'd been out all night, but she had returned safely, and that had been on a Saturday when there was to be a football match in the town. Nobody could be spared for a follow-up visit.

Frank gave me these explanations in a friendly, almost matter-of-fact tone of voice.

Well, then, I'd been wrong, hadn't I? I thought, miserably. I'd been completely wrong. Not only that, I'd made something of a fool of myself. Go back to Germany and see a doctor, and say: I think I'm overtired, or some sort of stress, or maybe I'm starting the menopause and getting over-emotional, and certainly over-imaginative. Can you prescribe something for me, please?

I've been so wrong, I told myself; such a very long way off the mark. My judgement has been completely at fault. What other mistakes have I made, then?

Frank was silent. He'd told me what had happened, what he'd discovered, and he'd been very kind about it. There'd been no recriminations, not even a mild joke at my expense, which I surely deserved.

'I'm so sorry I wasted your time,' I said, and my voice wasn't very steady.

Oh, no, this was too much. On top of it all, I was beginning to cry. I couldn't stop myself.

'Oh, damn.'

I pulled my arm free, and fumbled in my handbag. I always had some paper handkerchiefs. Where the hell are they, then?

'You didn't waste my time.'

Here. Here they are. Already opened, thank God.

'Don't cry.'

'I'm not. Not much, anyway.'

'Celia, you didn't waste my time. Did you hear me?'

'Hmm.'

I stuffed the damp piece of soft paper into my pocket, keeping my face down, turned away from him. He was being so kind, and I'd been such a fool.

'Anyway, thank you very much for asking. For questioning him, I mean.'

I was smiling at him now. I didn't mean this to sound as it did, a light-hearted valediction, thank you for your trouble it was so kind of you goodbye.

'I'll question him again,' he said, and he smiled at me. 'Are you feeling better now?'

He didn't want to say goodbye. He offered me his arm again, rather a formal gesture, but the smile made it friendly, so I took it, and we walked on.

Still, I was glad of the dark.

'So,' he said, 'we have a girl who won't kiss her boyfriends, but stays out all night with a man. By the way, I haven't checked your side of the story yet. I suppose I'd better. It's time for a bit of serious stirring, I think. I've no doubt you've been telling me the truth. I think you found out a lot about young Tamsin. And I think you're right. I'm sorry I've been pushing at you about this. I needed to be a bit more sure before I went back to Superintendent Pritchard. I want this case reopened, and I think he'll agree.'

'But haven't you got your answers?' I asked. 'You said he was telling the truth. What do you mean? I don't understand.'

'Yes, Giles Baker answered my questions, and he told me the truth,' said Frank. 'It was like a thin piece of cotton over a rotting corpse. It looked clean and white, but it didn't hide the stink. That man is a paedophile, or worse, and I want him nailed.'

'Frank?'

Such a strong metaphor, from this quiet man. A rotting corpse covered with a thin piece of cotton, and as he turned to look at me I saw the anger which had been hidden only by the veneer of his friendliness and his courtesy.

'Poor little girl,' he said. 'I should have looked a bit deeper. I thought it was spite, that effort to make it look like murder. That's why I didn't bother. It wasn't spite at all. She wanted something investigated, and she tried to make us do it. Well, Celia, she succeeded. In the end.'

13

He wouldn't tell me much more. He said
he'd already driven a coach and horses
through the rules by going as far as he had,
and we should leave it at that. I'd been
convincing, and he'd never been happy, and
the two together meant Tamsin would get
her investigation.

He followed me up the stairs to my room,
and it seemed perfectly natural that he
should do so. I hung my coat in the wardrobe and put the kettle on, and then I sat
beside him on the bed and asked him what
I should do about Tamsin. What was there
for me, now that he had taken over?

He didn't, as I'd half expected, tell me to
leave it to him, although he did seem a little
doubtful.

Pointers I might pick up from her friends
could only help, he suggested. When she'd
been away, where she'd gone, that sort of
thing.

'Amsterdam,' I said. 'One of them told me
she'd been to Amsterdam, and she'd been
bored.'

'When?'

'I don't know.'

'Who told you?'

'I don't know his name. It was one of the boys in the Wimpy Bar.'

I made coffee, and he watched me, and then nodded. 'When you were being a reporter,' he said. 'I remember.'

'Is it all right for me to do this?' I asked, sitting beside him again, and he nodded.

'Certainly,' he said, with a perfectly straight face. 'You're a snout.'

He watched me as I laughed, and I knew he would kiss me then, and that if I did not stop him he would kiss me again, and I told myself I still loved my husband, but it didn't matter. Being close to Frank mattered, my hand against the side of his head, his on my shoulder, pushing me back onto the bed, smiling down at me, waiting a moment to see if I would say no, stop. And then kissing me again, a hand on my breast and my arms around him, and feeling him smile.

Running through my mind were the words of a song, love is much more comfortable the second time around, and it did seem so. There was no hurry, no urgency, and there were long moments when we lay looking into each other's faces, quite calm, a little deliberate in our movements, more friendly than passionate.

He was a gentle and considerate lover, always very aware of me and of my reactions to what he did. It was as if his body asked

264

questions, do you like this? Shall I do that again? There was no effort to impress, no need then for strenuous physical exertion, only a desire to please, friendship, and perhaps a little affection.

This was another reason why I had come back to England. I'd known he would be pleased to see me again, and I had known, too, that it could lead to this. I did still love my husband, and sometimes I could believe he still loved me, but with Frank there was no love, there was something that seemed even better. There was time.

Frank had time to be with me, to listen to me, to talk to me. Now, he had time to make love to me, slowly and gently, and to watch me to see if I liked what he did, and to smile when I smiled, and to whisper to me, not words of love, but gentle and kind words, spoken slowly and with meaning. His fingers traced the lines of my face, my lips, the bones in my cheeks, the hollows of my temples, as if he was learning them, liking what he felt, wanting to remember. My own hands were running slowly up and down his spine, feeling the bones moving smoothly under the skin, feeling the muscles flexing. It was as if our bodies were speaking, and we were listening, very intently, very aware of each other, because this conversation was important and nothing should be missed, nothing forgotten.

When it was over we did not move apart, but lay close together, silent and still, and I thought of nothing but the warmth of his breath against my neck, and I wondered if he would want to stay for the night, or if he would leave now, and what would happen between us when next we met.

Would that be tomorrow?

'I have to go,' he said.

'Why?'

He kissed me, and said tomorrow would be a long day, but then he replied with the answer I should have expected.

'I'm married, too.'

I nodded, and sat up on the bed, and felt only a brief twinge of disappointment. There could be no future for us, but I'd expected none. I would go back to Anthony next week, and take up what I now thought of as my real life. But here in England I had a little time.

I asked him before he left if he would tell me what he found out, and he said he'd tell me what he could. Then he kissed me again, and said he'd probably tell me more than he should. Would I please try to be discreet about it?

He was only half joking.

'I won't boast about you,' I promised, and he smiled, and kissed me again.

I lay awake for quite a long time after he'd gone, thinking about him, and wondering whether, if I'd agreed I'd been wrong about

Tamsin, he would have dropped the case. He'd said he'd wanted to be sure. But he had believed Giles was a paedophile, or worse, whatever worse could be.

I remember, just before I fell asleep, wondering if I would dream about Tamsin that night, but if I did I forgot my dream as I woke, still lying on top of the bed, with my clothes strewn around the room, apart from my dress, which Frank had laid tidily on the chair. It looked like a scene from a wild orgy, as though we had torn them off my body in a frenzy of lust. It bore no resemblance to the almost decorous interlude that had in fact taken place.

Today, he would ask to reopen the case, and he believed he would be allowed to do so.

What would happen then?

He had said he would tell me, as much as he could and more than he ought, and with that I would have to be satisfied, but as I dressed I remembered the remark the boy had made about Tamsin and Amsterdam. I could ask more. I could continue to play detective.

During the morning I had a better idea, and I telephoned Helen.

'I can't talk for long,' I said. 'These international calls cost a fortune.'

Understand, bitch? I'm calling from Germany.

'How are you? Are you coping?'

I forced concern into my voice. I tried to tell myself that she probably was genuinely grieving for her daughter, no matter how little she had done for her.

'I'm all right,' said Helen.

'You are seeing the doctor, aren't you? You're not trying to get off those pills too quickly?'

On her favourite topic, her own well-being, Helen began to relax. She was seeing the doctor every few days, she was still taking the pills. She would never get over this, of course, but they did help. She thought she needed a holiday, she might go away for a little while.

'Would you like to come to Germany?' I asked, but Helen had more luxurious ideas than Germany. She needed sunshine. Giles had suggested the West Indies, or perhaps South Africa.

'Talking about travel,' I said, 'have you still got Tamsin's passport?'

'What?'

'Helen, I wouldn't ask if it wasn't an emergency, but I really do need a British passport for a young girl. I don't want to say too much. I really don't want to implicate you. But if you have got it, and could send it to me, I would be grateful. You could say I must have stolen it while I was staying with you, if it gets found out.'

It had sounded good, that. It had been quite convincing, at least in my ears. How had it sounded to Helen?

'Tamsin never had a passport,' she said. She sounded puzzled. And then she began to get angry.

'That's illegal. You're trying to get somebody into England illegally, aren't you? Well, Celia, let me tell you, I don't break the law like that. That's awful, you asking me for Tamsin's passport. That's awful of you.'

'All right,' I said. 'I'm sorry I upset you. Forget it.'

'How *could* you do that? She's hardly cold in her grave, and you're asking that. It's like exploiting her. I'll never forgive you for that. And trying to make me break the law, when I'm all upset. It's dreadful of you. I never want to speak to you again.'

She hung up, and I replaced the receiver slowly, smiling to myself, although I felt a little shocked, as I had expected. I hate angry words and raised voices. Always, after a confrontation, I feel cold and sick and shocked, but this time those sensations were mixed with elation.

How had Tamsin got to Amsterdam without a passport?

And if she hadn't gone, why had she lied?

I would have something to tell Frank that evening, something that might help.

I met Mandy Clarkson later for the sandwich that she said was all she had time for at midday. I asked her if Tamsin had ever taken time off from school to go to Holland, and she said she thought she had, some time in the Spring. There'd been some special excuse, some event that was of particular interest, so she'd been given permission.

Mandy was curious, so I told her about the boy's comment. At the time I'd thought it strange, that a young girl would find Amsterdam boring.

'I don't believe she ever went,' I said. 'Could you look up the files? Find out when it was, and who asked permission for her to go?'

She nodded, and said she'd brought me something. She reached into her bag, and gave me a rolled-up piece of paper, thick white paper. Then she said she had to go.

'Thanks for the sandwich, Celia.'

I knew before I unrolled it that it would be one of Tamsin's paintings.

But it was still a shock, when I looked at it, and saw the tree I had drawn on the blackboard.

I snatched my hands away from it, and it rolled itself up again, curling slightly crookedly across the table so that it lay diagonally across the white cloth.

It had been painted in watercolours, and I had used chalk, but I remembered the way my hand had felt as I shaded the outline of the low branch that should have carried a rope, and I had seen those same shadows on the tree Tamsin had painted.

Write this off to imagination if you can, I thought, and then, I don't know much about trees. It could be coincidence. It could. It was only a tree; trunk, branches, leaves, and that was what I had drawn. And what she had painted.

Feelings of anger were beginning to stir in my mind, and I tried to suppress them.

There's no point in getting angry simply because you don't understand something. That was silly. How many different ways are there of drawing a tree, if you don't know anything about them? And if you haven't got much talent.

Cautiously, I unrolled the paper again, and I studied the tree, and I found plenty of differences. It had simply been an odd coincidence, that I had drawn a tree roughly the same as the one Tamsin had painted. This branch at this angle, and that at another, and the bend in the trunk. But that was all.

And there was my choice of colours, which hadn't been quite what I would have used only a few days earlier, but then, I had been thinking about trees, hadn't I? I had noticed that the trunk of a tree wasn't really that flat, uniform brown. So, I could grant myself the credit of some powers of observation, and a little intelligence to go with it.

However, thinking quite rationally about it, I could see why Mandy had said it was spooky. It really was quite a coincidence.

There was a date at the bottom edge of the page, not in Tamsin's handwriting, printed lightly in faint pencil. The number was smudged, and I couldn't read it, but the month was September. This tree had been painted, or chosen to be displayed on the wall, in September, a month before she'd killed herself, and I was quite sure this was the tree she had used.

Had the idea come to her as she painted it? Had she seen, in the branch that swung down in the curve we had both drawn, the gallows that would end her life?

Or had she chosen the tree first, and then painted it to say something else to anybody who might look?

I didn't like touching the picture. For all my efforts to rationalise what had happened, the experience was unfamiliar enough to be unpleasant. When I unrolled the paper again and studied the painting, I could feel my own hand and arm moving as I drew the lines, as I smudged the colours with the tips of my fingers to make an effect I really couldn't remember ever having used before, or having learned. I could, if I allowed myself, imagine the feeling of a brush between my fingers, the difference in

272

the techniques you would need to gain the same effect. Smudging the chalk by rubbing at it, gently; washing one colour into another with the side of a paintbrush.

I'd been half listening as I'd drawn the tree. So had Tamsin, when she painted it. As she painted she listened with her mind, with her memory, with the feelings she had for the subject of her picture. If she'd gone on, she would have become so familiar with the techniques she needed she would have forgotten them. They would have become unconscious, so she could concentrate completely on what she was hearing with her mind, with her memory, with her feelings.

I hadn't realised before that the tree was beautiful.

It was warm, and welcoming. Trees had no warmth, I knew that. Lay your hand on the trunk of a tree and it is hard, rough, and cold. But if you could stand by a tree for a hundred years, with your hand against it, so that you knew it well enough to be part of it, you would feel a strong pulse under that tough skin of bark. You would feel the warmth of its life, and you would share in its slow dreams.

It was dark, too. There was a dark welcome from this beautiful tree. Come to me. Come to me for strength and for safety and for shelter and for death.

Come to me.

Stand by the tree with your hand on the hard, rough, cold bark, and feel the strong, slow pulse and the dark welcome.

I shuddered, and pushed the picture away again, watching as it rolled, more slowly this time because it had been lying flat. A waitress who had been standing near me came over and asked if there would be anything more, madam.

'No, thank you. Or, yes, a cup of coffee, please. But bring me the bill at the same time.'

This was not what Frank had meant when he had said, a little doubtfully, that I could go on asking questions.

Did it have any value at all, what I was learning from Tamsin's picture?

The coffee was lukewarm and gritty. I was the only one in the café, and they wanted to close and clean up, get ready for the evening trade. I pushed the cup away, rolled the picture again and the slid the thick rubber band over it. I would take it home next week, and keep it somewhere safe, and one day, when I was very old, and strong enough, I would look at it again, and see whether it still carried the same message, and perhaps then I would know enough to understand.

Will I ever be old enough and strong enough to see into the mind of a thirteen-year-old girl who looks at a tree, and finds it beautiful, and accepts its offer of death?

Tamsin had walked along these pavements on her way home from school, on the fine days when she didn't need to take the bus. Today it was cold and windy, and there was a gritty dust under my feet, a little like grey sand.

It must have been lonely, once she had made her decision. It would set you apart.

I'm going away. I am going away for ever.

Once you knew you would kill yourself it would set a distance between you and everybody else, even if it was only you who knew it. Once the decision had been made, the process of leaving would begin.

In Germany three years ago, almost to the day, certainly to the week, I had seen a man alone in a half-built street walking on grey sand on the road. That had been a cold day, too. There had been wind, gusting in spiteful little eddies around his feet, lifting the sand. He was wearing a heavy coat, grey or brown, very thick and stiff, and his arms were wrapped across in front. Despite the heavy coat, he was cold.

He was the only one on that road. Beside him, there were stacks of brick behind wire barriers. There were half-built houses. Land had been cleared, scraped free of grass and trees and open to the sky, bleeding its broken soil into the tearing wind.

He was small and thin, and he was walking

275

quickly, picking his way between ruts on the unmade road, his head down as he faced into the wind. As he heard the sound of my car he turned his head to look, and I saw that he was black.

There weren't many black people then, not in that little town. In Bonn they were more common, from the embassies, from the university, but out here I didn't think I'd seen a black man before, and I wondered what he was doing, on this building site, walking into the wind, trying to avoid the puddles in the ruts.

There was something infinitely sad, and yet very valiant, about that man, made for the sun, and struggling against a north European winter wind.

He, too, had been lonely, an exile from his land.

'Cold!' I exclaimed to Mrs Sam when I met her in the hall, and she agreed, smiling, that it was cold.

'Did you find the winters difficult when you first came over?' I asked her, and she said yes, but it had been a long time ago. It was better now. A sari was draughty in the winter, but her husband had bought her an Arran sweater, a proper one, made in Scotland by hand, and this had kept her warm.

'I should think it kept you poor, for a week or two,' I remarked, and she found that hugely amusing, throwing back her head and laughing, slapping at her thighs. She would tell her husband, he would think this very funny.

It had been a good investment, her Arran sweater. She still had it, twenty years later, still wore it. Goodasnew.

She offered me coffee. It seemed I was a favoured guest, since she'd made it so clear on my arrival that coffee could not be served in the afternoons, and it would have been ungracious to have refused.

'Yes, I would love a coffee. Thank you.'

We drank it in her tiny sitting room at the back of the building. There were religious icons and pictures, and Mrs Sam was pleased and surprised that I could identify the gods, and knew a little about them. And for me, did they have meaning?

'No, I have no religion. No real beliefs.'

'Oh, oh. So sad.'

It was easy to talk to Mrs Sam, and I needed to talk. I went on, explaining.

I wouldn't say there was nothing to believe in. It was only that I didn't know what, and didn't think it really mattered. So many people saw their religions as a way of bargaining with death, and death didn't need to strike any bargains. Death would have you whether you believed in a god, or not.

Mrs Sam was disposed to argue. Religion

was not about death, religion was about life and how to live. Thinking about death, I was right, wasteoftime.

I'd been thinking about little else that afternoon, so I took Tamsin's picture out of my bag and handed it to Mrs Sam, said she should look at it and tell me what she thought.

She unrolled the picture carefully onto her coffee table and held it flat with her hands. I noticed her fingers were long and slim. They were motionless on the white paper, very controlled. She wore heavy rings, with turquoise laid into them, and the fingers looked as if they wouldn't be strong enough to carry such a weight.

I watched her hands, because I didn't want to look at the beautiful tree again.

Such a lovely tree, and on a piece of ragged waste ground behind the railway lines. Did anybody ever look at it, and think, that's a beautiful tree? Did anybody ever notice it? In a garden you would see it, and think of the graceful shape. Against a sooty brick wall with brambles snarling behind it, it was just a tree. It would probably be cut down soon. That piece of land would be developed, in a thriving town with new businesses moving in and wanting premises. They called that a brownfield site, didn't they?

'Who painted?' asked Mrs Sam, and I

said, my niece.

'Clever girl,' she said. 'Lovely painting.'

'She died. She killed herself. She hanged herself from that tree.'

The slim, brown hands moved aside, and the painting rolled itself up again. Silently, Mrs Sam replaced the rubber band.

'Why?' she asked, and I thought I saw the sparkle of a tear in her eye.

I told her, this is why I came back, to try to find out. Because I couldn't understand. Tamsin, it was like two people, and only one could be real. But there was no doubt, she was pregnant, and almost certain about the virus. She, at least, believed she was infected. So, how did that happen? To this girl, who could paint that tree.

And I did you an injustice, Tamsin. I said, when it came to painting, you were good, but not outstanding. I was wrong. This was a talent that could have become great. Given the right guidance, you could have been one of the great painters. You could have done it.

There were stories about Tamsin, I said, and Mrs Sam's head was tilted to one side as she listened. Well, more than stories, it was true. Out late at night, not coming back all night, refusing to say where she'd been. But she wouldn't have sex with the boys at her school, she wouldn't even kiss them.

'Ah, I see.'

Mrs Sam's face was old, and wise, and kind. There was a gentle innocence about it that had nothing to do with ignorance.

Her mother wouldn't listen to her. When she killed herself she tried to make it look like murder. The police thought it was because she was angry with the man, or the boy, who had made her pregnant and then left her. They thought she'd done it to get her own back on him. But it wasn't that. There wasn't anybody. They said it was suicide, and that was all. Nothing more. Goodbye, Tamsin, that's the end.

'Every life comes to an end,' said Mrs Sam. 'This is a great blessing. All the monsters die. The dictators, the great and evil ones, the day must come when they are not there any more.'

She lifted the little enamel coffee pot and gestured towards my cup. I shook my head.

'Also, when a life has gone wrong, there is death. Like a painting, if it is too bad, start again. New piece of paper. Learn from the bad painting, make a better one next time.'

'Karma?' I suggested, and she smiled and wagged her head, the very Indian gesture that can be used as a polite way of saying, you are talking nonsense.

'You, my girl, you forget this karma business. This is not the way for you. Want to learn about all that, fine, but you please don't forget. Thousandsofyears. You come along, two books, two weeks, you know everything. Except maybe those thousands-ofyears being Indian.'

'What would you do about Tamsin?' I asked, and she didn't hesitate.

'What you are doing. Try to find out. Stop him. But don't forget, if you don't find out, one day death comes for him too. But you try.

'You like cricket?' she demanded. 'My husband, if India's playing, television stays on. Idle old bugger, I say, sit there, watch television all day. Okay. Ball hit, goes to the boundary, four runs, maybe six. That's all. You think a fielder don't run like buggery to stop that ball going to the boundary because it's only four runs? Cricket's only a game, don't tell my husband I say so, maybe he'll beat me. Game or something like this, you try, but you don't spend the rest of your life worrying if you don't win, because death comes one day.

'In the end, there is death. You can fail. Death can't.'

14

I showed Tamsin's painting to Frank that evening, and it didn't take him long to recognise the tree. When he did so, he looked startled. He glanced up at me, and then bent forward to examine it more closely, and to study the date pencilled in the corner.

'That is the tree, isn't it?' I asked, half hoping he would say no.

'It looks like it. It's extraordinary. Did she do it on an outing from the school? Does the art class do that?'

I didn't understand what he meant at first, and then I realised what he was asking. Had she sat in front of that tree with her paper and her paints, perhaps surrounded by her friends?

'No, it was done from memory,' I said, and then thought, I don't know that. Or, if I do, it isn't a statement I can defend.

'I think,' I added, quickly. 'I'll ask, shall I?'

'I don't suppose it's important. It's interesting, though. I've never come across anything like that.'

He looked at the painting again, and then rolled it up and handed it back to me.

'It's good, too,' he remarked.

We were sitting in my room. I didn't want to go out. I was tired of restaurants and cafés, and I wanted quiet and familiar surroundings. I wanted to hear what he had been doing, what he had discovered.

I wanted him to make love to me again.

'What did Superintendent Whatsisname say?' I asked.

'Pritchard. I've got three days.'

Was that how it worked? Was time allocated to every case? I knew they had started to use the term 'prioritise', I hadn't thought about what it meant.

'Will that be enough?'

It was an impossible question, and he didn't try to answer it with anything more than a smile, a shrug, and a brief comment that it would have to be.

I told him about my telephone call to Helen, and Mandy Clarkson's belief that Tamsin had been given permission to go to Amsterdam for a special reason, but I knew these discoveries were comparatively unimportant. I wanted to get them out of the way, so that I could hear Frank's news.

We were facing each other across the table, Mr Sam's new lamp casting light onto the printed cloth, from where it reflected onto our faces. Frank had taken off his jacket, and he was leaning forward, with his hands clasped in front of him. I was looking into his face and smiling at him, but I was more aware of his arms. I remembered them from the previous night, when they had been naked around my shoulders, warm and firm. Now, the blue cotton of his shirt stretched across them, but their shape showed through, and my eyes kept drifting down to them, as I remembered.

I liked his arms. When we had been lying together on the bed, I had run my hands along them, up and down over the skin, feeling the hairs rough and springy under my fingers, feeling the curve of the muscles, the hard angles of the bones in his wrists and elbows. We had been talking, listening to each other, but he had watched my hands on his arms, and I knew now, as he saw my eyes on them, that he, too, was remembering.

He began to talk, and I listened carefully, but I had to make myself concentrate on his words.

Giles Baker was a rich man, but the money hadn't been inherited, so Frank was looking for the source of his wealth. How had he made his money?

Why did it matter? I wondered, and then I realised. A paedophile, or worse, he'd said.

A trader.

It was very complicated, and those sort of complications were usually deliberate. Tax evasion was the most common motive, money-laundering, and the particular sorts of crimes that involved illegal sales; drugs, arms, stolen goods.

Pornography.

Giles didn't have a criminal record, which was a pity. Digging was difficult, and not always strictly according to the rules.

'Have you questioned him again?' I asked, interrupting him, and he said he had; he, and Sergeant Bull. Giles had been impatient. It was quite a good act.

'Look, I'll co-operate as far as I can, but I'm a busy man. Now, what do you want, and why?'

He'd said his business interests covered travel, through travel agencies in which he held controlling interests; a certain amount of import and export, at which point he'd complained bitterly about regulations, and he'd been very vague about what it was he'd imported, or exported. He'd said it depended upon demand, and upon what his contacts asked for. When they'd pressed him he'd said that yes, of course he had business records, but that side of things was handled in Holland, and that's where they were.

'Why?' Sergeant Bull had asked. The sergeant was a good policeman, but he knew little beyond the boundaries of his experience. Europe, to him, suggested a looser attitude to sex crimes, and a safer place in which to commit them.

Because that was where he paid his taxes on that part of his business, Giles had replied. It was all perfectly legal and a damned sight cheaper than paying them here. He traded as a limited company, and what's more he traded as a multinational limited company.

At that point he had seemed to lose patience with them, although it might have been part of the act. If so, he was very good indeed.

No, he was not a sole trader, he had several associates, and he would not give their names without a good reason, because he didn't see why they should be bothered with enquiries from the police. He wasn't entirely keen that they should know he was the subject of their investigations himself, and before he answered any more questions he wanted to know why they were asking them.

'And what has all this to do with Tamsin?' he'd demanded.

All these questions had taken quite a long time. Giles had been ready for them that time. The first time Frank had tackled him, with the accusation of having fathered Tamsin's baby, he'd been taken by surprise. He hadn't recognised Frank, and he'd thought the case, such as it was, had been closed.

'He's no fool,' said Frank. 'He isn't going

to panic, either.'

Then he leaned back in his chair, clasping his hands behind his head and smiling at me.

'I've been dealing with that all day,' he said. 'Chasing him, and thinking of you. Let's talk about something else.'

'You will get him, won't you?' I asked.

'I intend to.'

It was a good enough assurance, from him. But three days seemed a very short time.

We lay side by side on the bed, and we did talk. I thought, only a few years ago I would have found this strange. I would have wondered, doesn't he find me attractive? Is there something wrong with him? Now, if it occurred to me at all, it was simply that we had nothing to prove. We wanted to talk to each other.

I was aware of my little clock, behind me on the bedside table, ticking quietly, marking the passing seconds. When I look back on this, I thought, I will remember that. I will remember lying on this bed facing this man, listening to him. I will remember his head propped on his hand, the way his knee bends so his foot lies across the calf of the other leg. The way he reaches out, now and then, to push this lock of hair away from my forehead, and the way, a little while later, it falls back again, and makes him smile.

Sport, and football hooligans, we talked about that for a while, the way the teams were nothing more than a tribal banner under which the young men fought, and whether it was worth even trying to stop them. He spoke of containment, whatever that meant.

I asked, if it's nothing to do with football, why don't they advertise the fights instead of the matches, and he answered, do you think they don't?

I told him what Mrs Sam had said about cricket, and the way she ran words into each other. Wasteoftime, runlikebuggery.

'I bet she doesn't know what buggery means,' said Frank, and I answered, I bet she does, then.

I tried to remember how long it had been since Anthony and I had talked like this, using idle words, and a conversation that drifted into different channels, to be pursued or abandoned, as we liked.

Years, probably, I thought, and it was this loss more than any other that had done the damage. Anthony was more intelligent than Frank, better-educated, even better-looking, but it felt so good, to talk to a man again, and to listen to him.

I told Frank what Mrs Sam had said about death, and he thought about it for a while, wondered whether it might apply to capital punishment, decided not. He was against capital punishment, but thought he would rather be dead than locked up for ever. What about me?

Locked up where? I asked. And with whom?

Locked up with me? he suggested, and I said I'd rather be alive, and he pushed my hair off my forehead again, and leaned forward and kissed me.

'Three days,' I said, remembering. 'I have to go back to Germany in four.'

He frowned a little at that, but he kissed me again, and then, without saying anything more we both sat up and began to take off our clothes.

He was still frowning as he turned to me again.

'Will you come back?' he asked.

'I don't think so. No, I don't think so.'

He stroked my cheeks, and lay above me, looking down into my face.

'I won't see you again?'

I didn't want to answer him. I knew it would be better to say no. I had needed this interlude, this break in the loneliness, and perhaps he had, too, although neither of us would speak of it.

He didn't repeat the question, but this time he held me closer, as though he wanted the contact between our two bodies to be as great as possible, wanted no distance between us, because of the distance that was coming in only a few more days. It was not so slow, not so lingering, as it had been on the previous night. There weren't many words, but the kisses were harder, his grasp of me stronger, the movements powerful and growing faster, almost as if he was being driven by panic. Not much time, not much time.

'Frank?'

'Hmm?'

No, don't protest. If this is what he needs, then so be it.

It was over quickly, a great groan, and he was shuddering, and there was sweat on his back and on his face. He rolled away from me and lay on his back, one arm across his eyes as if to shield them from a bright light.

'I'm sorry,' he said.

'Oh, please don't,' I said. 'Please don't start that.'

'It can't have been much good for you.' And then, almost in the same breath: 'You might have to come back for the trial.'

And say what? I thought, but instead I asked if he didn't protect the anonymity of his snouts. It was meant as a mild joke, but it seemed to irritate him. He jerked his head and grunted, his eyes still hidden by his arm, and he didn't answer.

I lay beside him, silent, wondering what had gone wrong, and how it had happened so quickly.

Had he thought I would stay here? Leave Anthony, and live over here, in England? Or had he not thought at all, and been taken by surprise by the realisation that we had only a short time together?

'What do you want me to do tomorrow?' I asked, and his answer was almost brusque.

'Whatever you like,' he said.

I don't know if he meant it as a rejection. That was how I heard it. It doesn't matter what you do, so do whatever you like.

I let the words run through my mind, trying not to be hurt or angry. Had it not been for me he wouldn't have looked at this case again, even if he hadn't been happy about it at the time. But now his words had a dismissive tone. Run away and play, leave it to the grown-ups.

I wished I hadn't given up smoking.

I wanted him to go, now.

As soon as I thought it he sat up, and reached for his clothes, his head still turned away from me.

What had gone wrong, then? What had I done, that he should suddenly be so distant and so cold?

I could have asked him, what's the matter, and listened to the inevitable reply, nothing. They were the opening moves in a game I had played before, and never wanted to bother with again.

I had done nothing wrong. So, you deal with this, I thought. I will play a different game, with different rules.

'I'll try to find out about that trip to Amsterdam,' I said, and not in a tone to suggest I would listen to alternative suggestions.

He kissed me good night, but even then he would hardly look at me, and I watched the door closing behind him, and felt angry, and disappointed, and, once again lonely. This time I did not fall asleep where I lay, but got up and tidied the room, set the chairs straight, remade the bed, and then sat at the table.

Tamsin's painting lay there, and I wondered whether she had known, as she painted it, that she would use the tree to kill herself, or whether that had come later. I had seen something dark in it, but then I knew what had happened, and my imagination had been over-stimulated.

Still angry, I went upstairs to the bathroom and showered, and then climbed into bed, and tried to sleep, but it was a long time before I did so.

I had nightmares.

These were something different, these dreams of Tamsin painting herself hanging from the tree, and I woke crying, and knowing they had nothing to do with her. This was me, my own misery coming back to haunt me in the night.

It was dark, and I didn't think I had slept for more than two or three hours, but I got up and dressed, wrapped myself in my warm coat, and let myself out of the house. Walking would help.

What had I done wrong? Why was he angry with me? And what right had he to treat me like that? To become brusque and cold when I'd told him how long I'd be staying.

But I'd expected too much. As the sky lightened I recognised that, and although I still felt hurt the anger subsided. Frank Welland was, after all, just another man. The fact that he'd wanted me didn't make him anything special, or in any way different. It was my own vanity that had suggested otherwise.

I walked a long way, down a hill through the outskirts of the town, and a little while later I found a footpath beside a lake. I was lost by then, but it didn't matter. Eventually I'd find a road with a signpost, and then I'd make my way back. But I didn't know what to do.

I thought, I might as well go back to Germany now. The police have taken up the case again, and they have a prime suspect, so there's nothing more for me to do. They can do it all, better and faster. I've done all I can.

There's nothing left for me to do.

With the decision, my mood lightened. I began to walk more quickly, and to take an interest in my surroundings. There were bare trees silhouetted against the grey sky, and I looked up at them, enjoying the contrasting shapes of the stark black branches against the soft clouds, the one motionless, the other shifting gently in the beginnings of a morning wind. There was a flash of scarlet in the bushes, a brilliant colour that turned out to be nothing more than a sweet wrapper, but that had for a moment been a thing of beauty.

I've done what I promised, I thought. I came back. I've stirred it all up, Tamsin, and things are beginning to happen.

Let me go now? Tamsin?

I was running this conversation through my mind as I strode along the path, listening for traffic that would tell me I was approaching a road.

He'll catch him, Tamsin. He said he intended to. Giles won't be able to do any more damage after that, he'll be in prison. That's what you wanted, I think. When you went to the waste ground, and kicked at the straggly bush, broke those sappy branches, made what you thought looked like the signs of a struggle, were you thinking of this? Of his arrest on a charge of murder?

It was going to be a fine day. The grey sky

had pale blue streaks where the sun was rising. The clouds were moving away, and the sun was beginning to break through just over the horizon. How far had I come, then? I must have been walking for hours.

My calves were aching, and I thought I might be developing a blister on the side of my foot. I stopped and listened for traffic, and heard it somewhere to my left, just over a hill. The footpath ahead of me seemed to curve in that direction behind some trees, so I set off again, walking fast.

I was beginning to get hungry.

It won't be a charge of murder, Tamsin. I think nowadays people would see it as something worse. Murderers, they're ten-a-penny, aren't they? A life sentence, out again in a few years, there doesn't seem to be much horror attached to it any more. It's much more fashionable to be horrified by the story of an abused child.

It was a blister. I felt it burst, a patch of dampness against my foot, and I thought, damn. That's going to be sore, by the time I get back. I should have worn trainers, not these walking shoes. They're too new.

I turned another corner in the path, and scrambled up quite a steep bank, to find myself looking down on a road, with a rusty barbed-wire fence bordering it. Two of the posts were rotten and sagging, so I slid down the scrubby grass and pushed one of them over.

Which way was the town? I could only think, vaguely, behind me. I'd walked away from it, and I hadn't noticed. So, I thought, let's assume that most of the cars are going towards the town, not away from it at this time of the morning. Count them, how many out of ten are going to the left, and how many to the right? And hope that it wasn't a silly idea.

Ignore the blister, and keep walking, I told myself. Keep enjoying it. It's lovely, this time of the morning, with the air still clean and clear.

Anyway, Tamsin, I've done what I came to do. I played detective a little bit, and handed it all over to a real one.

Who turned out to be nothing so special after all.

I stopped then, looking around me, and thinking. Tamsin, I mused. Thirteen years old, only thirteen. I shouldn't be talking like this to a thirteen-year-old.

Why should I have thought that Frank would be special? Just because he fancied me, to use that rather nasty phrase which trivialises even lust, doesn't mean he has impeccable taste.

But I'd thought he was nice. I'd hoped he was nice. And he is, quite. But he is also very ordinary. I had better be thankful I realised that before I became close enough to him to make parting from him painful.

I'd thought he liked me. Not very many people do like me, not really. I'm not bad-looking, and I'm quite intelligent, but I don't think I'm a kind person. I will not put up with fools at any price, let alone tolerate them gladly. I try to help people if they need it.

Making excuses for myself, rationalising everything I had done, I walked on down the little road and only a mile further on came to a big dual carriageway, with signposts. I turned left again, walking on the grass verge, but now the traffic was heavy, and exhaust fumes blurred the air, so I could not convince myself I was enjoying my walk. I was becoming quite tired, and thirsty, too.

I'll go home tomorrow, I decided. I'll telephone Anthony and ask him to meet me at the airport. I'll write a brief letter to Frank Welland, asking him to let me know the outcome of the case, no matter how it ends, and that will be that. I will be able to do what I felt that coroner was doing, draw a line under it all, and think, The End.

Back in Germany I will miss England. I always do. There is something about this land that I've seen again today, early morning in early winter, a unique beauty.

On the other side of the road I saw a signpost, mildewed wood but still upright, probably a footpath. I could cross the fields, and it would be cleaner, and quieter, and maybe even quicker. I really did want to get back now, and have some breakfast, and do something about the blister.

I stood on the verge watching the traffic, waiting for a break in it so that I could cross, and a car, a little red car, coming from the town, slowed up as it approached me, slower and slower, and I turned to look at it, and looked straight into the face of Helen, staring at me through the side window. She was sitting in the back seat, and I saw her raise her hand and turn around to wipe the condensation off the rear window, so she could watch me crossing the road.

Then the driver accelerated away, and I walked on towards the footpath, wondering if anything would happen as a result of that chance encounter.

15

I felt mildly disturbed by that unexpected glimpse of Helen. The look of shock and anger on her face, for the brief moments I had seen it, made it clear that if we met again it could only be on the most hostile of terms.

I told myself I cared nothing for her opinion, that I could go where I liked, could come to this town if I wanted, and had no reason to worry about her. Nevertheless, I do dislike confrontations, and I dreaded the idea of meeting her.

Mrs Sam exclaimed in concern when I came in.

'So cold today, going out for a walk this early. Come into the lounge and sit by the fire. Five minutes to get warm, and then a nice hot breakfast.'

'I saw Tamsin's mother,' I said.

'Oh? Not a happy meeting?'

I told her about the little red car. Helen had been in the back of it, I said, and she'd seen me. No, there hadn't been a friendly wave.

On top of all this I hadn't slept well, and my blister hurt, but I didn't want to be unfriendly to my nice Mrs Sam, so I hung my coat in the hall and did as she had suggested, sat by the fire to wait for my breakfast.

A little while later she called me to the telephone. It was Frank, to tell me that Helen had made a complaint against me. I was in the country, she'd said, to try to steal passports.

'I'm sorry about last night,' he said.

'That's all right. But I am going back to Germany now.'

He didn't answer for a while, and I wondered whether I should say goodbye.

'Don't you want to know how all this turns out?' he asked.

'I was going to write and ask you.'

'Please don't go before I've seen you again. I might have some news for you this evening.'

Did I want to go back to Germany? I wondered. Whatever I did, I never had managed to think of Germany as 'home'. I was tired, and I was disappointed, and angry with myself. I didn't know how to answer him.

I wanted to see Mandy again. I certainly wanted to keep in touch with her, the nice woman who might have been like my daughter, if I'd had one.

'Celia?'

'I'm still here.'

Frank had left a sour taste in my mouth. I

had liked him, I had seen something in him that I'd needed. What there was had gone, and the need hadn't really been answered. Instead, there had been a two-night stand that in the end had meant nothing. I didn't know what to say to him now.

'May I see you this evening?' he asked.

'I wanted to take Mandy Clarkson out to dinner, if she's free,' I answered.

'This afternoon, then? Or tomorrow?'

Oh, stop it, I thought. Looking for salve for your wounded ego, because last night you were a lousy lover, and now you want to prove you can do better.

But I do want to know what happens, what you've found out. I want Giles in prison.

'Tomorrow morning?' I suggested. 'I could meet you in town.'

What I meant was, I will not go to bed with you again.

I am not yours, for you to believe you may keep for as long as you wish. You have no rights over me. You particularly do not have any right to resent it, when I tell you when I am going back to Germany.

I had thought I was running the words over in my mind, and suddenly I was speaking them. I was saying these things to him, and he was listening.

'I will not go to bed with you again, and I damned well will not tolerate your childish possessiveness. I come and go as I please, do you understand? And my foot hurts. Oh, hell.'

I hadn't even meant to think about that.

'What? What did you say?'

I had stepped from high drama straight into farce; from moral outrage into a whimper about a blister.

'Oh, I went for a walk in the wrong shoes, and I've got a blister on my foot.'

'Is *that* what's put you into this filthy temper?'

I decided to change the subject.

'What have you found out about Giles?' I asked, and he seemed quite glad to tell me.

He had decided that the fringes of the pornography trade would be the most likely hunting ground. There were difficulties, but they were not insuperable. He wanted to find out whether Giles had used his own name, and whether there were any levers to make people talk about him.

Pirated videos at car boot sales was the lowest end of the market, and it was fairly well known. There were at least a dozen names and faces, most of them low-level and low-life, amateurs with little video cameras sneaking into the local cinemas and filming the film, complete with walk-on parts taken by the audience, with black shadows between the screen and the camera, whispers, and the crackle of sweet papers drowning out the soundtrack. There were often suitcases stuffed under the seats of the cars with other boxes, other films, for customers who knew what to ask for, and how to phrase the requests. Gerry said you might have something. Something modern.

Modern. New. Young.

Children.

'Haven't looked at it myself, squire. Wouldn't know.'

Anything on a tape recorder could be denied.

'Told him I hadn't looked at it. I didn't know what it was, wouldn't have touched it if I had. Not my sort of thing, know what I mean?'

'I know all this,' I said to Frank. 'For God's sake! I was a journalist. This has been going on for decades.'

'Sorry,' he said. 'Forgot.'

They'd raided a stall a few weeks earlier, some little bit of local scum with a few faked-up rubbish films; tarts in black leather prancing around with whips, wouldn't fool a child, and this scum had talked. He'd said there was something coming in, real stuff, through Holland. Two names had been mentioned, both the men had been questioned, and one of them did have a record; so there'd been a somewhat casual attitude to a search warrant, and some photograph albums had been taken.

Tamsin's picture had been in one of them.

There hadn't been anything in the albums that could be described as over the top. The photographs had been nasty, but not horrible. The police had charged him, but had let him out on bail. Now he was in again, sitting in a cell about fifty yards from the office, and his flat was being searched, very thoroughly, with a proper warrant to back it up, and the negatives had been found. A WPC was going through them now, looking for Tamsin's picture.

When the name Giles Baker had been mentioned, this creature had sworn he'd never heard of him, and he'd been lying.

Frank said, when he was hunting around in the dark there was nothing he liked better than a liar. It told him he was on the right track.

'What did the photograph show?' I asked. I had to know.

She'd been in the nude, lying on a bed, her head propped on her hand. There'd been a sort of 'come on' smile on her face. Nothing nasty, apart from the fact that she'd been a bit younger; maybe twelve, possibly eleven.

Most of the photographs had been of that sort of thing: nude children posing, some in fairly suggestive attitudes, but there'd been nothing you could call serious pornography.

'Who is this man?' I asked, and Frank became dismissive. A pimp with a taste for hitting women. A piece of garbage, with a couple of convictions for stupidity.

'What?'

'Assault, one of ABH. We think he's pushing drugs, but we haven't found anything for that. He's a nobody.'

They were looking through his associates, and they were going to find a link to Giles Baker. Now they'd uncovered the photographs, he thought he might be given a little more time, should he need it.

My breakfast was getting cold.

I would meet him the next day, I said. I did want to see other people.

I wanted to see young Andrew Harper again. I thought he deserved to know the truth. I could say, maybe she did love you. She certainly cared enough about you to want to protect you.

Mrs Sam took my plate of eggs and grilled tomatoes back to the kitchen, to refresh, as she put it, which meant two minutes in the microwave, and I realised that I had a truly ferocious headache. I held the cold glass of orange juice against my forehead and wondered how it was I had only just noticed such a serious pain. Little points of light seemed to be breaking up and flicking at my eyes, like fragments of agony.

What had happened?

My life was like this now, I thought wildly. Look at it from the outside and it's all smooth, and intact, like this cold glass, even like my face, as it must be with the eyes closed. But it's not like that at all.

I was happily married to a successful man, we had a nice house, two cars, there must be plenty of money there. And she takes such an interest in asylum seekers, good works on top of everything else. What a very lucky woman.

Oh, God, this hurts. What can have happened?

He doesn't love me. I've driven him away, with my savage temper and the harshness of my judgements. I hate that house, cleaning it, or telling somebody else to do it, and then doing it myself again; that bloody Filipino girl, forty minutes to clean a bathroom and the tidemark left intact.

I am so lonely. I cannot compromise.

'Mrs Masters?'

Fragments of light, fragments of thought. Fragments of life.

'My dear, you are ill. Come, please. Come with me. Come.'

Lousy sex last night. He was like a machine, pump pump pump thud groan stop. Sorry. Bloody well should be, too. Moody, just because I'm going home, what did he expect?

'All men are lousy at sex sometimes. Better not to tell them.'

Oh, but definitely I must see a doctor

when I get home. I can't even distinguish between thinking and talking aloud now. And Mrs Sam knows Frank was in bed with me, using her nice hotel like a dirty brothel, behaving like a prostitute. What's the matter with me? Why is my head hurting so much?

We were in her tiny sitting room again, and I was looking at the print of Krishna with the gopis, the cow girls, very, very curvaceous. Krishna, as always, was blue. Wouldn't somebody have noticed that? Wouldn't one of the girls have said, Krishna, you really are extremely handsome, but why are you blue?

What would Krishna have replied?

Take off your sari, and I'll tell you.

Never mind being a god, he was a young devil, that one.

'Drink. Drink this.'

It was white and powdery, in a wine glass, a nice piece of crystal, possibly Waterford. It had a rather sharp taste.

'I should call a doctor, isn't it? Shouldn't I?'

Mrs Sam was so concerned, she was losing her almost perfect English, lapsing into the sentence structures she had learned at school. Somebody should tell India about this use of 'isn't it'. It is altogether too widespread an error.

'No, not a doctor.'

Why not? Why not, then? Why wait until I

go home? Here, I can talk about it in my own language. I am haunted by my niece, I have this weird imagination and a few fluky coincidences. There is the hostility between me and my sister-in-law and I saw her this morning, and now, for some reason, I am apprehensive about that. I have been unfaithful to my husband, and he wouldn't care even if he knew, and I don't care enough to wonder whether or not to tell him, even though I do still love him, I think.

There are African refugees who will, by now, be asking where I am, because they have difficulties and want to ask for my help.

They exploit me, that lot.

I don't blame them. Why shouldn't they? It would take them hours with their dictionaries and their borrowed textbooks to translate those letters. It's five minutes for me. The bus or the train into Bonn costs money they don't have, and sometimes they're caught travelling without a ticket, a sixty-mark fine because they tried to save ten. I go in two or three times a week, I can take them with me, and suppose I do have to wait for them because they're useless about punctuality? I'm only going home to the ironing and the polishing and the dusting and the cooking and the gardening and all the bloody pointless things that make up my days.

Mrs Sam's cool fingers were on my

temples, surprisingly strong, pressing and lifting in time with my pulse, and I tilted my head back and closed my eyes and tried to ignore the flashing points of light and the little spears of pain.

'Why not? Why no doctor?' she asked.

'I'm not really ill,' I said. 'I'm haunted.'

My mind is definitely wandering, and Mrs Sam patted me once, a little briskly, on the shoulder, and said she was calling Doctor Patel, nomorenonsense.

I had migraine.

I never had migraine, I argued, and the fat little man with the pebble glasses said I had it now and no mistake, lie in dark room and be quiet.

Mrs Sam brought me something she called nimbu pani, lemon juice with salt, which was wonderful. I had never tasted anything so good.

I don't get migraine. I'd always thought it was just a headache, a big excuse for the words; I can't come in today, I've got a migraine. For God's sake, I'd thought, a day off just for a headache, you feeble little bitch. But this pain made me retch. From now on, if somebody tells me they've come in to work in spite of having a migraine I won't believe them. Every time I try to stand up it's as though I'm being clubbed down by the pain, my stomach heaving from it.

Please, stop. Please go away.

'Go to sleep now, my dear. It will pass.'

I haven't given Mrs Sam her money for today. For tonight. She hasn't asked. I must pay her. I must see young Andrew Harper and tell him he was right, she wasn't like that. And Mandy.

I dozed off, and only woke now and then at Mrs Sam's soft knock on the door, for another glass of her wonderful sharp panacea, her cool hands on my forehead.

'Go to sleep now. It will pass.'

Late in the afternoon, when it was growing dark, I woke again, feeling cold, and noticing it. I must be getting better, I can notice cold instead of pain. I can sit up without nausea. I can reach for my sweater.

I slept again, and it was completely dark when I woke, but it had gone, that dreadful headache had left.

God, I thought, that was horrible. I would not have *believed* a headache could be like that.

I got up and washed my face, changed into clothes that were not crumpled and thought, I must find a launderette; I'm running out of clean underwear. I must telephone Mandy, and ask about Andrew Harper. I should contact Anthony. I must book my flight home, perhaps the day after tomorrow.

I seemed to be full of energy, and I wondered if it was a reaction to the migraine. I had heard somewhere that a migraine, once it had gone, left a sense of euphoria, and I had also heard that only intelligent people suffered from it.

Mrs Sam clucked at me when she saw me, why you outofbed?

'I'm better. I'm fine, really. I didn't pay you yesterday. I need to make a few telephone calls, and I haven't got any coins.'

'Oh, forgot. Somebody telephoned for you. I said you were out.'

'Who was it?'

'Didn't give a name. I asked, but he said, didn't matter.'

It made me uneasy. I never like it when somebody calls and I don't reach the telephone in time, I always wonder who it could have been. Anthony says, if it's important they'll call back. Don't worry about it. He can let it ring, if he doesn't want to answer. I find it infuriating. If I telephone from Bonn and there's no answer I've been known to yell at the receiver, pick the bloody thing up, I *know* you're there. Once I suggested a code; I'll let it ring three times, then I'll hang up, then I'll ring again. You'll know it's me, so please answer.

I must have been in the garden, he'd say.

Could it have been Anthony?

I telephoned him at the university, which meant he had to take the call because his secretary had answered. It's your wife, she said, without putting her hand over the mouthpiece, so he couldn't tell her to say he was out.

'Hello?'

'Did you try to telephone me earlier?' I asked.

'No. How are you?'

'The police have reopened the case. They think Tamsin may have been the victim of a paedophile.'

'Oh, poor child. How horrible. Do they think it's Giles?'

'I told you, didn't I? What I thought Tamsin felt about him. Anthony, it's much worse than that. There's certainly more than one. It's probably a ring.'

I heard him draw in his breath, and then he asked whether Helen had known.

'I don't know,' I said. 'I think she took good care not to.'

She'd telephoned him that morning, demanding to know what I was doing and where I was staying; didn't he think I'd done enough damage?

'What did she mean by that?' he asked, and I said I thought it was just a cliché, the sort of thing she would say.

'She drove past me in a car,' I said. 'She saw me. Did you tell her where I was?'

'No, I didn't. I hung up on her.'

She must have been very abusive, for Anthony to have done that. It wasn't like him at all.

After we'd rung off I thought, if it wasn't Frank who telephoned and didn't leave a name, then somebody's looking for me, and has found me.

When I called the police station he wasn't there, and nobody knew if he was trying to contact me.

'Could you ask him to call me when he gets in?' I asked, and the man said he'd leave a note on Frank's desk. He didn't know when he'd be back.

I wanted to get out, and Mrs Sam would take a message, so I telephoned Mandy and asked if I could come and see her that evening, because I'd be going back to Germany the next day, or perhaps the day after.

She sounded as if she'd be pleased to see me.

This time, I called a taxi, but I asked him to stop somewhere on the way where I could buy flowers, a little pot of something bright but easy to keep, to put on her windowsill.

Mandy's tiny flat seemed like a haven of sanity, despite the chaos of papers on her table, and she was pleased to see me. I almost felt like hugging her, she looked so clean and warm. She poured us each a glass of red wine, and I raised mine to her.

'To your bonny brown eyes,' I said. 'It *is* good to be here. I've had two horrible days.'

'Tell me,' she invited, and I said I would tell her a bit, but I'd leave out the man who turned out to be nothing much if she didn't mind, and she laughed, but before I could begin she said that Tamsin had been given permission to go to Amsterdam to see an exhibition of Dutch Old Masters. She'd been away for four days, but she hadn't talked about it at all when she'd come back.

'Would you have expected her to?' I asked.

'Not to me, perhaps. But in the art classes? She only said it had been okay. That wasn't like Tamsin. If there was one subject that would get her going it was paintings. She would talk about paintings, Celia.'

It only strengthened my suspicions. It wasn't proof, but I didn't need proof, not for myself.

'Four days,' I said. 'That's about long enough for an abortion, isn't it?'

And seeing Mandy look so sad I reached out and touched her cheek, trying to make her smile.

'They'll get him,' I said. 'I'm almost completely sure they'll get him.'

I told her the police were trying to link Tamsin with her uncle, and thought there was a paedophile ring involved, and Mandy winced. I went back over what Frank had said, about cheap videos sold from market stalls and at car boot sales, the lower end of the business, and I remembered what I'd learned as a journalist about the pipelines through which the professional material came, the books, films and photographs, the videos, and the contacts.

I remembered how they'd distributed the telephone numbers and names for those who wanted to do for themselves what they had seen others doing on film.

Travel agencies, Frank had mentioned, in which Giles had claimed a controlling interest, and I thought I remembered something there. It was always who you knew that mattered.

'Just a minute, Mandy,' I said. 'Somebody who worked for a regional radio told me about this. It was about ten years ago.'

'About what?' asked Mandy.

'Peter Holmes,' I said. 'I remember him now, he was a fat little man, he had a very high opinion of himself, but in his case it was justified. He was digging into adoption agencies in the Iron Curtain countries. Their problem was visas, getting the children out. But somebody with travel agencies, that might answer it. Don't travel agencies arrange visas?'

'I don't know.'

They'd have the contacts, wouldn't they? Even if they didn't fix them themselves, they'd know who did. It wouldn't take much. I mean, money, bribes. I couldn't see it at first, Tamsin being here, what's the travel agency bit? Why do you need a travel agency? But I think Tamsin just happened to be available. Was she pretty, Mandy? I only ever saw photographs. She didn't look very special.'

Mandy shook her head.

'A bit prettier than average,' she said. 'She had rather a heavy jaw. But she moved well, she was quite graceful, if that doesn't sound too old-fashioned.'

'He's made a lot of money. I don't know how much. He says he trades as a multi-national company.'

Mandy blinked.

'*Can* he do that?'

'I suppose so. There are other people, he's not on his own.'

'I'd always thought they were huge. Philips, and ICI, like that.'

'He wouldn't have made much money if it was just Tamsin, and anyway there was a photograph album. Frank said, *one* of the photographs was of Tamsin. How many children would there need to be? They don't all have to be in England, do they?'

I was becoming confused again. This was only in my own mind, and I was losing trust in my mind. Tamsin had been pregnant, some boy had seduced her and then ditched her. Then, this wasn't her first pregnancy, if I was right, that the trip to Amsterdam had been a cover for an abortion, and she was

HIV-positive, and it wasn't a boy because she wouldn't. So, Tamsin was the victim of a paedophile, and now it was getting serious, and then Frank had said, a trader.

No, he hadn't. I'd put that together from other things. Giles wasn't the father, he couldn't have been, but he was involved. That meant more than one man.

The main part of his business was in Holland, or so he said, and there were travel agencies, and Giles was a rich man.

How big was this?

I began to feel a little scared; not just apprehensive at the prospect of a confrontation with Helen, or perhaps Giles himself, but genuinely frightened. The police had opened Tamsin's case again, and had questioned Giles, and Helen had seen me, when they'd thought I was in Germany and that everything was over.

I borrowed Mandy's telephone and called the police station again, but Frank hadn't been back. The note was still on his desk.

'Celia, what's the matter?'

'It's probably nothing,' I said, 'but somebody telephoned the hotel and asked for me some time today when I was in bed with a migraine. It wasn't Anthony, and the only other man who knows where I am is Frank Welland. He's the policeman who's dealing with Tamsin's case.'

That's all he is, I thought. Leave out the

rest of it.

'Whoever it was didn't leave a name,' I added.

'So?'

'I think Welland would have left his name. I can't be sure, but I think he would, when Mrs Sam asked. I can't get hold of him, so I can't check.'

Mandy was looking even more puzzled.

'Helen saw me this morning. Tamsin's mother, I mean. I was out for a walk, I was on the main road to Birmingham, and she went past in the back of a little red car. It slowed down. It slowed down so she could look at me, do you know what I mean? There wasn't any other reason for it to slow down there. So, she knows I'm over here, and she's probably told Giles. Who's not only a paedophile. Or maybe he isn't, not personally. But he's involved in that.'

I drew in a deep breath.

'Mandy, tell me I'm talking nonsense.'

Her eyes were a little wide.

'I don't know yet. Go on.'

'It wasn't Anthony, and if it wasn't Frank, who was it? And why?'

'But Helen doesn't know where you're staying,' protested Mandy.

'That's what worries me. If she'd known I'd think, okay, Giles wants to telephone me and call me names, for stirring up trouble. Not very pleasant, but not serious. But they didn't know where I was. So Giles, or some-body, has gone to the trouble of telephoning local hotels looking for me.'

'There are hundreds of hotels around here,' said Mandy. 'Well, perhaps not hundreds, but a hell of a lot.'

'It wouldn't take long to reach Bracken-hills, going down the list,' I said. 'But he didn't know that. He, they, whoever, was prepared to go through them all. I suppose. Would you go to that much trouble just to have a row with somebody?'

'I try to avoid rows,' she answered, but she was speaking mechanically, simply answer-ing my question while she concentrated on her thoughts.

'I think you'd better stay here tonight,' she added, and this time she spoke emphatic-ally.

'I should have thought more carefully about what Frank said. But I was angry with him, and then I got that bloody migraine. I've only just realised what this could be. Oh, Mandy.'

'Come on, Celia. It's a long story to build up from one telephone call.'

But it wasn't really, not now I'd remem-bered, although I didn't want to tell Mandy about it.

Peter Holmes had disappeared, and nobody had ever found out what happened to him.

16

I stayed in Mandy's flat until the early hours of the morning. It was a Friday, so she didn't have to get up early, and she seemed to be enjoying my company, although she had caught some of my nervousness. Seeing her looking worried, with the little frown between her brows, I tried to laugh it off.

'It's me being paranoid,' I said. 'Perhaps it's a side effect of migraine, one that isn't well known. I'll write about it in *The Lancet* and become famous as a result.

'Anyway, what can they do? I don't talk to strangers and I won't get into a little red car, or any other car, come to that. They're not going to abduct me, are they?'

The thought of Peter Holmes did sometimes insinuate itself into my mind that night, but I pushed it aside. Men did go missing. Woman trouble, one of his colleagues had suggested, but the only trouble Peter had had with women was that he couldn't get one. He was too short, too fat, and far too self-opinionated.

Money, then? I wondered. He'd earned a lot, but perhaps he'd spent a lot.

Nobody had bothered much. It had been

a nuisance, finding a replacement for him, and they'd had to make do with a boy straight out of college who'd known nothing and hadn't had many ideas about how to investigate anything. He'd been replaced as soon as a woman with a bit of experience had turned up.

I tried to do what everybody else had done about Peter Holmes; I tried to forget him.

When it was nearly midnight Mandy and I did a bit of marking together, the same routine as before, with me making little pencil crosses in the margins so she could skim through the exercises quickly, and not read them all. We drank the bottle of red wine, and it and tiredness made us mildly hilarious a bit later, so we found ourselves giggling at silly jokes, and even at things that weren't funny at all.

'Stay the night,' she said again when I finally thought it was time to go. 'Doss down on the sofa. Pretend you're a student. We'll have black coffee in the morning and compare hangovers. Do you remember the cliché? "I swear I'll never touch another drop"? Celia, do stay.'

But I wouldn't. I told her I'd bring a flask of black coffee with me next time, and wake up the neighbours by banging on the door, and she began to giggle again as I telephoned for a taxi.

'Dear Mandy. What a lovely daughter you

321

are. To whoever your mother may be, I wish it was me.'

While we waited I asked her about Andrew Harper, and she said she didn't know much about him. If I wanted to write to him she'd give him a letter. She thought it was a lovely idea, to tell him he hadn't been wrong about Tamsin, but she was worried that he'd be upset by what had happened to her.

'More upset than by not knowing why she killed herself?' I asked, and Mandy didn't know.

'Perhaps not,' she said doubtfully.

'If you don't know the truth, it can be anything and everything,' I said. 'All the horrible possibilities keep coming to mind. Once you know the truth, you can say "At least it wasn't this, or this, or this." Just one horrible fact is better than a hundred horrible possibilities, isn't it?'

I was arguing as much to persuade myself as her. I would just have to be very careful, what I told him, and what I didn't.

On the way back to the hotel in the taxi, I thought, I'll ask Mrs Sam. She'll know what I should tell him, and what would be best left unsaid.

I let myself through the front door with the key she'd given me, and looked on the notice board.

There was no telephone message for me.

He hadn't gone back to the police station, then. He hadn't seen my note.

When I went into my room and turned on the light I saw that everything had been cleaned and tidied, but that Tamsin's rolled-up picture still lay on the table where Frank and I had left it. I didn't want to unroll it again, and feel the sense of shock and sadness, but I wished I could force Giles to look at it. I wished I could hold his head down close to it, like rubbing a puppy's nose in its own dirt, look at that. Look at what you did, you filthy thing. Be ashamed of yourself.

One day, I promised myself again, when I am old and strong, I will look at it. I may even frame that picture, and hang it on my wall, and sit in an armchair with gnarled fingers resting on the arms and stare at it, and remember my dreams.

I will remember Tamsin, who cared enough to be angry, and who might have been one of the great painters, and who had been stopped.

Would I have loved you, if I'd known you?

I'll remember this autumn. I'll remember the questions and the confusion, and the doubts. I'll remember the decision to see a doctor, because my mind wasn't under my control. I had lost the ability to distinguish between reality and fantasy. I had found myself speaking my thoughts aloud. It was all rather embarrassing, and a bit frightening, too. It was probably yet another manifestation of stress.

Yes, that was it. I didn't think my husband loved me any more, and so I found I was looking for love from another source, and what better than from somebody who couldn't deny me? Tamsin was dead, and could say nothing, neither rejection nor acceptance. I can love Tamsin, and believe she would have loved me. I'm doing no harm.

At least I don't dream about her any more, I thought as I fell asleep, and then Tamsin and I were in her room, looking around at the bright colours, and she was saying, 'See how everything goes together? Do you see how it goes together?' 'No,' I answered, 'I don't see how they did it. I don't see a connection.' 'Look again,' said Tamsin, and then we were walking down a road together, looking around because we thought we might have been seen, and we shouldn't be there, on that road. Something was watching out for us, searching for us. Run, said Tamsin, but I said no, don't run. Don't try to get out of sight. If you don't want to be seen, don't hide. Don't go into the garden shed and get under the pile of sacks. Take out a spade, and be seen beside the shed, digging the garden.

I think you ought to run, said Tamsin. I

think you ought to run away.

I'll stay with you, I answered.

Tamsin was sad. That's nice, she said, but I can't stay with you. I'll miss you.

Then I was on my own, on a traffic island, and a little red car was driving round and round, circling me, and Helen was in the back seat shouting at me, haven't you done enough damage? Haven't you done enough damage?

Go away! I shouted at her. Go away. You let it all happen.

But the car went on, round and round and I couldn't see who was driving. There was only Helen, wiping the mist off the windows, shouting.

I don't care about you, I thought, and I woke up, remembering her wedding.

The room was quiet and empty. I switched on the bedside light and looked at my clock. Half past five. In Germany I'd be getting up now, half past six, time to start the day. Anthony would sleep on, having worked into the early hours, sometimes all through the night.

There was no feeling of Tamsin. It wasn't surprising that I should dream about her, after such a day. I'd been thinking about her. This was different, it was just an ordinary dream, it meant nothing.

Dreaming about the dead foretells a death, somebody had once told me, and my mother had said it was superstitious nonsense, an old wives' tale. I shouldn't talk to the servants.

Daddy had laughed at that, and even she had had to smile. Servants, Mrs Binns, who came in once every two weeks to do 'the rough work', as it was known, scrubbing the stone floors in the pantry and the kitchen corridor, and other things I couldn't remember. She'd been full of old wives' tales, Mrs Binns. Give a tooth for every child, pearls for tears, never take flowers from a funeral, they want to go again. This is unlucky, that is lucky, that's a *very* old-fashioned remedy, by which Mrs Binns meant tried and tested, and found to be good.

Rub a stye with a gold wedding ring and it'll get better. Stuff and nonsense, my mother had said, but it had worked for me where Golden Eye Ointment had failed. Pure chance, according to my mother. Mrs Binns said she didn't know why it worked. Might be the purity of the gold was too strong for the bad of the sore, sucked it out, or drove it away, something like that.

Mrs Binns had been stubborn and un-educated and not very honest. My mother made sure none of the silverware was left in the kitchen on her days. It's not kind to put temptation in her way, she'd said. Mrs Binns refused to pay taxes, or so she claimed. If

326

that lot in the government wants money they can get out and earn it, like I has to.

Why was I remembering Mrs Binns? She'd had a black tooth in the front of her mouth, a hairy chin, and half a crown for me on my birthday when I was small. There'd been nothing when I was bigger, when I'd turned into A Right Little Madam. That was after I'd started school, and learned to read.

Mrs Binns had died, and my mother's regret had been tinged with exasperation. Typical of that sort, she'd said. Wouldn't take care of herself, and look what's happened. Well, you can't force them, and God alone knows who's going to replace her. I certainly can't do all that work alone.

She was old, Daddy had protested. She didn't die to spite you. Poor Binnsie.

Mrs Sam had a cleaner in the mornings, a quick young woman who wore skin-tight leggings and had a gold ring through one nostril. I'd seen her through open bedroom doors, briskly shaking out bedclothes or vacuum cleaning carpets. I thought there was somebody else who worked in the kitchen, I'd heard a woman's voice.

Some of the refugee women had asked if they could work for me. It was illegal, but I'd agreed on two occasions, when I'd thought the families were in desperate straits. Both times I'd regretted it. They

327

didn't steal, and they did their best, but one of them had continually begged me to let her have clothes, mine or Anthony's, and I'd felt uncomfortable about refusing, so I'd given her some. She'd sold them to the other refugees, and kept the money. The other had been too old, and too exhausted by her experiences, to manage the work. I'd been relieved when her daughter had come over to tell me she was ill, and couldn't come any more.

I decided I would rather do the work myself, and Anthony didn't like having strangers in the house, although he hadn't minded when I'd brought half a dozen young men over and let them loose on the garden. But then, he had promised to help in the garden, when we'd decided to move, and it wasn't a promise he'd kept.

I've always thought promises were important. I'd told him I couldn't manage the garden by myself, but he'd liked it, and the terrace, and he'd thought of summer evenings sitting there and relaxing. He'd forgotten he couldn't relax. Five minutes in a garden chair and he was fidgeting, and thinking of things he told himself he should be doing. If he wasn't asleep in that chair, from exhaustion, he couldn't sit there. He hadn't thought of autumn, with the work to be done. He'd looked at the big lawn and seen comfort and space where I'd seen the necessity for a bigger mower. The beech hedge had been pretty, and he'd liked it, where I'd remembered how fast it grows and how often it needs clipping.

'You promised,' I'd protested when I'd been working alone for two hours, and Anthony had looked at his computer screen, and sighed, and said all right, I'm coming. So I'd weeded for the rest of the afternoon in a weary cloud of guilt. He'd been working so hard, he hadn't been sleeping properly, and now I'd asked for his help with a task I could, if I worked as hard as he did, have managed myself.

So I tried to protect him from my own accusations. He'd promised, but he hadn't known then how much work he would have to do, with this consultancy. It wasn't really his fault, that he'd had to break his promise, even though he could have turned down the offer. He could easily have turned it down. He already had more than enough to do.

He broke his promise.

But I didn't. I didn't think I had. Daddy had been very strong about that. If you say you'll do something, you must. There may be worse things than people upon whom you cannot rely, but they don't come easily to mind. They are, in fact, a damned nuisance, Celia.

Daddy had once turned up at the local summer show in a taxi, with his leg in a

329

splint and a pair of hospital crutches on the seat beside him. He'd volunteered to judge the children's pets class, but he'd come off his bicycle on the corner by the church and broken his ankle. He'd taken a taxi from the hospital, gone to the show, and returned to the hospital later that evening to have the plaster cast put on. I'd gone with him, and the doctor had pretended to be angry, but I think he'd rather admired Daddy for that. I'd never forgotten it, everybody saying how marvellous it was that he'd come to the show, and the way the doctor had said he was bloody mad, it must have hurt like hell and serve him right, but he'd clapped Daddy on the shoulder on his way out.

Nobody was going to clap me on the shoulder on my way back to Germany. I'd made a promise to a dead child, because I'd imagined she'd asked for my help. Anyway, I'd kept the promise, I'd done what she wanted, but there was something else to do. Something had been said.

I sat up and swung my legs over the side of the bed, and tried to remember what it was. I was running things through my mind; write to Andrew Harper, have a word with Mrs Sam to ask her advice about what to tell him, there was that to do. Book my seat home, telephone Anthony to tell him when I'd be back, can you meet me at the airport this time? I'll pick up the Tin Wimp some time in the next couple of days, I don't want to bother with buses. If the aeroplane were to land late I'd miss the bus anyway. The connections never made allowances for delays.

There was something about it. Something about connections.

The dream, in the bright room with Tamsin, and she'd asked me if I couldn't see it, and I hadn't been able to. Look, she'd said. Was that what she'd said? Dreams go hazy after only a few minutes if you don't make the effort to remember. Even then, sometimes they go away. Very few dreams stay in the memory.

She'd been showing me something. She'd been showing me the room. Her arm had moved in a wide arc as she'd told me to look.

Look at the room, and see a connection, and try to remember.

But the colours had blended so perfectly, there wasn't a connection. It was all very smooth, the transition. It was the work of an artist.

Belgium. A friend of Giles's from Belgium, that was what Helen had said. See the connection? Tamsin had asked, her arm sweeping to indicate the whole room. See?

Yes. Yes, I see. Thank you, Tamsin. I'll pass that on.

And over breakfast I remembered his

name. Neville. Certainly an interior designer, it shouldn't be impossible to trace
him. Giles had given them those rooms for
Christmas and had taken Tamsin away on a
holiday while Helen stayed in a hotel.

Frank could take her in and question her,
why not? Neville from Belgium, you can do
better than that, Mrs Simpson. Come on,
try again. Even if Giles refuses to divulge
the names of his associates, Helen can be
bullied.

What's the harm in giving us his name,
Mrs Simpson? If he's done nothing wrong?

'She's the sort who'll scream for a lawyer,'
Frank said later that morning when I met
him, but he made a note of the name.
Neville from Belgium, he'd need more than
that. He'd forgotten those rooms, I could
well be right. A bribe to a mother, don't ask
too many questions if you want me to take
care of you both.

He hadn't telephoned me the previous
day, not after our first conversation. Was I in
a better mood now?

I looked at him a little warily, but the
question seemed innocent. At least there
was nothing but polite enquiry on his face.

'Somebody telephoned me,' I said. 'The
only men who have that number are you
and Anthony, and it wasn't Anthony.'

He poured himself another cup of coffee
and stirred it, looking thoughtful.

'Any ideas?' he asked.

'Giles. Helen would have told him she'd seen me.'

He would have thought of that for himself. I suppose he was checking; could there be another answer?

'Am I in any danger?' I asked. As soon as I'd asked I thought, what a very melodramatic question.

'I don't see why. Even an idiot wouldn't think that taking you out of the way would stop the investigation. Giles isn't an idiot.'

I sat back in my chair and looked at him, trying to see what it was about him that had attracted me. That still, to some extent, attracted me, and I thought, he's very solid. He's there, sitting opposite me, and he's aware of me, and he's listening to me. His mind doesn't wander away to some topic it finds more interesting. With Anthony, there's a feeling of absence. Frank's completely different. He's here, mind and body. A heavy, muscular body, very strong, and even when he isn't looking at me he's concentrating on me, thinking about me.

'Have you been given any more time?' I asked. Was it today or tomorrow that was the end of his three days?

'So long as nothing else comes up. If I can find a connection with this Neville character it might help.'

He'd been working on the one suspect he

could pin down, the man with the photographs, and that man had given them the name of the photographer, who'd put up a stone wall of defence. All the kids came through private requests. Please take photographs of little Sally, Mavis, Tim or Cuthbert. Yes, in the nude, it wasn't illegal to take nude photographs of children. Nobody had ever laid a hand on them, not in his studio. It wasn't pornography. It wasn't illegal to make his own prints either, and he could hand them on to whoever he liked. He couldn't remember the names of the kids, he wasn't interested, now piss off.

'Is he right?' I asked, and Frank pulled a doubtful face. Grey area.

'Children are beautiful,' he remarked. 'Young children are lovely to look at. Anybody can appreciate that, although there's so much suspicion nowadays you hardly dare even glance at them.'

It was when it became sexual that the border was crossed, and these photographs, he didn't think they'd gone over the line. Close to it, perhaps.

'Not much progress, then,' I said, and Frank disagreed. They'd found the photographer. In a little while they'd have gone through a lot more photographs, photographs that were certainly over the line, and when they found one that had been taken in the same studio there'd be another fish in

334

the net. They were watching that studio now, and that damned pervert with the hightech cameras.

'It's a little bit at a time,' said Frank. 'Making connections and looking through things, and doing other work as well, irritating though that may be. There were over thirty children in that album. I don't suppose they'll all end up like Tamsin, but one or two of them might, if we don't stop them.'

We were in a dark little coffee house in the old part of the town, sitting at the back of the room. The tables were in a Jacobean style, the chairs wheel-back, in what might have been genuine dark oak. The copper warming pans on the wall seemed as if they'd been put there because of a rule, but the coffee was good, and the waitress did keep her distance.

'Is there anything more for me to do?' I asked him, and he smiled at me.

'Did you mean it, when you said you wouldn't go to bed with me again?'

'Yes. Yes, I did. I still love my husband. I shouldn't have done that.'

He didn't try to argue, but he picked up my hand and kissed it, a slow and thoughtful gesture, and he watched my face as he did it.

'Like having a tooth out,' he mused. 'It hurts, but not as much as it would do later.'

'What a very romantic metaphor.'

He laughed.

'It was a compliment,' he said. 'It was becoming very difficult to keep you out of my mind.'

He laid my hand back on the table, carefully, as if it was something precious and fragile, and he shook his head.

'Perhaps you should go back to Germany,' he said. 'I wish things could have been different. I would have liked to have met you away from my work.'

Was this the last time I would ever sit opposite a man who wanted me to be with him?

'I'll go tomorrow, then,' I said. 'Will it be all right if I telephone you every few days for news?'

'Please do.'

I didn't want to leave. I felt somehow comforted, almost contented, by this new, and last, phase of our relationship. Now I could listen to him talking to me, and not be wondering why it was only talk, and his hand on the table only inches from mine, any touch being nothing more than friendship.

Perhaps I'm getting old, I thought, and didn't mind the idea.

There was a little sadness when we parted, on both sides. Frank put his hands on my shoulders and bent his head to kiss me, and

I rested my cheek against his for a moment. But we were both smiling as we turned to go our separate ways, and I hoped, and believed, there would be no regrets on his part, as there would be none on mine.

That brief affaire had been no part of my promise to Tamsin, but I would never have learned what the police were doing without it.

The thought almost made me laugh.

I would be even sorrier to say goodbye to Mrs Sam. She had been so kind to me, and she was so wise. I would never forget her beautiful old face.

I would probably never come back to this town. What would bring me, now? So when I parted from her, that would really be for ever.

The day before, I had been nervous, perhaps even a little scared, because somebody had found me, had tracked me through a telephone directory. I'd told Mandy I wouldn't get into a little red car, or any car come to that, and I wasn't the sort to talk to strangers. I had half expected a telephone call from Helen, or from Giles, which would probably consist of abuse and accusations. Had it occurred I would have hung up, gone to my room and made myself a cup of tea, and tried to put it out of my mind. I had also thought one of them might come and see me.

I would only have seen them in the lounge, I'd told myself, and if it had become too unpleasant I could have asked them to leave, even threatened to call the police if they didn't.

So I had made contingency plans, in case of a confrontation, and having made them I had put the thought of that telephone call out of my mind. As I walked down the road I was trying to remember the times of the flights back to Bonn, and the trains between this town and London, and the connections to Heathrow. The rail journey had taken just over two hours. But I remembered that tomorrow was Sunday, and it might take longer, so I should think about a late afternoon flight, and not plan on being back in Germany before the evening. Anthony and I could have a meal together in Bonn on the way home, because there might not be anything in the house.

It could be an opportunity to try to talk to him. Perhaps, if I could start up one, just one, interesting conversation with him, something to keep his attention on me, and not on whatever work he was doing at the time, I might yet revive our marriage. It had to be possible. It had to be worth it, too.

So the train of my thoughts had moved on, away from Giles and Helen and the police investigation, and into the realms of my own future. I had dealt with everything else as far as I could, and planned for what contingencies I could foresee.

What had not occurred to me, not for one moment, was that they might use violence.

They didn't ask me at all. There was no trap, no polite invitation; there was a car pulling up behind me, running footsteps, and then, as I turned to look with the beginnings of alarm stirring in my mind, there was an arm across my throat, a hand over my mouth, and the two men picked me up and threw me into the back of the car. There was another man there, and as I fell across the seats and halfway over his legs, he wound his fingers into my hair and dragged my head back, so that I was forced to look up at the blade of the knife he held.

'Make a noise and I'll take your eyes out,' he said.

17

A first I was too surprised to be frightened, but that didn't last long. There were four of them, and I was absolutely helpless.

The car was already moving as the last man jumped in, onto the back seat beside the one with the knife, pushing me aside as he did so and saying something to the driver. I thought he spoke in Dutch, but I could hardly hear.

They didn't make the mistake of driving away fast. From that moment on there was nothing dramatic. Unless they had been very unlucky, nobody would have noticed anything. It had happened too quickly.

'May I sit up?' I asked.

'No.'

My back was twisted, my legs forced down over the edge of the seat by the second man, and the one with the knife had not relaxed his grip on my hair. I was becoming aware of pain, not only from his hand wrenching at my scalp, but from my back, and from the pressure of the edge of the seat on the side of my thigh.

'I'm very uncomfortable,' I protested, and then the man seemed to snarl down at me, silently but horribly, and he twisted his fist. I felt hairs pulling out of my scalp, and I tried to cry out with the pain, but the man beside him was ready, and slapped his hand down across my mouth.

'Be silent,' he said. 'No more words.'

Frank had said there would be no point in this. Nothing would stop the investigation. What did they want?

I could almost feel their hatred and anger.

I closed my eyes. I couldn't think, looking up at that wicked little knife, or looking past it at the face of the man who held it. I had to think. I had to try to make a plan.

I wondered when would I be missed. At the earliest it would be on the following morning, when Mrs Sam might ask herself where I was. Even then she might do nothing, perhaps not for another day.

We were out of the town now. I thought we were on a country road. There were curves and bends, small hills, and I couldn't hear any other cars. We were moving faster, too.

I wanted to ask them where they were taking me, what they hoped to gain, but when I opened my eyes the man with the knife was still looking down at me, and what I saw in his face reminded me they had told me to be silent. He might be quite glad, if I were to speak again. It would give him an excuse to hurt me.

I was feeling sick with fear, but I was

341

beginning to grow angry as well, and that helped. At least it helped to keep my mind off the pain in my back and my leg, although the sharp burning in my scalp was less easy to ignore. I thought I could feel blood there.

These were the men who had had power over Tamsin. Frank had said there were thirty different children in the photographs, and these were some of the men who had been involved in that filthy business.

These were some of the men he was going to catch, and put in prison.

Over all these thoughts the question came again and again: what are they going to do to me?

The car slowed, and turned sharply to the left. I could hear gravel under the wheels, and it stopped. The man who was sitting beside the driver got out, and I felt the one with the knife shift, probably turning to look along the road. I heard the sound of a gate opening, and the car moved forward a few yards, stopped to let the man in, and then there was the sound of gravel again, and an uneven surface.

'Sit up now.'

It took me a few moments to struggle up onto the seat. There was a cramping pain in my side. I raised my hand to my head, and then looked at it. There was a thin smear of blood on the ends of my fingers. He really had wrenched a clump of my hair out.

We were driving along a track, and there were trees on either side. Beyond them I caught the occasional glimpse of fields, but mostly it was neglected woodland, with brambles and fallen branches.

I wanted to ask them where we were going, but I didn't dare to speak.

The car was a Mercedes. Now that I was sitting upright, I found it was very comfortable. The interior was upholstered in a soft grey fabric that felt like suede. It reminded me of the chair in Tamsin's room.

There was a building ahead of us which looked like an old stable block. I could see an arched gateway with a little clock tower over it. Then, as the car rounded a bend in the track, I saw the back of the house, long and low, built of grey stone. There were two white vans parked by the door, and the driver moved the Mercedes into a space on the other side of the steps, and turned off the engine.

He said something to the man beside him, and again I thought he might have spoken in Dutch, but I wasn't sure. I couldn't hear him very well, and I don't speak Dutch. I can catch the occasional phrase because of its similarity to German, but I can never be certain I have understood correctly. What I thought he said was, 'I hope this isn't a mistake.'

The man with the knife held my elbow as

we went in, his fingers digging in spitefully. Two of them went in front of us, and the other followed to close the door. I heard a key turn, the heavy 'clunk' of a strong lock.

We walked along a stone-flagged passage, and it felt familiar until I remembered my childhood; the corridor between the kitchen garden and the pantry had been stone-flagged, and it had smelt like this, as though there might soon be moss growing in the cracks. It was not exactly the smell of damp and dirt, but it was like a warning that they could easily make an appearance here.

There were double swing doors at the end of the passage, and on the other side the flooring was parquet, old and scarred, but recently polished. Through another open door I could see a hallway, where there were black and white tiles, and stone columns up into an arched ceiling, and a big oak door.

The next corridor was panelled in dark wood, and then one of the men in front of us unlocked a door and threw it open, and I was so dazzled by the brightness of the lamps that I stumbled as we went in, trying to shield my eyes and being pulled up short by the man with the knife.

I blinked, and shook my head, and looked around.

Lights seemed to be blazing down from every angle and the background was white, reflecting the glare.

The man let go of my arm and I put my hands up to my face.

'You are now in a studio,' one of them said, and added, in such normal tones of everyday courtesy that it took me several moments to take in the import of the words:

'You may scream, if you wish.'

There were cameras, and what I thought was probably sound-recording equipment, but I didn't know much about studios. I recognised microphones, and there were some things on stands that could have come out of an electronics laboratory. They might have been television cameras of some sort, but apart from them I had no idea.

It was a huge room. Further back I could see stage sets, put up in angles. There was a piece painted to look like a stone wall, and an area that might have been intended to be an operating theatre.

'Go over there. Go. Now.'

It was certainly a European accent, even if I couldn't place the language. I turned to look at him, and he was pointing to a set that might have been made for a talk show, a grouping of chairs around a small table. The other three men were already seated, but as I approached, the one who had held the knife stood up and walked away.

I went towards one of the seats, and immediately he was in front of me.

'You. Not.'

I looked at him, not understanding what he meant, and then one of the others spoke.

'You may not sit down.'

The words were spoken in pure public school English.

For the first time I felt a slight sensation of hope. They were being rude and childish, and that suggested stupidity. It was just possible that I might outwit them, and escape.

'You will stand there, and you will answer our questions.'

The languor of the voice was affected this time. The man was pretending to be an officer, giving orders to a subordinate, but I could not believe he had ever seen military service.

I looked at him, trying to keep my face expressionless, trying at the same time to memorise his features, in case I should ever have a chance to use what I could remember.

He was quite tall and thin, but not as tall as he would have liked to have been. He tried to look down his nose, but had to tilt his head back in order to do so.

I closed my eyes, and told myself I must not fall into the trap of allowing my hatred to colour my observation.

Light brown hair, rather large ears. Well dressed. Tall and thin, yes. About six foot, although that was hard to say now he was sitting down.

I listed the characteristics, trying to memorise them.

I will know you again, I told myself.

Thin hands with a signet ring. He's wearing brogues, and there's a scratch across the bright brown polish of the toe of the left one. It's a deep scratch, and it seems to be recent.

'What has that policeman found out?'

I should have been prepared for that question, I thought. Instead of spending my time in that car feeling frightened and sorry for myself, I should have been thinking. I should have...

'I am waiting, and my patience is very limited.'

He had certainly rehearsed this conversation. I wasn't prepared for it, but he was.

'He didn't tell me.'

Had I thought ahead I would certainly have been prepared for the blow that caught me on the side of my head and knocked me to the ground. The man who had had the knife had been standing just behind me, and as soon as I'd spoken he hit me.

I was crying. The realisation enraged me, but I couldn't help it. I was so frightened, and he'd taken me by surprise, hitting me from behind like that.

He let me lie there for a few moments, and then he told me to get up.

'You are quite remarkably stupid, but I am

not,' he said. 'Now answer my question.'

It was theatrical. His words, his manner, even the way he was sitting, it was all saying, I am an officer and I am in command. I am in control of this situation, and you are my inferior.

Slowly, I pushed myself off the floor, taking as much time as I dared, and trying very hard to think of a convincing lie.

'Now,' he said. 'That policeman. What has he found out?'

'He was asking me...'

There was another blow, on the back of my head, and this one sent me staggering forward as the man shouted at me.

'Don't try to *think*, you fool woman, just *answer* the *question*. What has he *found out*?'

'Peter Holmes,' I said.

Whatever reply he had been expecting, it hadn't been that one. He checked the words he had been about to speak, and looked at me, blankly.

'What?'

'Peter Holmes,' I repeated, and then, as if I was confused, 'I think that was the name.'

'Peter Holmes?'

'Yes. Yes, that was the name. It was. Peter Holmes.'

'And just who the *fuck* is Peter Holmes?'

'He's a journalist. He was looking into some story about missing children and he's disappeared.'

Keep talking, I told myself. Start babbling about him, whatever you can remember.

'He was a radio journalist, and he'd said there was a story about East European orphanages and the way visas were being bought, to get them out. The children. He'd got a couple of contacts in a travel agency, and he was trying to get his radio station to put up the money to bribe them to say how it was done. Welland was asking me...'

'*What* travel agency? What was the name of the travel agency?'

'He didn't tell me.'

I was expecting the blow that time, and I ducked, but that made it worse. The first one missed me, it went straight over my head, but it seemed to enrage the man. As I straightened up he seized my hair again and hit me in the face, twice, the first an open-handed slap on my cheek that stung enough to bring the tears to my eyes again, and then he hit me in the mouth with his fist.

As soon as he let go of my hair I fell to the ground. I wasn't feeling dazed, he hadn't hit me hard enough for that, but I was trying to gain some time.

'He didn't tell me,' I sobbed. 'He didn't tell me the name. I don't know.'

There was a taste of blood. My lip had split against my teeth.

That man, the one who hit me, who'd had the knife, he was shorter than the other one, with dark curly hair, and it was beginning to recede. He had dark eyes, quite deep-set, and his eyebrows met over the bridge of his nose, which was straight and jutting. He had a cleft chin.

I will know you again, too, I thought.

'What did he say about the travel agencies?'

'Nothing, he only said Peter Holmes wanted to bribe...'

The man kicked me in the back of the thigh, short and spiteful, but he caught the nerve centre and made me cry out.

'That's enough for now,' said the man with the public school accent. 'I'll tell you when I want the rough stuff.'

He looked down at me.

'Go on about this Peter Holmes.'

'He's disappeared.'

He disappeared nearly twenty years ago, and Frank Welland has probably never heard of him, but I can remember quite a lot about this, and I can hold them off a bit, talking about Peter Holmes. As one of the Africans had said, tomorrow is always a better day to die.

They didn't care that I knew we had come to a studio. Once we were off the road they'd said I could sit up, because nobody would see me, and it didn't matter. They intended to kill me.

I couldn't help knowing what they meant

to do, but I also knew that, if I let myself think about it, I'd panic.

I could only manage this by thinking of a few minutes at a time.

'Who are you?' I asked, and he raised a hand.

'One more question from you, and I'll let him do whatever he likes. Tell me about Peter Holmes.'

The other two men were sitting back in their chairs, watching and listening. They were older, their hair was grey.

'I'm trying to remember,' I said. 'Please, just give me a minute.'

'Stand up.'

I began to cry again. I didn't try to stop myself. The more frightened and helpless they believed me to be, the more they might relax their guard.

For whatever that might be worth.

'He hardly told me anything. He was asking me *questions*, not telling me.'

'He kissed you. He was your lover.'

Then he looked up at the other man.

'Kick her again,' he said.

I tried to roll out of the way, and so he kicked me twice, the first one sliding off the side of my calf, and the second one, far harder, into my ribs.

Bastard, I thought, as I curled myself up on the floor and groaned. I will survive this, and I will identify you, and I'll gloat over you while you stand in the dock, you bastard.

Daddy had once told me that anger is a very good anaesthetic, but I couldn't remember when he'd said it, or why.

I kept my face hidden. I didn't think I'd be able to hide my rage.

They must have followed me, from the hotel to the café, and then again when I'd left it. I should have been more careful. I should have been watching for them.

'I want to go to the ... toilet,' I said.

My mother had despised the word. For God's sake call it a lavatory, she'd said.

'You can go to the *toilet* later,' he sneered.

I know you, and I know your type, I thought. You went to a very *minor* public school. Your father was a junior civil servant and your mother was a pretentious featherhead.

'Peter Holmes worked for a radio station.'

'You've already told me that. You are becoming *boring*.'

I knew he had rehearsed that, too.

'He lived near here, but I think the radio station was in Shropshire. I think he said that, but I'm not sure. He showed me a photograph, and he said Holmes was small and fat. He asked if I knew him.'

'Why should he think you knew him?'

'Because I'm a journalist, too.'

For the second time I'd caught him by surprise.

'You're a *what?*'

'A journalist. I'm a journalist.'

The two men sitting beside him caught the word as well, and began to murmur to each other. I raised my head and looked at them as the one who was questioning me gestured at them to be silent.

'Who do you work for?'

'I'm freelance.'

'Stand *up*,' he said, but it was only to give himself time to think.

I did climb to my feet again, and then stood with my head lowered, looking at the other two out of the corners of my eyes.

One of them had a broken nose. He had a thin face with a narrow jaw; it looked as if it was the wrong size for the rest of his features. He was sitting with one leg crossed over his knee, and there was a patch on the sole of his shoe. I thought he was the one who'd driven the car.

'What are you writing about?'

I'd had a moment to think by then.

'Teenage suicides. The numbers are rising, year on year. I thought there was something odd about Tamsin's suicide. I mean, just because she was pregnant, why would she hang herself? Hundreds of teenagers get pregnant every year, it's hardly even unusual. I wanted to find out why.'

'And what *did* you find out?'

'Not much. It wasn't her first pregnancy.

She was just another little tart. I still don't know why she killed herself. I thought there might have been a drugs angle, but I haven't found it. I can't find out which of the boys got her pregnant, either.'

I thought I might have gone too far. Would he believe I was really that bad at my job?

'Who were you writing for?'

'Nobody commissioned it. I thought it was an interesting topic. I'm going to send it to an agency.'

He seemed to relax a little, or perhaps I imagined it, because I was hoping for it.

'What is this place?' I asked, and he flicked a finger at the man behind me.

'I'm sorry,' I said, but it was no good. He slapped me again, harder this time, on my ear. It hurt more than any of the other blows, a dreadful sharp ache that frightened me. It felt as if he had done some serious damage.

'Oh, *please*, stop *hitting* me. I'm trying to answer your questions.'

I didn't have to act any more. I only had to think about the pain in my ear, and what it might mean. The tears were real.

'Please, let me go to the toilet now. Please.'

'Dear God, you are a drag,' he said. 'I'd thought we might film this, but you're just too boring. You're too old, and you're not pretty enough, and you are bloody boring on top of all that. We couldn't even place it in a specialised market. I can't think of a single freak who'd be interested.'

He made another gesture, flicking his hand at the men beside him.

'Take her to the bloody lavatory.'

Only one of them stood up, and for a moment I felt a little hope, but he wasn't that stupid.

'Both of you,' he said.

We went out of the same door, and as it closed behind me one of them pushed me in the back, hard enough to make me stumble, and I heard him laugh. I thought of all the dirty names I knew for perverts, and I tried to keep my head low, I tried to go on sobbing and crying despite my contempt and my rage.

I tried very hard not to be too frightened.

They made me walk ahead of them, and when I turned to ask which way I should go one of them slapped my face and pushed me again. Each time we came to another corridor one of them would push me to make me go where they wanted. They were talking to each other, but very quietly and quickly, and the sound of their footsteps drowned most of the words. I couldn't understand anything, apart from the occasional laugh.

The house was huge. We went down a flight of stairs and along another corridor, and again the floor was stone-flagged. We were back in the kitchen area. I wondered why they had brought me here, so far away from the studio. There had to have been lavatories nearer than this.

Then one of them unlocked another door, and the other one pushed me through, and we were in a storage cellar, a half basement, where the only light came through a high window that had been almost completely obscured by dirt and cobwebs. There was no lavatory, there was only an open drain in the corner.

'That,' one of them said. 'Use. For you.'

They both laughed again.

It wasn't difficult to cry. I could tell myself that decency is a state of mind, I could believe it, but these were the men who had driven Tamsin to suicide and they intended to kill me, and now I had to squat over an open drain and urinate in front of them.

There was an old boiler at the back of the cellar, a monster that had probably consumed half a ton of coal every day. I couldn't see further than the dark outline it made, but there was the smell of a draught, and I heard a creak, wood on wood.

This was a big house, far bigger than the one in which I had spent my childhood, but it wasn't dissimilar, and I knew big, old English houses. I thought I could probably guess my way around this one.

Above us, or near to it, would be the

kitchen, because the kitchen range and the boiler would use the same chimney stack. There might be a service lift to bring the coal up from the store.

The pain in my ear had subsided to a dull throbbing. My lip was beginning to swell, and there was a sharp ache like a stitch in my side where that man had kicked me. How often had he hit me? Would they believe it, if I passed out?

They were watching me, not because they wanted to, but to try to humiliate me. As I stood up and pulled up my slacks the one who had driven the car said something to the other one, something derogatory, and sneering.

'I need a doctor,' I said. 'That man's done something to my ear.'

I think they understood what I said, but they ignored it. They both jerked their heads towards the door, and stood aside for me to walk between them.

They didn't believe I would ever need a doctor again, because they were going to kill me.

Holding my hand against my ear, I went through the door and as they began to follow me I turned as if to plead with them, and slammed it shut in their faces.

I had hoped for a latch that I could wedge, but there was nothing on that side except a handle, so I didn't even try to hold it closed.

I sprinted down the corridor as fast as I could, hearing them shout, and then hearing their footsteps as they ran after me.

Up the flight of stairs three at a time, and I turned right, away from the front of the house, towards the corridor we had first come down, towards what I hoped, what I prayed, would be the kitchen.

They weren't far behind me. I could hear them running, and one of them called out.

But I was faster than they were. I was younger, and fitter, and I had taken them by surprise.

I crashed through the swing doors, and then I could smell the cold and the damp I had noticed when we came in. There were doors to either side, and I tried them, frantically twisting the handles, begging for one of them to open.

They were all locked, but the last one gave a little as I pushed at it, and I felt part of the frame move. It had been damaged and not properly repaired. I stood back from it, paused for a moment to take a couple of deep breaths, and then I kicked the wood beside the lock, once, twice, and the third time it cracked, the frame splitting, and I pushed my way through into the vast kitchen that had once served the house.

The windows were small and high, and they couldn't have been opened for decades. I had hoped to set a false trail by smashing through one of them, but I could see immediately that it wouldn't work; they would not believe I was agile enough to force my way out through such a small gap.

Instead, I ran straight towards the huge cast-iron range against the back wall, to the white painted cupboard beside it, and it housed, as I thought it might, a service lift. I pushed it down and scrambled onto the top of it, grabbing the rusty steel cables, and praying they would hold for long enough. As it began to move I pulled the cupboard door shut behind me.

There was something wrong with the counterweights; after only a couple of feet the lift almost fell down into the cellar, and I scraped the palms of my hands raw as I tried to slow its headlong descent. It crashed to a halt, jarring all the breath out of my lungs so I could only crouch where I was, trying to gather my thoughts, trying to listen, trying to breathe.

They were in the kitchen, and they were searching. I could hear them moving around and speaking to each other, and there was a tone of alarm in their voices that brought a brief flash of vindictive triumph into my mind.

I pushed at the door, pushed harder, and felt it grind on coal dust. Gritting my teeth, I braced myself against the back wall and pushed with my feet against the old wood, a steady pressure that might force it open without making too much noise. It wouldn't be long before one of the men looked into the lift shaft.

The door grated sharply, and then swung open. I wriggled through the gap between the top of the lift and the frame, gasping as the edge of the wood scraped against my ribs where I'd been kicked, but then suddenly I was through, and free, and standing beside the enormous boiler.

I knew I didn't have much time. The men would search the small labyrinth of pantries and still rooms that led off the kitchen, but they would soon realise there was no way I could have escaped through them, unless one of them had an unlocked outside door, and I would certainly not rely on such luck.

There were two huge coal chutes into the cellar, and I could feel a draught from the shutters that covered them. They should be secured by bolts on the inside, and there probably wouldn't be any external locks. Normally, there wouldn't be any need for them. Most houses were only protected against intruders, not escapees.

Would they guess I had come back to this cellar?

They were stupid, these men, but eventually they would search.

There were no more sounds from the kitchen. They would have gone back to the studio, and confessed that they had let me escape.

They would all know that, if I were to get away, they faced long prison sentences. Quite soon they would become desperate, and very dangerous.

I didn't think they had dogs. I could only hope they didn't have guns.

It was gloomy in the cellar, but my eyes had become accustomed to the lack of light. The chutes were steep, and smooth, as well as filthy. Somewhere, there should be some sort of hook on a pole with which the bolts could be worked.

I found it behind the boiler, propped up against the wall. The bolts were in deep shade.

If they catch me, they will kill me.

This thought kept rising to the surface of my mind, and even though I tried to push it away because it frightened me, it brought with it a degree of elation. I was in desperate danger, and I was fighting for my life, for the first time ever, but that was all right. That was good. I was good enough to win.

They were stupid, and I was not. This whole action, abducting me and questioning me and knocking me around, it had been incredibly stupid. There was nothing they could gain from it, apart from a few snippets of information to help them guard themselves against police questioning.

But even though they were stupid they were dangerous, and if I didn't escape from them they would kill me. I must not panic, I thought. I must think, and I must get away.

The pole in my hands had a familiar type of hook on the end of it. It was brass, a little like a boat hook. I thought it meant they weren't normal bolts on the shutters; there would be a spring, with a loop of metal to release it. There'd been one like it in the hay loft at the stables where I'd learned to ride.

I didn't know whether those men would concentrate on the grounds or on the house. If one of the doors had been unlocked they might assume I'd be outside, trying to reach the road. If not, it wouldn't be very long before they came down here. All the doors in the kitchen corridor had been locked, and if they had been as careful in the rest of the house, they'd be able to search it quite quickly.

The springs were stiff and rusty and the first one broke as soon as I put any pressure on it. The catch was still lodged, and immovable now. If the other spring broke, I would have to think again. I would be trapped.

I went over to the door, opened it carefully, and listened.

At first I could hear nothing, but then there was the sound of running footsteps, and a voice calling.

I closed the door again, and went back to the coal chutes. This time I worked more slowly and more carefully, moving the spring a little at a time, trying to free it, not forcing it. It grated, but then it did begin to move. It was clogged with rust and with coal dust.

If I could climb out, if I could reach the woods, I should be able to get to the road. If I could get to the road I could flag down a car. It wasn't very far. I should be able to find a path, and run.

The catch grated again, and I felt something give. I pushed with the pole, but the shutter hardly moved at all. One of the screws must have broken.

I heard another shout, and I tried to ignore the growing feelings of panic. They'd be down here soon. I had to get out.

Another screw broke, and then the whole catch fell free, clattering onto the chute and sliding down to land at my feet. Cautiously, I pushed at the shutter, listening as I did so.

Nothing.

It lifted, and there was daylight flooding into the cellar, and nobody had seen.

The chute was too steep for me to scramble up it, so I slid the hook over the edge of the frame and used the pole to pull myself up, hand over hand, until I could grasp the frame and push the shutter open. I waited there for a moment, watching and listening.

I was looking into a walled kitchen garden, but there was a big arched gateway through which lorries could be driven. So far as I could see, that was the only way out. The walls were too high to be climbed, and there was nothing stronger than brambles growing against them.

There would be windows overlooking this garden. Every room down this side of the house would overlook this garden.

I knew that, if I allowed myself to think about it, I wouldn't be able to go through with it.

I pushed the shutter, pressed against it with my head, grasped the frame with both hands, and then I launched myself through onto the gravel drive. Something, probably a stone, dug painfully into my shoulder as I rolled over and scrambled to my feet, and then I ran for the gateway.

I heard a shout, and an answer.

I'd been seen.

I sprinted around the corner of the gate, running as fast as I could on the gravel, knowing it could be heard and telling myself there was nothing I could do about it. They would have seen the direction in which I was heading, and they would be after me.

There was another car between the Mercedes and the two white vans.

I was heading for the stable block, and I knew that would be the next place they would search. I could easily be trapped, in there. Instead, I dodged around the back of the garden wall, and found myself waist deep in nettles, and only inches away from a rusty tangle of barbed wire.

Don't panic, I said to myself. Don't panic. Think.

By now they would all be coming after me. They would know I was out, and the direction in which I had run. They would not be watching the garden.

I jumped for the wall, and gripped the top of it, almost crying out with the pain as my hands, rubbed raw by the steel cables of the service lift, ground into the old brick.

Bastards, I thought. You traded in children's misery and you mean to kill me, and I loathe you and I despise you, and I will gloat over you as you face a contemptuous jury.

With every word I pulled myself along the wall, hauling myself as high as I could, pushing the wire away with my feet, using my anger and my fear to give myself the strength to escape.

When I heard running footsteps on gravel, I braced myself against the wall, and then threw myself back, hoping, almost begging, that I was clear of the wire. I couldn't see what lay under the nettles.

The noise of their feet on the gravel must have drowned the sounds of my fall. I was quite lucky. I landed almost clear of the wire, only my arm scraping against the rusty barbs, but I managed not to cry out again.

The impact of the fall sent a savage bolt of pain through my ear, and I rolled over, pressing my hand against it, trying to fight back the tears.

If I could only find a gun I would kill you, I thought.

There were more footsteps, running past the end of the wall towards the stable block.

I lay still, catching my breath, waiting, and listening.

Perhaps, if I could stay here until it was dark, I would stand a better chance.

But there'd been another car alongside the Mercedes, which meant at least one more against me, and maybe they could telephone for help. How many could they bring? And would they think of dogs?

'*Celia!*'

It was Giles's voice. I raised my head, listening.

'Celia! Please, come out!'

The other four had been stupid, but not Giles. Now he was here it would be much more difficult.

'I'm so *sorry*. It's been a misunderstanding. These ridiculous cretins, God knows where they got this idea. Celia, I promise you, you're quite safe. Please, come out.'

Then there were other voices calling.

'*Saur-eee, Ceelia! Saur-ee.*'

'*Mrs Masters!* I really am most dreadfully sorry. It's been a ghastly misunderstanding. Do, please, come out. Please. Honestly, you're perfectly safe.'

It was becoming so tempting, to believe them. My ear was hurting, my hands, my arm where I'd scraped against the barbed wire, even the back of my shoulder where I'd landed on a sharp stone as I'd escaped from the cellar, and now they sounded like reasonable people. I'd been in some sort of nightmare of violence and stupidity, and the voices offered sanity.

I did so want to believe them. It would be so good, to stand up, to call out, here I am. They would help me back over that horrible wire. They would take me to a doctor, or the hospital. They would take me away from here, apologising, explaining, and could there be an explanation?

No.

'*Celia?* What do you want me to do? Would you like me to call the police?'

How did he imagine I should answer him?

It hadn't been Giles who'd abducted me, and I could well believe he would be furiously angry when he heard it had been done.

'*Celia?* They've told me they hurt you. For God's *sake*, let me help you!'

I heard the sound of another car, the rise and fall of the note of an engine, and then

367

wheels on gravel, and two doors slamming. They'd called in more people, to search for me.

I can't get away, then. I can't escape. So I might as well trust them, and Giles would know about Frank Welland. He would know he couldn't get away with...

No.

There are nettles, and brambles, and broken branches here, I can't get through without making a noise. All they have to do is listen. How long can I stay here, lying in these nettles, and they keep stinging me, and my ear hurts so much, I think he burst the drum. If I don't get help soon the damage might be...

No. Don't trust him. Stay there.

Tamsin?

You saw it, it's a studio. Do you think they'd let you go, now you know? You can hire that place. By the hour, by the day, by the week, you can use their sets and their equipment, you can even use the grounds. Call the police, he said. Two actors in uniform and a white car with a blue lamp.

Tamsin, is that you?

Now that my anger was subsiding the pain was becoming worse. I did so want to believe them. I did so want them to help me, to explain, to say, let's discuss it later, please. Let's go to the hospital first, and get your ear treated, and those cuts on your arm

368

and those horrible raw patches on your hands. I wanted to get back to sanity, to questions I could understand, and answer. When did you last have a tetanus injection? Are you allergic to penicillin? Does that hurt?

There's no sanity here. There's misery here, not sanity. Those men, they're stupid, but he's not. He's just horrible, but he's not stupid. They haven't caught him yet, but now he's been here, and you can say it. He was there. This is where it happens, not that little photography shop. That's nothing.

Her voice wasn't very steady. I'd never heard her sound so wretched. The memory of her pain and her fear was almost overwhelming here, where it had happened.

'Cee-lia! Saur-eee!'

Tamsin, I can't get away. I thought I could, but I can't. There are too many of them now, and I can't stay here any longer. Everything hurts too much, and I'm cold. I'm really getting cold.

'Celia? They've arrested Neville Jacklin. I didn't know he was a bloody pervert. How could I know? I wanted the best for Tamsin. God, Celia, she was my *niece*, I *loved* her. I wanted him to do her room, that's all. I should have seen it, but I didn't. They've got the little bastard now, they'll send him to jail. It's all over, Celia. They've got him.'

Him, maybe. They may have got him, but

there are seven at least looking for me now, and perhaps more on the way. I've got no chance.

'Listen, Celia. I was bloody furious when I heard what you'd told the police, about me and Tamsin. Of course I was, it was disgusting. Anybody would have been. I said a lot of things about you. Some of them went a bit far, but I was bloody angry, and I had every right to be. Listen. Konrad heard what I said, and he misunderstood. Where he comes from, this wouldn't be so unusual. He thought he was carrying out my orders. For God's sake, Celia, those three used to be Romanian policemen, they didn't exactly work to judges' rules, or whatever they're called. Listen, I really am sorry. I said I'd like to get you on your own and kick the shit out of you, he thought it was an order.'

And Mister Minor Public School? I thought. Doesn't he speak good English either?

'Celia, I'm trying to expand my travel agencies into East Europe, that's why they're here. Mark's been in the Eastern Bloc for about ten years, and frankly I could kill him for what he's done today. I don't understand it myself, so I can't pretend to try and explain it to you. Konrad told him I'd given the orders. Listen, Celia, I'll call the police if you like, but it's going to make a hell of a mess and take months to sort out, and it really wasn't my fault. Naturally, I'll pay you compensation. It wasn't my fault, but these idiots are my responsibility. What do you say to five thousand? Would that be fair?'

This was becoming confusing. I couldn't seem to summon up my powers of reason. He sounded so convincing, calling out to me, explaining and apologising. These men, they come from Eastern Europe, or they've been there for a long time, and things are different over there. I'm so sorry, let me help you, I'll take you to hospital.

The tone of his voice was right, too. He was reasonable, but becoming a little exasperated. Look, Celia, what do you want me to say? I'll call the police, shall I? It'll be a bloody mess, but I couldn't blame you.

I wanted to stand up and say, all right, here I am. Now, take me to hospital, and we'll talk about the police on the way.

All that was stopping me was Tamsin, or my stupid imagination, and was this the right time to let my imagination take control?

Don't believe him. He's horrible, and everybody believes him until it's too late. Keep still. Lie still.

But Tamsin, I'm hurt. I do need a doctor, my ear's badly hurt.

'Cee-lia! Saur-ee!'

'Mrs Masters, I really do apologise. I completely misunderstood, I thought I was following orders.'

Lie still. I've been here. I've been here before. I believed him, too. I've heard those voices before, don't worry, come with me, that's a good girl, come on, now. Do you know what they did to me, because I believed them?

I could hear footsteps on gravel. I could hear voices, I'd thought they were speaking Dutch, and it was Romanian. They were looking for me, still searching.

He was still calling out, Giles, offering his apologies and his explanations, and beginning to sound seriously annoyed.

'Celia, I can't stand here all day shouting like this. For God's sake, do be sensible. What on earth do you imagine is going to happen to you? I only want to *help* you, I want to take you to hospital. Stop being so bloody melodramatic, you're not taking part in some stupid James Bond movie.'

Go away then, I thought, and Tamsin said yes, *go away. Celia, please lie still.*

I felt something moving under my arm, some insect on the edge of hibernation disturbed by my weight, or a worm, and I tried to shift away from it. I saw one of the tall nettles against which I was lying move, so I stopped, watching it, listening in case anybody else had seen.

It was such a still day, with the grey clouds almost motionless overhead. Sound carried easily, and any movement could be seen, if somebody was looking in the right direction.

I can't stay here much longer, I thought, and Tamsin was in my mind again. *You must, Celia. You must keep still.*

Giles had stopped calling. There was silence, a listening silence, seven men or more listening for me, perhaps to come and help me, over the rolls of barbed wire, away from the horrible nettles, back into the house and then to hospital, where everything would be clean, and sane, and normal again.

No. No, they won't, they're not like that.

Where was Giles? Was he watching, with the others? Were they all watching for me?

So this silence, what did it mean? I could hear nothing, apart from the distant sounds of rooks, and from even further away the drone of traffic. It was so quiet it could only mean that they were watching and listening, waiting for any sign from me, any sound that could lead them to me.

It was the silence of the hunter.

But I could not keep still any longer. I had to move, I had to get away from the wire and the nettles, and the cold that had gone beyond unpleasantness and discomfort into the unbearable.

Quiet. Be quiet. Please.

Very slowly, I rolled over onto my stomach,

and I began to inch my way forward, crawling on my elbows and my knees, stopping every few seconds to listen. They wouldn't shout if they saw the tall nettles moving where there was no wind. One would simply touch the arm of another, and point, and they'd nod, and quietly, and very confidently, they would come to get me.

I was listening for footsteps.

Just ahead of me there was a broken fence, the wooden railing of what had probably once been a small paddock, in the days when that stable block had held horses. Beyond that were the loose boxes and tack rooms, now falling into disrepair, or filled with unwanted junk.

How do I know?

Be careful. Be careful, they're watching.

I *am* being careful. I'm being as careful as I can. I think this is stupid. This is England, not some lawless corner of a half-starved baby nation trying to climb to its feet. People don't...

People don't rape children and film it? People don't tie you up and sell you and hire you out to men with cameras and tape recorders? Where have you been? Children run away from home, and people find them and pretend to be friends. They say, you can stay with me for a few days.

All right. Tamsin. I'll be quiet.

Friends. People pretend. Children disappear, Celia.

But you didn't disappear.

No, but I wasn't always alone when I was here. There are more photos, they haven't found them all. I talked to them, the others who were in the pictures. They told me what happened to them, and that's why I didn't run away. I know what happens to children who run away.

Oh, Tamsin.

She was quiet after that. It had been a great effort for her, to come here, and she was very tired.

That house, I thought, that was where they'd find the backgrounds for those photographs. They hadn't been shot in little High Street photographers' studios, they were the sets built for the films, stored in that big house, quite innocent.

We used that one for *Pride and Prejudice*, part of it was filmed here. And that, oh, yes. It was a series of horror films, who was it who hired the place? I'll have to look it up. A French farce, a war film, and those, well, that was a bit nasty. We wouldn't have them back again. Borderline pornography.

He would have an answer for everything.

No, no idea they'd photographed children here. What do you mean, anyway? What's wrong with photographing children?

I crawled under the broken fence, and I was in a patch of dead and tussocky grass, away from the nettles, but far more exposed, should anybody be close enough to see me. I began to move more quickly, still keeping hard up against the fence, hoping it and the weeds that grew high against it would give me some cover.

Perhaps they thought I'd got away. Perhaps they'd given up.

Would Giles be able to talk his way out of this? Frank Welland had known he was lying, but you can't put that forward as proof. A cotton sheet over a rotting corpse, that was how he'd described it.

Be careful, be careful. A faint and fading whisper.

I *am* being careful, Tamsin. Just shut up.

And then I heard footsteps, and they were running, and I knew I'd been seen.

I scrambled to my feet and ran towards the stable block, stumbling on the grass, stiff and awkward from the long minutes I'd spent lying on my back in the cold nettles.

'*Cee-lia! Stop! We saur-ee!*'

Liar, I thought. Liar. Bloody liars, you bastards, you're going to kill me if you catch me.

There were cobblestones in the stable yard, and the buildings were almost completely derelict, with doors hanging open from rusted hinges, and from this side I could see holes in the roof, rotten rafters standing black and crooked behind the broken tiles.

As I ran I felt panic rising. I couldn't run

fast enough, I was too stiff, too cold.

There were loose boxes down three sides of the quadrangle, but I knew I'd be trapped in them. There'd be no connecting doors. Ahead of me was something like a storage shed, and beside that there'd be the tack rooms. There'd be another door, it might lead out onto the track.

There was another door, and it was locked. I pushed against it, but it was no use. That door had probably been the last item in the entire block to be repaired, and whoever had mended it had done a good job.

I could hear two people in the yard, and as I listened there was the sound of a car turning in through the arched gateway. Another one followed it.

I was trapped. Giles had sounded so reasonable, so persuasive, and I had nearly stood up and answered him: here I am. Help me. Now there were two cars in the court-yard. Giles's men had chased me, and they had trapped me, and no matter how desperately I might have hoped, I could not make myself believe they had done so in order to help me.

Come on.

It's no good. They've caught me.

Look. Look around.

Two broken bridles hanging on a hook, a rusty iron stove, an old coat and a pair of boots, a couple of jackets, a helmet, a saddle rack with a broken strut, a moth-eaten blanket, what I am looking for, Tamsin? Buckets and an iron hook hanging from the ceiling for cleaning bridles, a halter with a frayed rope, empty tins, half a packet of rat poison.

The coat. Put it on.

It's red. It'll show up like a beacon, why should I put it on?

The coat and the boots, and up into the hay loft because the roof's broken.

I did it, because I didn't know what else to do, and they were going to kill me so nothing mattered any more. I might as well pretend Tamsin was there, telling me what to do, and why shouldn't I do it? Tamsin had been here before, and she knew her way around, so I might as well listen to her, and it really doesn't matter if I am going crazy.

You said it to me. You said, don't hide in the shed, get a spade and stand beside the shed and dig the garden.

I don't understand.

But I was climbing the splintered ladder up into the hay loft, wearing a red coat with a torn sleeve and carrying the boots, and I seemed to follow her across the wooden planking to the place where the rafter had rotted and the tiles lay broken all around.

You're going for a walk. There's a track down there. People go for walks down tracks, don't they?

It's too far down. I'll hurt myself if I jump

378

down there.

They'll kill you if you don't.

I pulled off my trainers and stuffed them into the pockets of the coat, dragged the old rubber boots onto my feet. They were too big, and one of them had a split along the welt.

Hurry, come on. They'll hear you if you're not quick.

Climbing onto the roof wasn't very difficult, although it was certainly dangerous. I couldn't know whether the rafters would bear my weight. And it was quite a long drop down onto the ground.

I slid down the tiles, feeling something sagging underneath me, and I tried to dig my feet into the guttering as I reached the edge, but it broke away, and I fell. I did manage to land fairly well, on my feet and rolling, but I jarred my knee painfully and winded myself too, so for a moment I lay there catching my breath and ignoring Tamsin, who was nearly frantic at the delay.

Come on, come on. They're in the tack room, they'll find you.

Pull yourself together, I thought as I stood up. Don't let your stupid imagination get completely out of control.

There was only another broken fence between me and the track, and I climbed through it and began to run towards the woods.

Don't run. Walk. You're just a woman going for a walk.

She was right. I mustn't panic. I must be a woman going for a walk, something you'll see everywhere in the countryside, a track through fields and woods and a middle-aged woman walking along it. All I need is a dog. A black and white mongrel. I should be carrying a lead.

I'm nothing out of the ordinary. If you look out over the track, from the hay loft or anywhere else, I'm just a woman going for a walk in the country. A woman who wouldn't turn round and look back. Why should she? She's often been along this track before, walking. Walking her dog.

There was a bit of rope in the pocket of the coat. I took it out and carried it in my hand. Dog lead, see? And the dog's run ahead, into the woods.

Somebody called out behind me, a sharp and interrogative shout.

No, I don't think so. Nothing to do with me. I've got to catch up with my dog, I don't want him getting onto the road.

'Nuff-ield!' I called, pitching my voice high, this woman has a rather shrill voice. *'Here, Nuffy. Come on, boy. Good dog, Nuffy.'*

He's a little black and white mongrel, mostly terrier. I've got to catch him before we get to the road, because he's not very bright about cars. He was probably chasing a rabbit, that's why he ran off.

'Nuffy! Come on, Nuffy!'

I'm not worried, not yet. There's the wood between me and the road, he'll be in there, sniffing about. So long as I can catch him in the wood, he'll be all right. He'll come when I call. He usually does. Well, quite often, anyway.

Walk slowly. I'm quite old, you see. I can't walk very fast. Nothing to do with a bruised knee, it's just a touch of arthritis. Of course it makes me limp a bit.

'Nuffy!'

Only another fifty yards to the wood, and then through that and I'll be on the road. I'll have to be careful there. They could be driving on that road, and they've already got me once, throwing me into the car.

I will have to be very careful.

Slower, please don't walk so fast.

All right, Tamsin. Have you seen Nuffield?

Oh, for God's sake, this is impossible. I can't control this at all now, I don't know what I'm thinking, or what's real, or what's just my imagination and I'm beginning to believe in ghosts. Any moment I'll see that silly little dog and he'll be a ghost, too. He must have been dead for thirty years, old Binnsie's daft little mongrel.

Don't cry.

Have I done enough now, Tamsin? When I've told the police about this, about what they did, will that be enough? With what they've already got, will they trap Giles with this, or will he get away with it? He can say he'd never dreamed they'd take him seriously, his angry threats, he'd never meant them to do anything about them. He'd been angry because of what I'd said. I'd accused him of incest with his niece, wouldn't anybody be angry? He'd said he'd like to kick the shit out of me, and Konrad or whatever his name was had heard him and thought he was giving an order. Konrad didn't speak very good English, and unfortunately, where he came from, this wasn't such an unusual event. It wasn't the first time he'd been given an order like that. And he passed it on to Mark, who should have known better, but he's been out of the country for ten years.

An English jury might well believe it, at least so far as Giles was concerned.

I was in the woods now, looking around for my dog, still calling out now and then. Were they watching me? Or had they gone back to searching in the stables for Celia Masters? That old woman on the track, it was lucky she hadn't seen anything, wasn't it?

'Nuffy!'

She was too busy looking for her dog. She shouldn't have let it off the lead, if it won't come when it's called. People are silly about dogs in this country. They won't train them and they let them run loose, and then they get upset when they lose them, or when they get shot chasing sheep.

Poor little dog, it was only playing, only having a bit of fun.

There's the road ahead now, I can see it, I can hear it. Where's that bloody dog?

Come on, there's no bloody dog. There's no need for the bloody dog now, you can drop that bit of rope. You can take these old boots off and put your trainers on again.

There was a house, a shabby little house with grey stucco walls, and there was smoke coming from the chimney, and it wasn't far away. I began to run. Only a little way down the road and I could be at that house, and I would be safe. If only they are still looking in the stables.

Where can she be? Go through those loose boxes again, look behind the old bits of furniture, look in the hayloft, and be quiet if you find her in case that stupid old woman in the red coat comes back down the track.

If they're driving on the road they may see me. If they get close enough to the old woman in the red coat they'll look, and they'll stop, and they did it before, when I wasn't tired and hurt. I'm not strong enough to fight them.

But it's easier to run on the road, there aren't any ruts, and it's a flat surface. I ran as fast as I could, trying to listen for a car, hearing nothing but my feet thudding on the tarmac, seeing nothing but the little house with the smoke drifting from the chimney, praying it meant there was somebody at home.

I went through the gate and along the path, and I rang the bell and then I knocked on the door, and when the old man opened it and looked at me I managed to speak quite clearly.

'Please, may I telephone the police?'

But then I burst into tears.

18

The doctor said he didn't think the damage to my ear was as serious as I'd feared, but he wanted to have an X-ray of my skull. There was a lump, and I couldn't remember how I'd got it. Had that man used a weapon? Every time I tried to think about it my memory seemed to blur, as if it had gone out of focus.

He patted me on the shoulder and said I shouldn't worry. It was concussion, and it would pass.

Then Frank turned up at the hospital, and kept apologising, and I couldn't stop crying.

'They were going to kill me,' I said, and he looked at me helplessly, and didn't know what to say.

I didn't want sedatives or tranquillisers, or whatever it was they kept offering me. I wanted those men locked up, and I wanted to tell Frank what they looked like, so that he could catch them.

'We've got them,' he said. 'Don't worry about it.'

It was too easy. Why did he say it like that?

Because they were denying everything, and he wasn't sure what he could prove.

They said Mark Fraser had been the only one in the car, and he'd asked me to come and talk to Giles about my accusations. I'd agreed.

'I wouldn't get into a car with a stranger,' I said, and Frank shook his head and said he knew I wouldn't.

There'd been an argument, Giles had explained. It was hardly surprising, when one considered the accusations I'd made. I'd stormed out, too angry to look where I was going, and had fallen over a boot scraper.

'It's unbelievable,' I said.

That was how I'd got my bruises.

I held out my hands to Frank. They'd been cleaned and bandaged by then, but somebody had told him.

'How does Giles explain this?'

None of them knew about the steel cables in the service lift.

'Never mind,' I said. 'Never mind. Frank, search that place, that's where they took the children. They'd run away, and they said they were friends. But they weren't.'

I stopped, because my memory was beginning to fade again, and I thought, no, please, I have to be able to think. I have to be able to say this.

'What happened to me...'

'Yes?'

'It doesn't matter. It doesn't. But there were children there.'

'You saw them? Celia, did you see any children there?'

That wasn't what I'd meant. I'd been going to tell him something about hearing the men talking. But he'd asked.

I drew in a deep breath, and felt my teeth baring.

Yes, you bastard, I can lie too.

'*Yes.*'

Let me think, let me think.

'Frank, let me think. I've got to try to remember them, haven't I? Describe them?'

'Celia?'

I knew he didn't believe me, but I also knew he wouldn't be able to ignore what I said, even if it was a lie.

I didn't only remember Tamsin's misery and fear, as she had relived it in that place. I remembered what she'd said about the other children.

But Frank was quite clever, and I would have to be careful.

'It was after I'd got away from them,' I said. 'Look, they'd knocked me around, hit me on the head. I was a bit groggy. So bear with me, Frank. I've got to try to get this right.'

He was watching me, and he didn't answer.

He knew exactly what I was doing, and I would have to play on my confusion, on the fact that I'd been hit on the head. Anything

I got wrong, I'd say, I'm sorry. It's all a bit hazy, because I'd been hit on the head, you see.

'After I got away,' I said again. 'Yes, and if you want to get them for what they did to me, you'll find blood and skin on the cables of the kitchen service lift. My blood and skin. Well, I got back down into the cellar that way. But the children weren't there, it was later I saw the children. But they're going to find it difficult to explain that blood, aren't they? That's why my hands are bandaged, you see.'

I stopped, and thought, and looked at him. I couldn't read his face.

'The children, they're not there any more, are they?'

'No,' he said. 'There are no children there.'

His speech patterns had become precise again. I noticed it, and remembered the first time I'd seen him, how I'd been struck by the way he phrased what he said.

'They were getting them out. I heard them. I heard a child crying.'

I had to think. Where could I have been, to have heard a crying child, and to have seen children?

'They thought I'd got away, I suppose. Obviously, the first thing I'd do as soon as I could was phone the police. So, they wanted to get the children out. They would, wouldn't they? But will you be able to find traces? They won't have had time to destroy everything, will they?'

'Probably not,' he said.

'I was lying in the nettles,' I told him, speaking slowly as if I was trying to remember and thinking as fast as I could, thinking they'd be able to find traces there, where I'd thrown myself back from the wall. There was some evidence. 'I heard a child. I went back to the wall and pulled myself up, so I could see over the wall. It was stupid, they could have seen me, but I heard the child, and I was confused. I thought they might be hitting the child, because they'd hit me. I know it doesn't make sense, but I was still a bit dazed.

'There were two white vans, and one of the men was pushing a child into the back of a van. Sort of, holding her by the arm, lifting her up so she could get in.'

'Her?' he asked.

'I think it was a girl. I'm not sure why, now. One of the other men came out with two more children, and then I realised they might see me, so I got down. A bit later I heard cars driving away. I didn't see them. Are the white vans there? I thought they must be taking the children away in the vans, but I didn't see them. I only heard them. One of the children was crying, so I looked.'

He'd been watching me, all the time I was speaking. I was aware of his eyes fixed on my face, and I wondered if that was how he looked when he was questioning a suspect. I couldn't tell what he was thinking. I wanted to ask, do you believe me? But I knew that, if I did, his answer would be, no.

'Could you estimate the age of the children you saw?' he asked.

You're not writing anything down, I thought. You only asked that question because I'd stopped talking and the silence had gone on for too long. This is all lies, and I don't care. Tamsin said there'd been children in that house, so search it. Find something, you. Go and look at those cables, and that man with the white coat who'd stood in Helen's beautiful kitchen, he can...

'Neville Jacklin,' I said, and then I was staring Frank in the face. This is the truth.

'Giles said you'd arrested Neville Jacklin. That was the name he used. That's the interior designer, the one who's in Belgium. Have you arrested him?'

'No.'

But now he was alert again, and I almost shouted at him in vindictive triumph.

'That's the name, Frank! Bloody Giles made a mistake at last!'

'Neville Jacklin?'

'Yes. When he was shouting at me to come

390

out, he said the police had arrested Neville Jacklin. Let me think.'

They had hit my head, they really had. And Tamsin had been there, telling me to keep still. I had to remember, and I couldn't, and I felt the tears begin again.

'I can't remember. I can't bloody *remember*.'

'All right. Give yourself time.'

'He said something about Tamsin's room.'

'But that was the name? Jacklin? Are you sure?'

I was sure, and Frank knew this was true. He left me alone and went to find a telephone. Neville Jacklin, who lived in Belgium, and Giles had been trying to persuade me to come out, and at last he'd made a mistake and given us the name.

Perhaps it didn't matter that I couldn't remember anything else.

What could they prove against Giles?

A nurse came in and told me they were ready for me in the X-ray department, and when I came back from there a while later Frank had gone. He'd left a message. Somebody would call at the hotel later that evening, and take a statement.

I began to cry again.

The nurse was very sweet. She brought me a cup of tea and a box of paper handkerchiefs, and said I really should have victim counselling to help me get over this. I'd been attacked and threatened, and I should talk about it to somebody who'd been trained to help people like me. She sat with me for a while and talked about ordinary things. She told me about her little boy, and said it was difficult to manage when she was on the same shifts as her husband, who was also a nurse but in another hospital. He thought they should get an *au pair* to help, but she didn't like the idea of leaving Damien with a stranger.

The doctor came back and said there was no fracture in my skull, and I could go as soon as I was ready. The nurse told him I was still a bit shocked, but it wasn't that that had made me cry. It was Frank's message, that somebody would call and take a statement. I'd lied to him, and he knew it.

I went back to the hotel in a taxi, and Mrs Sam exclaimed in consternation at the bandages, and about my face, which I hadn't seen. When I looked in a mirror I saw that my eyes were sunken and bruised, and I was very white.

'What happened?' she demanded. 'You had accident?'

She was the only counsellor I needed. I told her everything, including my lies to Frank about the children, and she listened, and nodded, and when I told her about Tamsin speaking to me and her misery at being back at that house there was nothing in her lovely old face to suggest there was anything strange in the dead coming back.

'You were lucky to get away,' she said when I'd finished. 'The police have caught these men now?'

'Yes, but what can they prove against Giles?'

She wagged her head at me.

'This is their business, and they are not too stupid, these policemen. They will look in that house and find something, even if they put it there themselves.'

I was startled, and a little shocked.

'I'm *sure* they wouldn't do that.'

'Then we must both hope they won't need to.'

I didn't want to argue with her. I sat quietly, looking at the picture of Krishna with the gopis, wondering what I could say when somebody came to take my statement. I began to feel desperately tired, and it wasn't only because of what had happened to me. It was because I realised Giles was probably too clever for me. I'd despised him, and looked down on him and his flabby, self-indulgent sister, and now it seemed that he was much cleverer than me, and would probably get away with what he had done. It was my word against his, and it wouldn't be enough, in a criminal trial.

'If there were children in that house the police will find out,' said Mrs Sam. 'They will find something about children.'

But it wouldn't matter. There was always an explanation. Other people had used the house, and it was impossible for anybody to know what went on all the time. If children had been abducted and raped and filmed there, who could prove that Giles had been involved? One of those companies that hired the house by the hour, the day, the week, any one of them could have brought children, and there is the explanation for the child-sized shoe in the cupboard, for the broken toys.

The photographs would match, and Giles would be horrified, and enraged. He would ask the police to tell him if they found out which company had done it, so that neither he nor any of the concerns in which he held an interest would ever do business with them again.

Of course they could have the keys to the house, and there would be no need for a search warrant.

And Mrs Masters?

Mrs Masters was a peculiar woman of a certain age, who had never liked his sister and had always thought herself superior to both of them. But why she should be exaggerating this story was beyond his understanding.

Although, of course, he had not been present when Mark Fraser had questioned her, and if Mark had gone too far, then it was regrettable, but hardly Giles's fault. As he had already explained, Konrad did not speak very good English, and when he, Giles, had said he'd like to kick the shit out of that bitch Celia Masters, Konrad had misunderstood. He had gone to Mark Fraser, and said Mr Baker wanted Celia Masters beaten up, and Mark had taken some sort of compromise action. He knew Giles wouldn't have ordered a beating, but unfortunately he hadn't been able to get hold of Giles at the time to ask what he meant. So he'd followed Mrs Masters and seen her go into a café where she'd met a friend.

There might be a long pause at that point, I thought. Frank had kissed me goodbye. It hadn't been a particularly passionate embrace, but it would have indicated something a great deal more than a friendly farewell to a witness.

Would Giles say anything about it?

'Women. Are you married, Mr Welland?'

Man to man, amused and condescending incomprehension. How could you possibly interpret that as a threat?

So when Mrs Masters had left the café, Mark had drawn up alongside her in the car, and asked her to come with him to meet Giles. He'd said Giles was, of course, very upset by her accusations, but also anxious to find out the truth about Tamsin's death, and would like to discuss it.

And Mrs Masters had agreed, and had got into the car with him.

Giles would have no idea why she was now making these appalling accusations. But then, he also had no idea why she believed he had had a sexual relationship with his own niece.

This would never even get to court, let alone see him convicted.

'My dear?'

I had forgotten her.

'Yes, Mrs Sam?'

'You have done all you can. It is no small thing, finding that house. Okay, we know, not exactly detective work, getting kidnapped and all this nonsense, but I think, one very big step. Perhaps you have not been Wonder Woman, but it is surely so that you have been one damned big nuisance to these people.'

She leaned forward and put a hand on my knee, looking into my face very earnestly.

'For sure you have saved a child, probably many more than one. Even if the police say now, drop case, no damned good, they have to find another house. How long do you think that would take? Many, many months for sure.'

'Do you think they will drop the case?'

'Oh, no. Nonono. This is too big, now.

What I mean, perhaps you haven't won, but you have been a nasty thorn in their side. My dear, it is not a small matter, to have slowed them down. Months to find another house, and in those months, no children.'

I knew she was right, and that it was no small matter, to have saved even one child, but it wasn't enough. I believed Giles was the man they had to catch in order to stop this filthy business, and I didn't think they could do it.

I would lie, when I made my statement, and I would lie in court. I would say I had seen children, and that I had heard a child crying, but it wouldn't be enough. There were four of them and only one of me, and my excuse for not going into details was that I was dazed, because I had been hit on the head.

I had been dazed enough for my imagination to have taken a strong hold on my mind. After all, I had become obsessed with the death of my niece.

I could almost hear the words as they would be spoken by a barrister. I could almost see the jury considering the idea. She hadn't actually been lying, that well-spoken woman who had stood in the witness box and claimed to have heard a child crying, and to have seen children being put into the vans. Her evidence can be discounted without any suggestion that she was deliberately committing perjury.

What more could I do? I wanted Giles in the dock, in prison for a long, long time, not out looking for another house to use, looking for more children.

'I hate house-hunting,' I said, and remembered going with a friend and her family to look at flats in Cheltenham when they'd come home from Canada. Sue, Chris, and two children whose names I couldn't remember, and they seemed to be looking for perfection. If Sue liked a flat, Chris didn't, and if Chris said this one was ideal, a child would complain that there was nowhere to put a bicycle, and so we would go on to the next on the list. I couldn't remember why I'd been involved, but I did remember Sue telling me that finding a home was a family thing.

Daddy had been born in the house where I grew up. He'd told me, when I was very small, that one day the house would be John's, not mine, but if I didn't marry somebody with a nice house he'd buy me one, so it would be fair. The house, Daddy said, was a family home. It was a family thing.

I was looking at the picture of Krishna with the gopis, and they all had impossibly long and languorous eyes. I was aware of that on the surface of my mind, that and the lines of their bodies, the curve of the hips, and the glowing colours, but underneath

398

ran the echo of the three words, insistent, singing to me, a musical phrase that would not be ignored.

A family thing, a family thing, a family thing.

Why Tamsin? Why take such a risk, with a child from his own family? How had this come about?

A family thing.

I sat forward in my chair, and Mrs Sam looked at me questioningly.

'Why Tamsin?' I asked. 'Why did he take such a risk?'

Tamsin had said there were runaways. Peter Holmes had been investigating East European orphans, but Tamsin was Giles's own niece, and I had been so close to this I hadn't for one moment wondered why.

He'll never say, but there's more than one member of a family, and he's clever, but I'm damned if I'll believe Helen is.

'If Frank won't confront her, I will,' I thought, and then realised I had spoken aloud.

Mrs Sam didn't have time to ask me what I meant, because the doorbell rang, and she went to answer it. It was a man I'd never seen before, and the spotty policewoman who'd been at Helen's house on the night I'd first arrived. The man introduced himself as Detective Sergeant Reece, and told me that I already knew WPC Ingles.

Would I please come down to the station to make a statement?

Hadn't Frank said somebody would come to the hotel? I thought he'd said that. But there were other guests around, and I didn't want these people in my room, so I said I'd get my coat.

There seemed to be a lot of people at the police station, crowding around the front desk, and, after we'd been let through, in the corridors.

'Is it always this busy?' I asked, and Reece said no, but offered no explanation. He showed me into a room, not the one with the antique table, and said he'd be back in a minute. The policewoman, Ingles, stood by the door with her hands behind her back, and looked at the wall.

'What's happened?' I asked, but she said she couldn't say. I wondered whether she meant she didn't know.

It was another man who came back, and said his name was Royston. He didn't seem to want to look me in the eye, and he ignored the hand I held out to him. He put tapes into the recording machine, and repeated his name, and that of the policewoman, time and date and my name, and then he glanced across at me before looking down at the table, and asked me to say, for the tape, what had happened.

'Please take it from the time you left Chief

Inspector Welland at the Copper Kettle café,' he said, and then I understood.

I should have known, too, that Giles would not have been content with making trouble for Frank. When I'd made my statement, and promised to come back the next day to sign the transcript, Reece drove me back to the hotel, alone this time, and said as little as common courtesy would allow. Mrs Sam met me in the hall and told me Anthony had telephoned, and had asked me to call him back.

Helen had been in touch, he said. She'd told him I was having an affair with a policeman. He thought he should let me know.

He sounded vague and non-committal, as if this was a matter of no great importance and he was thinking of something else as he spoke, as indeed he might have been.

'I love you,' I said, and he replied, dutifully, that he loved me, too.

'Can this wait until I get back?' I asked, and he said, of course.

I sat by the telephone in the hall looking through the directory, and I found only one entry under Welland, F.J. Helen would have found it, too, once Giles had told her to look.

They'd been prepared to kill me, but somehow I was less shocked by that than by the damage they'd inflicted on us in this way. Anthony had been told, and I was quite sure Frank's wife would also have heard.

Had they taken Frank off the case? Would it make any difference if they did?

He came to the hotel quite late that night. He was very subdued, but he greeted Mrs Sam before we went up to my room. He sat at the table, and asked, politely, whether I felt better now.

'Oh, please get to the point,' I said, and he nodded.

His wife had gone to spend a few days with her sister. She didn't intend to leave him, or to do anything very much, but she was upset, and wanted a little time away from him.

It was a woman who had telephoned her, but hadn't given a name. At first she'd refused to believe it, but the woman had said Frank was no longer in charge of the case, telephone Superintendent Wallace if she didn't believe it.

'Have you been taken off the case?' I asked, and he said no, but he wasn't in charge of it any more.

'Not because of you,' he added. 'It's too big now. It's international, for one thing.'

I said, 'I think Helen might break down, if she was questioned. If she was shown some of the photographs, the nastier ones, if you've found any.'

Yes, they had found some very nasty photographs, but unfortunately they hadn't found Helen. She'd gone, and Giles said he'd no idea where, but he wasn't in the least surprised.

'Why not?' I asked, and Frank said Giles was blaming me. The police were trying to find her, but it wasn't very likely they'd succeed, since Giles owned travel agencies. If he was half as clever as Frank suspected, Helen was abroad, and wouldn't have travelled under her own name or with her own passport.

'She'll have to come back one day,' I commented, and Frank raised his eyebrows and asked why I thought so.

'Oh, bugger,' I said miserably, and he smiled, the first time he'd done so that evening.

'Amsterdam,' I said. 'I don't know why. But it's all been Amsterdam and Belgium, and what about Neville Jacklin?'

'He's in Bruges,' said Frank. 'I hope he's answering questions. It's a little glimmer of hope, that.'

'Is Giles going to get away with this?' I asked, but it wasn't a question Frank could answer. The investigation was very big now, with all Giles's associates being watched, not only here but in Belgium and Holland too.

'Whatever happens, you've been a bloody nuisance to him,' he said, and I remembered Mrs Sam saying much the same thing.

'Frank, why did he take the risk of using his own niece?'

'I don't know.'

'Neither do I, but I can't get away from the idea that it's important. Wasn't it a stupid thing to do? When there were other children he could use?'

But he didn't seem to be interested. He simply shrugged, and asked me whether Helen had contacted Anthony, and when I said of course she had he nodded, and looked away from me.

'It wasn't much of a marriage anyway,' I said.

It might have been salvageable, though. It might have been. It had been good, once. She probably had destroyed what there was.

'Will he divorce you?'

'I don't expect so.'

Would I mind very much if he did? I could leave Germany and come back to England. I could work again, become a journalist again, possibly even work on this story. Take it up where Peter Holmes had left off.

I shivered, and Frank looked at me.

'How many of these bloody paedophile rings are there, anyway?' I asked.

'Not many this big, I hope. Why?'

I told him about Peter Holmes, and he said he doubted if his disappearance was linked with his investigations. Not unless he'd been very unlucky.

Frank was so depressed he didn't seem to be able to take any of my ideas seriously. Everything I suggested he dismissed, not rudely or brusquely, but as if I had offered him something that was too heavy for him to carry, as if he was too tired to deal with it now.

'I'd better go,' he said, but he made no move to do so. Back to an empty house, even sitting here had to be better than that.

'This case won't be solved in one sudden move,' he said. 'It'll be like chipping away at a coal face, a little bit at a time. It seems there are quite a number of people involved. If I'd begun to guess it was as big as this, I might have been more careful about where I met you. I never dreamed he'd have the organisation to have us followed.'

'How many people?' I asked, and he answered that my statement had mentioned other cars arriving, as well as the vans leaving.

He didn't look at me as he said that.

'I'd better go,' he said again, and this time he stood up.

I saw him out, and went back to the room and lay on my bed, staring up at the ceiling, trying to think. I would go back to Germany in a couple of days' time, perhaps tomorrow, and I would tell Anthony about Frank. Anthony would listen, politely.

Perhaps I would tell him I'd been lonely. He might understand that. He might sympathise. Or it might sound like an excuse, an attempt to shift the blame onto him.

I fell asleep, still lying on top of the bed, and woke suddenly, very early in the morning, feeling stiff, wanting to wash. I was dirty, and ashamed, and very tired. Something filthy had happened, something had shocked me and hurt me, and I'd thought I could trust him because he'd been nice to me, but he'd tied me up.

'This is only until you're used to it,' he'd said. 'I don't like doing this.'

There were tears drying on my cheeks. I'd cried in my sleep. I'd cried.

But he'd been frightened too, because Giles had been so angry, and I'd thought he'd come to rescue me.

Don't tell. Mustn't tell. Yes, we'll go home. Of course, sweetheart, darling, my precious, don't cry, poppet, my little one, my sweetie. Trust me, I'll make it all right. I will, darling, but don't tell. You wouldn't want Mummy to get into trouble. People don't understand. Trust me, darling. Trust me, I'll make it all right, but we must keep it a secret, it's a family thing. Keep it in the family, and trust me to make it all right.

Don't tell.

There's only me and Mummy, and what do you think would happen to you if we went to prison? They'd take you away and put you in a horrible place. I know about places like that. They're dirty and cold and horrible, and you don't get enough to eat, and you'd have nobody to help you.

I didn't mean this to happen, sweetie. Not to you, my darling.

Don't tell Mummy. She'd only be upset, and there's nothing she could do. She might tell somebody else, and then we'd all be in terrible trouble, because they wouldn't believe she didn't plan it. I can't explain it all, you wouldn't understand, but darling, you mustn't tell Mummy. Keep it in the family, and trust me to make it all right. Trust me. There's nobody else you can trust, is there? If anybody else knows, you could end up in one of those places they call children's homes, and you'd be there for years, and you'd hate it, and there'd be nobody to help you.

I sat up on my bed and drew a deep breath, and thought, I must keep this. I must not forget any of this, because it's the last time I'll hear from young Tamsin. She can't do any more.

I felt dirty. I'd been degraded, and frightened, and in the end betrayed. But now I was free of all that, and all that remained was revenge, and that was what it was, simple revenge. For what he had done, and allowed others to do, I would be revenged on him.

I stood up, shivering in the cold morning air, and I found a pen and paper and I sat at the table and began to write, as fast as I could before the memory of the dream faded, as memories of dreams so often do. I wrote it as facts. This happened, then he said that and the other one answered and then they did this, and he promised, and that one paid, and the cameras were there and there and there. And the two other children were brought in, and I never saw them again. The other men, who paid, and promised, and did this, or that.

And that man, the first one.

Get him.

By the time I'd finished I was crying and shaking, and I had never known such anger could exist.

I packed my suitcase, and I crept down the stairs and I left an envelope and a short letter.

Mrs Sam, I will never forget you and your kindness. I love you for what you did for me, and for understanding about Tamsin. Here's the money I owe you, and I'm sorry it's a few days late. I think, if you listen to the news, you'll hear the end of this story, but for now I have to be quick, and can't go into details.

I telephoned for a taxi, and asked him to take me to the police station and wait for me there.

'Hurry,' I said to the sergeant. 'Please, if

you want that statement signed, please hurry.'

I had a plane to catch.

I flew to Brussels, all the way thinking of nothing but the dream that had made it clear, and that somehow I would use what she'd told me. I couldn't plan, I could only wait, and hope, and see what happened.

In Brussels I found a taxi that drove me back along the motorway to Bruges, to the police station, and it seemed appropriate that it was raining. There'd been enough tears, it was time for the heavens to cry.

But I cried, too. There was anger and sorrow, and something like rage against a god, if such a monster existed, that could allow such things.

'Have you still got Neville Jacklin here?' I asked, and with those words began the arguments, and the confrontations with all the men who wanted to ask me questions that I had already answered, and all I could say was, please, if you will let me confront him, you might get even better answers.

This would not be allowed. We regret, madame.

'Has he answered your questions? Only a few moments, and I think I can break him. What have you got to lose? Please?'

There were the same men asking the same questions, but I'd become stubborn and even more angry, and then I shouted at them.

'I only need a moment. If it works at all it will only take a moment.'

Madame, we are not permitted.

Oh, please. I have spent so long trying to trap these men. Look at my hands, I did that trying to escape from them because they were going to kill me.

Oh. madame, yes that is very bad. We are so sorry, we wish we could help.

Only a moment to see him.

Madame. Madame, it is so kind of you to come to us. We cannot allow you to speak to a prisoner, but if you would care to see around the precinct, since you have come so far? A matter merely of courtesy, you understand?

So they showed me their building, where they worked, and after a while they led me down the stairs, and two of them went ahead of me while another talked, politely, watching the end of the corridor, and then took my arm to make me hurry just a little, and we went around the corner and there, between the two policemen, just going into another room, was a small man, who glanced up at me. Small, and grey, nobody important, a nothing, a prisoner in a police station, who wasn't even looking at me any more, but I didn't need the touch of the man's hand on my elbow to know who it was. I drew in my breath, and I called out in a voice that wasn't mine, that I'd never heard except in dreams and fantasies, I called out to him.

'*Uncle Neville!*'

He stopped, he seemed to stagger between them, and I called again, in the voice I could never have known, I called his own words back to him.

'*This is only until you're used to it.*'

He screamed then, and again, and again, but I don't know how long he went on screaming, that shrill sound of terror, because somebody was dragging me away, and I hardly knew what was happening, only that she'd won, and he'd broken, and that he was the one she'd wanted me to get. That one, the first one, and after him the one who'd betrayed her.

19

He was screaming, and there was an alarm bell ringing, too much noise. I tried to get to him. I fought the policeman who was holding me, and I nearly broke away from him. He shouted at me to stop.

I will kill him, that screaming man who did those things to her.

They pushed him into the room and they were confronting me and talking to me, and other people were coming into the corridor. The young policeman who was holding my arm and trying to stop me was speaking to me, urgently, and then I listened.

'Enough, madame. Let them talk to him. Please, madame.'

Yes, they must talk to him now, immediately.

I watched as men went into the room, and I heard him again, and then I turned and walked away, back towards the corner at the foot of the stairs, to where more people were crowding and asking what had happened.

She's done it, I thought. She got him.

'Madame?'

'Yes. Yes, it's all right now. I'm sorry, did I hit you?'

'No, madame.'

'You can let me go now. It's all right. I won't go after him.'

An older man was following us, almost running, and he asked what it was I'd said to Jacklin. I stared at him, and tried to look bewildered.

'I'm sorry,' I said. 'What do you want to know?'

'Madame, you said words and he shouted. Which words?'

Impatiently, he spoke to another man, who asked again.

'Madame, what did you say to Jacklin to frighten him?'

In the confusion, none of them had heard. None except Jacklin, who would probably never tell them.

'I'm not sure,' I said. 'I knew Tamsin used to call people Uncle and Aunt, you see. I thought, if he was the one, she might have called him Uncle Neville. So I shouted that name, and he looked at me.'

'Yes, we heard that, madame. But after, what did you say?'

What would I have said? His own words, that had come to me in a dream, shouted in her voice. There could be no explanation for those words, not to these men.

I frowned, looked away, gnawed at my lip, all the signs of concentration, of trying to focus my mind while they waited, and at last

I shook my head.

'I'm sorry,' I said. 'I can't remember.'

He was not prepared to believe me, and he spoke impatiently, almost angrily.

'Madame, you have demanded him.'

Again, in frustration, he turned to the man beside him and spoke quickly, gesturing at me.

'Madame, you asked to see Jacklin,' the other man translated. 'You have said you can make him talk to us. You can, you said, break him. You have known what you will say. Now, please, what words did you say to him?'

'I don't know,' I insisted. 'I had meant to say something about driving Tamsin Simpson to suicide, but when I saw him I said something else, and I don't know what it was.'

They were all looking at me intently, and the man who had followed us made a gesture of disgust, turned, and walked away.

'I'm sorry,' I called after him. 'I'm sorry.'

'Please come with me now.'

A young woman had spoken, smiling at me, so I followed her up the stairs, and in the dark glass doors ahead of us I saw myself. A white face with blackened, sunken eyes stared back at me. Dark and tousled hair framed that face like clouds. I hardly recognised myself.

'Madame?'

She led me into a room, a comfortable room with upholstered armchairs and a sofa, and said I should please sit down. A doctor was coming to see me. I should be calm, all was well.

My hands seemed to be convulsing, clenching into fists and then relaxing, only to clench again. I sat in one of the chairs and stared down at them, willing them to be still, and gradually the uncontrolled movements slowed, and stopped.

'The doctor will be soon,' the young woman said. 'Be calm, madame.'

I couldn't be calm. I was feeling quite frightened. This might only be delayed shock, but I had never had these strange sensations before, of being so completely out of control that I could hardly believe in myself. It was as if I had changed into somebody else.

'Be calm, madame.'

'Yes.'

I will try to be calm. I want to be calm. I want to be myself again.

Oh, please, I want to go home.

He hasn't much time for me now, and maybe I've hurt him, even though I didn't mean to. That wasn't what I'd meant at all. But he's so sane, Anthony. If I can be with him, I think I will be all right. I think I will be myself again. Quite soon.

The doctor was a young woman with curly

hair and a round, smiling face. She looked hardly old enough to be out of school. She asked me questions, which I answered mechanically, and she took my pulse and looked carefully into my eyes. Cool fingers on my head quickly found the lump, and I spoke before she did.

'It's been X-rayed. There's no fracture.'

'Good, but there is concussion. A shock to the brain?'

'I understand.'

Another simple explanation had been presented. There was always another simple explanation, it seemed.

'I will tell them,' said the doctor. 'Sometimes, with a concussion, there are behaviour changes. This is not your fault. I will give you something to make you calm, and you should sleep.'

I wondered what she meant. I wanted to ask, what is not my fault?

'That you do not remember what you said.'

It was the policewoman who answered the question I had not known I'd asked.

I am still not in control. I speak when I don't mean to. My thoughts turn into speech, and I don't know it.

'I want to go home.'

Was that thought, or spoken? Say it again.

'I want...'

'Soon, madame. Now you must rest.'

The policewoman took me to a room where I could wash, but I felt dirty deeper than my skin, although I longed for a shower. I wanted to be home, clean, in my own bed between cool sheets, my life normal again.

Perhaps he wouldn't let me come back.

'Sleep now, madame. Please, drink this that the doctor gave.'

I lay down on the sofa and she covered me with a soft blanket and said she would not be far away, should I need her. I thanked her.

There was a blue light in the room, and I watched it as I felt the drug taking effect, felt myself becoming drowsy, the throbbing ache in my hands changing to a slow warmth, felt the anger and the fear draining away, and sleep taking their place.

There were no dreams that I can remember.

When I woke the policewoman was sitting in a chair by the table, reading a book by the light of a shaded lamp. She looked across at me, waited to make sure I was truly awake, and then offered me coffee, or tea. She said she had spent some months in England and knew how to make tea properly.

'Then I would like tea, please,' I said, but as she stood up I remembered.

'Jacklin?' I asked, and she said she was not permitted to discuss. But she smiled at me

417

after she had said that, watching me to see that I noticed her smile.

She brought me tea, and, as she had promised, it had been made in the English way. As I drank it she talked politely of other things, of her holiday in Cornwall last year, of her liking for English books. Not until I had finished did she ask me if I was now well enough to discuss the case with the detectives, who were waiting to talk to me. If I felt well enough.

'Yes,' I said. 'Yes, of course. I'll try.'

There were three of them including the man who had been angry and impatient with me. They all stood up as the police-woman showed me into the room, and the impatient man bowed to me and smiled.

'Are you feeling better now?' he asked, and I knew the polite enquiry had been trans-lated for him, and rehearsed.

'Thank you, much better,' I replied.

The youngest of the three held a chair for me, and when I was seated they, too, sat down. The one who had asked if I was feel-ing better introduced himself as Caniard, and gave the names of the others, which I immediately forgot. The young man who had held my chair sat beside and a little behind him, opposite me, and smiled at me. I thought it was he who had translated for Caniard in our confrontation. The third man sat on a chair against the wall, stretched out his legs and crossed them, and then nodded to the other two.

'Please will you tell us what you know of the relationship between the man Jacklin and your niece, Tamsin Simpson?'

There was hardly anything I could say, and I had to be careful. What did I actually know, and what had I dreamed?

So I gave them what few facts I could, and told them what I believed, and what I had guessed.

When I had finished there was a long silence. It was as if they were still waiting.

'If you ask for Detective Chief Inspector Welland,' I told them, 'he'll give you all the background. He knows far more than I do.'

The younger man glanced enquiringly at Caniard, who nodded.

'Monsieur Caniard permits me to inform you, madame, that we are working very closely with the English police, and the Dutch, and we believe we have much for which to thank you.'

I thought, Tamsin told me what to say.

As I thought that it brought back the memory of that last dream, of the ropes and the little man apologising and explaining that he didn't like doing it. This is only until you're used to it.

'What has Jacklin said?' I asked.

With the other evidence they had, it was enough to keep him in prison for a very long

419

time. There had been, at last, explanations of some papers they had found in his house and his place of business. Also, it would now be difficult for the man Baker to deny the connection.

I closed my eyes and sat back in the chair, and felt myself smile.

'There isn't much more I can tell you,' I said.

'Can you now remember what you called out to Jacklin?'

I had tried to make my voice sound like that of a young girl, I explained. I had been lucky with my guess about his name, what she would call him. I thought it was his name that had frightened him.

They shrugged. Perhaps. If I truly could not remember, then it could not be helped. A pity. *Quelle dommage.*

They did not believe me, and could not understand why I would not tell them what I'd shouted at him. They were puzzled, and possibly even a little suspicious, but it seemed the doctor had, as she had promised, told them I was concussed, and not entirely responsible for my actions.

'Have you found any children?' I asked, and my voice felt tight and dry in my throat.

'Yes, madame. We have found three children. We may find more.'

So, I thought, whatever happens it had been worth it. No matter what I do now, three children make it all worthwhile.

'Have you finished with me?' I asked. 'I would like to go home now.'

The doctor had not thought me well enough to travel, they said. So, while I was sleeping they had telephoned my husband, and he was now on his way, in the car, to collect me. If the roads were clear, he should be here in not more than perhaps two hours. It would be more comfortable for me to travel home with my husband, in a car.

I looked down at my hands, clasped on the table in front of me. The bandages were still clean, although fraying a little.

It was only this time yesterday, I thought, that I'd been in the hospital where they'd washed my hands and then put those bandages on them. It seemed a long time ago, and so far away.

But that was in another country: and besides, the wench is dead.

Marlowe. I shivered. So bleak, so final, and truly so far away.

'Madame?'

I smiled at him.

'That was very kind of you,' I said. 'That was truly very kind.'

My hands convulsed, clenching again, and there was a sharp pain. I gritted my teeth and stared at them, willing them to be still. Do as I wish. Be still.

Anthony was on his way, in the car. He

would take me home, they'd said.

Yes, he would do that. He would take me home. I would have what I'd wanted: a shower, clean clothes, my own bed, a sleep between the cool sheets.

'Is there anything more I can tell you?' I asked. 'I think I've told you everything now. You or the police in England.'

There was nothing more, they said.

Nothing more for me to do. Now I could truly say goodbye to Tamsin. Sleep well, Tamsin. I believe, now, I did know you, I really did know you, but perhaps it doesn't matter so much. I may not believe it later. In a week or a month, you may be somebody I dreamed. Even so, dream or reality, you are somebody I could have loved.

Sleep well, Tamsin.

I was taken back to the room where I'd slept, and another policewoman brought in a tray, with good, strong Belgian coffee, hot croissants with butter and jam, and a glass of orange juice. She apologised that she had no bacon and eggs, and I managed to laugh.

He would be here in less than two hours, and we would go home, and the journey would be almost silent, because we had so little to say to each other now, and because his kindness would not allow him to question me while I was tired, and possibly ill.

I would have to stay for a little while, and

422

I knew he would be reasonable, no matter what we decided. And if I left, I would have to make plans.

Nobody would need me. The refugees could manage perfectly well without me. In Germany, who needed English? Most of the people who worked with them knew enough English to tell them what their documents said, and what they should do. I'd never met a German lawyer who didn't speak good English.

I felt my hands move again, but I checked them quickly, and they were still. I stared down at them.

I will be in control again. I will. I will be myself again, for whatever that's worth. I will not be controlled by anybody else. My mind is my own.

A long, deep breath, and I brushed at my cheek with the back of my bandaged hand. There had been a small sensation, it wasn't a tear.

I might have to go back to England for the trial. I had promised myself I would see those men in the dock, and listen to them sentenced.

I had promised I would plant a tree.

I had promised fidelity to a husband I loved, and I hadn't even thought of that promise, when I broke it.

Does it matter? Will he mind?

I brushed at my cheek again, and this time

did not bother to pretend there were no tears.

I drank the coffee. I felt a little better after that.

At some time, when I had completely recovered, Anthony and I would have a civilised discussion about our future. We would make a decision. It would be one on which we had both agreed.

Somebody should come and tell me what's happening. I've done a lot, and I think they could tell me, not just vague generalisations, but a few details about what he's said, him that they called 'the man Jacklin', they could tell me. And if they're so closely in touch with the police in England they could also tell me about the man Baker, and the woman Simpson too, if they've found her.

But nobody came, and when the door opened again it was to admit Anthony, shown in by the policewoman who had brought me my breakfast, and who now took the tray, and by then my eyes were dry and clear, and I smiled at him, and offered him my cheek for a kiss. Make-up had, to some extent, covered the pallor of my skin, if not the dark bruises around my eyes. My hair was tidy; the tousled and cloudy look I had seen in the glass doors had gone.

Gone for ever.

Caniard and the young man came to say

goodbye, and to thank me for my help. They were both smiling now; the suspicion seemed to have vanished. Caniard said something to Anthony, and he replied in his effortless French, too fast for me to understand, something that made both men laugh.

But I couldn't leave without asking them.

'Has Jacklin told you enough?'

They looked at each other, and Caniard smiled and nodded to me before the younger man spoke.

'He has told us what he did. Also, others who did the same, he has given names. The man, Giles Baker, he has said this name. In England, we have told them what he said, and they say it is good. It is very well, what he has told.'

'Thank you,' I said, and he bowed to me, and showed us out of the door.

Anthony carried my suitcase to the car and opened the door for me, smiling at me, but people were watching us and I didn't know whether the smile was for my benefit or for theirs. It was a strange and uncomfortable feeling, wondering if he was putting on an act.

As we pulled out into the road he asked if my hands hurt, and I said no, not very much, but my head ached a little. Had they told him I'd been concussed from a blow to my head? He was concerned about it; would

I like to go to the doctor on the way home? It might be a good idea for him to look at my hands while...

'Have you heard anything about the case?' I interrupted.

Only what he'd heard on the radio, he said. There'd been arrests in England, Belgium and Holland, and more were expected. It had been described as a lengthy operation, involving the police forces in all three countries.

I smiled when he said that, not only at the wording, but also at the dry irony of his voice.

'Have they charged Giles?' I asked, but no names had been given.

He turned on the radio at that point, and found a news programme, in Dutch. I could hardly understand a word of it, but Anthony seemed to be listening, although so far as I knew he didn't speak much, if any, of that language. I spent the rest of the journey looking out of the window, and such conversation as we had was brief, and of nothing important.

It isn't a long journey, across Belgium and into Germany, provided the roads are good, and perhaps because it was monotonous not too much time seemed to have passed before we were pulling up outside the house. Anthony carried my suitcase up the steps, and I had my wish of a shower, and clean clothes, although by then I was well beyond tiredness, and didn't want to sleep.

But I did want to know what was happening, and I wanted to know what Anthony was thinking and whether he saw any future for us. He had, once again, retreated into his study, to the safe haven of his work, and I was left to realise that, had there been any chance for us, the concern he had expressed when I'd told him I'd been concussed would have manifested itself in something a little stronger than a mere suggestion that we should visit the doctor.

So I telephoned Frank Welland, because it didn't matter now, and I asked him what had happened.

He told me that Giles was in custody, although he hadn't yet been charged. He was still pretending to cooperate. He claimed to have known nothing of what had happened at the house, even though one of his companies owned it. His lawyer had advised him to say nothing more, and he was putting on a very good pretence of wanting to be of assistance, but of feeling himself bound to take the expert advice he'd been given.

There was no news of Helen. She could be anywhere in the world by now.

'What did you say to Jacklin?' he asked, and I felt that I did owe him the truth. I told him about my dream, when I had been Tamsin, and Jacklin had tied me and made his apology, his plea for understanding.

'I could hardly tell the Belgian police that,' I said in the end, and Frank agreed. His own voice had the totally non-committal tone that I had come to associate with disbelief.

'Why did Giles use Tamsin?' I asked, and Frank said the story was, at last, beginning to come out. It had been an accident. Giles had never intended Tamsin to be involved. Now, he was accusing Jacklin of raping her. He probably had been genuinely fond of his niece. Jacklin had been in England, and had seen Giles with Tamsin in an ice-cream parlour. Giles had been in the habit of taking Tamsin out, quite often, when he was in the area. He'd done that since she was a little girl.

Jacklin had come over to say hello, but Giles hadn't introduced him. Giles hadn't wanted Tamsin to meet him, and he'd got rid of him as quickly as possible, and said nothing to him about who Tamsin was.

The reason Giles had given for not wanting them to meet was that he'd never liked Jacklin, although the man was brilliant at his work, and a profitable associate. Jacklin had interests in hotels in Europe, and Giles needed those hotels for his tourist business. But he claimed he'd always felt there was something unpleasant about Jacklin.

Only two weeks after that chance meeting,

Giles had taken Tamsin out again, but had called at the house to collect something, some papers, he said. He'd told Tamsin to wait for him in the car, and Jacklin had come out and seen her. He'd been drunk at the time, and he'd seen the child on her own as an opportunity. He'd taken her into the house.

Giles had been delayed, and when he came out to find Tamsin had gone it was too late. He'd found them both in one of the rooms.

Somehow, he'd persuaded Tamsin to keep quiet.

'It's not difficult, with a child of that age,' said Frank, and I closed my eyes and caught at something stirring in my memory, some fragments of promises, the dread of a future of fear and loneliness.

Giles's discovery of the two of them should have been the end of it, but Jacklin had become besotted with Tamsin. Only she would do, and most of the European end of the business rested on Jacklin.

None of this had come from Giles, but now Konrad was beginning to talk, and Mark Fraser was contributing a few small items of information.

According to Konrad, Jacklin had offered Giles a choice. Giles would organise things for him with Tamsin, or Jacklin would arrange to have her abducted. It wouldn't be the first time that had been done.

'Oh, stop,' I said, and Frank fell silent.

'The Belgians tell me that Jacklin's got AIDS,' he said later, and although I'd already guessed that, I felt myself smile.

Jacklin was claiming to have loved Tamsin, and said that she loved him, too. As soon as she was old enough he would have married her.

When he said that, I thought I'd be sick.

Jacklin was claiming he had bought Tamsin. He had paid Giles, more than double the usual fee. But he loved Tamsin, and he'd designed her room for her, and done the work for nothing, because he loved her. The kitchen and the bathroom had been done to keep her mother quiet, and for that Giles had paid.

'Did Helen know?' I asked, but he couldn't answer. If not, it was because she'd been very careful not to find out.

'I told you she refused to listen to Tamsin,' I said. 'That night when she was drugged half stupid, she almost told me. She said Tamsin told disgusting lies. They weren't lies. I hope she rots, that woman. I hope she rots.'

Frank wasn't very interested in Helen. Everybody's efforts were now being concentrated on Giles, and there was still some doubt. He was too calm, too much in control. Knowing that he was lying, when he spoke at all, was a long way from proving it.

'Can you record off your telephone?' I asked, and he said of course he could.

'Hold on a moment, please.'

I'd written down everything I could remember. As soon as I'd woken in the early hours of the morning, only this morning, I had written down what had happened and what had been said.

'If you play this to him,' I said to Frank, 'it might help.'

And so I read my notes. I read them in a flat and toneless voice because I could not bring myself to think about them. Words, they were only words, used to pass on information, only words.

Don't tell. You wouldn't want Mummy to get into trouble. It's a family thing. Trust me. Trust me. Places they call children's homes. Trust me. You'd be alone, years and years and nobody to help you.

Trust me. Don't tell.

It seemed to go on for a long time, the words repeated, again and again and I read them in my flat voice and heard them in his, persuasive and plausible and frightening. How much more so for a child?

Don't tell.

When I stopped Frank was silent, and then he spoke sharply.

'Where did you get that?'

'I told you. I dreamed it. Frank, I dreamed what I shouted at Jacklin, too.'

'Celia, this is important. Don't give me stupid stories.'

I didn't answer him. There was nothing more I could say, and besides I could hardly speak at all now. I could remember hearing his voice, and I could remember feeling her fear and her misery.

I put down the telephone, with Frank's voice still sharp and angry speaking into it, and I sat quietly for a while, thinking of what had happened, and then thinking of Helen, and of my contempt for her. She, too, would be listening to the radio, waiting for news, wondering if she would hear her brother's name.

Where would he have sent her?

I didn't greatly care. She was unlikely to be able to build herself a life, no matter where she was. Helen would always be discontented, and would always look outside herself for something to blame for her unhappiness. Somehow, she would find a way of justifying herself.

On the late news that night I heard there'd been more arrests, more people charged, and then the telephone rang, and a few minutes later Anthony came downstairs and told me it had been the police.

They'd wanted to tell me they'd now found enough evidence to charge Giles, and the list of those charges was very long. They would oppose bail, and since they'd found forged passports in one of his offices, they didn't expect he'd win his application for it.

'He won't be free again for a very long time.'

Even Anthony, that gentlest and kindest of men, did not try to disguise the satisfaction in his voice.

'Have they found any more children?' I asked.

He didn't know.

'It was your friend Frank Welland,' he said. 'I didn't ask him anything.'

He turned back to the door, but I spoke before he reached it.

'Please don't go.'

I wasn't looking at him. So much of my time recently seemed to have been spent looking down at two bandaged hands, clenched or curled in my lap. I really should change those dressings now. They were beginning to look grey at the edges, the cotton splitting and fraying and they were still damp from the shower. I might not even need bandages any more. The wounds hadn't been deep. Friction burns mostly, the doctor had said.

Anthony was waiting for me to speak again. The door was open, but he'd turned back into the room and was standing, and even though I wasn't looking at him I knew the expression on his face. Polite enquiry, and behind it, only discernible to those who knew him very well, a little apprehension.

Was this to be a confrontation? Was this going to demand those reserves of restraint and control upon which he so hated to draw, and which he had had to use so often against me?

Was he again going to have to face my anger?

No, I thought, but you may have to face my misery, if I don't manage to hide it.

I began to talk to him about Tamsin. In the end, despite everything, we had won, we had beaten them, she and I. I'd told him before I'd gone back to England about my dreams, and about my feelings that she'd wanted me to go back. At the moment I did believe she'd haunted me, even though I could see that I might not always believe it. One day I would probably accept the other, simpler explanations for everything that had happened.

It had been a very strange time, and there were things that I did regret. I didn't mean my injured hands or the blows to my head.

I stopped speaking then in case Anthony wanted to say something, but he hadn't moved from his position by the door, and the silence went on.

Perhaps what made it worse, I said at last, was that I hadn't really cared very much about Frank Welland. I'd liked him, I'd enjoyed his company. But I couldn't claim there'd been some sort of overwhelming passion. There'd been nothing on that sort of level at all. I didn't know whether it made any difference?

I looked up at him then, and he was watching me, his head a little on one side, not smiling, but listening, carefully, to what I said.

'Frank's married, too,' I told him. 'Helen telephoned his wife. It was a piece of sheer spite. They'll be all right. She's not leaving him. He was worried about how you'd take it. He asked me.'

I looked down at my hands again.

'I couldn't answer him,' I said, 'because I didn't know.'

Now, I would say nothing more. I would wait here, sitting in this chair, looking down at these hands, until he responded, in one of the many ways open to him.

I had to wait for quite a long time, but this wasn't because he was deliberately keeping me in suspense. That wasn't the way he would behave. It was because he was choosing his actions and his words carefully, and because he knew that what he did next would matter.

He closed the door, and came into the room to stand in front of me, waiting until I looked up, and I hadn't meant it to happen, but there were tears in my eyes as I looked at him.

He reached down and touched my cheek, and he smiled at me.

'I never wanted you to be hurt,' he said.

Epilogue

It was over a year before the case came to court, and by then I was back in England. I'd told Anthony I thought we both needed a sabbatical from marriage, and he'd laughed at the choice of words, but then agreed. After a few months I might go back to Germany. Or I might not. We'd meet somewhere, we decided, and see where our lives were leading us, and whether our paths could converge again.

It had been a civilised discussion.

There were many promises I had made, and I kept them all. I saw those men in the dock, and I felt the rage and the contempt of the jury as the 'guilty' verdicts were pronounced, and I listened to the judge saying he could hardly bring himself to speak of the crimes that had been committed, so he would confine himself to passing sentence.

Giles will not be out of prison for twenty years.

Frank asked me whether I wanted the charges of abduction and assault pressed, or whether I'd leave those in case the unthinkable happened, and one of the men was acquitted. Leave it, I said, and in the end we didn't need them.

There were men I'd never seen who were called as witnesses, and whose names were given as Mister X, Mister Y. Soon they, too, would be standing in a dock, but in the meantime they had elected to turn on those who had led them.

There were children, too. Teenagers mostly, some of them needing interpreters, and they were the ones who spoke of having been promised adoption, a happy family life in a new country, a rich country, where they would have, as of right, everything they had lacked in their homelands.

There was a girl from Durham who'd run away from home to London, and had been offered a place for the night by a woman she'd never seen again, who'd said she ran a hostel for young runaways. Instead of a safe place in a hostel she'd been driven for miles in the back of a white van to a big house in the country, and she'd been tied up and raped while somebody took photographs and filmed it. There'd been other children there. One of them was called Tamsin. Tamsin had given her some money, so she could get on a train if she could escape from the men who guarded her. At least it was a chance. But Tamsin had asked her not to tell anybody what had happened, if she did manage to get away.

She'd come forward when she'd heard that

Tamsin was dead.

She still hadn't gone home. She was a heroin addict now, feeding her habit with prostitution and occasional theft. That man, she said, pointing at one of them sitting in the dock, had given her heroin.

Tamsin had been nice to her. Tamsin had been her friend.

That afternoon, when she'd finished giving her evidence, I went to a garden centre and I bought a silver birch sapling. I stood in the road outside, with the young tree in my hands, feeling both elated and foolish. I had nowhere to plant it, but it was mine and Tamsin's, and it needed to go into the ground.

I asked the man who'd sold it to me if he knew a friendly farmer who'd let me plant my tree on his land, and he looked at me in astonishment.

'Farmer?'

'Yes, a farmer. There must be some around here.'

I went by taxi, and I explained to a young man that my niece had died tragically, but she'd loved trees, and I'd made a sort of promise to plant one for her.

'All right,' he said, as though it was the most natural thing in the world, a complete stranger arriving at his farm with a tree. 'Somewhere nice, then. We'll need a spade.'

Tamsin's tree is on the edge of a lovely

little wood at the top of a field where the hay had just been cut. The tree didn't look very beautiful when I left it, because it had a blue plastic case around the trunk to protect it from the hares that would otherwise kill it by gnawing off the bark. Next year it will have a wooden guard around it to keep the heifers from eating it before it's strong enough to grow again.

I hadn't known about protecting young trees from hares and cattle, but the farmer said he'd take care of it for me. Come back in a couple of years, or better make it three, and that tree would look a treat.

His kindness, and the promise of the lovely young tree, gave me enough hope to go back to the court the next day. It felt like plunging into filth after I'd only just made myself clean again.

It was a bad day. A prosecution witness admitted he'd lied, and said he thought some of the other witnesses had done the same, because they believed they'd get lighter sentences for telling convincing stories. The defence hammered at the point until it seemed as if the whole case hung on the words of the discredited witnesses, and that without them there was nothing.

I was staying with Mrs Sam for the three weeks of the trial, not in the little room I'd had on my last visit, but in a bigger and lighter one at the front of the hotel. Mrs

Sam had greeted me with a smile, and a comment that I was too thin, better eat British Raj curry and chips.

That night I told her about the liars, and she said of course, what did I expect? Angelsfromheaven?

'Liars tell lies,' Mrs Sam scolded. 'You must expect. The judge will certainly know. So, what does this mean, this telling of stories? It means the liars will not be quite so lightly treated as they had hoped. Nothing more. The truth is, these monsters have been caught, and will be locked away to do no more harm. Now, you stop this crying.'

'I'm not crying,' I said.

'Nono. A bad cold again, middleof-summer. I know.'

'I want a bath,' I said.

I wanted them punished. All of them.

Helen had telephoned me, only a few days before I left Germany.

'It's no good asking where I am, I won't tell you. Why have you done this to us? What did we ever do to you? All these lies, you're wicked. You're a wicked, wicked woman.'

I let her go on for a while, and my anger this time was cold, and very clear.

'Tamsin was dying anyway,' I said. 'Didn't Giles tell you? That nice man from Belgium gave her AIDS. In her case it developed quite quickly. Sometimes it takes years, but I'm sure you know about that. Wherever you are, I hope they've got clinics. It's quite easy, to catch the virus, and she probably didn't know at first. Or what do you think, Helen? A child of that age. Would she have known?'

I put down the telephone, and I went into the living room and poured myself a very large whisky. Helen was one of the stupidest women I had ever known, and I thought she would probably believe me. I hoped so. I hoped she would think that she, too, might have AIDS, caught it from Tamsin, who had caught it from Jacklin. A tiny fraction of the misery her daughter had suffered, but it was all I could do.

How many other children had he infected?

I wasn't needed as a witness, and there were days when I could hardly bear to stay in the courtroom. I was writing the story for a magazine, one I'd worked for many years earlier, and they'd asked for a different viewpoint, as they always do. The irony of the beginning of the end being signalled by the death of a child who'd hardly even been involved was enough for me, and would be for them, I hoped.

There'd be little I could say about Tamsin, I told them. After all, I never knew her.

The publishers hope that this book has given you enjoyable reading. Large Print Books are especially designed to be as easy to see and hold as possible. If you wish a complete list of our books please ask at your local library or write directly to:

Magna Large Print Books
Magna House, Long Preston,
Skipton, North Yorkshire.
BD23 4ND

This Large Print Book, for people
who cannot read normal print,
is published under the auspices of

THE ULVERSCROFT FOUNDATION

... we hope you have enjoyed this book.
Please think for a moment about those
who have worse eyesight than you ...
and are unable to even read or enjoy
Large Print without great difficulty.

You can help them by sending a
donation, large or small, to:

**The Ulverscroft Foundation,
1, The Green, Bradgate Road,
Anstey, Leicestershire, LE7 7FU,
England.**
or request a copy of our brochure for
more details.

The Foundation will use all donations
to assist those people who are visually
impaired and need special attention
with medical research, diagnosis
and treatment.

Thank you very much for your help.

Other MAGNA Titles
In Large Print

ANNE BAKER
Merseyside Girls

JESSICA BLAIR
The Long Way Home

W. J. BURLEY
The House Of Care

MEG HUTCHINSON
No Place For A Woman

JOAN JONKER
Many A Tear Has To Fall

LYNDA PAGE
All Or Nothing

NICHOLAS RHEA
Constable Over The Bridge

MARGARET THORNTON
Beyond The Sunset